THEY CHALLENGED THE GODS
TO KEEP THEIR NOBLE HERITAGE.

PANTHER BURN—Mightiest of all the Cheyenne, a warrior feared by his enemies, yet still betrayed by brothers. Passionate and daring, his own life and the fate of his people depended on his fighting spirit, his courageous heart and his matchless skill with rifle and bow.

REBECCA BLUE THRUSH—A beautiful Cheyenne woman torn between loyalty to her people's traditions and the glowing promises of the white invaders. Her fate was entwined with that of the renegade warrior who offered both a timeless love and a terrible choice.

COMMANDER JUBAL BRAGG—Tall, lean, and vicious, he was haunted by his past: a bloodlust for vengeance against the Cheyenne and a vow to capture the one Indian warrior he hated with an insane obsession.

SABBATH MCKEAN—A frontier scout with a temper as fiery as his flaming red hair, he judged a man by his character not by his color, but even if he dared to call Panther Burn his friend, he might someday be sent to kill him.

JAMES BROKEN KNIFE—Coward, traitor, and white man's cur, his desire for the warrior's woman was a sickness in his heart, and his final betrayal an act of ultimate cruelty.

MICHAEL SPIRIT WOLF—Brought up to follow the white man's ways, he might reject the legendary chief who fathered him . . . but would he lead him to his death?

KATE MADISON—Proper, proud, and passionate, she was a physician in a strange and savage land, the woman who would bring two turbulent worlds together.

Sacred Is the Wind

Kerry Newcomb

BANTAM BOOKS
TORONTO • NEW YORK • LONDON • SYDNEY • AUCKLAND

SACRED IS THE WIND

A Bantam Book / December 1985

Quotations on pp. 98–99 taken from
The King James Version of the Bible.

ISBN 0-553-25183-X

Published simultaneously in the United States and Canada

Bantam Books are published by Bantam Books, Inc. Its trademark,
consisting of the words "Bantam Books" and the portrayal of a
rooster, is Registered in U.S. Patent and Trademark Office and in
other countries. Marca Registrada. Bantam Books, Inc., 666 Fifth
Avenue, New York, New York 10103.

PRINTED IN THE UNITED STATES OF AMERICA

H   0 9 8 7 6 5 4 3 2 1

For Patty, Amy Rose, and now Paul Joseph

Writing is an odyssey. I would like to thank
those who helped me along the way.

Linda Grey, editor and friend, for wisdom and expertise.
Aaron Priest, the best agent anywhere, who really
cares and cares.
Ann and Paul Newcomb, my parents, and brother Jim,
whose love is a support like no other.

The story's about done. I hope I haven't bored you. It's a sorta queer world, ain't it? Sometimes I think it jist was to be so, an' no help, an' sometimes I conceit I ought to done better; but anyhow, all I git outen the whole experience is that a man must keep peggin' away.

—J. H. Beadle,
Western Wilds and the Men Who Redeem Them, an Authentic Narrative

Love is a far off country
Yet a land I yearn to find
A home to joy and sorrow
But seldom peace of mind.

I seek a bright warm country
A place in my true love's eyes,
Where the sparkle of love's laughter
Bring stars to starless skies.

Yet in this country distant
Though the cold moon never chills
I am told the price of happiness
Is the thunder in the hills.

—Anonymous

Prologue

March 1865
Montana Territory

No dreams. Only silence of the heart. No song, only waiting. Storms raging over Spirit Mountain, north winds whipped into a tempest, spinning down from the Bitterroots where eagles roost in the crevices of the Great Divide, north wind, new wind, bringing rain to the forests below Spirit Mountain and the village of the Morning Star people who claimed the mountain as their own. The mountain, not the *maiyun* dwelling there, for who can claim the Spirits. Men can only do their best, can only lift their hearts in prayer and raise their voices to be carried off by the wind. It is for men and women to tread the paths of their days beneath the ghostly scrutiny of the *maiyun* and the love of the All-Father, the Great Spirit, the Beginning and the End.

In the last days of the buffalo, in the last days of the horse, Panther Burn had done his best. And it had not been enough. His features bunched in concentration as he tried to keep the faces of his friends from returning to his mind.

"*Ta-naestese!*" he muttered. "Go away. Go away." He turned on his side and dug his shoulder into the bulrush mattress from which he had not moved for the

1

past hour, ever since his father had sent him here to await the verdict of the council. He sighed, deeply, almost a moan. He glanced up, at the entrance to the tipi. Steps sounded, Panther Burn propped himself up on the backrest of willow shoots, waiting for the rawhide flap to be pushed back and the tall lean length of Yellow Eagle, his father, to scramble through. The coals crackled, popped, sent an ember arcing toward him. He caught the glowing morsel and ignoring the pain extinguished it in his palm. He listened as a shadow fell across the entrance, hesitated, then glided past; the footsteps faded. It might have been his mother. For Crescent Moon would never have shamed her son by entering and offering again the venison stew both her husband and Panther Burn had earlier refused. This was not a time for full bellies. Not when, elsewhere in the camp, another mother mourned her dead sons.

Panther Burn dropped the spent coal from his hand. There was an irregular crimson patch of burned flesh in the center of his palm but the pain was nothing compared to the hurt within his heart. Blood trickled toward his fingers, he wiped his hands on his buckskin shirt, the one his mother had made him before he left on the hunt. A warrior's shirt, he had thought then, as now . . . only now he would have torn it from his body if it weren't for causing his mother grief. And one mother grieving in the camp was enough . . . all because of him . . . his pride . . . his honor.

It began with a hawk.

It was a sprawling land of emerald meadows in those days, a lovely cloud-swept land, a killing ground, a realm of beauty and death. Nothing stirred among the deep thick stands of pine, no glimpse of movement save overall the sudden swift shadow of a hawk. The cry of the hawk rang out over the rolling landscape to dash against the Absarokas in their snowcapped granite robes of silence, the shrill cry returned in a succession of ghostly echoes. It is said that among the craggy battlements where the pine forest gives way to hard barren ground, the spirits wait, walk, dwell, and now and then sit content as if in audience to the deeds of men. It is said, and the Cheyenne believe, that the spirits argue in voices of thunder, they weep in the wind, they slumber in the gentle rains washing the earth in forgetful tears. But on this second morning of the Muddy-Face-Moon, men not *maiyun* hunted in the foothills of the mighty peaks to the west. Panther Burn of the Spirit Mountain Cheyenne raised his coppery arms in unabashed prayer. He faced the east and thanked the All-Father for the gift of morning. A young man of twenty years, he stood just under six feet tall. His dark black hair hung past his shoulders; a single braid would have been lost in the thickness of his hair had the strand not been interwoven with two gray eagle feathers. His eyes were like flint chips, capable in anger of flashing sparks of light. He was naked to the waist though a beaded medallion fashioned of porcupine quills and blue and white trading beads hung around his neck. He stood strong and lithe in buckskin leggings, breechcloth, and beaded moccasins. His voice rang out, rich in tone, strong and commanding, his invocation cut through the stillness like an arrow in flight. In the deep band of purple-black above the golden glow of sunrise swelling upward from the horizon, a single star continued to flicker as if with a life of its own, joining in this warrior's song of the soul.

"All-Father . . . thank you for today," sang Panther Burn as warmth gradually eased into his chilled torso. "Thank you for this new beginning. Thank you for the mountains and the rivers." He lifted his gaze to the dying dazzling sky jewel overhead. "Thank you for the morning star. Where it sings, I am with my people. I am never alone." His hand drifted to the medallion against his chest. Within the round patch of stitched buckskin the beads had been worked into a striking design, a square cantered on a corner and set off by four lines, one to a side, radiating outward like rays of light—the Morning Star. His hand touched the medal-

lion, gently gripping it as he repeated the song-prayer.
When he finished, darkness had been leached from the
sky. The March sun offered but a false promise of
summer's warmth here in the high country. Panther
Burn glanced down at the camp nestled in a pine grove
at the base of the hill. Three figures, his companions on
the hunt, were up and about, each tending to his own
business, each welcoming the morning in his own way.
The wind sighed in the buffalo grass, whipping black
strands of hair against Panther Burn's cheek. There was
power here in the Lonesome. And magic. But Panther
Burn was not ready yet to understand the ways of magic
and the spirit. He only knew that his heart was filled
with life. He felt ready for brave deeds, great heroics
that he might join his father in the Dog Soldier Society,
hotame-taneo-o, the bravest of the brave. But Yellow
Eagle, his father, had ordered his son and these three
others to continue the hunt while the Dog Soldiers
carried war to the mighty Crow. What honor was to be
gained in the death of *vaotseva*, the deer? Full bellies
for the people of his village, yes, but what of the heart,
what of the spirit? Heart and spirit know hunger as
well. The shadow of the hawk swept up the hillside,
passed across the brave, rushed down to lose itself amid
the treetops.

An arrow thwacked into the earth at Panther Burn's
feet, shattering the young man's moment of reflection.
Panther Burn flinched, leaped back, much to the amusement of one of his companions below, who held his bow
aloft and shouted up the slope.

"I have counted coup on the panther," laughed High
Walker. He was a year younger than Panther Burn and
one of the pranksters of the village from which they had
all set out three days before. One packhorse was already loaded with rawhide packets of smoked venison.
Another kill and the four young hunters could return
home. High Walker continued to bait his friend. He
trampled the dirt with a quick dancing step. "Now I
may join the Clan of my father," he laughed, "I have
counted coup and proved my worthiness." Little Coy-

ote, High Walker's brother, the eldest of them and a man seldom given to smiles, ignored the antics of High Walker and busied himself with the Hawken rifle he had used to bring down their first kill. He sang his morning prayer in a soft voice, all the while readying his weapon. With his ramrod he tamped home a charge of powder and lead shot, placed a firing cap over the nipple, and gingerly lowered the hammer to hold the primer in place; he grew quiet, prayer completed, rifle loaded. Knows His Gun, the third brave by the camp-fire, was a slim, diminutive young man. Small-statured and conscious of it at a trace over five feet tall, Knows His Gun generally followed, seldom led. His character was flawed with an insolence that befitted a man broader, taller, and better able to contend with the enemies his attitude might help to create. Contrary to his name, he was the only one of the four without a rifle, a fact of which he was bitterly aware.

"Perhaps I should count coup as well," Knows His Gun remarked as he reached for his elk-horn bow. Little Coyote nudged the weapon away with his foot. "The panther will laugh with High Walker because they are friends," Little Coyote said, his solemn expression misleading. On closer observation his brown eyes regis-tered concealed amusement. "But he might return your arrow to someplace other than your quiver. And right up to its turkey feathers." Knows His Gun started to complain that he was not afraid of Panther Burn but he held his tongue, for everyone knew Little Coyote as a man wise in the ways of truth, capable of recognizing lies when he heard them.

"Better to give thanks for this morning," Little Coy-ote added, glancing upward as the hawk suddenly ceased its lethargic spirals above the treetops and shot from the sky like a bolt of lightning. A tanager, its red head and bright yellow plumage gleaming in the dawn's glow, glided from the top of a hundred-and-seventy-foot-tall ponderosa pine and headed toward its nest among the branches of a smaller pine halfway up the slope oppo-site the camp. The tanager's high-pitched cry was cut

5

short by an onrush of lethal talons as the hawk knifed through the air. Dark and deadly, its rust-red tailfeathers streaming back like living flames, the hawk snatched its prey from the sky. The impact sounded like a pistol shot to the men below. Its cry of triumph ringing down the wind, the hawk soared upward over the hilltop and lost itself among the conifers. Little Coyote glanced around and noticed Panther Burn standing like a statue on the hillside enrapt by the sight, a look of eagerness shining from his coppery face and flint-chip eyes. At last Panther Burn appeared to sense Little Coyote's stare, for the statue came to life and broke into a hurried trot down the last few yards of hillside.

"I hope you remember your father's words," Little Coyote said, a premonition of impending disaster lurking on the fringes of his thought.

"Too well," Panther Burn replied, tossing the arrow back at High Walker, who danced out of harm's way. "Yet it was I who cut the sign of our enemies, the Crow. It was I who alerted our village."

"And you who watched your father and the other Dog Soldiers ride out to track these Crow dogs who have entered our hunting grounds," Knows His Gun remarked offhandedly yet not without the knowledge of how his words stung the son of Yellow Eagle.

"And it is for us to bring food to our people," Little Coyote said. "Which we will not accomplish standing here." Little Coyote stooped over and took up Panther Burn's Hawken rifle, noting with satisfaction that it was already loaded and primed. Panther Burn might yearn to disobey his father, but at least he was setting a good example for the others.

"I think the others were afraid of how bravely we would count coup upon the Crow," High Walker said, siding with Panther Burn. "They are afraid we would cover ourselves with glory and shame them with our bravery." He slung his bow and quiver over his shoulder and took up his Hawken and gave a loud cry that echoed over the hills. Their horses nearby grazed unperturbed, already well accustomed to the antics of

6

the young braves. Bees darted among splashes of pink and white bitterroot. The world ignored High Walker's challenge.

"Our horses are fast," Knows His Gun piped up. "Our arrows fly swift and straight." He was as eager as any of them to make war against the Crow.

Little Coyote shook his head in resignation and started toward the horses while High Walker and Knows His Gun disguised the remains of the camp. Panther Burn fell into step, taking his rifle from Little Coyote but keeping to one side as if unwilling to walk behind even a friend. He respected Little Coyote and preferred the company of this quiet young man. But despite his love for friend and father, Panther Burn's heart yearned to prove his worth to Yellow Eagle, to all the people of the Spirit Mountain Cheyenne. He longed to wear the buffalo hat of the Dog Soldier and be accorded the respect due the members of this society. Little Coyote read his friend's thoughts but said nothing. He tossed a blanket over his horse and tied his rawhide bridle around the mare's pink-flecked muzzle and proceeded with Panther Burn to gather the other ponies.

"I too would build my lodge among the Dog Soldiers," Little Coyote revealed at last. "It is just that I am one who can wait. This, my friend, is a good day." He led three horses now while Panther Burn had bridled the other three. "And I am not ashamed to be a hunter."

Panther Burn paused. His pinto, a sturdy brown-and-white-patched stallion, nudged him forward, eager along with the other two mares to continue abreast of the horses trailing Little Coyote. Panther Burn lifted his eyes to the treetops as a dark-plumed crescent shadow swept up from the ponderosas, climbing in long lazy spirals to the sky, casting its shadow over the unforgiving earth.

"Ah, my friend, there are hunters," said Panther Burn, "and there are . . . hawks."

*   *   *

Panther Burn balanced his Hawken rifle across the back of the pinto and pulled on the rawhide shirt his mother had stitched for him. Crescent Moon had labored many hours over the shirt, stitching the Morning Star symbol on the left, over the heart and the stark red-beaded design of fire on the right. It was a shirt befitting a warrior, not a hunter, and Panther Burn had been loath to wear it even at the risk of disappointing Crescent Moon, but a brisk north wind changed his mind and he donned the soft rawhide shirt. The wind reminded him that this month was also called by some *punu-ma-es-sini*, the light snow moon. For three hours now he and Little Coyote had been riding together, leaving Knows His Gun and High Walker to hunt on the opposite slope of the ridge. Half an hour ago Panther Burn had cut buffalo sign and with Little Coyote followed the tracks in silence. The scattering of cloven hoofprints took them through a dry wash and up a long arduous climb along a gully that forced Panther Burn to take the lead and Little Coyote to follow. The surefooted pinto beneath Panther Burn chose his steps carefully. The animal had been bred to the rocky slopes, perhaps had climbed these same ridges, before Panther Burn had caught him and turned the animal from a wild mustang into a half-wild mustang. Good graze at the top of the draw, Panther Burn thought to himself as the pinto quickened its stride; good graze and water luring the animals into hurrying up such a winding broken path as this. Savage-looking chunks of broken granite jutted out from beneath a veneer of topsoil. Brush against one of these and lose a chunk of flesh from your leg, strip it to the bone. Step wrong and a ledge could break away, sending horse and rider tumbling down the gully, leaving both broken, buried in gravel, carrion for wolves. The pinto angled to the left. Panther Burn almost lost his balance, his fingers tightened on the reins, his legs firmly clasped the stocky frame beneath him. The animal sidestepped again, leaped a break in the granite, and trotted up the remaining few feet to bring Panther Burn out on a broad plateau carpeted with tall yellow grasses dotted with tender emerald shoots. The land gradually sloped into a broad fertile valley. Spring storms had washed life into the valley. Though patches of snow still clung to the shadows lining the battlements better than ten miles across from where the two braves stood, the green shoots clinging to life here by the gully increased in gay abundance, spreading outward in an avalanche of newborn life. Despite the chill north wind stirring the dry yellow stalks of yesterday, spring had come to the land between the ridges. Tall stately pines masked the apron of land beneath the granite battlements. Bitterroot formed pools of pink and white flowers throughout the valley. And dotting the tableau, serenely oblivious to the hunters on the ridge, a herd of buffalo wandered over the rich feeding ground—one older male, a younger bull, half a dozen cows, and four calves.

Neither brave spoke, their glances to one another conveying all the information they needed. Panther Burn had first discovered the tracks that had brought them to the valley. It was for him to make the kill. Holding his rifle by the rawhide-wrapped stock he gestured toward the older bull. Little Coyote nodded. They would approach the grazing animal from either side, Little Coyote to head the animal toward Panther Burn, whose responsibility it was to make the kill. Panther Burn was grateful that Little Coyote had suggested leaving the packhorses in the care of High Walker and Knows His Gun. It made two less horses to have to worry about. Buffalo are a peculiar lot. Oftentimes an entire herd will stand placidly feeding while all around them hunters fire their guns, dropping animal after animal. Another day and the slightest commotion might set them off in a thunderous onslaught of hooves and slashing horns, trampling everything in their path. Those days were gone, Panther Burn ruefully reminded himself. *Ve-ho-e*, white men, had brought an end to the vast herds sweeping the plains, white men who killed for sport, who took the hides and left the prairies choking on the stench of rotted meat. *Ve-ho-e* had made the rifle Panther Burn carried. And though it shot further than a bow and perhaps killed quicker, he wondered if the price might not be too high for such a weapon. For the rifle was not of the people. Such thoughts confused him. And now was not the time to think of right or wrong.

The herd below ignored them as the Cheyenne braves slowly descended the slope and reached the floor of the valley. Panther Burn tried to swallow, his mouth was dry as granite shale. One of the calves had ceased its playing, stopped to stare at the approaching riders. To the calf's poor eyesight, the hunters appeared to be two more buffalo albeit strangely shaped ones. The young bull was better than a hundred yards away, cropping the green shoots sprouting up through old growth around a pool of melted snow. As Little Coyote made his way around opposite his companion and began to double back, the wind shifted, carrying his scent to the old bull. Six feet tall from hoof to humped shoulder blades, ten feet long from horn to tail, to see its great shaggy head rise suddenly and a great and terrible bellow issue from its throat was enough to strike fear into the bravest heart.

The bull lunged forward, veered toward Panther Burn, recognized the blocked route and lowered his head, charging forward, eyes blazing, slaver on its lips. The move was unexpected. So was the bison's speed. Panther Burn jerked on the reins and the pinto danced to one side as the bull lunged past, its curved horns narrowly missing the pinto. Little Coyote galloped past in pursuit. Gravel and dust spattered Panther Burn's face as he wheeled the pinto and took off after Little Coyote. Alerted by the bull, the rest of the herd fled the meadow, heading toward the shelter of the rocky battlements to the north. Panther Burn eased the hammer down on the percussion cap and whipped his pinto into a reckless gallop that gradually closed the distance on Little Coyote and the buffalo bull. He watched as Little Coyote raised his rifle. The bison veered to the left, its horns slicing toward Little Coyote's mare. The

Cheyenne was forced to fire his rifle while yanking on the reins to guide his mount out of the path of those raking horns. Flame, powder smoke, and lead ball spouted harmlessly over the bison's hump. The mare almost lost its footing, forcing Little Coyote to rein up to keep them both from tumbling to the ground.

Panther Burn was a blur of motion passing his friend at a dead gallop. The dark mane lashed his cheeks as he leaned forward, riding low and close to the mustang. The bison was fast. The sturdy little pinto was faster. But time was running out. The bull was leading Panther Burn toward a rock-strewn section of the meadow that would make pursuit even more treacherous. The pinto seemed to sense the urgency, and calling up a reserve of strength, pulled slowly forward, inching up until horse and rider were alongside the bull. Panther Burn raised his rifle, gripping the reins with his left hand, aiming the Hawken with his right. But he held his fire, waiting, daring a broken neck so as not to waste his shot. He had seen the animal's cunning and resisted the urge to fire. Suddenly the animal veered to the right, trying the same trick it had used on Little Coyote. Panther Burn yanked on the reins and the pinto veered in step with the buffalo. For a moment, stallion and bull were parallel, charging at breakneck speed across the mountain meadow. For a single moment, flashing hooves and slashing horn, sinew, flesh, and shaggy fur, horse and buffalo and man were a single entity, unstoppable and one, in wild and deadly flight upon the plain. Death or life in a matter of inches, in split-second timing, the difference between thought and instinct.

The Cheyenne sighted behind the shoulder, hesitated to allow the bull its stride as its hooves pounded forward, rib cage extended, leaving unprotected and vulnerable the bison's swiftly hammering heart.

Panther Burn fired.

* * *

Memories slither out from shadows, memories glare with serpent's eyes from the dreaming embers. Only the keening drums toll the notes of tragedy. Tap-tap-tapping like some beating heart in the throes of sleep, moving into endless sleep. *Let me walk the spirit trail with my friends, All-Father, hear me!* Panther Burn looked up at his mother. She might be real, or a phantom of the night come to trap him. He had been lured into a trap before.

"I bring living water." She spoke in a soft tone. She stared into her son's agonized gaze. His fault . . . his fault . . . his most grievous fault. She wanted to offer her solace, but knew there was no comfort for him and did not wish to humiliate him by trying. Crescent Moon bowed and stepped out of the tipi, leaving behind the clay jar she had carried up from Crazy Wolf Spring. Panther Burn crawled over to the jar and cupped a handful of water to his mouth, cupped another and washed his face, the icy cold water bracing in its effect. It made him feel better. And feeling better returned his pride. What had he done save make war on the enemies of his village? What wrong had he committed? Was he not of the Morning Star people, the blood in his veins, Cheyenne blood? Enough of torture. Let the elders decide his fate. He had done what must be done. He would not hang his head and walk the path of shame, not for his father or any other chief of the village. The drums continued, signaling that the elders were still in council. So be it. He stood. Sucking in a draft of air, he recognized the smell of cooked buffalo meat. Memories of the hunt returned, and more than the hunt . . . the ride back. He would never forget the ride back.

Around the flagging campfire, Knows His Gun leaped the flames, loosing an ear-splitting war whoop as he touched earth, leaped again over the cookfire. Landing, he stumbled so that the brown bottle of whiskey he held slipped from his grasp. High Walker reacted with an agility that belied his squat stocky frame. His hand shot out and snared the bottle in midair, and continuing in a single motion, swept up to tilt the bottle to his lips. He took three swallows as Knows His Gun recovered his balance and lurched toward his companion.

"You'll drink it all, thief!"

Little Coyote and Panther Burn glanced up from the travois they had built to haul the meat to the village. They watched as Knows His Gun leaped for the whiskey, as High Walker knocked him back and stole another mouthful of the raw, throat-scorching brew.

"It seems the trader who visited our village during the last moon brought more than blankets and gunpowder," Panther Burn muttered.

"Knows His Gun will have visions in the morning." Little Coyote chuckled.

"Just so long as they are visions of him doing his share of the work." Panther Burn finished tying off the leather fastenings that bound the lodge poles into the woven pattern of a frame and glanced up at the black cliffs overhead, great brooding battlements of wind-gouged granite blotting out half the sky.

"At least the light of our fire is hidden from half the hills."

"You are like the *ve-ho-e* trader who weighs his gunpowder, his grain, the glass beads which the women prize so. My friend, you weigh your thoughts and trade them for trouble, only trouble, always trouble."

"We have seen Crow sign these days," Panther Burn replied. "In the presence of his enemies, only a fool says, 'I am safe, there is nothing that can harm me.' " He glanced at Little Coyote, wondering if his friend had taken offense. The words had been spoken with unintended harshness. It was not Little Coyote's fault that Yellow Eagle had ordered them out on the hunt. The two men continued in silence to stare into the light of the campfire where High Walker and Knows His Gun were locked in desperate struggle over the remnants of the whiskey. Know His Gun was astride High Walker's chest, both hands locked on the bottle that

High Walker refused to release, laughing all the while. Panther Burn reached down and wrested the bottle from them both. He threw the bottle beyond the circle of light, sending it crashing among the rocky debris at the base of the cliff.

"Ahhhh!" Knows His Gun staggered to his feet and stumbled toward the edge of the circle, then looked back at Panther Burn. "You had no right."

High Walker tried to stand but his own brother shoved him back, shook his head in warning. Knows His Gun wiped a forearm across his features. His hair hung unbraided and clung in sweaty strands to his cheeks. He wore a breechcloth and nothing more. His nakedness wreaked of spilled whiskey. Knows His Gun blinked to clear his vision as Panther Burn knelt by his own blankets and began arranging his Hawken rifle, shirt, and other gear. Knows His Gun straightened, his small but muscular physique swelled with false courage.

"I am no woman to be ordered about. I am not your slave. You had no right to take my whiskey." He cleared his throat and spat on the ground, almost losing his balance. He steadied himself. "We have never walked in the same path, you and I, so you taunt me, you insult me."

"We have never walked in the same path." Panther Burn nodded without looking at the smaller man. "But I threw the white man's crazy water from camp because you had had enough. You and High Walker, both. And we are not safe among the lodges of our people on this night."

"Liar. Black liar. I say you seek to shame me." Knows His Gun slipped a knife free from its scabbard at the small of his back. Neither Little Coyote nor High Walker made a move, each was loath to precipitate violence against one of their own. Knows His Gun moved forward, the knife blade extended from his fist. "I am Knows His Gun . . . swift as the hawk, strong as the silvertip . . . a scourge to those who would be my enemy . . . come, I am not afraid of you, come and kill me if you can."

"It will hurt," said Panther Burn, his black eyes deep and merciless. His voice was soft, spoken for the man with the knife, a gentle voice that cut through the whiskey-fed bravado and sowed the seeds of fear, more deadly than a knife thrust. Knows His Gun could not withstand the bleakness in those dark eyes, the bitter truth in the quiet solemn voice. It would hurt . . . a lot. And then he would be dead. The knife blade wavered, and lowered at last. Knows His Gun turned and walked back to his bedroll and slumped down upon his blankets. He closed his eyes, groaned, and passed out, his last thought that it was better to sleep in shame than die.

High Walker sighed and stretched back out on the ground. Little Coyote continued to his own blankets, where he checked his rifle before reclining. Warmth radiated from the glowing coals of the campfire, the sky overhead was clear and ablaze with stars, his belly was full, it had been a good hunt. He looked over at Panther Burn, who sat staring at the coals.

"Knows His Gun was drunk with whiskey," Little Coyote said. "Do not let it trouble you." He folded his hands behind his head. "It is my way to brood over such things, not yours. Tomorrow we start home, the hunt is over. *E-peva-e*, it is good."

"The song to welcome us to our village has yet to be sung," Panther Burn replied. He continued to stare at the blood-red coals. Panther Burn's uncle had looked into such a fire as this and found the name for his newborn nephew amid the dancing flames, had been given a vision of a mountain cat watching him from the livid coals, a panther burning . . . burning in the night.

"What are you telling me?" Panther Burn challenged the pulsing coals, the voice of his thoughts, soundless as starlight, unnoticed by his companions.

Immense stands of white pine circled the broad clearing. Clouds overhead looked like vast snow-covered granite peaks grown miraculously airborne and drifting

15

eastward, casting sullen somber shadows on the earth below, dampening the festive brilliance of the sun. A day homeward from the valley of the buffalo, the four hunters drew abreast of one another. Behind them, the two packhorses trailing their travois obediently halted. The Cheyenne waited, under cover of the forest. They watched from the edge of the clearing as a single rider entered the meadow almost directly across from them. Still two hundred yards away they could see he was not Cheyenne, but Crow. A lone Crow warrior, perhaps lost, foolishly revealing himself to the young Cheyenne braves.

"We are hunters," Little Coyote whispered, turning to Panther Burn, fearing that where he led the others would follow.

"We are Cheyenne," Panther Burn replied. "And here rides our enemy so contemptuous of us that he makes no effort to hide himself."

"We have much meat to bring to our village." Little Coyote glanced at the others, then back to his friend.

"I think I will count coup on this Crow and gain a lodge of my own among the clan of my father. Yellow Eagle himself will call me Dog Soldier," Panther Burn said.

"I too will ride against this Crow," Knows His Gun spoke up.

"And I in turn," added High Walker. "Come, my brother," he returned to Little Coyote, "is it not your wish as well to be counted among the bravest of the brave? Let us count coup on this Crow warrior and capture him. We will bring him to our village so that all may witness our brave deeds. The young women will make songs for us, will sing to us near the rushes of the river."

Panther Burn checked the surrounding forest, saw no other movement. This had to be the handiwork of the All-Father providing him the opportunity at last to prove himself. He reached behind and unfastened the extra packets of smoked buffalo hump and allowed them to drop to the pine-needle-carpeted earth.

16

"Will you come, my friend?" he asked of Little Coyote. The pinto pawed impatiently at the ground as if sensing the rider's anxiousness. Little Coyote glanced down at the packet on the ground.

"I do not find it so easy to discard my responsibilities," he said, a strange sadness in his eyes.

"I will return for them," Panther Burn replied. The other two braves were likewise freeing their mounts from unnecessary encumbrances. Panther Burn kept the rawhide scabbard over his rifle the better to strike his enemy without killing, thus braving death and counting coup. Knows His Gun notched an arrow, then remembered at the stern glances of the others what must be done. He returned the arrow to his quiver. He would use his bow to strike the Crow warrior. High Walker handed his Hawken rifle to Little Coyote and tore a limb from a nearby piece of deadwood, then flashed a grin.

"Use a switch to strike a Crow dog," he laughed. Little Coyote did not appear amused. Something was troubling him, but the others ignored his somber expression.

Panther Burn looked upward at the limitless reaches of cloud-dappled heaven. He pointed and spoke. "You see, my brothers, the sky is empty. Today, I will be the hawk." He breathed in the sweet cold air. The March wind ruffled the gray feathers fastened in his hair. He felt a part of earth, tree, sky, wind . . . and the world seemed to pause, to hold its spirit breath as if waiting in readiness.

The figure in the meadow drew closer now. A man on a brown mare, clad in buckskins, black feathers woven into the striking topknot of hair curling forward over his forehead, he carried a rifle and a war shield painted yellow and fringed with six black feathers. The world waited as if drawing the rider in the meadow closer still. At last Panther Burn could contain himself no longer. Loosing a wild cry, he drove his heels into the flanks of his pony. Horse and rider shot from the clearing.

"Haaa-yaaaa-iiii! It is a good day to die," shouted

17

Panther Burn, brandishing his rifle in its scabbard. "Come, my enemy. We will do battle this day." The Crow warrior drew up sharply, then wheeled his horse and took off back the way he had come. Surprised at such behavior, Panther Burn glanced over his shoulder and was dismayed to find that High Walker and Knows His Gun had not waited, but followed him out of the clearing, ruining the plan. Panther Burn had figured on the Crow standing his ground. Now there was nothing to do but outrun the others and close with the Crow in hopes of engaging him in combat. Panther Burn leaned forward over the pinto, the pony's mane streaking back to whip his rider's cheeks. Ahead, the Crow seemed to falter as if losing a grip on the reins. Gaining ground, Panther Burn urged the pinto on. He could hear the drumming hooves behind him and would have turned to wave off his companions had he not feared losing control of his own racing horse. A fall might well result in a broken neck. So he relied on speed to overtake the Crow's brown mare before the likes of Knows His Gun could join the fight. The Crow angled to the left. Panther Burn followed, trying to cut the brave off. The Crow swerved again, bringing himself within range of the others. Cursing, Panther Burn slapped the rifle across the pinto's flanks to coax the last ounce of speed out of the animal. Suddenly Knows His Gun cut across his path and Panther Burn swerved in the nick of time, barely avoiding a collision. The Crow unexpectedly changed course again. Knows His Gun fought his horse, managing to bring it under control. He was hopelessly out of the chase, but High Walker, the last suddenly finding himself first, plunged directly toward the Crow brave and raised his switch to count coup. The fool was charging head-on without regard to safety.

"No!" Panther Burn shouted too late as the Crow raised up his rifle, a breech-loading Springfield, and fired over his war shield. High Walker was blown backward off his horse. He landed on his shoulders, arms and legs outstretched, still holding the pine branch, his body rolled heels over head, came to a halt and settled in the tall grass. Panther Burn slowed to look at his dead companion. High Walker's face seemed frozen in a mirthful grin, as if the circumstances of his own death struck him as a poorly conceived joke. Panther Burn ripped the rawhide scabbard from his rifle. He would count no coup this day, but take a life for a life. The war cry welling in his throat died unspoken as he looked after the departing Crow, now riding directly toward the pine grove from which the Cheyenne had emerged. Black powder smoke masked the clearing, rifle fire erupted from the shadows. Panther Burn watched in horror and helpless understanding as five Crow warriors emerged from the clearing, leading off the packhorses and travois. The Crow who had lured Panther Burn and the others from the woods turned now and issued a challenge at the two braves in the meadow. The other Crow, one of whom seemed to be sorely wounded, appeared torn between attacking the remaining two Cheyenne and leaving with the stolen travois. Knows His Gun whipped his horse and retreated at a gallop toward the cover of the forest. Panther Burn, utterly sick at heart, leaped down from the pinto. He would make his stand and die here. He raised his rifle and signaled for his taunting enemy to attack him. The Crow argued among themselves and for a moment Panther Burn braced himself for their onslaught. Eventually reason overrode battle lust. The Crow swung their horses around and disappeared into the timber, the last of their jeering insults faded on the thin air. The melee had ended as quickly as it had begun. Panther Burn started walking toward the edge of the forest, his legs trembling with every step as he led the pinto back the way they had come. "Little Coyote!" The Crow had set a trap and he had fallen right into it. His fault, his alone. "Little Coyote!" He entered the line of trees, fearing the worst. "Little Coyote . . . ?" And he found it.

Little Coyote lay where he had died, two steps away from a deadwood barricade. The broken shaft of an arrow jutted from his side, a war club had caved in part of his skull and masked his countenance with brains and blood. The two rifles were gone and his body had been speedily stripped. He lay naked, facedown among the pine needles. So boyish-looking now, so helpless. Slowly Panther Burn squatted by his friend, reached out and placed his hand on Little Coyote's cold right arm. Within reach, as if in final rebuke to the living, caught among the brittle branches of the deadwood, where it had been tossed in a dying last effort, dangled the packet of meat Panther Burn had so easily discarded.

Yellow Eagle, war chief of the Dog Soldiers, emerged from the lodge of his elders, his heart heavy within him. Yet such emotion was not for him to show, not while the eyes of the mother and father of Little Coyote and High Walker were fixed on him. He strode purposefully from the center of the great circle and up the slope toward the lodges of the Dog Soldier Society among which Panther Burn would no longer be allowed to live even though his mother lodged there . . . even though his father was the leader of the clan. Panther Burn would not be hounded from the village, but if he were to stay, no society would have him, and he must make his camp outside the confines of the great circle. His recklessness had caused deprivation for the food he had lost and grief for the lives. The blame had fallen on him. Knows His Gun escaped guilt, for he had not been the leader of the hunt, and as he had proclaimed before the council, Knows His Gun had only ridden out into the clearing to bring Panther Burn back from his foolhardy attack. Yellow Eagle shook his head and continued up the hill. If only Panther Burn had offered some defense for his actions. Dogs barked in the darkness. Unseen in the night, a woman wailed and mourned and beat her breast. The mother of Little Coyote and High Walker loomed before him. Yellow Eagle paused.

"My sons . . . where are my sons?" the woman shouted, holding up her arms. She had lacerated the flesh of her forearms, blood covered her rawhide dress. She stumbled, other women stepped forward to bear her off toward the orange glow of a campfire. A man of sure quick steps, a man casting a long shadow, Yellow Eagle betrayed no emotion but walked with the bearing of authority. The Dog Soldiers' own reputation for courage in battle carved a path for him through the curious onlookers eager to know the decision of the elders and chiefs. Dishonor had sullied the lodge of Yellow Eagle, casting its shadow on all who would dwell within. And yet, in his heart, a father is loath to cast away his son. Easier to scar himself, endure any physical suffering than to stare at the flesh of your flesh and say, "I have no son."

Yellow Eagle paused before his tipi, dreading to the deepest recesses of his being what must be done.

"Panther Burn!"

Nothing.

"Panther Burn!"

Nothing still.

The chief of the Dog Soldiers leaned forward and stepped into the lodge. A solitary figure huddled by the dying fire. Crescent Moon lifted her coppery face.

"He is gone," she said.

Before her, like an offering of hopeless expiation, resting in the nest of crimson coals, lay a bloody knife, bloodier still the blackened morsel of severed flesh, near the blade . . . the finger Panther Burn had cut from his left hand in grief.

"Your son is gone," said Crescent Moon.

Her deep brown eyes were dry. The tears were in her voice.

BOOK ONE

1

A thousand miles wasn't enough. Fifty-two days on horseback, riding south, always south, leaving Montana and Wyoming territory behind, crossing into Colorado, avoiding the occasional ranch house or scrub farm, avoiding all men, red or white, for fifty-two days. March into April, always on the move. Now with May—*vehpotse-ese*, the Leaf-Moon—but three days off, still that from which he fled rode with him, the guilt, the weary hurt. Wasn't it enough that he had left Spirit Mountain and his people (his no longer) behind? What did the ghosts of Little Coyote and High Walker require . . . death for death? Running did not undo what had been done. Panther Burn could not bring back the dead, nor would he end his own life. And yet in a way he had, cutting himself off from his parents, his village, to journey south. Leaving had salvaged what remained of his honor. There were things worse than exile.

Gray rain fell in slanted sheets from the sky the color of gunpowder. Soaked to the skin, Panther Burn lowered his head to the elements, allowing the pinto its head. Water matted the brave's black hair, streamed down his face and neck. He tugged his blanket over his head;

though the material was too drenched to provide warmth it at least buffered his features from the stinging downpour. Today, tomorrow, or the next day, he was bound to reach the Warbonnet and then it would be a simple matter to follow the creek upstream or down until he cut sign and reached the village of the Southern Cheyenne and the hearth of Beartusk. Panther Burn had not seen his uncle for almost three years and yet he knew he would be welcome at his campfire.

Thunder rumbled overhead, shook the muddy ground, caused all the world to tremble. The pinto shied. The Northern Cheyenne's fingers instinctively tightened on the reins as he spoke harshly to the animal. The pinto under control again, Panther Burn adjusted the blanket over his shoulder and head. Balancing his rifle scabbard across his lap, he rubbed water from his eyes, squinted, trying to see through the fading daylight, hoping to spot a tree, a large rock, any type of outcropping. But here on the broad rolling valley floor, cover was scarce. He should have remained in the foothills and waited out the storm. Ruefully he remembered how he had watched it build in the west, great battlements of clouds piling one atop the other, blotting the sun, looming darker, ever darker. But patience was something he hadn't packed in his war kit, and wagering he might win his race across the wide treeless valley and reach the low hills and timber to the south, he'd broken camp and headed out. A fool's escapade, and one currently teaching him a bitter lesson. But the hills and forest line couldn't be much farther ahead. His stomach growled. The brave tried to will his hunger away. For two days now he had seen not the slightest trace of game save for a couple of jackrabbits that had dodged his arrows with ease. Relying on the Hawken had spoiled his talent with the bow, he bitterly noted. The rifle, a fine weapon for deer and buffalo, was much too large a bore for rabbit. So the brave went hungry. He rode on, bowed forward, enduring, with as little conscious effort as possible.

Come all this way to drown, he thought to himself. And started to laugh. And then he stopped as the pinto halted in its tracks. Panther Burn glanced up in alarm and saw a dark expanse directly ahead; in the grim light, through the slanting rain, the blackness loomed wide and tall, gradually gaining definition as the downpour lessened in its fury. The shape took on edges, a roof, became the opening of a barn, its doors open.

"Well, don't just stand there, Injun, come in out of the rain," a voice issued from inside.

Panther Burn paused, suddenly grown cautious, his right hand slipping inside the buckskin scabbard covering his rifle.

"You understand me?"

"I understand," Panther Burn replied to the shadow before him.

"Then suit yourself, hoss. But I'm closin' up."

One of the broad panel doors began to swing shut. Panther Burn nudged the pinto with his heels and the animal trotted in out of the slashing wind-whipped dusk. The cessation of rain hammering at him was a relief and the Cheyenne sighed as he jumped down from the pinto to the straw-littered floor, swaying once and steadying himself against his horse.

Panther Burn allowed his eyes to adjust to the gloomy interior. The pinto waited patiently as if being out of the storm was enough reward. The Cheyenne's grip remained firm on the Hawken in its beaded buckskin covering. Saddles, bridles, stalls, thick pine beams, mud-chinked timber walls all took on definition in the feeble light. The owner of the barn drew closer.

"Heard your horse there a-plodding through the mud. I'm a keen listener. Always been. Eyes ain't worth much, no sir. They git any dimmer, this ol' hoss will have to seek tamer pasture." As the barn took on definition, so did the man within. A hard-bitten old-timer, back bowed, thinning gray hair, broad-shouldered and long of arm, clad in a plaid shirt and worn woolen trousers tucked into black boots. He stretched out a leathery hand to the rain-soaked Cheyenne. Water dripped from Panther Burn's fringed buckskins. The eagle feathers woven in his braid were sodden. He brushed the black hair out of his eyes. His coal-black eyes were alert, suspicious, his entire frame hungry yet wiry and poised. His gaze lowered to the Colt dragoon thrust in the old man's waistband.

"My name's Wister . . .. Jed Wister. I could've started the ball when you were sittin' out there in the rain." The old man patted the revolver. "But . . . I got no quarrel with any man, be he red or white, black or yellow . . . long as he comes in peace a man's welcome at Foot o' the Mountains. That's what I call my place here." The old man noted the Indian's newly healed left hand where Panther Burn had cauterized the stump of his severed finger and covered it with a healing poultice of elk mint, whiteweed, and tallow, wrapping it in buckskin until the wound had ceased draining. The old man knew the purpose of such a self-mutilation but did not inquire. He ended his speech and turned his back on the brave and started down the straw-littered aisle that separated the two rows of stalls.

"There's coffee and hot grub at the house," Wister muttered as he neared the rear of the barn. He doubled over, and lifted a trapdoor. "Got me a tunnel here so we don't even need to get wet. Dug it myself, which is why I don't walk so straight-up, erect-like no more." His pocked features managed a grin, and frankness, too, that Panther Burn found to be an unusual quality in a *ve-ho-e*, a white man. "Bed here or follow me to the house, whatever you've a mind to." Wister took a lamp from a nearby timber support, knocking a bridle to the floor in the process. He muttered something about useless old-timers, and returning the gear, struck a match on his belt buckle and lit a little coal-oil lantern. The glare colored the homely set of his wrinkled face a sickly yellow. He started down.

"Wister," the Cheyenne said, stomach betraying him with an audible growl, "I will camp at your fire. I am called Panther Burn."

The old man chuckled and waved him over. "You speak pretty good English. Understand it good, too?"

28

"White missionaries, traders, soldiers at Fort Bozeman, I learned from all," Panther Burn flatly explained.

Wister nodded. "You'll do, lad. Find a stall for your horse and come on."

Foot o' the Mountains was a long, low-ceilinged house lost in the shadowy base of a massive chunk of granite that rose out of the valley floor. Climbing out of the tunnel that connected the main house to the barn, Panther Burn entered the cluttered main room where Jed Wister served up his grub and tended to the thirsty requests of his customers behind a bar built of sturdy timbers with the bark still on, rough-hewn like the men who visited Foot o' the Mountains. Oil lamps dangled from the ceiling on short stubby chains. Barrels of flour, grain, dried apples, and salt pork were stacked along the far wall. Tables and ladder-back chairs built by the same hand that had felled wood to build the house were set about the room with little regard to pattern. Pipe and cigar smoke coiled and swirled like serpent-wraiths about the foot-thick beams overhead. The room smelled of beans and bacon, of wet clothes and rye whiskey, of tobacco and sweat; it smelled of burning pine timbers and worn leather, of fur pelts, gunpowder, coal oil, and coffee. Three men clustered around one table closest to the fireplace. In the darkest corner of the room, barely discernible in the glow of his pipe, another figure sat with his back to the supply barrels. Panther Burn could not tell much about the man in shadow but the other three were dressed in uniforms like those he had seen worn by the cavalry troopers at Fort Buchanan in the Dakotas; short-waisted blue coats trimmed with brass buttons, brass buckles on black belts, breeches dyed a lighter shade of blue than the coats and tucked into calf-high black boots patched with dried mud. One of the men wore a campaign hat with one side of the brim pinned up to hold a scarlet plume that jutted back at a rakish angle.

His two companions sported short-brimmed caps and

red bandannas around their throats. The uniforms had been stripped of any identifying insignia.

"Help yourself to grub. It's hanging over the fire," Wister said, rummaging behind the bar and placing a tin cup of strong black coffee on the countertop alongside the Cheyenne. The rain outside hammered down in increasing cadence. A bucket in the center of the room slowly filled, drip by drip, as water worked its way through a broken shingle. "Been meaning to fix that," Wister noted, staring at the bucket. "But then I been meaning to visit Paree, France, someday too. Reckon I'll get around to both in good time. And if I don't, well . . ." He did not bother to finish, before altering the course of his conversation. "Lessee, uh, that's Colonel Jubal Bragg and his younger brother Tom, and that house on legs there is Big Marley."

Panther Burn took the cup without reacting to the old man's attempt at conversation, his eyes never leaving the three "soldiers" gathered at the table as he crossed to the fireplace and sat on the stone hearth before the flames. He grabbed up a tin plate, and swinging the pot out from over the flames, ladled out enough beans and pork to feed a couple of hungry men. He shoved the cook pot over the coals and hung the ladle back on its hook. He tore a loaf of fresh bread in half, grabbed up a spoon, and started to eat, all the while remaining conscious of the three men in uniform. One of the three, the youngest and from his facial appearance related to the man in the plumed hat, slid back in his chair, and standing, crossed to the bar.

Tom Bragg was slight of build, clean-shaven; his cheeks were thin-skinned, tiny red veins showed at his cheekbones. His eyes were a soft brown, gentle like a woman's and sharply contrasting with the contemptuous set of his arched eyebrows and thin-lipped smile. He moved with a kind of cockiness that reminded Panther Burn of Knows His Gun. A second chair slid back and the one called Marley joined his friend at the bar. Looming over his younger companion, Marley was thick-shouldered, thick-necked, with legs like oak beams. When he turned, leaning back with his elbows on the bar, he revealed features as brutish as the young man's were cultured, almost feminine. Big Marley had been in more than one fight in his time: his bald head, cheeks, and jaw were thick with scar tissue and a nasty scar ran across the bridge of his flattened nose. The third man, Colonel Jubal Bragg, remained seated. He was as slight of build as his brother. His brown hair hung to his neck in carefully trimmed curls. The crow's-feet at the corners of his eyes, the hard set of his features, gave him a lean and dangerous look. Unlike his younger brother, the colonel sported neatly trimmed sideburns that framed his face. He sat stiffly, properly erect like a king holding court. Panther Burn sensed the presence of *masanee*, the crazy spirit, behind the man's cool, intelligent disdain so evident in his patrician features. Panther Burn did not like looking at the man with the plumed hat and so the Cheyenne lowered his gaze to the Hawken rifle balanced across his right leg, then to his plate of bread, beans, and salt pork. He almost gagged on his first sip of coffee but the hot bitter liquid warmed him to the bone, and the food, though a far cry from antelope steaks and pemmican, subdued the gnawing hunger in his belly.

"I say, Wister," the man in the plumed hat at last spoke up, his tone that of a man forced to endure the indignities of Wister's humble dwelling. "As colonel of the territory militia, entrusted with the protection of the settlers from Denver to Castle Rock and as far north as the Graybull, I find myself perplexed by your behavior. Letting one of the very savages whose depredations I and my brother Tom here and Sergeant Marley have been sent to protect you against . . . letting this . . . buck within your very walls smacks of extremely poor judgment, and I am kind in my phrasing, sir."

"Beggin' your pardon, Colonel Bragg, but I didn't ask for any part of your help," Wister replied. "May be some scared folks over in Castle Rock. But not me. I been on good terms with Injun folk 'ceptin' maybe the Ute, which a blind man could see this lad ain't."

31

Tom Bragg tilted his head and threw a shot of Wister's rye down his throat, gasping at the liquid fire. "Red meat looks alike and smells alike to me." He flashed a grin at Big Marley, and pushed away from the bar. He hooked his thumb in his army-issue gunbelt, his left hand closed around the wire-wrapped hilt of the saber slung at his side. Jubal tugged at his sideburns as he assessed the situation. He glanced over at his brother, admiring Tom's bravado if not his discretion. On the murder of their parents by the Cheyenne, Tom, six years younger than his brother, had been sent to Philadelphia to be raised by grandparents, while Jubal, at fourteen, had hired himself out to a freighter in St. Louis. He had grown to manhood in the West and was no stranger to violence.

"Lookee here, Tom . . . uh . . ." Wister stammered, trying to intercede. "The rule here at Foot o' the Mountains is any man is welcome. And no trouble. This here's neutral ground."

Big Marley looked over his shoulder at the old-timer. He shook his head, placed a finger thick as a sausage to his lips, indicating Wister ought to be quiet.

"I ain't talking about a man," Tom said. He checked the gloom-shrouded figure in the dark corner, imagined him to be impressed. Basking in the power emanating from his older brother's presence, young Tom Bragg threw out his chest and swaggered over to the colonel's table. The whiskey burning in his gut fueled his courage all the more. Too young to receive a commission in the recently concluded War Between the States, young Tom had abandoned an Eastern education and left his grandmother's side in Philadelphia to join his influential brother in the Colorado Territory. Here was adventure and glory to be won. Here in the West was a place for men of valor. He had come to the frontier to fight Indians, and the brave by the fire was the first real Indian he had seen alive and up close. Only one week west of the Mississippi and already an opportunity had presented itself.

Oblivious, or so it seemed to the colonel's brother,

Panther Burn ignored Tom's baiting and finished his meal. He was troubled not by the words of Tom Bragg but by the kinship he felt for the *ve-ho-e* youth. Panther Burn too was a man who had something to prove . . . to his father . . . and to himself.

Movement in the corner of the room diverted the Cheyenne's attention. The man at the table by the supply barrels rose and approached the hearth, plate in hand. He was dressed in buckskins, frayed at elbows and wrists, a beaded belt girded his middle, there was no narrowing of the waist. The man was broad in the shoulders, chest, hip, and thigh, solid-looking as if carved from stone, and though he stood no more than five and a half feet tall in his calf-high moccasins, he moved with a grace and quickness, with such an aura of formidability that it seemed as if he towered over a man like Marley. Thick red hair hung to his shoulders, a closely cropped beard covered his jaw, and thick red eyebrows lent a brooding quality to his deep-set russet-colored eyes. He wore no weapon save for an "Arkansas toothpick," a knife whose broad fifteen-inch blade, double-edged and razor-sharp, flashed in the light of the fire. He stepped in front of Tom and leaned across Panther Burn, who resisted an impulse to raise his rifle in alarm. The red-haired man stabbed a chunk of albescent salt pork out of the iron cook pot with his knife and used the broad blade to scoop a portion of beans on top of the meat. He turned and winked at Tom and spoke softly in a deep gravelly voice, menacing in its gentleness.

"Pilgrim, folks around here have enough trouble with the Ute coming over on the dry side, raiding and killing, without you starting trouble with the Cheyenne. Jubal Bragg"—the man looked past Tom to the officer of the militia seated at the table—"you and I seldom see eye to eye. But in this case maybe you better listen up and have your brother take off his war paint before our guest here puts his on." The red-haired man licked the bean drippings from the blade.

Tom's facial expression wrinkled in distaste for the

man's lack of manners. "Now, you look, Sabbath McKean, I'll thank you to mind your own damn business."

"Suit yourself," the red-haired man said. "Just strikes me as a shame. A fella ought to be dry behind the ears before he goes off and loses them." The knife blade flashed in the firelight and rose again with a morsel of fatback speared on the point. Tom started to draw his saber but halted at his brother's voice.

"Enough, lad. You've had your say," Jubal said, silencing his brother. He glanced at Sabbath to see if the scout was satisfied. McKean nodded.

"Rain appears to be letting up. Why don't you take your brother and Marley here on to Castle Rock," he suggested.

"Where a kinder visit awaits us, I daresay," Jubal added. The colonel stood, revealing himself to be a tall, narrowly built man, slender as Tom Bragg but with an air of authority his brother lacked. Two silver dollars clattered onto the tabletop. The colonel returned a third to the belt pouch at his waist. The big man at the bar straightened and snorted in disgust.

"One of these days," he growled, "I'll learn ye what color your skin is."

"Anytime, Marley," said Sabbath McKean, half the big man's size and twice as dangerous. The colonel stepped in front of Tom, gestured for his brother to precede him to the back room and the stairway to the tunnel. Tom grudgingly relented, backing away, turning and leading the way. Marley tugged at the brim of his cap and glowered at Wister.

"One day you oughta learn to make rye whiskey, you old fart."

"Rye? I thought you ordered *lye*," chuckled Wister, enjoying himself now.

"I trust you will be ready to scout for us when the militia is formed," Colonel Bragg said to the man called McKean. Panther Burn looked from one to the other. "Some of your friends and neighbors will be riding with us."

34

"I'll join you in Castle Rock," replied McKean. "At least until we push the Ute back over the divide."

Bragg nodded. The officer looked after his brother. "Tom will learn. He's a good lad and damn if he hasn't spirit. Those Eastern schools couldn't smother that." He tipped his hat to the scout, spun on his heels, and pointedly ignoring Wister, walked smartly from the room, his pace crisp, direct, as if on parade. At the back door, Tom waited, mustering what he hoped to be a menacing stare that he fixed on Panther Burn and the white man standing by the fire before following his brother out of sight. Sabbath McKean sighed and much to the brave's surprise spoke in Cheyenne.

"So young, so very proud . . ." Sabbath mused aloud, the phrase one he remembered from his time among the Cheyenne.

"Many are the bones drying in the wind," replied Panther Burn in kind, "that once were men, young and proud." The white man nodded, grinning in admiration at the young brave's grit and returning to his table in the shadows. Panther Burn relaxed, grateful the confrontation with the militiamen had not resulted in a fight. The soldier's animosity puzzled him, for it was said that the Southern Cheyenne walked the path of white men. Wister rounded the bar and crossed to the abandoned table, grabbing up the silver coins and dropping them in a pouch beneath his shirt. Panther Burn shifted further from the hearth but within its warmth. The thunder had indeed ceased, and though he could still hear the rain on the roof, it truly had lost intensity.

"Wister . . . ?"

The old man turned.

"I will sleep by the fire."

"Help yourself," the tavern keeper said. "Plenty of floor space. And I reckon the excitement's about over. 'Lessen maybe the creek in back rises up and washes us all away."

Panther Burn's gaze narrowed. "The *o-he-ke* . . . the creek . . . what is it called?"

"Why, uh, let's see, in your lingo . . ." Wister glanced

over at the man in the shadows for help. The gravelly voice drifted over to them.

"*Mamaa-estse*," said Sabbath McKean.

Panther Burn felt the weariness leave him at the name the white man had spoken. *Mamaa-estse!* The Warbonnet! He leaned back upon the warm hardwood floor, closed his eyes, and drifted into sleep, exultant that his journey was over, never realizing it had only just begun.

2

Halfway into the following day, Panther Burn lay beneath a green canopy of weeping willows. He cautiously settled down in the moist sand along the banks of the Warbonnet. Here where the creek became a broad sun-dappled pool with its golden gleaming stones shimmering below the jeweled surface of the water, four young Cheyenne women frolicked in the shallows. He grinned, shimmying underneath the leaf-tipped streamers, and worked himself into a better position with a more unobstructed view. He counted four actually in the creek-fed pond and seven more lying in various states of undress along the opposite bank, sitting by the water's edge, washing their hair, braiding their thick strands, chattering to each other. One of the four in the water leaped upward. Panther Burn caught his breath at the sight of her lithe tawny limbs and torso rising from the surface of the pond. A flash of coppery skin, small firm breasts crowned by nipples the color of chokecherries. As the young woman slid once more below the surface, Panther Burn grudgingly lifted his eyes to the line of trees beyond the pond, where the creek spilled over a deadwood dam. Columns of smoke rose above the treetops. Sabbath McKean had instructed the young brave to follow the creek downstream in order to find the Southern Cheyenne village. He had not lied and in fact had even expressed an interest in accompanying the Northern Cheyenne. But at the last minute, McKean decided to continue on to the white man's town of Castle Rock, for he was wary of the intentions of Colonel Jubal Bragg. As memories of departure from Foot o' the Mountains faded, the Cheyenne brave returned his attention to the pond. In front of him, beyond the rotting logs, he noticed a pile of buckskin clothing. A thought came to mind as to how he might announce his arrival among his uncle's people. His features brightened in a grin.

Rebecca Blue Thrush burst upward from the pond, her long black hair whipping outward, fanning the other young women with a fine cold spray. Esther Madison, a Cheyenne woman who had taken the last name of her Anglo husband, laughed and shielded herself. Hope Moon Basket, a round-faced portly girl, dove toward Rebecca, determined to meet the challenge, and caught her off guard, knocking her off balance. Rebecca disappeared beneath the water, only to regain her footing and emerge choking and coughing water from her lungs. Esther Madison and Faith Little Shield rushed to help, but Rebecca waved them off, and cupping her hand, swept it across the surface and splashed Hope in the face. She sputtered, caught her breath, and splashed back. Esther, petite but resilient as whipcord when it came to girlish rough-and-tumble play, joined the fray, siding with Rebecca while Faith fittingly supported Hope. From the safety of the opposite bank the other girls cheered on their favorite combatants and wagered their recently gathered berries and roots on who would be the first to cry "enough." Few were foolish enough to wager against Rebecca Blue Thrush. For the young woman had gained a reputation for persistance—some called it stubbornness—among the people of her village. Rebecca Blue Thrush had beaten even the young men of the village during a race but three months past. It had been a long and arduous course winding from the banks of the Warbonnet to Foot o' the Mountains and back to the village. Rebecca had not been the most fleet of foot among her peers. There were young men and women far quicker. But she had gained victory from simple endurance, a refusal to quit after others had fallen away with twisted ankles, bleeding feet, aching, tortured lungs. Some called it pride, finding blame in her out of anger for besting the young men in the race, others suspected her of spirit help. After all, wasn't she the daughter of Star, the medicine woman? While the young women on the creek bank tried to goad and bait one another into betting against Rebecca, to the surprise of everyone, she turned out to be the first to retreat from the onslaught of her good-natured adversaries. A collective sigh of disgust rose from the creek bank, for no one had cast their lot with poor Hope. Rebecca turned toward the bank where the willows swept the water's edge, stirred by a gentle breeze. Hope Moon Basket continued to splash until Esther cried out for her to stop. Immediately! Then Esther looked to her companion, sensing Rebecca's concern.

"*Saaaa* . . . what is it, Rebecca?" Esther said, staring at the willows.

"I do not know. Something." Rebecca replied, frowning. She shook her head. Water dripped down into her brown eyes and she wiped a hand across her face to clear her vision and brushed back the water-drenched strands of hair. Now the girls on the riverbank fell silent as well. Faith, a solidly built woman whose figure had yet to betray the fact she was with child, stepped up alongside Esther Madison, who shivered as the chill of the spring-fed creek seeped into her slight frame.

"Our clothes," she whispered to Faith. "Our clothes . . . on the bank."

"Someone tell me what is going on or I shall leave," Hope complained, suspecting all three of her friends of mischief.

Blackbirds swooped low overhead, circled in a lazy arc, dipped en masse toward the willow grove, and then loosed their high-pitched trilling calls as they rode the air currents up from the trees, avoiding the grove and scattering. Rebecca started to shout a warning to the others, just as the horseman burst from concealment. With his rifle the ferocious-looking warrior scooped up one of the buckskin shifts and whirled it overhead, loosing a wild cry. The girls on the bank screamed and scrambled up from the creek to disappear into the woods. In the pond, the four bathers swam toward the opposite bank. The warrior's wild cries only fueled the efforts of the women in the pond. Hope Moon Basket, for the first time in her sixteen years, outdistanced her three companions and was the first to rise soaked from the creek, her chubby form quivering as she clawed her way up the bank. Faith and Esther were not far behind, though. Wet hair plastered to skull and neck and shoulders, they staggered from the shallows. Hope had already vanished down the path through the forest. Faith and Esther lost no time in following, for they could hear the warrior's wild war cry as his horse plunged through the creek in pursuit.

"Quickly," gasped Esther, stumbling, bracing a hand in the mud and regaining her balance. Her slight build accounted for her speed as she darted toward the trees. Faith did not look back and most certainly did not tarry at the water's edge, but figuring Rebecca to be right at her heels, scrambled up the last few muddy yards and headed down the path after her friends. She prayed those ahead had raised an alarm in the village by now. Esther turned and glanced over her shoulder at Faith a few yards back. She slowed, stopped. Faith Little Shield swerved off the path to avoid a collision and tripped over a surface root. She bruised a shoulder, tumbled, continued to roll until she had regained her footing.

"What is the matter with you," Faith said angrily, rubbing her bruised shoulder.

"Do you want to see us both captured by such a mad

one? Would you be a Ute slave? Hurry, you foolish girl!"

Esther pulled free and pointed back up the trail, her breath rasping.

"Rebecca . . . Where is Rebecca?" Faith turned, noticed there was no one behind them. And the cries of the savage were stilled as if he no longer pursued. And if he no longer pursued, then he had found what he wanted. Faith, though larger and far stronger than Esther, reached out to clutch her friend's hand.

Water glistened on their smooth naked flesh as they looked in horror at one another, then down the empty, ominously silent path.

Rebecca Blue Thrush crouched in a little over three feet of water, enough to cover her nakedness, yet shallow enough to allow her to fight if need be. Her fingers searched, closed around a smooth, fist-sized stone. Her hair splayed upon the water in shining black strands. Panther Burn cautiously approached, the buckskin dress dangling from the muzzle of his Hawken.

"Come no closer, foolish one. I will strike you down and leave you for the men of my village to have sport with," Rebecca said, hoping she sounded more formidable than she felt. At least she had bought time for the others and allowed them to escape. Panther Burn drew closer, the water came only to the underbelly of his pinto.

"Is this any way for people of the same blood to greet one another?" Panther Burn chuckled.

"The same blood?" Rebecca warily repeated. She raised the stone, ready to hurl it at him.

"And the same star," Panther Burn gently added. He guided his horse to one side, and turning toward the girl in the shallows, revealed the Morning Star sewn into his hunting shirt.

Rebecca, realizing he had played a trick, slowly lowered the stone. She grew suddenly aware that the water hid precious little of her nakedness and she

41

attempted to cover herself. Panther Burn tilted his rifle and the buckskin smock slid off the barrel into her anxious grasp. She slid the garment over her head and stood, pulling the dress around her as she rose from the water.

"It was a good game." Panther Burn sighed. Naked or clothed, he had never seen such a lovely girl. Coppery smooth was her flesh, her hair a dark cape falling to her waist. The All-Father had fashioned her features with delicacy, spacing the slightly slanted brown eyes, touching the lips pink like the first flush of bitterroot in spring. Panther Burn tried to hide his interest behind a gruff exterior, but Rebecca's keen gaze had noticed. And now that she was no longer in fear for her life, she too made a brief assessment. What girl would not be attracted to someone so strong-looking, so confident? Though his own attractive features were marred by a kind of arrogance, his black eyes flecked with gold betrayed a deeper quality of introspection that intrigued her.

"Come, girl, I will take you to your village," he said, leaning forward to extend his left hand. She noticed the raw-looking scar tissue where his little finger had been. She reached up and took hold of his wrist. He braced himself to swing her up behind him. But Rebecca had other ideas. She lunged to her right. The pinto half-reared, dug its hind legs into the rocky bottom. Panther Burn shouted in protest as the reins slipped from his grasp. Water gushed into his open mouth, cutting off his cry. It was his turn to stagger to his feet. Coughing and squinting through blurred vision, he watched as Rebecca, riding his horse, trotted the animal up out of the pond. Panther Burn grabbed one of his eagle feathers as it drifted on the surface of the pond toward the makeshift dam. He sputtered, stooped to retrieve his rifle, and poured the water out of the barrel.

"*Now* the game is finished," Rebecca proclaimed. Panther Burn stared at her a moment. He brushed his wet hair back out of his eyes, coughed, and spat another mouthful of water, then stood erect, the water just below his waist. He took a few steps, a few more, until the water was down to his knees. He stared at the sodden eagle feather in one hand, the waterlogged rifle in the other. His shoulders began to shake, he threw back his head and gave a great laugh. And continued laughing as he slogged his way to the bank. Climbing out of the water, he leaned his rifle against a log that had been washed up on the bank during a flash flood.

"*E-pave-e,*" he said, his laughter slowly subsiding. "It is good, warrior woman."

Rebecca carefully watched him, his reaction completely unexpected. She was surprised to find a warrior so able to laugh at himself. Now she could see through the facade of his attempted arrogance and liked what she found—a pride that might deceive from time to time, but also self-knowledge. She was unaware of the remorse that had kept his very soul in a viselike grip these past weeks. She had no understanding of how good it felt to laugh after hurting inside, after being unrelentingly in pain for almost two months on the trail south from Montana. Panther Burn glanced over his shoulder, surprised to find she had not ridden away when she had the chance. He removed his moccasins, squeezed the water out, and placed them back on his feet.

He started chuckling again, shook his head.

"My friends have probably alerted the village," Rebecca said.

The brave nodded.

"The men will come," the young woman continued.

The brave nodded again.

"Well, you had better come along. You may ride with me on my horse." Panther Burn glanced up sharply this time. "Uh . . . your horse," Rebecca corrected. He stood and crossed over to her. "Panther Burn," she said. He stepped back, startled she should know his name. "I remember now," she continued. "When your people and mine gathered to renew the medicine hat and the sacred arrows. Many summers ago. Yes, I remember. You uncle is Joshua Beartusk."

"It is so," Panther Burn said. "But he is not called such a strange name . . . Ja-shwa."

"He is now. We have all taken Christian names. I am Rebecca Blue Thrush."

"Ahh . . . Star's little girl." The medicine woman was highly regarded among even the Northern Cheyenne.

"Not little anymore," Rebecca said. Panther Burn looked up at her, appreciating the way her dress clung to the shapely wet form inside. Not little anymore, indeed.

"Christian names?" Panther Burn repeated with uncertainty. "What else has changed since our two peoples joined around a single ceremonial fire?"

"Return with me and find out," Rebecca said, a challenge in her voice.

"Why not?" Panther Burn shrugged, suppressing his misgivings as he leaped up behind Rebecca. He liked the way she warmed his hands, and and warmed to his touch, her body tensing, relaxing, tensing again where he placed his hands on her waist. "After all," he added, "I have already had my bath."

More than a dozen riders met them as the pinto trotted clear of the timber. Panther Burn reminded himself that he had forgotten to load his rifle with dry powder. Of course his mind had been occupied by Rebecca's closeness. It took him a moment to realize that these men were Cheyenne at all, for many were dressed as white men, wearing worn denims, faded woolen shirts, worked-in boots. Sweatstained hats shaded their features as the men circled the pinto.

"James . . . Peter . . . what are you doing?" Rebecca called to two of the young men who brandished rifles and cast angry looks toward Panther Burn as they blocked the path.

"We rode out to rescue you," the one called James, a bold-looking young brave, replied as he angled his own skittish mount through the settling dust. "Esther . . . Faith . . . all the rest came running into our village, crying out you had been taken and our people were under attack."

"By one brave . . . one Cheyenne warrior?" Rebecca asked, laughing.

James Broken Knife looked past the couple on horseback toward the trees as if expecting a ruse. Then he focused his humorless stare once more upon Panther Burn while his companions gathered around, studying this new arrival's more primitive trappings.

"What are you doing here, *hestoo-ve-estane?*"

Panther Burn bridled at being called a stranger. He was of the same people as those around him. Now that they could see he was no enemy, still they were hostile to him.

"He is Panther Burn, nephew to Joshua Beartusk," Rebecca said, feeling a little angry herself.

"Has he no tongue . . ." the one called Peter spoke up, looking around to his companions for support, ". . . that a woman must speak for him?" He was slim, compact, with a vain disregard for the Northerner.

"Perhaps he can only speak with his hands. See, he is dressed like a savage," another voice spoke up.

"What have you to say for yourself?" James said, balancing his rifle across his lap. He carried a percussion weapon, though not as heavy a caliber as Panther Burn's. The barrel was patched with rust.

The Northern Cheyenne reached around to take the reins out of Rebecca's hands. Holding them tightly in his fist, he glanced at the young braves who surrounded him. There was no paint on their faces, yet they had ridden out to battle. Their horses were unmarked, their weapons a mixture of flintlock and percussion rifles as well as farm implements—crude hoes and rakes. As for the braves themselves, their hair was cropped close in the style of many white men. And they circled him, resentment in their faces, but why? Baiting him with their taunts, why?

"You have called me a stranger. So be it," Panther Burn replied at last, looking around him, taking them all in with his sweeping appraisal. "For is not a wolf a stranger to a pack of yelping dogs?" He slapped his rifle down across the pinto's rump and the animal burst through the ring of braves and scattered them like leaves in a gusting wind. Before the startled young men could recover, Panther Burn had crossed the meadow, and cresting a narrow ridge, followed the emerald landscape down to the village of the Southern Cheyenne. If the young men who had met him coming up from the Warbonnet had made him feel unwelcome, the sight of the village left him dumbfounded—and truly a stranger. A haphazard arrangement of log cabins with a few tipis scattered among them sprawled across the trampled grasses. The village showed little activity. Quite possibly the girls from the river had yet to spread the alarm to the whole community, or perhaps they had not been believed. Women in gingham and calico dresses, children in ragged denims, old men in buckskins or faded overalls came out of their cabins to watch in curiosity. Rebecca noticed several of her friends, fully clothed now, and she waved to them to show them nothing was the matter. The breeze shifted and Panther Burn wrinkled his nose in distaste at the stench of kept livestock that mingled with wood smoke, tainting the very air. And he took notice that several of the cabins had fenced-in and partitioned pens in which were kept hogs and chickens. Farther beyond the irregular confines of the village he could see a small herd of cattle, the white man's tame buffalo, grazing in the afternoon, lolling in the sun. Other young men rode in or walked over to study the new arrival as Rebecca, enjoying being the center of attention, announced to everyone that Panther Burn had come from his people in the North to be with his uncle, Joshua Beartusk. Panther Burn had no use for such announcements but he was too distraught to protest. More curious young men approached, and none of them looked like Cheyenne warriors. Where were the societies, the Crazy Dogs, the Red Shields and Fox Men? Panther Burn stared at the American flag where it flew from a flagpole rising upward for thirty feet from the approximate center of the camp. Why such a banner and no scalps of their enemies hanging from the pole, and why was such a thing where the ceremonial fire was to be kept burning?

And the circle? The great circle of life that every Cheyenne village and camp became the living symbol of, that every Cheyenne took his strength from, that was the basis for every aspect of life . . . where was the circle in this jumble of white man's cabins strewn upon the meadow?

Esther and her husband, Samuel, a tall spare-looking white man dressed in a black frock coat and trousers, white collar and black shirt, waited before a cabin door as the two on horseback approached. Samuel held a broad, flat-brimmed black hat in his hands. His blond hair was parted in the middle and cut close to his skull, emphasizing his overlarge ears. Rebecca pointed to the cabin where the couple waited.

"I live there."

Panther Burn tugged on the reins and warily approached the cabin. Esther gave a cry of relief and ran forward. Rebecca slid down and hurried to embrace her friend. Panther Burn glanced over his shoulder and noticed James Broken Knife and his companions skulking back into the village. A few of the braves paused to inform the curious of Panther Burn's identity.

"Oh, Rebecca, I thought you were behind me," Esther blurted out. "And when I looked around . . ." The two friends hugged one another. "I didn't know what to do."

"It's all right," Rebecca said soothingly. "You see, it is only a friend from far away. From the Northern village up beyond the Yellowstone."

Reverend Samuel Madison stepped forward.

"The peace of Christ be with you, brother." He held his hand up toward Panther Burn, who backed his horse away, keeping a close eye on this strange-looking *ve-ho-e*. "I assure you, I mean no harm," Samuel said.

"Christians names . . . white man's lodges, *ve-ho-e-otova-a*, the white man's buffalo, out in the meadow, war ponies used to scar the earth, to plant white man's crops, this is your doing?"

Samuel glanced around at his wife, then back to the brave on horseback. Recalcitrant braves were nothing new to him. Such young men as this, so desperately in need of God's word, had been the reason he had left his well-to-do family and the comfort of his father's house to spread the gospel of the eternal Father.

"My doing and that of my wife. We have a house here and in Castle Rock, although I prefer to be with Esther's people baptizing my Cheyenne brothers and sisters, teaching you to live in the new ways, in peace with the white man." He reached out and took Esther's hand, smiled at her, his long, bony features brightening, becoming almost handsome.

Panther Burn nodded and looked past the reverend to Rebecca. "Where will I find the lodge of my uncle, where are the Red Shields?"

"These people live at peace," Samuel interjected. "They no longer have need of war clans."

"There is the house of Joshua Beartusk," Rebecca said, pointing to a cabin on the westernmost perimeter of the village. Its log walls were in desperate need of mud-chinking. "But will you not greet my mother first?" Panther Burn looked aside, sensing another's approach. The woman called Star walked up alongside the pinto stallion. She was of the same height as Rebecca and as lithe-looking as her daughter despite the streaks of silver in her long black hair. Star wore a beaded buckskin dress, worn smooth, soft-looking. A necklace of porcupine quills and blue trading beads circled her throat.

"My mother, this is Panther Burn, the son of Yellow Eagle," Rebecca said.

"So you are the one," Star replied. She stared at Panther Burn; a look of apprehension crossed her face. Panther Burn shifted uncomfortably. At last the older woman spoke. "I will tell White Bull, our chief, of your arrival. It is good he should know." She placed her hand upon his leg and fixed him with her unwavering gaze. "What have you brought, Northerner? Ah, never

mind. You cannot know. Full bellies and lovemaking
are the only visions of the young." She chuckled. "Well,
Northerner, there will always be a place at our cookfire
for you."

"*Ne-a-ese*," said Panther Burn, at a loss for words.

"No need to thank me," Star replied, eyes suddenly
twinkling, a derisive tone in her voice as she glanced
over at Samuel Madison. "It's what any 'Christian' would
do." She started off through the village in search of
Simon White Bull. Several women emerged from their
cabins to gather about her to learn what she had learned
about the new arrival.

Panther Burn looked at Rebecca a moment more,
holding her gaze with his own, then he turned his horse
and walked away toward his uncle's cabin.

The door to the cabin swung ajar, pressed by the
invisible hand of a summer breeze. A couple of chickens scratched and pecked at the rain-damp earth, clucked
suspiciously at Panther Burn as he dismounted and
ground-tethered his stallion. The chickens scattered as
the brave stepped up to the door, leaned into the
shadowy interior.

"Beartusk?" he said in a soft voice. Something stirred
in the darkness, trotted toward him. A mongrel dog, its
short bristly fur the color of dried corn, stuck its muzzle
into the daylight and sniffed Panther Burn's leggings.
The man in the doorway reached down and scratched
the dog's neck and scarred ears.

"Who have you been fighting today, old dog?" Panther Burn chuckled.

"Who has he mated with today would be the better
question," a voice said from the interior of the cabin.
"Who is it? What man comes to my door?"

"The son of Yellow Eagle," Panther Burn replied.
"Have I changed all that much since our people renewed
themselves by the banks of the Graybull?"

"No. I have."

Panther Burn shoved the door farther open until an

expanding rectangle of sunlight spread across his uncle's wrinkled features where he sat at a table, dressed in a worn woolen shirt and trousers tucked into battered brown boots. Scraggly gray hair hung to his neck. A clay bottle and two cups rested on the tabletop. He waved in the general direction of the door and then reached down and took up a cup on the second try. His other hand crept across the splintery surface of the table until it discovered a clay bottle, then gingerly he poured the cup full of potent-smelling spirits.

"Uncle, what has happened?" Panther Burn entered the cabin and crossed to the table, tripping, as he walked, over the worn-out shell of a tribal drum. The gut head hung in dry brittle tatters. Panther Burn nudged it aside with his foot and continued to the table. He sat on the three-legged stool opposite Joshua Beartusk. "Uncle . . . what has become of the Circle?"

"Broken," Joshua replied, sliding the cup toward his nephew and then filling a second for himself. He smiled, revealing a row of yellow teeth. "Old Warrior!" The dog, lying in the doorway, clambered to its feet and padded over to its master, placing its head in Joshua's lap to be petted and scratched. When Joshua finished, the animal stretched itself out on its side at the old man's feet. "We live as the white man now," Joshua continued. "We take his Christian names, we raise his chickens, we grow his crops, we fatten ourselves on his tame buffalo, we wear his clothes, live in his houses . . . and catch his sicknesses. Three years ago, great fever." His leathery-looking hands patted his face, then cupped the back of his neck. "Terrible hurting, here. Two moons later I was blind. A half-man." Joshua sighed and drank from his gourd cup. Panther Burn took one sniff of the bitter-smelling brew and set it aside. "Still we live in peace," Joshua added.

A blind peace, maybe, Panther Burn thought to himself.

"Now you must tell me about your father. Does he fare well? And my sister Crescent Moon, how is it with her? You must tell me everything. I am glad you have come." He reached out and felt for the younger man's hand, took it in his. "A Red Shield cannot have a wife, children, no . . . you and your parents are all the family I have. It is good not to be alone."

A Red Shield, this broken blind old man? A feeling of shame swept over Panther Burn for his thoughts. He gripped his uncle's hand tightly and told him of life by Spirit Mountain, of all that had transpired since the two tribes of the same people had joined in celebration, now more than five years ago. He told his uncle of battles and hunts, of horses caught and buffalo chased and how sweet the chokecherries were last year; told him everything except the real reason why Panther Burn had left his father's village and journeyed two months alone to be with Joshua's people.

As evening shadows shrouded the land, turned the treetops to black spear points against a blood-red sky, Joshua crawled beneath the blankets, and curling up on his pallet, began to snore. Old Warrior padded over, whined a moment, then settled down to warm himself against the old man's soon sleeping form. Panther Burn stepped out of the cabin, stretched, and walked out from the village, an easy thing to do, as Joshua's cabin was on the edge of the sprawling, orderless arrangement of cabins. He ran through the buffalo grass to the crest of a knoll about a hundred yards from his uncle's cabin. And there, safe from the prying ears of the rest of the village, he began to sing.

In beauty was it begun
In beauty let it be finished.
The first of stars,
The last of sun
Come moon-woman, magic woman, lead us to our rest.
By the All-Father was it begun
By the All-Father it will be finished.
In beauty.

Though he sang softly, the gentle wind carried his voice to the edge of the village. And there were some who took notice, who paused by their cookfires to listen, to remember. And one in particular, standing in the lee of Joshua's cabin where she had come to bring food to the old blind man and his nephew, Rebecca Blue Thrush listened to the song, her heart inexplicably reaching out to the singer. And she dared to dream.

3

The Cheyenne attack had been sudden and merciless, catching the settlers off guard just as the wagon train broke circle along the banks of the Tongue. As arrows filled the air and clouds of black smoke and flame exploded from rifles hidden in the tall yellow grass, Dolph Bragg shoved his two sons out of the back of their prairie schooner and handed his elder boy, Jubal, a revolver and pointed toward the riverbank.

"Run! Care for Tomm . . . eeee." Jubal's father stiffened, his expression contorted in agony, then he slumped forward and slid partway from the wagon, his pants leg caught on a rake. Aurelia Bragg was there, coming from around the wagon in time to catch her husband and lower him to the ground as she screamed his name and clawed at the bloodied patch on the back of his coat. Her brown hair, unpinned, streamed in the wind like the tattered canvas covering the wagon, like the flames licking skyward from the surrounding wreckage. Her mad eyes bored into Jubal.

"Run," she shrieked, echoing her husband. Jubal could only stare at his father. Aurelia Bragg reached out and slapped her son across the face, rocking him back against his brother. Tom, only eight, stared with mute uncomprehension. Cries of the wounded and war whoops of the Cheyenne breaking from cover mixed with the brittle exchange of gunfire as an age-old tragedy played out the final minutes of its final act.

"Mama!" Jubal screamed. His face was red from her hand so moist with the blood of his father. Jubal pushed himself off the ground. He didn't want to leave. Not without his mother. Fear had turned his flesh icy cold. He shivered and tried to find the strength to speak, daring another blow to try to change his mother's mind. But his voice was lost in the din. Bullets thwacked into the wagon bed, showering the boys with splinters. Somewhere up ahead a keg of gunpowder, secreted in the flaming wreckage of a covered wagon, exploded, rending red flesh and white into unidentifiable fragments. Tommy Bragg began to cry. Jubal dragged his brother to his feet and wasted precious seconds dusting him off.

"It's all right," he said.

Twelve years later, Jubal still remembered saying, "It's all right." Just as he remembered turning back to his mother, only to find her sprawled across his father, part of her skull torn away by a piece of shrapnel as large as a wheel hub from the obliterated wagon. Jubal grabbed his brother by the arm and ran. He ran then with the sounds of slaughter at his heels. He ran and did not stop until he reached the riverbank. A brave struggled up from the water's edge. The two boys barreled full tilt into the warrior and knocked him backward down the bank, the boys came tumbling after. A jumble of arms and legs, a twist of torsos, separating at last. The moment froze as it ever did, for this was the climax of his nightmare . . . the brave's face streaked with yellow war paint, his war club raised as he emerged, dripping from the shallows, Tommy curled against his older brother, as Jubal, his father's cap-and-ball revolver gripped in both hands, worked the hammer back, the barrel trembling. "Fire . . . for God's sake, fire!" a voice screamed. Jubal hesitated, staring into the face of the Indian, transfixed, as the savage's face seemed to change, puzzling him. Then, the moment broke. Kill him! Kill him! The brave's shrill war cry hung on the air, he lunged with his knife. The boy squeezed the trigger.

A shot, a flash of gunpowder illuminated the wall nearest the bed. The lead slug blew a foot-long strip of wood away. Jubal screamed, fired again. A water pitcher exploded into a thousand china fragments. The door to the room flew back and Tom in pajamas rushed in from the hallway. Jubal spun toward the light. Marley loomed out of the blackness and knocked Tom to the floor as Jubal realized too late that he was no longer at the scene of the massacre but safe in his own bed at the Hippolyte Hotel in Castle Rock. He squeezed the trigger on his Colt dragoon. The revolver roared a third time and an inquisitive resident of the hotel ducked and retreated down the hall as a chunk of the doorsill turned to sawdust; the bullet ricocheting toward the other bedroom doors that hurriedly slammed shut.

"Colonel!" Marley shouted.

"What the . . . ?" Tom muttered, trying to rise. Marley shoved him back down to the floor.

Perspiration dripped from his jawline, beaded Jubal's forehead, rolled into his eyes, stung there. Jubal did not care. He lowered the gun, his hand trembling until it reached the bedding. Even in the gloom the room began to take on definition, a caneback rocker, a nightstand, two hurricane lamps at either end of a couch that Marley had been using for a bed. Moonlight pressed against the drapes, seeped in silver slivers where the velvet failed to meet.

"C'mon," Marley said, lifting Tom by the scruff of his pajamas and propelling him toward the door.

"But my brother . . . see here . . . let me go . . ." Tom tried to protest but Marley's momentum carried them both out of the room. Only then did Big Marley loose his hold. Tom pulled away and tried to head back into the room. Marley grabbed him again and this time did not stop until Tom was safe and secure in his own bedroom.

"Dammit, man, let me be," Tom shouted, furious at such manhandling. He teetered on the edge of the bed but managed to regain his balance.

"The colonel ain't gonna want to talk to you right now."

Tom's room was simpler, smaller. Its furnishings consisted of a four-poster bed, a dressing table, two ladder-back chairs near the fireplace, assorted chromolithographs on the walls, two out-of-date calendars, heavy burgundy curtains over the single window, a lopsided nightstand on which a pitcher and washbasin balanced precariously. It was a room to sleep in, nothing more, but comfortable in a rough sort of way. Temporary quarters, not a home.

"How dare you lay a hand on me," Tom snapped. The veins in his cheeks stood out in stark relief, a map of scarlet beneath his pale flesh. He tried intimidation, but somehow could not bring himself to muster the authority to make the bigger man retreat, something in the way his gaze could only reach Marley's jawline. Failing that, Tom returned to his bed and sat on the edge, his hands folded in his lap. "What the hell happened in there?" he said in a resigned voice. Marley nodded, appearing to approve of the younger man's unspoken surrender. Marley, who seldom slept fully out of uniform, hooked his thumbs in his suspenders, cleared his throat, looked for a place to spit, then swallowed.

"Long as I've known him, and that's been since sixty-two, when he pulled me out from under an overturned caisson and killed the three Johnny Rebs a-fixin' to stick me, long as I been by him, he's had them dreams. Or dream. Always the same one, always bad. About your ma and pa."

"Oh," Tom said, nodding. He frowned, then shook his head. "And he wakes up shooting."

"Sometimes. Sometimes not. This was the first time in about six months or so. Seems I remember around

56

Christmas . . . Well, it don't matter. Only that he ain't got any talk in him for a while afterward. He'll be all right. I reckon it's bringin' you up from Denver that's kinda opened an old wound."

Tom sighed, shook his head, then opened a flask he kept by his bed. He tilted the slim silver bottle to his lips. Marley watched with thirsty deference, but Tom lowered the flask, screwed the top back on, gasped, and took a deep breath. The bourbon settled his nerves. He returned the flask to the table by the bed and swung his legs beneath the covers. Marley started toward the door.

"Funny. I can't remember a thing about that day. Oh, I recall being put on the stage for Denver, and the train in St. Louis, arriving in Philadelphia and being curious why Jubal hadn't come with me to our grandparents'. But what happened before . . . well, it's all sort of blank. Funny . . ."

Marley paused in the doorway. "He saved your life, like he saved mine. That's all you need ever keep in mind. Don't never forget." The door swung shut with a finality that only emphasized the big man's parting remark even as it plunged the room into darkness. Marley continued across the hall and back into Jubal's suite. He gently closed the door and felt his way along the wall to the nearest lamp, then struck a match and touched flame to wick.

"Not too bright," Jubal said from his bed. He was sitting up, a Navy Colt revolver still gripped in his right hand.

"You up to beaver?"

Jubal nodded, but the shadows of his past seemed to fill the room. It was always like this, after the nightmare. A tide of memories impossible to stem. Apprenticed to a freighter for one year and working at full pay for another, Jubal Bragg had put aside enough for traps and supplies and at sixteen had headed west to the mountains. But trapping did not appeal to him, nor the lonely reaches where a man stands alone beneath the sky. Almost a year to the day he left, Jubal returned to

St. Louis and the freighting company. He worked his way up from mulewhacker to manager. An older, wiser young man, Jubal saved his money, shrewdly chose his acquaintances and culled the favor of the city's wealthy merchants.

He saw to his own education while learning his trade and establishing a reputation for honesty and competence. At last Jubal garnered enough support that by the close of 1859 he had formed his own freighting company and moved to Denver City. Jubal held the belief that this burgeoning settlement by the banks of Cherry Creek and the South Platte River was destined to become the "Queen City of the West." Denver grew, though not without a struggle. And so did Jubal's fortune. Success was inevitable to a man determined not to fail. At war's outbreak in 1861, twenty-two-year-old Jubal Bragg received a contract to supply the Union garrisons operating in the Colorado and New Mexico territories. War ensured a tidy profit with every shipment of food, tack, lumber, clothing. . . . Then came the Indian attacks, depredations against settlers and soldiers alike. In response, Jubal organized a militia, commissioned himself colonel and organized the locals throughout the territory to defend themselves against attack. With the Civil War come to an end at a courthouse in Appomattox, the territorial governor had requested that Bragg's militia continue to defend the outlying areas until government troops could be dispatched in adequate numbers to Colorado. Wealthy merchant, local hero, at twenty-six Jubal Bragg had everything—money, prestige, power . . . and nightmares.

"Colonel?" Marley cut through the reverie, the solid resonance of his voice dispelling the shadows of memory.

"Yes, Sergeant Marley, I am up to beaver. Why, I'm as sane as any madman."

"You ain't mad, Colonel. You just got bad dreams from time to time."

"Well-said, Sergeant Marley. Well-said. I'll drink to that." Jubal climbed out of bed and wrapped himself in a brushed-velvet robe. Marley lit another lamp to further dispel the gloom as Jubal reached for a decanter of brandy and two glasses, leaving the revolver on the table by the spirits.

"I suppose the manager will be around. We had better have an explanation ready."

"Everyone knows you hereabouts, Colonel. I reckon you can just do what you please."

Jubal filled a glass for himself, one for Marley. He walked over to the window fronting Main. The hotel was the point from which two intersecting streets, Main and Commerce, radiated outward in a V. Houses sprawled beyond the center of town like a stain of civilization cluttering what had once been a sea of buffalo grass. The window faced west and in the moonlight Jubal could make out the outline of Castle Rock, those great battlements of granite rimmed with silver and jutting upward from the plain like some medieval buttress. The playthings of nature rupturing the proud earth in some forgotten cataclysm. Jubal sipped his brandy, watched Marley's reflection in the mirror as Marley drained his glass at a single gulp, then busied himself with reloading the Navy Colt. He swabbed the empty chambers, added powder and tapped in wadding and a lead slug, and sealed the chamber with a dab of bear grease, lastly replacing the firing caps and easing the hammer down.

"It's cognac, dear fellow, for heaven's sake don't bolt it down like that. The masters of Charente are turning in their graves." Jubal took another sip. The brandy leached the cold that had plagued his bones since arriving in town from Foot o' the Mountains. It had been an eighteen-hour ride that had taken them into night of the following day, but the rooms at the Hippolyte had been kept waiting, of course.

Jubal shook his head and sighed. He had studied brandy in the same way he had studied the arts and law and what tomes of science he could lay his hand on. All to create an image that would one day completely subvert his true self, hide forever the reality of an unschooled frightened orphan left alone in the world by the act of a murderous band of savages.

He watched as Marley crossed over to his bed and placed the revolver on the nightstand. "Loyalty is as rare as oysters in the desert," Jubal said.

"Sir?"

"You are one of a kind, Sergeant. That's all."

"No sir. I got me two brothers back in Arkansas. Plowboys, let me tell you. Hell, they'd a liked to come west, only they're too stupid to find it." He chuckled and stretched back out on the couch. This night Marley slept in his trousers, long johns, and woolen socks. "If it's all the same to you, Colonel, I'll get back to sawin' logs. I got me a whole pile to cut through afore sunrise."

"To hard labor." Jubal lifted his glass in salute. He inhaled from the glass and took a sip, wishing for a proper snifter. Cognac in an ordinary glass was almost a sacrilege. He stared back out at the town. Most of the buildings were dark, although light spilled into the street from the Judge-Me-Not Saloon. Movement caught his attention. He continued to watch until he could make out a cowhand and one of the gals from the Judge-Me-Not, dancing what appeared to be a kind of shuffling waltz. Jubal could hear no music, which lent an unearthliness to the scene. Watching, though, made him feel sad, but he continued. He had never had time for any kind of personal relationship, though he'd bedded his share of tarts. And Tom was his only family. At least having a brother made him feel not so alone. Tom was his link to the past and maybe to the future. At least they were together now. Tom Bragg was brash, but he'd learn. God, how he had complained about leaving Foot o' the Mountains. Still, it was better than sharing the morning's fire with a murdering . . .

The Cheyenne! Jubal dropped the glass. It bounced off the rug and rolled to a standstill, leaving a trail of cognac. Now he remembered! The Indian in his dream, the face changing. It had never changed before. It was the brave from Wister's place. But why had the dream changed now? Jubal had seen other Indians before. A number of them he had personally dispatched to their ancestors. Never enough, though. Never enough to balance the ledger for the deaths of his parents. But the Cheyenne . . . why had he entered the nightmare? Why him and none of the rest? Jubal felt the hairs rise on the back of his neck. Something about that cursed buck. He had sensed it from the moment the brave had entered the room. And when their eyes had met, what link had been forged in that single moment? Jubal had sensed it and he was certain the Cheyenne had, too. Jubal rubbed a hand over his features, wariness stealing into his bones. He glanced toward the lamps, decided to leave them turned up, and headed for his bed. Marley was already snoring, his great bulk draped over the length of the couch. No point in waking the man, for Marley would understand no more of this than did Jubal. The colonel climbed into bed, propped himself upright against his pillows, closed his eyes, and reconstructed the young brave's dark, handsome features. Lost in his thoughts, Jubal absently tugged at his sideburns, conjuring an image of the Cheyenne that was at once intense and malevolent.

"We will meet again," Jubal said. "I think we do not even have a choice."

That night, Jubal Bragg did not sleep.

That same night, two days' ride from Castle Rock, in the village by the Warbonnet, Rebecca's mother was singing. A soft, eerie tone had drifted on the early-morning air and roused Rebecca from her troubled sleep. She listened now, working herself down in the straw-filled mattress as if burrowing for sleep. Star continued to sing. "One has come. He is the end of days. He is the beginning of others. This one among us. The sign, the warning, as told in the thunder voices. When they speak again, many will go to you, All-Father. Accept the spirits of your children. One has come. He is the end of days. He is the beginning . . ."

Rebecca opened her eyes and glanced around at the

sparely furnished but comfortable room that served as bedroom, kitchen, and sometimes bath. She had neglected to draw the curtain that partitioned her bed from the rest of the single-room cabin. Her mother's partition was also pulled back to reveal Star's empty bed. Rebecca's mother knelt by the hearth, stirring the orange glowing coals in the fireplace with a willow switch. Rebecca raised up on elbows as a flurry of sparks shot upward from a popping ember. The sparks danced and dazzled in the gloom, like the eyes of demons, like the spirits of the dead called forth, no, loosed upon the morning, only to wink out, a dozen at a time. Star continued to sing, repeating the words of her song, but softer still until her voice could no longer be heard. And yet, Rebecca still believed that Star was singing. She somehow felt her mother's voice, heard within the litany, as incessant as heartbeats. And Rebecca shivered. For suddenly the woman, the mother who had meant warmth and comfort and love all Rebecca's life, seemed to be altered. Oh, her physical presence remained the same, but somehow the spirit was changing before Rebecca's eyes and she wanted to cry out in her terrible fear. She knew her mother was a medicine woman, and had seen her counsel the distraught, grind herbs and roots into powders and unguents to cure the ill. But she had never been audience to . . . mystery. Until now. And why now? In these early hours before sunrise, why? Am I mad or dreaming or both? Rebecca silently asked herself, lest she disturb her mother's incantations and cause her to lose control. And it would not do for the medicine woman to lose control, for as the embers exploded and cracked apart, the sparks whooshing upward seemed to coalesce into a single glowing visage, that of a . . . wolf . . . peering out of the shimmering light, its fire-orange eyes fixed on Star. The medicine woman's lips no longer even moved, yet Rebecca could hear the prayer-song. It seemed to fill the room now, it seemed to whirl and coil like gusts from a storm, increasing in its fury, a wild and swirling torrent of words and tones whose meaning Rebecca could not understand. *One has come. He is the end of days* . . . Panther Burn? THE END OF DAYS! How could the cabin still stand, how could the roof contain such a din? Rebecca brought her hands up to cover her ears, to no effect. For the song echoed from within, the tumult had been unleashed in Rebecca's own flesh and bone and mind.

Stop, she told herself. *I will not listen. Oh, Mother, my mother, make it stop!*

The wolf spirit leaped from the fireplace, its body formed of shimmering pinpricks of fire. Its glowing paws closed around Star, became one with Star, the medicine woman of the Southern Cheyenne. First the paws, then the snarling jaws, the sleek, gleaming torso, the livid eyes, all one with Star. Forms blurred. The singing stopped. And Rebecca, still unable to scream, watched as the spirit form merged and vanished, leaving only an old woman kneeling at hearthside, stoking embers to life. A shadow seemed to fill the room, a darkness from which there was no release. Rebecca, eyes closing, sank back upon her bed.

A dagger of sunlight slashed the bonds of sleep and Rebecca awoke. She blinked, turned her head aside, away from the patch of sunlight that slanted through a space in the log wall where the chinking had worked loose. Rebecca glanced over and saw her mother, asleep in bed, her breathing even, silver hair splayed across the down pillow Esther Madison had brought her from town. Asleep as if nothing at all had happened. But what had happened? Only the visions of sleep. Nothing more. Rebecca rose and stood beside her bed. She padded across the floor and listened as she walked, to the crow of roosters announcing to the world the arrival of another day. Dogs barked. Calves bawled in the meadow. Rebecca stared down at the gray lifeless-looking embers. See, Rebecca chided herself, only a few coals retain their life. She looked over at Star's huddled form and smiled. Only the visions of a troubled sleep and nothing more. She knelt on the granite hearth to stoke the fire in preparation for breakfast. Pain! Sudden, brutally swift. Rebecca gasped and sprawled backward onto the floor. She stifled a sob, stared at her outstretched legs, and gingerly examined her bare knees where the flesh was red and blisters were already forming from contact with the searingly hot stones. She glanced over in dumb astonishment at the fireplace. It was as if a roaring blaze had filled it for the length of a night and a day, and the granite slabs absorbed all the heat. But if that were the case, then would the coals not still be aglow and pulsing with fire-life?

"I have a poultice for your knees," Star said as she climbed out of bed. She walked over to a nearby clay pot and brought it over to Rebecca where she sat naked on the floor. Star, as naked as her daughter, knelt by Rebecca and placed a finger to the young woman's lips as she started to speak, hushing her. Star dipped her fingers into the jar and scooped out a dollop of amber paste and tenderly smeared it across the blistered flesh. And as she ministered to her daughter, the medicine woman began to sing a song of healing and truth and the paths all must travel to find them both.

Star sang and Rebecca listened. And learned. And began to sing.

Panther Burn woke with the fading image of Rebecca Blue Thrush to warm his heart. His dream had been hot as a dozen summers. He had lain with her upon the moist inviting riverbank and held her in his arms and tasted of her kisses, brushed aside her halfhearted restraints and protests to join with her in the timeless fulfillment of youthful passion.

He woke to log walls, a hard floor, a cold hearth. He rose on his elbows and glanced over at his uncle's sleeping form, curled upon a pallet, a huddled gray figure with his face to the wall. This had been a warrior, a Red Shield, valiant as the Dog Soldiers in battle with their crimson-stained flesh and spears and shields. Beartusk . . . Joshua Beartusk, Panther Burn silently repeated. These people had changed. They had forgot-

ten the Circle in their effort to live at peace. Panther
Burn turned and grabbed a dipper and helped himself
to a mouthful of water from a nearby clay pitcher. He
promptly spit the water on the floor. No woman had
entered while they slept and filled the pitcher with
living water fresh from the creek, nor cleaned away the
scraps of last night's meal that Rebecca had left for
them. Were the Red Shields no longer held in respect,
that they would have to attend to such woman's work?
Panther Burn rolled off his blanket and stood, stretching the kinks out of his body. He stepped to the doorway and stared out at the village framed in the doorsill.
Maybe it had been a bad idea to come. These were his
people, yet he felt a stranger among them. He should
leave. No good would come of this. He should leave
this very minute and go . . . where?

Where?

He stepped through the doorway, suddenly aware
that the pinto was no longer tethered outside the cabin.
Stolen! His face grew flushed. His heart began a savage
cadence. He glanced to either side to see if perhaps the
horse had pulled free and wandered off. Old Warrior
followed him out of the house, wagged his tail, and
trotted off into the village without so much as a single
look toward the brave staring down at the stake in the
ground. Panther Burn remembered looping the lead
rope through the wooden stake. And he had made
certain it could not pull free. No, someone had stolen
the animal during the night or early morning. But who?
Nothing in the village aroused his suspicions, only misgivings at how different his uncle's people had become,
and in the way they lived. Smoke began to stream from
chimneys as the people prepared their breakfasts. Children burst out-of-doors, their joy filling the newborn
day with the music of life. Panther Burn studied the soft
ground before the cabin, hoping to pick the pinto's
hoofprints out of the churned earth. So intent was he in
his examinations that he failed to notice the braves led
by James Broken Knife. Five in number and all in their
early twenties, they were part of the group who had

ridden to Rebecca's "rescue." Clad in blousy cotton shirts and dungarees, they balanced farm tools on their shoulders and stared resentfully at his buckskin regalia. Panther Burn recognized James Broken Knife as he stepped forward. The Southern Cheyenne tilted his hat back to reveal his chiseled features.

"*Ha-hey*, my brother of the Spirit Mountain folk. If you are to live with us, then you must work with us. We have enough tools to share with you." James Broken Knife folded his muscular arms across his chest. His grim smile matched the chill in his voice. His face was square, solid, but there was a brittle edge to the way he carried himself; peace had eroded some of the hard texture of what once had been a warrior.

"To dig in the earth?" Panther Burn laughed softly. "I will leave woman's work for the women." James's smile wavered and his features darkened. He took a step forward. Panther Burn braced himself for the man's attack. Another shadow fell between them and both men turned as Rebecca came toward them. She walked stiffly for her knees still throbbed and she carried a loaf of fried bread and a clay pitcher of tea brewed from the dried leaves of sarvisberries. Rebecca slowed as James turned to watch her, then ignoring his icy stare, she continued forward, forcing him aside and Panther Burn too. She entered the cabin, placed the food and drink on the table, and returned to stand in the doorway behind Panther Burn. Behind her, Joshua Beartusk continued to snore.

"What are you doing, foolish girl?" James asked.

"Bringing food to a blind old man," she replied.

"Why?"

"Because I wish to do so." Now it was her turn to grow angry. Panther Burn noticed he had suddenly been forgotten by the leader of this group of farmers.

"Come with me. We must talk." James Broken Knife tossed his rake back to one of his companions. He started off into the village, thinking to escort the girl back to Star's. He paused and looked around, surprised to find Rebecca was still in the shadow of the cabin. She had not moved. "Rebecca . . . you will walk here with me."

"*Saaa* . . . I am not some Ute slave to be ordered about," Rebecca retorted.

James Broken Knife turned and rejoined his friends. He took up his crudely fashioned hoe, then looked from Rebecca to Panther Burn, who could not conceal his amusement, and back to Rebecca.

"We will talk at nighttime," James told her. He tugged the brim of his hat down to shade his features and walked off toward the plowed ground where the earth had been scarred to grow crops just east of the village. Panther Burn grinned at Rebecca.

"I do not think your friend likes me."

"Many people do not like you."

"I have only been here a night. I have met few people. Yet so many already wish me to leave."

"They are afraid," Rebecca said, stepping out of the doorway and closer to him. She noticed several of the women from a nearby cabin watching her. No doubt they would embellish her visit as only ardent gossips could. Well, after the strange things she had seen with her mother, Rebecca no longer cared. One of the women, dour-faced Sarah Scalpcane, would undoubtedly have Panther Burn embracing Rebecca before the story was complete. "You have hurt your legs?" Panther Burn's inquiry interrupted the girl's speculation.

"A burn, nothing more." She remembered her mother's ominous incantation, foretelling the arrival of one who would signal the end of days. "They are afraid of what you might bring," she continued. She did not want to speak of her mother's magic. "They fear you bring trouble with the *ve-ho-e*. And not only the white men in Castle Rock, but the ranchers and the soldiers. You must understand, we live in peace now. But we have peace only because the white man is not afraid of us. We have adopted his customs, his names, his God. And we are no longer feared. Now the Ute have crossed over the mountains. They have raided and killed and made the white man fear again. But not us. Not yet.

Because we do not walk in the old ways." Panther Burn started walking. He crossed around the cabin and stared off into the meadow. "Are you listening to me?" Rebecca asked, following.

"I am looking for my horse. It has been taken," Panther Burn replied, studying the lay of the land. "But I hear you, Rebecca Blue Thrush. The *ve-ho-e* used to hate and fear your people. Now I think they only hate." He spotted the pinto among a small herd of mustangs, grazing near a juniper thicket. He started off across the meadow. "Maybe you will hear a flute outside your cabin this night," he shouted back to her. "Maybe it will not be James Broken Knife." He did not wait for her flustered reply. After all, he had a thief to catch.

The mustangs lifted their heads as Panther Burn approached. They studied him with care before deciding that despite his strange scent he meant them no harm. The pinto continued to graze and the others followed suit. A thin young boy sat with his arms wrapped around his drawn-up legs and from his position near the thicket seemed to be watching over the herd. The youth also watched Panther Burn, so wide-eyed and awed by the Northerner, that some of the fire left Panther Burn's anger. The boy stood, retreated hesitantly toward the thicket.

"You, there, boy," Panther Burn called out, hoping to sound older than his own twenty years. "Whose horses are these?"

"They are mine, Northerner," a voice said from behind Panther Burn. The brave turned to see a solidly built, gray-haired, elderly Cheyenne astride a horse. He wore a plaid shirt and denims with the trouser legs rolled up over his rock-scarred boots. The man removed his flat-brimmed hat and wiped the perspiration from his leathery-looking face. "It is a poor hunter who allows a man to approach him unnoticed from behind. His lodge will always be empty and his wives forced to

beg at the common fire." The brave replaced his hat. "I
am Simon White Bull, chief of the Southern Cheyenne."

"And I am Panther Burn of the—"

"I have been told who you are. The son of Yellow
Eagle. Songs of your father's wisdom and bravery are
sung even around our campfires."

"What you have said of the hunter is true," said
Panther Burn, not wanting to speak of his father. "Next
time I will listen for you behind me. Yet such talk of
hunting seems strange to hear. I am surprised there are
any hunters left in the village. It would seem the men
tend the white man's buffalo or hunt with hoe and
rake." Panther Burn pointed to the newly plowed ground
where the men led by James Broken Knife were busily
weeding and planting seeds. "And I can find no common fire."

"We do not go hungry. We can stay here and build
strong homes and the old do not perish in the winter,"
said Simon. He glanced at his horses, taking a mental
count. In the process he noticed the pinto. "That is not
my stallion."

"It belongs to me." Panther Burn whistled softly and
the animal raised its head, neighed, then left its grazing
to trot over to its master. Panther Burn rubbed and
patted its neck. "It was taken from where I had tethered
it last night."

"Is that you, Zachariah Scalpcane?" Simon White Bull
asked.

The boy came forward. "Yes," he replied.

"Zachariah has no father, and no horses to keep. My
sons are dead and I have no one to bring them into the
meadow," Simon White Bull explained. "Zach, did you
take the pinto?"

The boy looked from Simon to Panther Burn. "Ye
. . . yes. I did not mean any harm. You were sleeping.
And your horse had come far. I thought it would be all
right to bring him along with the rest. I never let them
stray and I know where the grass is sweet." The boy
held himself proudly erect, his voice reaching for a tone
of authority.

"How old are you?" Panther Burn asked of the youth.

"Eight summers," the boy explained.

"His father was a brave man. As my sons were brave." Simon White Bull shifted his weight, grimacing as if an old wound on his hip were bothering him. "They were killed up at Buffalo Creek. The white men had their many-times-firing rifles and although we outnumbered them they killed many of our warriors and we could not even approach their circled wagons."

Panther Burn looked away from the boy toward the man who had declared himself leader of these people. "Was it then you decided to turn your men into women, to scratch the earth with their wooden tools, was it then you turned the Morning Star people into white-eyes fit for tending the tame buffalo?"

"It was then I grew sick of war and began to teach myself how to live in peace with the white men," Simon answered.

"We too live in peace, beneath Spirit Mountain," Panther Burn said. "Because the white man respects us and does not interfere too much in our lives. We live in peace as Cheyenne."

Simon narrowed his gaze. He did not appreciate being chastised. It showed in the suddenly stern set of his features. "You are a rude and troublesome young man who speaks of custom yet forgets to present himself to chiefs of this village on his arrival, who slights us with his unproved bravery. We are trying a different path here, Panther Burn. Do not try to stand in our way." Simon White Bull walked his mount in a tight circle around the Northerner, then keeping the animal tightly reined, walked the horse away from the herd. The warning in his voice had been impossible to ignore. Panther Burn watched the chief depart, recalling in that instant that Simon White Bull was a Dog Soldier. Or at least he once had been.

"I did not steal the horse." Zachariah suddenly spoke, distracting the Northerner from his gloomy thoughts. Panther Burn turned and looked at the eight-year-old. "I watched you ride into our village. You did not see

70

me. But I knew you were a warrior." He pointed to the eagle feathers. "One day I will wear such a symbol of my courage. And I will not be *enano-vo-estane*, a planting person."

"You would wear an eagle feather?" Panther Burn said, warming to the lad's high spirits and independence. Here was a kindred spirit, however young. "Then first you must prove yourself worthy," the Northerner explained.

"How?" Zachariah asked, his whole being alert, his face shining with enthusiasm. Copper face and brown eyes and cropped black hair, his young body thin but resilient-looking—Panther Burn took all this in and decided the boy just might do, if he had backbone. Time would tell. It always did.

"It is for a father to show his son the way of the eagle," Panther Burn replied, without thinking. Then he remembered that Simon White Bull had said that the boy's father was dead. Zachariah lowered his head and stared at the trampled earth. Panther Burn leaped up onto the pinto and stretched out his scarred left hand to pat the boy on the head. The Northerner looked around and saw Simon watching them. Good. "One day soon, the chief of the Southern Cheyenne will have to tend to his own horses." Panther Burn looked down at Zachariah. "On that day, we find your eagle feather. In this, I will be your father."

Joshua Beartusk leaned against the side of his cabin, his face tilted to the western horizon, allowing the afternoon sun to warm his features, his sightless eyes, to sink deep into his bones and leach the cold that unending darkness instilled. Old Warrior sat at his master's right leg. Joshua sighed and shifted his weight upon the three-legged stool. The mongrel dog yawned and stretched out its paws, and panting, looked up at the blind man before resting its muzzle back on the ground. It looked up and gave a fitful wag of its tail as Panther Burn rode back from the hunt.

71

"*Ha-ho*, my nephew, did the All-Father bless your hunt? Was your aim sure and arrows swift?" Joshua listened as Panther Burn stepped down. He heard the younger man struggle with the weight of something. The blind man held out his hands and suddenly the outstretched fingertips brushed the thickly furred hide of an antelope. Joshua licked his lips, already tasting the freshly killed game cooked over a slow-burning fire. Panther Burn placed the hide in the old man's hands. He had butchered the kill out on the trail. He returned to the pinto and removed the rawhide packets of meat and for a moment an image flashed through his mind of another hunt, of a reckless act, of dead friends. He willed the memories away and proceeded to unload the meat. Zachariah Scalpcane rounded the corner of the cabin and trotted up to Panther Burn.

"I saw you." The boy grinned. He was clad in leggings and breechcloth, and his naked torso was covered with dirt. A bruise formed a purple blossom on his lip. Panther Burn tilted Zachariah's face to one side. The boy read the question in the Northerner's expression. "Some of the other boys . . . I told them I was going to braid my hair and wear an eagle feather. They made fun of me so I fought them." He studied the ground a moment, then shrugged. "I did not beat them. They were too big. But it does not matter. They will be planters while I ride the warrior trail and count plenty coup." The boy puffed out his chest and strutted in a tight circle and then laughed at his own antics. Panther Burn grinned and dropped a packet of meat into the boy's outstretched hands.

"A warrior's first obligations are to see to the care of his mother's lodge."

Zachariah tucked the packet under his arm as the Northern Cheyenne handed him another. "You will bring this second packet of meat to the lodge of Star, the medicine woman." Zachariah nodded, understanding the older man's instructions if not their purpose. "Now go. I will come for you tomorrow or perhaps the next day.

You must be ready when I call. Will your mother agree to this?"

"When I bring her the food she will," the boy replied. "I shall go find Star first." As he started off, Joshua called out to the youth. The boy turned toward the blind man, who held out a hand, then pointed directly at Zachariah.

"Be sure you do not look her directly in the eye," Joshua warned. "Else she will turn you into a mouse!"

Zachariah stared at the old man a moment, then snorted in disgust. "I am not afraid. I have looked upon her many times. And I am not a mouse."

"Many times is not now," Joshua cackled, stroking the antelope hide, his leathery palm gliding smoothly over the deep brown-and-gold fur. "The Star of yesterday is not the Star of today. I am blind, and yet I know these things. Maybe because I am blind." He leaned back and laughed again. Zachariah retreated a step and then trotted off into the village, where the smoke of cookfires mingled with the scent of buffalo grass. Chickens scampered across his path as he continued toward Star's cabin. His mind wrestled with the problem at hand. Everyone knew Joshua Beartusk was nothing but a crazy old blind man. So only a fool would take stock in such ravings. But as Zachariah neared Star's cabin, it began to glow, bathed as it was in a vibrant ray of sunlight that cut a molten gold swath through the village, leaving half in shadow as a cloud passed before the sun. As Zachariah looked on, his heart suddenly filled with misgivings, the cabin's golden aura dimmed, grew somber and ominous as the cloud blotted out even more of the sunlight. Zachariah slowed, cautiously approached the door. Joshua's warning reverberated in his mind, overpowering the last vestige of his courage. Hands trembling, he placed the packet by the door, rapped twice, bruising his knuckles on the rough-hewn surface, and then scampered off toward his mother's cabin, his tension and fear easing with every step, his spirit soaring by the time he reached home.

Panther Burn had watched the entire incident, and,

seeing Zachariah race off after leaving the packet, smiled, then returned to his uncle's side.

"He ran away," Joshua chuckled. "Good. He has learned a valuable lesson today. Sometimes it is better to be a foolish boy than a brave mouse."

"Are you truly blind, Uncle?" Panther Burn asked in amazement, waving a hand before the old man's face.

"There are things a blind man can see that one with eyes cannot. I had forgotten," the old man replied. "I pray that I never forget again."

Panther Burn walked a few paces away. "I pray I can forget how I have looked upon this village from the hills and found nothing I could value." He sighed. "I will build our cookfire here. We will take our meal in the warmth of the sun." The Northerner squatted and drew a circle in the dirt. He looked up a moment, watching the tips of the sweet grass ripple in the gentle breeze. Then he turned his attention to the village that spread in a shapeless mass behind them. He shook his head in despair.

"What kind of people are these? Among the Spirit Mountain folk, your campfire would never want for wood, your belly for food; you would never be alone."

"Do not judge them too harshly, Nephew. I have not had need of their company. Our young men talk of planting, of how dry the earth is today or how it is too wet and the harvest will be poor, of corn and what will happen if it does not mature, if the cattle do not fatten, what then?" Joshua's features wrinkled in a grimace. "Planters!"

"But are there not other men, such as yourself, who have not forgotten what it is to hunt, to ride against one's enemies, to be strong and respected?"

"Old men with more lies. No, I have heard enough of old men like me. So have we all heard enough. Forgetting the old ways makes the new ways easier to accept. So we keep to ourselves. And guard our dreams." Joshua shook his head and sighed. "The white man's whiskey helps too. But I have none left. Now there is nothing to do."

"Nothing, eh? Not now, old man," Panther Burn said. "I will cook the meat I have brought. But you must do something as well." He reached inside his shirt and withdrew a juniper branch, walked over, and placed it in the old man's hands.

"My father once told me no woman could resist the tones of his brother's flute. That from the flutes you carved came the sweetest sounds, music like wild honey luring the young maids from their lodges. He used to tell me that the girls of his village were drawn to you like babes to bright beads when you played."

"A young brave's innocent pastime, before I took up the Red Shield." Joshua turned the branch in his fingertips. It was nearly straight, about eighteen inches long. He did not need eyes to carve a courting flute, his fingers knew the way, his heart held memories of fire, of his youth when once he too had longed. "I will need a . . ." Panther Burn placed his knife in the old man's hands before Joshua could even complete his request. "And sinew?"

"Taken from the antelope," Panther Burn replied. "And dried all morning." He placed a small clay jar in his uncle's grasp. "I boiled his marrow for the glue you will need."

Joshua continued to run his fingers over the wood, pursing his lips, humming faintly to himself, drawing out the spirit of the juniper branch that he might carve a flute in beauty. Suddenly he chuckled aloud.

"What is the matter, Uncle?"

"Your pretty speech about the view from the hilltop . . . you must have found something of value. Some*one* of value."

Panther Burn looked away in embarrassment, remembered his uncle was blind, but continued to keep his back to the old man. He began to build a fire in earnest.

"I can carve a flute," Joshua said. "But I cannot teach you to play." He began to whittle. "That is something every young man must learn for himself."

* * *

Sam Madison strode through the camp marveling at the beauty of the twilight. The sky was washed with purple and obsidian, stars like newly formed gems gleamed against the firmament. Few people crossed his path, for the families he had ministered to these past three years were gathered about home and hearth, enjoying evening meals, enjoying . . . peace. Samuel envied them. He wanted to be home as well, but Simon White Bull had summoned him and the reverend respected the chief too much to ignore his request.

A mongrel and her pups broke from the shadows to follow the white man, hoping he might have a scrap of food to discard. Fifty feet later they gave up and returned to keep their vigil in the shadows, their muzzles raised to the scent of the nearest cookfires. Sam quietly approached the chief's cabin, rapped twice on the door, and entered into darkness at Simon's invitation. The chief squatted on the floor; his silver hair hung past his ears and was raggedly cropped. His features were wrinkled, sadness haunted his eyes. He nodded at Sam and rose from the fire, a burning twig in his hand. He carried the flame to a lamp on the table and when the amber glow filled the room Sam could see that he was not Simon's only guest. A brave stood before the shuttered windows. He was of average height and looked to be the same age as Simon, and as solidly built as the Southern Cheyenne chief. But there the similarities ended, for their other guest wore only a breechcloth and buckskin leggings. A beaded quill breastplate covered his upper torso. The left half of his face, as he stepped forward, was covered with white paint, creating an illusion of being part skull, part flesh. His right eye was highlighted by a yellow circle. He wore a fur cap adorned with raven feathers. The brave's eyes widened in astonishment.

"A white man! What trick is this, White Bull?" Sam took the brave for a Ute; behind that garish war paint the Indian exuded hatred.

"No tricks, Coyote Walking. He lives among us. He has taught us much." Coyote Walking spat on the floor.

Simon's gaze narrowed. "Do not forget, we have been enemies longer than we have been friends."

"Simon, why have you called me here?" Samuel managed to say. He knew of the depredations in the area. The Ute and his followers had come down from the mountains to raid and kill. And he knew only the presence of Simon White Bull kept the Ute from plunging his knife into the reverend's heart. Samuel tried to hide his nervousness. He took a seat at the table near the fire. Plates had been set out and a clay tureen of stew dominated the center. Steam still drifted from a coffee cup, but Simon's wife, Husk, was nowhere to be seen. Blankets hung from the walls and the makings of a buckskin shirt had been left in the seat of the rocking chair Sam had presented to the chief as a gift.

"Husk is with her sister," Simon said. He sat across from Samuel. "Coyote Walking comes in friendship. We have raided one another's camps, stolen each other's horses, but now he comes in friendship."

"I do not like this," the Ute muttered, edging toward the door.

"Coyote Walking is a chief. He has seven braves down by the Warbonnet, hiding. He wants me to join with him, to lead my braves with him down the path of war. If I do not, he will return to the mountains, he will follow the passes toward the setting sun and rejoin his people." Simon glanced at Coyote Walking. "The Ute is valiant, but he has no stomach for riding against the soldiers that have come. But if my young men paint their faces for war, he will stay to fight at our side."

"Will he also help to bury your dead?" Samuel said. Suddenly the strength of his convictions had returned. He matched Coyote Walking's stare.

"The white dog barks," said the Ute. "Among my people, we know what to do with barking dogs. We drive them from our village with stones and clubs."

"You are not among your people," Simon White Bull replied.

"It is so. But I came here in friendship. If you do not join with us, then I shall leave. As an enemy."

"As an enemy? Then I am thinking you will not leave at all." The menace in Simon's voice gave the reverend a start. He had never heard his friend sound so dangerous. But then, he had been lucky. When he arrived in the village of the Southern Cheyenne, Simon White Bull had been ready for peace. Even Coyote Walking seemed impressed, for he lost some of his defiance and his gaze revealed his uncertainty.

"I shall leave as I came," he meekly answered. Simon White Bull nodded and an instant later the Ute had vanished through the doorway with hardly a sound to mark his departure.

Samuel exhaled loudly. "My God, Simon. The next time . . . well . . ." He rose from the table.

"There is food," Simon said.

"Esther is waiting for me," Samuel explained. "Tell me, why did you send for me?"

"I wanted you to see. This night, I chose the way of peace. Tell the others, the *ve-ho-e* who do not trust us, what your eyes have seen, what your ears have heard. The Morning Star people walk the path of peace."

"I will tell them," Samuel Madison said, reaching forward to place his hand on the chief's shoulder. "In Castle Rock . . . and in Washington, when I meet with the Great White Father."

"But will he listen?" said the Southern Cheyenne, his voice tinged with a kind of sorrow that seemed to spring from his soul, like blood from a raw wound. All his sons were dead. All his sons.

"Yes," said the Reverend Samuel Madison, and he prayed he was right.

"I see him," Samuel Madison said, watching from the window of his cabin. He had not been able to get the Ute out of his mind. He could not sleep and had come to the window for a breath of air. And spied Panther Burn, another brave who seemed destined to ride the warpath. Even in the late spring the nights were cool. A fire cracked cheerily in the hearth. Esther rose up from the pillow and patted the empty spot beside her on the mattress.

"Come to bed, my husband."

Samuel did not appear to hear. He continued to watch as Panther Burn paused, a blanketed silhouette outlined in the smoldering glare of a dying campfire, as if unsure of his destination, a man lost among his own people.

"He will be difficult to reach. There is so little time. Maybe I should delay our departure," the reverend softly suggested. He knew better, of course, for the letter he had received informing him of his father's demise had taken better than a month to reach him. Poor Father dead. And how amazing to discover the parent who had disowned Samuel on his decision to enter the ministry had recanted on his deathbed, in the process reinstating his only living heir to the Madison fortune. Wealth and influence were Samuel's for the accepting. Preaching the word and Christianizing the heathens were one thing, but it never hurt to have a little power to make yourself heard. "Well, we won't be gone long," Samuel added with a sigh. The figure in the ebbing firelight continued on and vanished in the darkness. "What is he looking for?"

Samuel turned from the window, allowing the curtains to settle back into place. The cabin he had built to live among his flock was a single-room structure, its wood floors covered with bearskins, the walls draped with blankets. Half a dozen chairs hung from the walls, two others sat at either end of a broad hand-hewn table made regal by two silver candelabra. Elsewhere, iron cook pots, a rocking chair, clay cups and bowls, a rack for weaving, a war shield and a coup stick, crossed tomahawks and tanned hides, candles, a reading stand and leather-bound Bible transformed the interior into kitchen, dining room, and parlor. The bedroom was but an alcove hidden behind a curtain of blankets, behind which he and his wife shared another creature comfort Samuel had not been able to sacrifice, a thickly mattressed four-poster bed freighted to him from his father's home outside Philadelphia. Clad in a nightshirt

that fell to his ankles, he padded across to the fireplace
and stoked the fire a moment, added a log to the flames,
straightened. His reflection filled the oval mirror he
had placed over the hearth. Alongside the mirror were
two tintypes, one of his mother, a severe-looking woman
with her hair pulled tight in a bun at her neck. The
other was of his father, fierce-looking and bearded,
resembling more some wild-eyed John the Baptist than
a shipping magnate whose business had prospered from
the recently ended Civil War. Samuel had inherited his
father's angular visage and his mother's stern, thin-
lipped features; and his mother's nature as well, for she
had been a kind and caring woman.

"Now what, my husband?" Esther left her bed and
walked over to Samuel, her cotton bedclothes sweeping
dangerously close to the fire. She dared the flames to
be at his side, sensing his misgivings.

"I was wondering to myself how someone like me
managed to find someone like you." Samuel chuckled,
putting his arm around her. Esther barely came up to
his chest as they stood near the hearth.

"*Saaa . . .*" she exclaimed. "You see with your eyes.
Not mine." Esther tugged at him. He followed her
lead, taking a step toward the bed. "Once my people
rode the war trail. Many moons passed. It was always
the same. With every season the women would mourn
the loss of their husbands and sons. Never, it seemed,
did we have enough to eat. In winter, the old died in
the snow. Then we learned to trade with the white man
for blankets and guns, tools and seeds, instead of raiding
his forts and dying before his guns. You came among us
and taught us the white man's ways. You came to my
people by the Warbonnet and showed us how to bring
food from the earth, how to plant, how to keep the
white man's buffalo that we might not have to follow
the vanishing herds. You told us of the one God. And
you met a girl named Bird Hat and baptized her Esther
and she saw in you the hope of her people, she saw in
you a good heart—and she saw in you . . . peace. But
what did you see in her, *ve-ho-e?*"

Samuel took another step, then another, following her lead. He spied his ungainly reflection on the wall and gently replied, "In you, my beloved, I saw beauty."

"Then you gave me another name," Esther said, pulling with delicate strength. "And I am Esther Madison . . . your woman."

"And soon I will be giving you another people. I wonder what Washington society will think of you." Samuel laughed. Suddenly he gripped her tightly, his eyes boring into hers. "But we will return. I promise you. Our place is here, in this village by the Warbonnet . . . beneath the Morning Star."

Esther nodded, allaying his fears with her innocence and her trust. She tugged again and this time he followed, without pause, to the bed where he might lie in warmth, holding beauty in his arms throughout the night.

Panther Burn slowed, glanced over his shoulder at the night-shrouded village surrounding him. Just on the border of a patch of light streaming through an unshuttered window he glimpsed movement. Panther Burn lowered the flute from his lips, stooped down and picked up a small stone, started forward a step, then spun and hurled the missile. It skimmed across shadow and light to shadow again and struck home. A gasp, a startled cry, and Zachariah Scalpcane limped into the lamplight.

"*Saaa*, you've crippled me," he moaned as he ruefully approached the one he had been following.

"It was a little stone." Panther Burn grinned.

"It felt big." Zachariah rubbed his shin.

"Tell me, lame warrior, why you follow me. What mischief are you about? Your mother will see your empty bed and worry."

"I think she will be glad it is empty," Zachariah said. He straightened and looked back toward the darkened mass of his mother's house, a patch of black against the star-filled night. "Peter Old Mouse has come to see her. Only he does not bother to stand on his blanket. My mother already has invited him to lie beneath hers."

81

"So you have decided to follow me," said Panther Burn. The Northerner tugged his blanket around his shoulders and stared down at the boy, finally reached a decision. "Will you help me if I ask it?" Zachariah brightened and nodded.

"My uncle is asleep behind his cabin," Panther Burn explained. "Wake him, gently, and bring him inside, to bed. Stay with him until I return. I place him in your care. Will you do this for me?"

"As you ask it," Zachariah said. "But what if he will not come inside?" A breeze pushed the boy's hair in his face; he brushed it back from his eyes.

"That is why I am sending you," Panther Burn explained. "Because you are a man of great resource." Zachariah seemed to swell with importance at the compliment. "But you have much to learn about stalking." Panther Burn ruffled the hair back from Zachariah's eyes. The youth backed away, then laughed with the man. He trotted off toward Joshua Beartusk's cabin, hesitated a moment to face Panther Burn. The boy clasped his hands over his ears.

"And you have much to learn about playing a flute."

"*Saaa!*" Panther Burn hissed and scooped up another stone, but by the time he cocked his arm for the throw, Zachariah had vanished in the shadows.

Rebecca was sitting at the table, across from Star. The lamp between them washed their faces in its pallid glow. Mother and daughter were beading the hem and sleeves of a buckskin smock. The soft brushed garment lay between them.

"Perhaps I should stitch some around the neck," Rebecca said, searching a tin cup for the appropriate color of bead. Star glanced up from the hem. She had finished one row of white beads and had begun another.

"You could use the white as I have done," she said, glancing up at her daughter. The older woman's heart filled with love and pride as she watched her daughter work. There was sadness too, but it must be hidden.

The visions Star had seen must remain unspoken, if Rebecca were to survive.

"I will do it," Rebecca said. "But such a dress as this will be, a girl might wear it at the two-called-together ceremony." The girl smiled and looked up at Star and almost glimpsed the medicine woman's hidden sorrow. "Mother?"

"It is such a dress," Star said, her expression cheery, "as you will have it to be."

Rebecca wasn't completely fooled. Her eyes narrowed as she studied her mother. Star's silent thoughts were a barrier that Rebecca was determined to breach. If not tonight, then soon.

"Mother?" she began. The quiet strains of a flute filtered in through the closed door, rescuing Star from her daughter's inquisition.

Panther Burn blew a trilling series of notes, his fingers opening and closing the holes in the flute. He watched the door and played and when at last the door opened and Rebecca Blue Thrush stepped outside, the Northerner offered a special prayer of thanks for the craftsmanship of Joshua Beartusk.

She stepped forward, hesitated, then came toward him.

"Why do you play your flute outside my door?" Rebecca asked, baiting him. Panther Burn stared down at the flute as if he were seeing it for the first time.

"This? Why, my uncle carved it. He said with this flute a hunter could charm the birds of the air into his trap. See, I have caught a thrush." He eased his blanket around her shoulders that they might stand together in it. Her body was warm against his, a good warmth, like that of a summer day. Panther Burn led her out of the village and onto the plain, where moonlit shadows danced in cloaks of silver. Fireflies shimmered and swirled as if surrounding the couple in an ever-changing cosmos, stars and planets evolving and exploding, lapsing into silent blackness and bursting into light once more. Panther Burn and Rebecca walked in silence upon the buffalo grass. Bluebells and buffalo grass, fireflies and starlight, all pieces of a timeless puzzle, fragments of a life lived in beauty if only one has eyes to see, ears to hear, arms to embrace, a heart to give. They walked and lost all track of time. At last Rebecca Blue Thrush broke their common reverie.

"Why did you come to this village?"

"Am I not a Cheyenne?" asked the Northerner.

"That is no answer," said Rebecca.

Panther Burn nodded in agreement. But it was the only answer he had for her. Then she took his hand in hers, touched the scar tissue where he had severed his finger in grief for his dead friends. He jerked his hand free as if her mere touch meant him harm. She looked at him, obviously stung by this sudden rejection, yet Rebecca did not have so much pride she could not be sympathetic. Given time, she was certain he would confide in her. Given time.

"My mother thinks the spirits guided you to us."

"Only if the spirit is named Sabbath McKean." Panther Burn chuckled. He looked back over his shoulder at the irregular cluster of lamplit cabins that made up the village. He did not want to talk of the past. Not when she was so close that he ached to hold her.

"My mother is a woman of power. I have seen her magic. At least, I think I have," Rebecca said. "My mother says that you are a sign of great and terrible changes for my people."

"My people too," Panther Burn corrected. "But I am only one man. How can I change the whole village? Maybe Star means I bring change for *one* of the people by the Warbonnet. Maybe you, Rebecca Blue Thrush."

His breath was soft upon her cheek. His hand strong, exciting, close. Yes, she could love this man, easily. For he was unlike any man she had known. Rebecca turned toward him.

"Why did you ask me to walk with you?"

"Because I want you," Panther Burn said. "When I saw you in the river I thought to myself, here is a woman to walk the hills with, to bear sons; she has strength, and courage and great beauty." Panther Burn glanced aside at her, amazed at this sudden act of courage on his part. Rebecca had not expected quite such a direct answer. She had asked almost in jest, out of a flirtatious whim, not really intending to confront him or her own feelings.

"Now tell me, Rebecca Blue Thrush, why did you leave your house and come with *me*?" Panther Burn asked, tilting her head so that she looked directly into his eyes. Rebecca tried to think of a light reply, anything to escape the intensity of the Northerner's gaze. Star's visions, her own misgivings—suddenly none of it seemed to matter. She had no words, only actions. Rebecca put her arms around his strong neck, her head upon his chest, her lithe body pressed against him, locked to him in an embrace.

Let this be my answer, she thought, trembling as they touched.

4

Friday, May 12, 1865

I have pursued my elusive quarry from one valley to the next, delving deeper into the high country. I had thought to make contact and bring to an end these terrible atrocities long before now. But alas, our scout, Sabbath McKean, informs me that ours is a hopeless pursuit, the Ute raiding party has crossed back over the Divide, their murderous souls glutted in the wreckage of burned-out cabins and butchered families. We have paused three times today to bury the dead, the last stop involving the remains of a couple of prospectors. We did not sort out who went with what but covered both gents over in a common grave, assuming they were partners. Tom has been keen for action, and has handled himself well, though he emptied his stomach more than once today. There is no shame in it, for every man will have his day in the bush. The sight of these poor victims left me atremble as well. But what upsets me more is that the heathens responsible shall go unpunished, for tomorrow we start back to Castle Rock. . . .

"Is it true then?" Tom Bragg stood just inside the tent, the canvas flap settling in his wake. He stepped forward and sat opposite Jubal. Blond beginnings of a beard fringed his jawline. His pale blue eyes began to radiate some of the intensity of his older brother. Only some, though. "We are turning back?" As he leaned his dusty elbows on the table and peered at Jubal, the lamplight lent a sickly coloration to their faces, as if each man were wearing an amber mask. "We can't." Tom shook his head, a note of incredulity in his voice. "It's wrong. Those men . . . today . . . the squatter family down in the valley . . . just poor dirt farmers . . . maybe their future held nothing but hardscrabble but at least it was something. Better than to end up . . . Goddammit, Jubal, there has to be a reckoning!"

"And I will see to it," Jubal said, rubbing a hand over his weary features. "I always see to it." After his parents' deaths, there had been no others. Bodies, yes. Corpses to be entered in his mind's mad tally book. Debits and losses, a ledger of vengeance only he could read. Or one day balance.

"How?"

"I will worry about 'how,' " he snapped. "I don't have enough men to send up in the passes and risk losing them to ambush or late snows, I just don't have enough." Jubal knew if he hadn't taken the time to wait for Tom in Denver he could have been after the Ute a whole week earlier and avoided this dilemma. Too late, now. Water under the bridge.

"So we do nothing," Tom growled. He drew the Colt revolver he had yet to even fire. At his left protruded the hilt of his as-yet-unbloodied saber. He worked the gun's cylinder, studying the loaded chambers. "It isn't fair." Click, click. The gun gave him a feeling of power. He liked the sensation.

"Fair?" Jubal chuckled. "Such notions are for Easterners, fine city folk in soft feather beds. The morning coffee's cold and life's 'unfair.' Or it is a fine day, we are safe and the Sunday chicken is plump and juicy and life . . . is 'fair.' "

"There is no glory in Sunday dinner," Tom said, returning the revolver to his holster, and reaching over, helped himself to a glass of brandy from his brother's decanter. He filled a coffee cup half-full. "No glory at all."

"No fortune either," Jubal added. "Nor sweet revenge." A moth fluttered into the tent and circled in on the lantern, drawn toward the light in an ever-tightening spiral.

"A single gray morsel of life," Jubal observed, "bent on suicide." His hand shot out, catching the moth in mid-flight. He tossed it toward the loosely dangling canvas flap, blocking the entrance. "You will find, little brother, out here in the West, a man or a moth can still make his own victories."

The moth darted away from the tent flap, forsaking night for the lure of the flame. It flew from freedom to death against the lamp's soot-streaked heated glass chimney.

"Or tragedy?" Tom noted, sipping from his cup.

"Exactly," Jubal said, reaching over to clap his younger brother on the shoulder.

"And what about the Ute war party?" Tom asked.

Jubal stood and stepped around the table and drew back the flap. Two dozen campfires scattered their red glow throughout the aspen grove where the hundred men of his militia were camped for the night. He looked toward the snowcapped battlements looming above them, where wind-scoured passes had offered an escape to the savages he had sought to bring to justice. So be it, he said to himself. But they weren't the only red devils around.

Three privates of Bragg's Colorado Militia warmed themselves at their campfire, extracting the last vestige of comfort due them before assuming their midnight sentry duties. Hec Knowles growled in his cups and decried the unfortunate roll of dice that had lost him his right to sleep. He dunked his hooked nose over the tin cup and breathed in steam. Dickey Rutledge, the youngest of the three, stretched his hands, palms open, to the campfire. "Don't seem right to be so cold in May," he muttered. His fuzz-covered cheeks seemed unnaturally pale in the glare of the fire.

"We climbed better'n a thousand feet today, I'll warrant," the third man observed. He was a hawk-faced, hard-looking sort with yellow teeth and a bulge in his cheek from a chaw of tobacco. All three had followed Jubal Bragg long enough to wear out a uniform apiece.

"I should've checked those dice," Hec reiterated for the hundredth time. A shadow fell across the trio as Big Marley loomed over the men.

"Bellyachin'," Marley said. "I heard it from over by the spring and knew it had to be Knowles, Rutledge, and Spike Cutter." Marley squatted and helped himself to coffee. "So what else is in your craw?"

Spike Cutter spewed a rust-colored stream of tobacco juice into the fire. "Since you're makin' a list, Sergeant. It galls me we been chasin' ghosts. Ain't seen red hide nor warbonnet of them butchers."

"Seems we ought to have left these Spencer repeaters back in Castle Rock," Rutledge added, nodding in agreement, his boyish appearance hidden behind a scruffy beard and caked trail dirt. "And brought shovels."

"And maybe a hearse." Hec chuckled.

"And four white horses," Spike finished.

Marley gulped the coffee down, tongued a lump of grounds out from between his teeth. His thoughts echoed their sentiments but protocol kept him from letting them know. He dropped the cup, spat out the grounds, and tugged the brim of his cap low over his eyes.

"You boys just see you keep awake tonight. Leave how to fight Indians to the colonel." He did not offer the men an opportunity to reply but continued on his way out of the camp and up the nearest slope to the ridge where he knew he'd find the one man who didn't waste time complaining. Marley took care to make enough noise to announce himself, stepping on twigs, letting low-hanging branches swing back into place. His sudden yelp, however, was unpremeditated as an owl startled from its roost buzzed him as it screeched off into the darkness.

"Big ox." Sabbath McKean made his observation from his cold camp. His voice carried over the stillness to the lumbering sergeant.

"Don't aim to give you the chance to shoot me for a redskin," Marley said. His stumbling efforts carried him over toward the scout. "Light a shuck to show me the way."

"Not hardly."

Marley cursed and crawled hand over fist until he gained the deadfall Sabbath McKean had chosen for his camp.

"So . . . you think some of them heathen rascals might've doubled back."

"No. Just a habit of being cautious," McKean replied. Marley grunted, sat upwind of the scout.

"Then we lost them for sure."

"This time," McKean said, clasping his hands behind his head and staring up at the stars.

"Curse their souls."

"Might as well curse the wind for blowing too hard, the sun for shining too hot, the rain for falling," Sabbath reflected, unruffled by his companion's anger. "Ute or Sioux or Cheyenne or any other Indian . . . they're just another element, no worse, no better. You and me and Jubal Bragg down there, we're the visitors."

"Them we buried ain't," Marley growled. "You know, one day, me and you are gonna have to tangle. Just don't seem right if we don't. Maybe when we've killed the last red nigger whelp."

"Why do you hate them so much?" Sabbath asked.

"Injuns. Hell . . . 'cause the colonel hates 'em," Marley said. "You got an extra stick of jerky?"

Sabbath dug in his war kit and found a hard, flattened chunk of meat about six inches in length. He tossed it over to Marley. It landed on the sergeant's round solid belly.

"Thanks," the sergeant muttered.

Sabbath nodded, though the man couldn't see. The scout knew deep in his heart that the Ute were crossing back over the mountains; their raid was ended, leaving behind them a few fire-gutted ranches and maybe a dozen slaughtered whites; leaving behind something else as well.

Hatred.

And hatred wasn't something men could just set aside or turn their backs on. It was a legacy that gnawed at the heart like a cancer. It could drive a man mad and turn mercy into bloodthirsty retribution. The militia was returning to Castle Rock with nothing to show for their troubles but hatred. He lowered his eyes to the western mountains, implacable, unyielding, a dead end to grand ambitions. Not a shot had been fired, but Jubal Bragg's little war was over.

Or was it?

Sunday. A time for worship and departure. Surrounding the couple in the center of the camp, the people of the Warbonnet village spread out in an ever-increasing throng to hear Sam Madison's words of departure. Against an azure sky, clouds floated in listless harmony like barkentines of old. To the west and north, distant snowcapped peaks filled the far horizon. It was a day of leavetaking and Samuel Madison's voice rang forth upon the clear spring air. He held aloft the worn leather Bible that he had carried into the wilderness seeking to atone for a wealth that was not of his choosing, seeking respite from the seductive trappings of his family's influence. Fittingly enough, he had read a passage from Exodus. Now, standing on the wagon bed, he could see that most of the village was indeed gathered to wish him well, to hear his parting words. "My brothers and sisters," he said, "it is thus with sorrow in my heart that I must begin my own exodus. I must leave you for a time. But I will be a hollow man in the city of the Great White Father, for my spirit remains here, with you. I will come back to you, but until I do, I leave my sacred

91

book as a sign that I am still among you, that I will always be among you. My Bible, the words of the one true God put down for all to have and hold." Simon White Bull stepped forward from the crowd, a grave expression on his face as he lifted up his arms and Samuel placed the Bible in Simon's outstretched hands. The chief of the Southern Cheyenne turned, holding the Holy Book aloft so all could see what had been entrusted to his keeping.

"And now," Samuel continued, catching a smile from Esther, whose uplifted eyes beamed with admiration and love, "I shall ask you all to pray with me, that the Holy Spirit watch over us and guard us and bring Esther and me safely back to you, our people."

Men and women sank to their knees on the fragrant earth. Samuel spotted Panther Burn sitting astride his horse on the fringe of the gathering. He was dressed for traveling, savage in his buckskins, his rifle balanced in the crook of his arm, his long black hair framing an expression of distrust and even contempt. Samuel lowered to his knees, returning his attention to his flock, ignoring the panther on the perimeter, though he sensed the Northern Cheyenne was no less dangerous than his namesake.

"Heavenly Father . . ." Voices lifted in prayer. The flap-flap-flapping of the American flag atop its pole in the center of the village.

Panther Burn wheeled his horse about and trotted back toward his uncle's cabin. It bothered him to watch all those Cheyenne kneeling and praying to the *ve-ho-e* God. Panther Burn knew how to speak to the All-Father, standing up and singing out alone, with all the spirits of earth and sky to listen. It was a good way. But a glance aside told him Rebecca had her own ideas, for she was kneeling with the rest. His disregard for the strange customs lessened then. He willed her to look in his direction, that she might see his readiness, for he had insisted on accompanying her to Castle Rock. After all, had she not stood in his blanket, had she not walked with him alone and spoken her secret thoughts in whispers soft as prairie breezes? She would not be distracted from her prayers, and Panther Burn continued on, passing through the conglomeration of cabins and tipis, where dogs licked their chops and anxiously inspected the racks of smoked beef, where hoes, rakes, and plows were stacked in place of spears and war shields, where men knelt and prayed to "Jay-ho-vah" instead of the Buffalo Spirit or Coyote Prankster or the One Spirit, All-Father.

He found Joshua Beartusk sitting outside his cabin, scraping the stone blade of his tomahawk until it tapered to a keen edge. Zachariah sat cross-legged at the blind man's feet, giving his awed attention to Joshua's tales of battles and hunts, the lives and deaths of warriors from long ago. An audience seemed to do his uncle good, Panther Burn noticed. In the week since his arrival, here at least was one positive sign, the rebirth of Joshua Beartusk. Oh, Joshua kept his jug of store-bought whiskey handy, but he turned to it less now. And Zachariah, who had once felt only disregard for the Red Shield warrior, now found his own burning dreams of greatness and honor refueled by Joshua's stories.

The blind man paused, hearing the pinto's approach and recognizing the cadence of the animal's gait. "So, then, you have not left," he called out. "Perhaps she has changed her mind and does not want you to come with her. Perhaps another has played upon a flute and called her to a blanket she finds more to her liking."

"Perhaps the All-Father has made a mistake," Panther Burn replied. "He should have left your eyes, Uncle, and stolen your tongue."

Zachariah stood and Old Warrior the mongrel hound lifted its furred head in disapproval, for the dog had been using the boy for a backrest, warming itself in the morning and napping to the droning voice of its master.

"I still want to go with you. We could ride to the mountains from the white man's village. We could follow the eagles . . ." All the enthusiasm of his youth was mirrored in the boy's trusting expression.

"Tell him, Nephew, that you hope to nest not with

93

eagles, but a different kind of bird. A thrush?" Joshua leaned forward as he cackled at his nephew's expense. Zachariah looked inquisitively at Joshua, then returned his pleading attention to Panther Burn.

"When I return," said the Northern Cheyenne, "we will go then, you and I. To the mountains." He reached out with his rifle and jabbed at his uncle. "And we will take this worn-out moccasin of a man with us. And lose him there." Joshua scowled and batted the rifle barrel away with the shaft of his tomahawk.

"Who would be there to protect you if we ran into a war party of Ute? Ha. Mock me, young one, and you will have more to mourn than the loss of a finger." Panther Burn straightened, his composure stiffening. Joshua sensed his wit had become too sharp and wounded his nephew and he turned his sightless gaze toward the sound of the horse as it whinnied and pawed the earth.

"Nephew . . . I . . ." Joshua sighed. Hearing the horse retreat, he sensed Panther Burn's departure. "Ahh."

"What is it, Joshua?" Zachariah said. "He just rode away, without . . ." The boy started after the Northerner, but Joshua caught him by the arm.

"Do not follow, little brave." Joshua ran a leathery hand across the badlands of his seamed and care-worn features. "A man must heal his wounds alone."

"Wounds?" Zachariah replied, looking around at the blind man. Joshua held out his tomahawk and fit the shaft into the boy's open palm. Zachariah's eyes grew wide. "It is a weapon for a great warrior," the boy responded, hefting it in his grip. "I will ride against my enemies. The blade is sharp and will cut deep."

Joshua nodded but he kept his face turned toward the fading sound of the departing horse.

"Not as deep as a man's words," said Joshua Beartusk. But Zachariah Scalpcane took no notice, hearing only the whisper of a stone ax slashing sunlight.

*　　*　　*

Esther fidgeted with a bolt of cloth she had brought for Star. She glanced out the window at the two figures on horseback, facing one another like monuments to enmity; Panther Burn, wild and untamed in his buckskins and shoulder-length hair, his braid of eagle feathers and brandished rifle, James Broken Knife in worn Levi's and plaid shirt, a flat-brimmed hat hiding his cropped black hair, a farmer, one of many to walk the streets of Castle Rock.

"You could tell the Northerner not to go," Esther lamely suggested, her delicate frame taut with concern. Rebecca perched on the edge of her bed. She was waiting to bid her mother farewell, for the stage from Castle Rock rarely left on time and she expected to have an extra day in the white man's town to ogle the dresses in Widow Chalmers's storefront window or to browse the fragrant confines of the Mercantile and spend a precious coin on a bag of penny candy. And just to visit. For it seemed she and Esther had had little time of late.

"You should not have invited James Broken Knife to come with us."

"But I thought the ride back . . . the two of you together . . ." Esther tried to hide her smile. Rebecca raised her eyes heavenward. "Well, it is time you took a husband," Esther finished defensively. She sniffed, muttered something about "thankless efforts." She checked the window to make certain Panther Burn and James were not at one another's throats. She spied Samuel bringing up his wagon. Dust churned from its iron-rimmed wheels and trailed behind him in lazy spirals. James waved to the reverend. Panther Burn continued to glare suspiciously at the white man.

"A little bird told me she saw you standing in the Northerner's blanket. That you walked from camp and were gone a long time."

"Saaa!" Rebecca hissed. "Little bird? More like a plump calf named Hope Moon Basket. I saw her watching us." Rebecca stood and walked across the room. She put her arms around her friend. "We walked. We stood together, in closeness. And the night called to us,

95

whispering our secret names. Then we returned to the village. Nothing more."

"The Northerner frightens me," Esther said.

"And me too," her friend replied.

"But . . . you will go to him again, if he plays his flute outside your door?"

"Yes," said Rebecca. But before she could open her heart to her friend, Star swept aside the blanket partition that screened her bed alcove.

"You two have the whole day to chatter," she said. "Esther, go to your husband. I would bid my daughter farewell in private." Esther nodded, squeezed Rebecca's hand. Star looked on, summoning every vestige of control, determined to hide the breaking of her heart. Because she had seen in the sacred fire . . . too much.

"Good-bye, Star, I will miss you."

"Me?" the medicine woman exclaimed with forced brightness. "Now don't let your husband hear such a thing. Or he will write it in his book. And make prayers against me."

"You misjudge Samuel," Esther replied. She glanced at Rebecca. "Please hurry." Esther Bird Hat Madison did not want to sit between James Broken Knife and the Northerner any longer than she had to.

Only when the girl was gone did Star take her daughter in her arms and hug her close so their hearts seemed to beat as one. Rebecca was startled by her mother's strength, for it seemed as if the medicine woman were almost trying to crush the two of them together. At last Star grudgingly freed her daughter. Standing at arm's length, Rebecca could see her mother was crying. She reached out in concern.

"With James and Panther Burn there can only be trouble," the young woman said, suddenly concerned at Star's behavior and searching for a reason to remain in the village. "Maybe it would be best if I stayed here. After all, Esther said she would come back to us. I don't have to go."

"Yes! You must! You must!" Star exclaimed, and her eyes widened. Her daughter was taken aback by the force in the woman's voice, by the look of inexplicable terror that seemed to explode across Star's face. Then in another instant it was gone and Star was smiling, almost serene.

"You must go and be with your friend while you can. The white father's village of Wash-een-ton is far and much can happen on such a journey." Star reached inside a beaded pouch hung at her waist and removed a small leather bag tied with a thong that she looped around her daughter's neck.

"You must never open this. For it will lose its magic if you do." She opened the bodice of her smock to reveal a similar bag.

"My mother gave this to me. Now I to you, part of my magic, the way of my spirit, our spirit." She patted Rebecca's arm, hoping to lull her daughter's suspicions. Rebecca gingerly touched the bag.

"What does it contain?"

"Ahh. Curious one. The same question I asked my mother and she asked hers. Well, each is different in some way, and each the same." Star led her daughter to the door. "Four things. The ashes of a sacred fire . . ." Rebecca remembered well the mystical flames her mother had conjured.

"My blood mixed with the ashes so that I will always be with you," the medicine woman continued. "And a handful of earth from the place where I bore you and brought you forth from my body." She brushed her cheek against Rebecca's.

"Now do as Esther said. Hurry."

"But that's only three," Rebecca blurted out, suddenly frightened and unsure. "Ashes and blood and earth, but what else?"

"That I will never tell and you will never know," Star replied. And for a second Rebecca thought she glimpsed in her mother's eyes something afire, something she had seen before, almost wolflike, burning. Yes, the spirit in the flames. Then the woman was Star again. And she smiled. "For life, my daughter, should never be without mystery."

5

"Blessed is the man that walketh not in the counsel of the ungodly, nor standeth in the way of sinners, nor sitteth in the seat of the scoundrel." Sam Madison quoted from the Bible but his thoughts were on a more homespun adage: "from the frying pan into the fire." Hoping to avoid passing through the heart of Castle Rock, he had guided his team down a little-used path that skirted the rock formations that gave the town its name and approached the V-shaped cluster of shops and stores from the north instead of the east. But the good reverend hadn't expected to find the encampment of Bragg's Colorado Militia straddling the wheel-rutted path. There had been tension in the town for the past few weeks. There always was when an outbreak of Indian raids occurred. But the suspicions directed toward Simon White Bull's village usually abated with the end of the troubles, when the Southern Cheyenne's warring kinsmen drifted on north or west over the mountains. But the militia was different. Bragg's men had built their reputation on pursuit and warfare. Ranging the territory, in constant conflict, they had no use for peace and less for "God's savage children," as Sam liked to call his flock. He knew Bragg's men were in the area but had hoped to avoid any confrontations between the peaceful Southern Cheyenne and the soldiers. And now he was bringing his wife and the others right through Bragg's camp. "For the Lord knoweth the way of the righteous: but the way of the ungodly shall perish."

Panther Burn heard but did not understand why the *ve-ho-e* was speaking in such a way. He did understand the angry expressions on the trail-weary faces of the soldiers who paused in setting up camp to come forward and watch, in silence, the procession through their midst. Nor could Panther Burn see the scene as they did: A buckboard, first, rambling over the hard-packed earth, with a white man at the reins, his stiff white collar chafing his neck. Beside him, a squaw, dressed like a white woman in a dusty gingham dress buttoned to the throat; behind them on a makeshift bench seat sat Rebecca Blue Thrush. They didn't know her name, but more than one man brightened, found himself willing to forgive the atrocities and murders of the past few days if such a girl as this would stay awhile. Being bone-tired had nothing to do with lust. James Broken Knife, for all his plaid shirt and close-cropped hair, was recognized for what he was after a moment's speculation. For Panther Burn, the soldiers needed no moment. Several paces behind the others, the Northerner held himself erect as men in their dusty blue uniforms, others in various stages of dress, paused amid the myriad chores that men of little rank are heir to, to stare in mute hostility at the Northerner's passing.

Other than the red imprint of the Morning Star on the pinto's rump, neither man nor beast wore paint. But Panther Burn knew he needed no war paint for such men as these to bridle at his presence. He recognized them for what they were—warriors such as himself. For all their numbers he was determined not to be cowed. Let these bluecoats know he was not like the others of White Bull's village.

The camp dog can be tamed.

The panther, never.

Not a word was spoken, not an insult uttered. Only the silent threatening stares of a hundred Indian fighters who had witnessed over the years only the evil that red men could do, like any men.

"God's peace be with you this day," Sam called out to those closest to him as he scanned the camp, looking for its leader. Many here were young men; too young for service in the Civil War, they had grown to manhood under the bloody tutelage of Jubal Bragg. Not all were young, though. Here were those who had once been farmers or ranchers—once but no more—men who had suffered loss, endured private tragedies in the clash between red culture and white. They marched to the same drums of vengeance as did their self-styled colonel.

And as if summoned by the reverend's thoughts, Jubal Bragg himself rode toward them on his way from town. He had come to see to the bivouacking of his men and to announce that the saloons and brothels on Commerce were open to them for the night. Samuel recognized the colonel from their chance meeting in Denver some years back. He still remembered Bragg's parting remark that he too was doing the Lord's work, only he was Christianizing the red heathens with the saber, not the cross.

Beneath the red sky of late afternoon Jubal glanced over his shoulder at Tom Bragg and Big Marley and spoke in a voice that did not carry to the reverend. But a few seconds later, Tom Bragg saluted and left the north road to ride at a gallop toward the camp. He passed the wagon, sweeping the white man and two women with a glance so filled with loathing that Samuel shivered despite himself. James Broken Knife suffered the same fate. Tom recognized Panther Burn and briefly considered an interchange with the Northern Cheyenne, especially since Sabbath McKean wasn't around to interfere. But Jubal had instructed him to hurry the men along with their camp and to post half a dozen pickets just in case there were any more like Panther Burn skulking about. Tom continued on, but he rode close enough to the Northerner's pinto to force the animal to dance a few steps aside. Then the youth was past and entering the camp.

With his temperamental brother safely dispatched, Jubal Bragg guided his mount off the side of the road and with Big Marley, ever faithful, at his side, awaited the buckboard as it left the outskirts of the campsite. As the wagon and the two braves on horseback departed, the soldiers broke their silence and returned to their duties, considering the irony of the moment—that they had followed a trail of carnage and never caught a glimpse of the Indians responsible, only to have some of the bloodthirsty thieves ride right through camp. And having the reverend lead the procession didn't fool the militia, not by a long shot. Samuel tugged on the reins and the wagon slowed as Jubal Bragg touched the brim of his hat.

"Well met, preacher. Glad to see you still have your hair."

"I never doubted I would lose it, Colonel," said Samuel, appraising the self-styled officer. "But then, a man has little to worry about from friends."

Bragg glanced over the women in the wagon, to James Broken Knife and last to Panther Burn. The two men recognized one another.

"Don't speak to me of worry. I buried a family up on Cross Creek and a couple of white men up on the Divide. They were 'befriended' by the likes of these. The dead have no worries." Jubal ran a hand over his features, a simple gesture of weariness that failed to erase the darkness, the *masanee*, Panther Burn had glimpsed. "Your heart's grown too soft, preacher. The frontier is no place for you."

"And maybe yours has grown too hard. I know all about you, Jubal Bragg."

"Ahhh," the colonel exclaimed, nodding. "I am the villain in this piece. Well, let me tell you something, Madison. You think you're a shepherd. Only you've mistaken the wolves for the lambs. But I see things as they really are. One day your brethren will go too far. They'll get caught with the blood on their knives. On that day I'll come back north . . ." His voice trailed off and he turned his horse and started down the path. He paused again and Marley halted as well. The eyes of Jubal Bragg bored into Panther Burn.

"Northern Cheyenne," said the officer.

"I am Panther Burn," the brave replied, undaunted.

"You do not hide behind illusions. Notice, Marley, the lack of a civilized ploy." Bragg relived, in a single incendiary second, his nightmare, and the face he had seen. The Northerner obviously had failed to under-stand all of Bragg's rhetoric.

But Panther Burn had gleaned enough. The word "hide" piqued him. Yet spirits spoke through this *ve-ho-e*. And Panther Burn sensed death. But his own or Jubal Bragg's, which?

A man of wealth and power with an army to call his own. A man with nothing of his own but the horse beneath him, the rifle in his hand, and courage like a heart afire. Bound by fate, by timeless tragedy, by a blood bond neither could hope to fathom yet both suspected.

Samuel Madison called to his horses. The axles of his buckboard creaked and groaned as he continued on his way. Rebecca, much to James's chagrin, shouted to Panther Burn. For she had watched the two men and sensed in her soul the ominous flow of events coursing between red man and white. And she was filled with fear for Panther Burn. Her left hand stole upward to clasp the leather bag dangling from her throat. Her voice shattered the tableau. Panther Burn looked away from the colonel, and prodding his own mount, contin-ued after the Madison wagon. Strangely enough, it was Marley who grunted in satisfaction. He had never seen the colonel behave so strangely. He watched the Rever-end Madison and his "flock" depart toward the outskirts of Castle Rock. From the line of travel he guessed they were heading for the whitewashed church on the north-east corner of the settlement. Well, who cared?

"I'll be glad to get back to Denver," he said aloud.

"We'll rest a day and start the men back," Jubal

instructed. He watched as his brother, having dispatched men for sentry duty, returned at a gallop toward them. "It appears Tom has energy for us all."

"He's got the fire in him, true enough," Marley dryly observed.

"A problem, old friend?"

"To be right honest, Colonel, and meaning no offense, a week of playing nursemaid is about all I can stand."

"He's all I have, Sergeant. Bear with it a while longer. At least until we reach Denver." Bragg grinned, dispelling the last of the Northern Cheyenne's legacy of gloom. Jubal needed to remind himself that only a few years separated Tom and himself, that they were brothers and not father and son. A small family, by most standards, but better than none at all. Though he hated to admit it, he was glad in a way that the Ute had slipped away. Tom was still too headstrong, too anxious for battle.

"I'll look after the pup," Marley said. "Just so long as I ain't gotta bathe him." Big Marley scratched beneath his cap, sent a stream of brown juice arcing to earth, and readjusted the plug of tobacco bulging his left cheek. "No need to worry yourself, Colonel. We're practically home."

"Yes, home," Jubal replied, and his gaze grew distant again, as if his vision had turned inward.

And Marley wondered what he saw.

6

Night came to the town of Castle Rock, bringing a noisy peace. Already word had spread the length and breadth of Commerce Street, from the bustling saloons and bordellos where the men of Bragg's Militia squandered the last of their hard-earned coins to the quieter environs of Main Street and the houses beyond, good news . . . for the war party that had plagued the area had crossed back over the Divide, been hounded by Jubal Bragg and sent scurrying. Families could return to their outlying farms. Folks could sleep without fear of waking to angry war whoops and burning walls and the cries of the dying. But before sleep must come celebration. So even in the more reputable homes, the town's distinguished citizens, men like the mayor of Castle Rock, the president of the bank, and the town barber, gathered with friends to toast the health of the militia and to wish them a speedy departure as well. The townspeople longed to return to normalcy. Now they wouldn't have long to wait.

At the north edge of town, in the shadow of a church steeple, the lights burned brightly in the parsonage of Reverend Charles Holstead. He too entertained visitors; Sam Madison and his wife had come to spend the night. And despite his misgivings, for hostility toward all Indians was on the rise, the pastor of Castle Rock's Church of Good Hope had welcomed these weary travelers. He would have done so even if Sam had not been his friend, because it was his belief that Good Hope must stand for something in this world. It must have value. It must reach out, beyond antagonism, and embrace with Christian love anyone and everyone.

Now with evening drawing on and the promise of a tasty meal to come, the unusually somber reverend had found an excuse to lead Sam off into the parlor, where, after hastily closing the oaken door, he hurried Sam into a nearby chair and slid another chair over alongside the first. Sam Madison watched in somewhat bemused suspicion as Holstead darted back across the room, peeked around the door to make sure they were safe from prying ears. Who was there to eavesdrop? Sam thought. The women were preparing the meal. As for James Broken Knife, he had already headed off toward town despite Holstead's suggestions to the contrary. And Panther Burn, the Northern Cheyenne, had remained in the stable out behind the parsonage.

Holstead assured himself that Esther and Rebecca were busy in the kitchen. He prayed they would stay there for a few more minutes, for what he had to say was for Sam alone. He was loath to alarm the girls. And because he thought of Sam Madison as something of a religious protégé, of whom the pastor of Good Hope was especially fond, Holstead was determined to make the young man see the light even if it meant risking insult. He had opened his house to Sam, his Indian wife, and her friends. But for all his devoutness and Christian belief, Holstead couldn't help but feel a trifle nervous. Given the present attitudes, what would his own church community say, when they found out?

"Reverend Holstead, you have me at a loss," Sam began. But the parson waved him to silence. Holstead settled his heavy body into an overstuffed chair, which groaned as he shifted his weight. Holstead's round, good-natured features dripped sweat. Moisture shone in the folds of his double chin and capped his bald pate with glistening droplets. Apprehension did him poor credit. In place of his usual smile, his lips were drawn tight against his teeth as he struggled with how to begin. His fears shamed him. But then, he had never laid claim to perfection, only a place in the struggle along with the rest of creation.

"Now, listen, son, it's a poor time to be in town. Not good at all."

"My wife and I—"

"Have done nothing," Holstead interrupted. "Except *be*. And that's enough right now. *Being* an Indian. *Being* married to an Indian. Listen, you know there are good people here, but it takes time for tempers to cool. Having the militia around doesn't help matters. Mind you, I had no wish to lose what's left of my scalp to some raiding party of hostiles, so I was glad for Jubal Bragg's presence. And yet I will be glad when he leaves, too. There is a malice in him that spreads like a disease. I've seen it infect an entire community before."

"Are you warning me against even boarding the stage in town?"

"I have a carriage and a fine strong team of Tennessee-bred mares. You could be in Denver by morning. And on the stage to St. Louis by nightfall. Just leave my carriage at the Methodist church. As for James and the girl, Rebecca, and that other one, Burning Panther or whatever . . . send them away. Send them away tonight."

Samuel shook his head. "We are all tired. I cannot just rush off into the night. Old friend, I shall impose upon your hospitality and be off at daylight. I am sure you exaggerate the danger." A Seth Thomas clock over the hearth tolled eight bells. Reverend Holstead tugged a watch on a brass chain from his vest pocket. The brass casing gleamed in the lamplight. The old man tapped the watch on the arm of the curve-backed chair and shifted his weight on the purple cushions. He returned the timepiece to his pocket, then rubbed the stubby fingers of his right hand across his face.

"Stubborn as a David," the reverend muttered at last, peering over his knuckles at the younger man.

"Right is on my side." Sam grinned. He settled back in the easy chair, which, like the others in the parlor, was sumptuously cushioned in purple and scarlet and stitched with a motif of swans and unicorns. The furniture was Holstead's pride and joy, for it had been delivered to him after a particularly devastating sermon on the nature of vice and God's fiery retribution against sinners. A certain madam had been so moved she had closed her coop of illicit love, scattered her flock of soiled doves, and become Holstead's church organist. Though the chairs had come from the brothel, the madam swore they had been purchased with honest money and prevailed on Reverend Holstead to accept them as a gift. Sam Madison never failed to be amused at the notion of the furniture's colorful odyssey from boudoir to parsonage.

Holstead sighed and stood. "Well then, I've said all I can say on the subject." He walked back to the door and opened it. In the dining room, the table was set. Platters of meat and vegetables trailed steam. "I suggest," Holstead cautioned, "we discover whether or not you married Esther for her cooking." He sniffed the air, savored the rich aroma of roast antelope and fried potatoes. "I think I already have my answer."

A man alone in the night. Panther Burn, the Northern Cheyenne, stood in the loft of the stable and looked out from the loading window upon the town of Castle Rock. He had been in towns before, but never one this large. How could people live like this in square lodges, with fences and alleys and streets all crisscrossed like the web of a spider? No wonder so many of the *ve-ho-e* were crazy. They had lost the Circle magic. And now they were trying to make the Cheyenne forget as well. The wind moaned through the eaves and a loose cedar shingle trembled overhead. It was time to leave, thought Panther Burn. This very minute. And go where? Back to a village of strangers, of *ve-ho-e*/Cheyenne? No. Why, then, the mountains. But go alone? He shifted his stance and looked down at the rear of the parsonage. The lamps in the kitchen were aglow and shadows passed before the unshuttered windows. He guessed it must be Rebecca moving quickly, with practiced grace among the tables and chairs and canned goods . . . Rebecca Blue Thrush, trying to be a white man's woman. His heart throbbed wildly in his breast. But a Cheyenne she was born, Cheyenne she was meant to be, to walk as one of the People, to live as one of the People. Panther Burn glanced at his scarred left hand. Even if he could never return to Spirit Mountain, he would always be Cheyenne, the Morning Star would always shine for him. And her.

Rebecca had stood with him in his blanket. Once he had called to her and she had come. From the moment he had seen her standing naked and proud in the War-bonnet, he had wanted her with him. This was why the Great Spirit had led him south, not to find another home, but to find her. Yes. It was so. He must tell her what had been revealed to him. Now! This very minute!

Panther Burn reached inside his buckskin shirt and his fingers closed around the flute. He patted the wooden instrument, and reassured, smiled and turned from the loading window. He hurried over to the ladder and scrambled down the splintery rungs to the earthen floor. He landed lightly on the balls of his feet and hurried up the center aisle. The pinto whinnied in its stall as Panther Burn approached. Suddenly the Northerner paused. He breathed in, alert now. The stable smelled of dirt, hay, manure, leather, and something more . . . something that had not been there before. He wrinkled his nostrils. The pinto nickered and stomped its hooves. Another horse scratched at the packed ground, then unconcernedly nuzzled a mouthful of oats out of a nearby trough. A brittle stalk of hay snapped as Panther Burn identified the new aroma: the still air reeked of whiskey. Panther Burn sniffed, turned as James Broken Knife lurched out of the shadows. The Southern

Cheyenne came in low and fast. Too fast to stop as Panther Burn danced out of the way. James crashed through the siding of an empty stall and grunted as he hit the hard ground. He rolled off his gut and onto his feet, his stance uncertain. He ran a hand over his close-cropped black hair and searched the ground around him for his hat.

"You call me farmer," James spat. "I will show you." His hand came away bloody. The hell with the hat.

"You will show me a drunken Indian. Nothing more," said Panther Burn.

James charged and once again Panther Burn avoided him, only this time he stuck out his left foot, caught James Broken Knife around the ankle, and sent the Southern Cheyenne sprawling into the middle of the barn.

"Enough," Panther Burn said. He had no stomach for such a one-sided fight.

"You will leave. Tonight. You are not welcome among my people. I swear you will not return to the Warbonnet." James groaned, wiped a dirty forearm across his features, blinked, and managed to focus on Panther Burn.

"Then we have nothing to quarrel about. I am leaving," said the Northerner.

James sat up, surprised at his easy victory. "And the girl Rebecca?"

"She goes with me," Panther Burn said.

"No!" James crawled to his feet, lunged forward, his powerful arms extended to catch Panther Burn in a spine-crushing bear hug. The Northerner ducked, and using all his strength, drove his right shoulder into the pit of James's stomach. The larger man gasped and dropped soundlessly to his knees. His breath came in short ragged gasps. He slowly curled forward, rolled on his side in a fetal position. He did not lose consciousness and his wide-open eyes burned with hatred. But the fight had certainly been taken out of him. Panther Burn turned his back on the fallen brave and walked over to the pinto. He led the fierce little stallion out of the stall and swung up on his back. He slung his Hawken rifle in its blanket scabbard over his shoulder.

"James Broken Knife," said Panther Burn to the figure huddled in the darkness. "You make a better farmer than a warrior. Go back to your garden, go back to your white-man's buffalo. Do not follow me, for I would not have your blood on my hands." Panther Burn did not wait for a reply, but rode from the barn. Once in the night wind, he reached again for the flute that Joshua had carved. What if this time she did not come? He was almost afraid to play upon it.

If the dining room was fragrant, the kitchen was all but heady with the mouth-watering scent of potatoes and steaks and freshly baked biscuits that Esther gingerly lifted from the fireplace oven. She tapped the iron pan and the bread tumbled out in a wondrous avalanche upon the table. Rebecca rearranged the piping-hot biscuits upon a platter and paused to tear one in half and dip it into a crock of honey and plop the morsel into her mouth.

"*Saaa!*" Esther exclaimed, catching her friend in the act.

"Just testing. I wouldn't want you to serve your husband something that might not please him. He might take a switch to you and drive you from his lodge."

Esther scooped up the remaining half of biscuit and gobbled it down. She nodded, pleased with herself. She had wanted to make a good impression on Reverend Holstead. Rebecca took up an empty plate and crossed over to the fire and began to fill the tin with potatoes, steak, and gravy. Esther looked on in disapproval. She leaned against the kitchen table, folded her arms across her bosom, her lips pursed as she tried to decide what, if anything, could sway her friend's affections.

"You bring the Northerner his meal?"

"Yes," said Rebecca. She returned to the table and placed a couple of biscuits on the plate, then met

110

Esther's worried gaze. "I have the feeling we are going to repeat an argument."

"I just don't see why he had to humiliate us and offend Reverend Holstead by staying in the barn."

"It is Panther Burn's way," Rebecca said with a shrug.

"Well, it is a rude way," Esther snapped. "And I suppose you will sit with him while he eats with the horses?"

"A little while. He does not like being so . . . close to so many white men."

"Then let him leave." Esther reached out and placed her hands on Rebecca's shoulders. "Stay here. After all, you came to be with me. We might not see each other again for a long time, Rebecca."

"And we will have the rest of the night and tomorrow morning to talk and walk and look in the windows of the shops in town." The flames in the fireplace leaped upward and a twig exploded, causing both young women to jump. Rebecca laughed at herself. Esther joined in, but halfheartedly. She tried to think of an argument to sway her friend from this course of folly. But even as she started to speak, the sound of a flute cut her short. A soft trilling song filtered in through the shuttered window, a melody Rebecca's heart had memorized, that called her to come out from the kitchen in the parsonage, out from under the roof of the white men to walk in the Cheyenne night.

"Don't go, Rebecca," Esther whispered. And she stared at the back door as if the devil himself were without the walls of the house. "You think you know him, but I tell you he is not like other men. Please don't go."

"I must," Rebecca replied, setting the plate of food on the table near a jar of nutmeg and a tin of sugar.

"But why?" Esther asked.

"You said it yourself," Rebecca whispered. "Because he is not like other men."

*   *   *

Rebecca waited in the wind. Dust devils danced in darkness. Leaves blew against her ankles. Invisible fingers caught at the fringes of her buckskin smock, tugged at the hem of her calico dress. Rebecca walked away from the house, stared up at the Church of Good Hope's black spire jutting toward the cloud-strewn sky. A wind promising a spring storm gusted out of the west, subsided, gusted again. But where was he who had called to her, playing his music upon the night? Had she imagined the flute? Well, then, Esther shared her madness, for they had both heard. Rebecca stood in an arena of moonlight bordered on three sides by parsonage, church, and stable. But from the open north came the sound, a drumming of hooves, a rider coming at a gallop. Rebecca shivered, tensed with uncertainty, for a second considered running back the way she had come. And then she saw him, materializing in the silver light, Panther Burn. She gasped as he bore down on her. Something inside whispered to her to run away. Run away from him. But she could not. He was proud and terrible with his long hair streaming wild like a cape and his eyes, black, blazing as he leaned to one side, his arm crooked out, encircled her, scooped Rebecca up beside him. She stifled a cry of alarm, her heart in her throat. Then the pinto vanished past the church and raced off into the wind.

"No," a voice slurred. "No . . . !" And James Broken Knife stumbled uncertainly out of the barn, where he had watched the abduction. What spell had this damn Northerner worked on Rebecca that she should not cry out? The Southern Cheyenne made his way into the moonlight, veering through the settling dust. "Has she no shame?" he muttered. An empty bottle slid from his left hand. The motion startled him and he jumped aside, lost his balance, and fell. James Broken Knife lay on his side until the world quit spinning. He cursed the bottle, cursed the Northerner for disrupting all his plans. His eyes focused on the hilt of a knife lying in the dirt. He reached out, brought it closer, and inspected the markings on the bone grip. Three wavy lines, the mark-

ings of the Spirit Mountain Cheyenne. The knife was
Panther Burn's. The Northerner probably lost it from
his sheath when he leaned out to sweep Rebecca up
into his arms. James Broken Knife scowled and tossed
the knife aside and rolled over on his stomach. Ah, if
only he could rid himself of the Northerner as easily as
casting the knife away. He crawled to his knees, then
managed to stand. Suddenly his flesh tingled and he
gasped as an idea wormed its way through his liquor-
clouded brain. He remembered, earlier, how Colonel
Bragg had seemed to take a special interest in Panther
Burn. James didn't know why. Nor did he care. Suddenly he had a plan, and that was all that mattered. He
would need more courage. Another bottle's worth. And
he would need . . . the knife! The knife he had thrown
away. Dropping to his hands and knees, he began to sift
his fingers through the dirt. The wind blew grit into his
eyes. The discomfort only served to sober him. James
crawled and searched, all the while telling himself he
could be rid of the arrogant Northerner. Rid of him for
good. And free Rebecca from his madness. But only if
he found the knife of Panther Burn. He searched franti-
cally and prayed. And a dark God heard. . . .

*Death and love in a night washed with stars. Toward
the distant hills, the dark hills, a man and woman ride
without a thought for the morning, she is a captive
beauty and he has stolen her away, like her heart,
stolen, this thief of love, of passion, this free and savage
spirit. Let the wind blow. Let the shadows dance before
the moon and cover the earth in a shifting patchwork of
silver and obsidian. A man and a woman vanish from
the trappings of civilization, of ordered conduct, of
gentle beds and tamed lives.*

*Let passion rule this night, for it is the song of every
wind. And the stars are the sirens of desire, glimmering
Circes that beckon to lovers on their odyssey, "Come,
sweet strangers, hear our call, dare the unsafe harbor,
and find in one another's arms perilous ecstasy." Be-*

ware, to listen is to lose caution and gain a lifetime of memories.

Gentle was the wind's caress. Tender the music of the trembling boughs. An hour from town had brought Rebecca and Panther Burn into the low-slung hills that swelled toward the distant Rockies, majestic in their robes of night. Panther Burn leaped down from horseback, and setting his rifle aside, he spread his buffalo robe and a blanket upon the fragrant earth. The scent of lodgepole and ponderosa pine mingled with the dusky perfume of bittersweet nightshade that Panther Burn crushed with his buffalo robe. He stood upon the ground cover and turned to find Rebecca still on horseback.

"Are you afraid of me now?" he asked. His hand outstretched to her. She shook her head no. "The white man is like a spider. One builds a web, the other a trap of fences and streets and dirty-looking buildings and more fences. Here we are free. Come stand beside me." She did not move. "Why do you wait?"

"I do not understand why I have come here." For a moment Rebecca considered riding away on the horse, stealing the pinto and racing back to Castle Rock. What madness had seized her that she had not fled this man when he galloped toward her? She should have run to the house. She should have called out for help. *Something. Anything.* She slid down from horseback. *Nothing.* She had reached out to him as if following an instinct so ingrained as to be unfathomable. It was true, she feared this Panther Burn. But she feared herself, her unspoiled confused heart, even more. She walked soundlessly to him, stood before the Northerner. "I do not understand why I have come here," she repeated in a hushed tone.

He took her in his arms then. His embrace, too powerful to resist, crushed her close to him. The heat from their bodies mingled, ignited the blood in their veins. Her small breasts thrust forward as he pulled her to him, crushing her against his chest. The world seemed to spin out of kilter only for a moment, then Rebecca felt the tanned buffalo hide against her back and the stars twinkled like jewels overhead. Panther Burn's face

114

eased across the backdrop of stars. His own eyes radiating a starry light. Rebecca fought her own passions. It was right to be here. And wrong. She wanted him and yet could not reconcile desire with her beliefs. And so she tried to push him away, but Panther Burn only caught her wrists and pinned her arms to the ground as he worked his way astride her struggling form. Rebecca realized the more she worked her legs, the higher rode her dress. She ceased to kick, but her body remained tense. Her long black hair was splayed out upon the robe. Panther Burn's spilled forward, masking his features in shadow. Slowly he lifted her arms and brought them together and he lowered his face to her wrists and his breath was warm upon her flesh. Then he threw back his head and gave a hearty laugh that reverberated among the moonlit conifers as he rolled off her struggling form. Rebecca sprang to her feet and ran toward the pinto. She paused to whirl around, her voice trembling with anger.

"Who do you think you are, Northerner," she blurted out, "to treat me in such a manner?" She began to back away from him now, afraid to take her eyes off the man lest he charge her.

"No!" Panther Burn said sharply. Rebecca froze in mid-stride as the Northern Cheyenne rose to his knees. And now his tone softened. "Woman, who do *you* think I am? Only that is important. I know myself. I know I would never dishonor you. I called to you. And you came because here, in our hearts, you know we share the same song. I would have us share the same life. There, it is said, and the words no longer burn in my heart." The cry of an owl echoed in the forest. The wind played a susurrant melody, haunting her thoughts, her memories. Yes, she had walked with Panther Burn before, but then it had been within sight of her village. And the very proximity of her people had guaranteed her safety, she had been able to indulge her passions without fear of them getting out of control. Alone with him she had panicked. Now she blushed for having displayed such weakness. His struggle with her had been a game.

"Do you play a game now? Are your words from the heart or the coyote spirit within you?"

"Come sit beside me and find out."

Rebecca glanced at the pinto, peacefully cropping the budding green shoots underfoot. Save for the eerie wail of the screech owl and the creaking of the branches overhead, the world lay silent, as if one with the man upon the buffalo robe. The eagle feathers in his braided hair wafted in the dying breeze. He did not move toward her, leaving Rebecca to make her own choice. She started forward, hesitated, then continued, surrendering to the need to trust him. She knelt before him on the robe, and when his arms encircled her, she allowed him to guide her over onto her back. He lay alongside her, one arm across her bosom, his scarred hand caressing her cheek.

"Little bird, I have no wealth, no horses, nothing to offer Star that I might ask her to bring you to me in the two-called-together ceremony."

Rebecca reached up and covered his hand with her own. "My mother's wealth is in her visions, that which no man can give her. And as for horses, Panther Burn of the Spirit Mountain . . . my mother has no need of horses." She laughed softly and nestled in his arms and listened to the distant chorus of a coyote baying at the moon. Poor spirit, so lost, thought Rebecca. "We will live among my people?"

Panther Burn stiffened at her question, but he would not lie to her.

"I am a Cheyenne. My heart runs with the buffalo, it will not graze with cattle." He knew his words stung her. Yet what could he do? Certainly not return to his father's tribe after leaving in such disgrace. But what right did he have to lead her with him into exile? "I will think on it," he added at last, reluctant to bring anything between them.

From far off in the granite peaks to the west came a murmur of thunder.

"Perhaps the spirits say it is good and give their blessing." Rebecca sighed.

"Ahh, then the *ma-heone ve-ho-e*, the holy white man, has not led you from the old ways." His breath warmed her cheek. She liked that. She would not, however, let Sam Madison go undefended.

"I am a Christian," she replied. "But that does not mean I am deaf. I can hear the spirits speak as well as you, Northerner." When he laughed, she tried to frown in response. But Rebecca could not hold it for long. And when he lay on his back, she turned into him, her lithe form extended along the length of his body. She smiled then and lowered her head to rest upon his chest, the beaded Morning Star near her cheek. Rebecca had never experienced such a mixture of peace and turmoil, for her physical need for him was almost unbearable. And yet the very peace of being close to him, a peace she was certain he also sensed, this too was good. She closed her eyes, as did Panther Burn, and without meaning to, they fell asleep, together in one another's arms; a man and woman happy in their innocence, undisturbed by the thunder in the hills.

Sabbath McKean had chosen to take his whiskey in the Babylon Saloon. The biblical reference did not bother him and the Babylon boasted the most spacious interior in all of the emporiums along Commerce. More room meant less cigar smoke per square inch. Sabbath liked to breathe between drinks. Unfortunately it appeared most of Bragg's Militia had the same idea, for the tables were ringed with uniformed men and the bar that ran the length of one wall, fifty feet from corner to corner, was jammed with an assortment of soldiers of every shape and size. Sabbath sat with his back to a wall, his slouch hat tilted forward, shading his hawk face. Quick was the temper in him, for Highland blood flowed in his veins and he sat like a king on his own private throne, as if daring any of the men in the Babylon to try to commandeer his table or intrude in any way on his whiskey-soaked solitude. He leaned forward and tilted the half-full bottle before him and measured a healthy portion of Kentucky lightning into his tumbler. He lifted the glass in salute to the voluptuous Greek maidens who cavorted seminaked upon the Elysian fields in a chromolithograph that dominated the wall behind the bar.

Smoke clung to the ceiling beams and choked the illumination from the oil lamps suspended there. Despite the abundance of lamps, an all-pervading soot-gray gloom obscured the room and stung the nostrils and set all eyes to watering. One of the Babylon's birds of pleasure, a woman named Francine LaFleur, danced upon a table while the piano player in the corner played "Rose of Alabam'." Francine was a better whore than a dancer but her admiring audience didn't seem to mind. Every time she lifted the scarlet satin hem of her dress and kicked out, hopping from one foot to another and showing off her legs and thick thighs encased in a stocking mesh, a chorus of deep-throated cheers would raise high the roofbeams.

One of the soldiers, unable to restrain himself, tipped her off the table and into his arms. The prostitute bore the man to the floor in a tumble of petticoats and trousers. The men surrounding the struggling couple cheered and toasted Francine. At last the militiaman staggered to his feet and with Francine LaFleur in his arms and his nose all but buried in her ample bosom the stalwart lover threaded his way through the crowded room and laboriously climbed the stairs to the bedrooms on the second floor.

"Sleep well, brave laddie," Sabbath muttered, and drained his glass. He had rumbled with Francine once upon a time and counted himself lucky that he lived to tell the tale. "That woman enjoys her work with a vengeance," he added with a chuckle. A shadow slipped into his periphery, spoiling his solitude. Sabbath greeted Tom Bragg with a glare. The scout's reddish eyebrows furrowed forward like enormous caterpillars crawling toward the bridge of his nose. Tom Bragg wavered unsteadily. The hilt of his saber managed to gleam even in this smoky den. A pistol shot caused Tom to jump. In the corner, the piano player took a Yankee suggestion and quit the "Rose of Alabam' " for a medley of "John Brown's Body" and "On the Banks of the Ohio." Sabbath glanced over and recognized Hec Knowles, Spike Cutter, and young Dickey Rutledge in a tight circle around the hapless pianist. Rutledge holstered his still-smoking revolver. He loosed a war whoop and began stomping and clapping. He grabbed the nearest girl, a mousy tart barely sixteen, and began to dance while the man she had been flirting with, a ploughboy judging from his overalls and coat, took a step toward the girl, looked at Knowles and Cutter, then thought better of the idea; he shrugged and backed down and headed for the bar.

"Well, scout, you really earned your money. Let those savages get clean away," Tom said. He leaned forward. His hands splayed out on the table as he steadied himself. "I think I'm going to be sick."

Sabbath groaned and shook his head. He grabbed his bottle and leaned back against the wall, relinquishing the table to the sour-looking youth. Marley shouldered through the crowd.

"What's the matter?" he said, eyes shifting from Jubal's brother to McKean.

"You make a good mother sheep," Sabbath muttered. Marley reddened. He clamped his teeth down on the stub of a cigar. "Your lamb here is gonna be sick," Sabbath continued. Tom pulled away as Marley reached for him.

"Take your hands off me," the youth snapped.

"These hands is gonna tuck you in bed," Marley said. "And maybe bust your chops so's you'll stay put."

"Nothing wrong with me. I just need to relieve myself." Tom retreated a step, located the side door leading to the alley. He turned to Sabbath. "We'll finish our discussion later." The young Easterner shoved his way past Marley.

"I wonder if I need to stand by and make sure he

don't piss down his boots," Marley said as he watched Tom move unsteadily to the alley door.

"Might help 'em to fit," Sabbath retorted. " 'Cause right now he doesn't fit them a'tall."

"They never will," Marley said. "Them boots belong to Colonel Bragg."

"You'd follow Jubal Bragg to hell," the scout observed.

"We all got to follow someone," Marley said. "Or something." He sat on the edge of the table and held out a glass for Sabbath to fill. "How are you gettin' to hell, McKean?"

A knife in the shadows, moonlight on steel, on the burnished face of a man who had come to avenge himself. James Broken Knife lifted the blade in his hand and braced himself against the rough wood of the wall behind him. He watched without recognizing Tom Bragg as the youth made his way out of the Babylon Saloon and sought out the darkness at the rear of the alley to relieve himself against the side of a rain barrel. The Southern Cheyenne swallowed. His throat felt dry, he ran his tongue around the stale whiskey taste inside his mouth and started forward. A rising wind moaned as it stirred the dust in the alley. James Broken Knife's solemn face was a portrait of wavering determination. There simply hadn't been enough courage in the one bottle he had finished. A man needed more, especially a man of conscience. He hated Panther Burn for the way he had turned Rebecca's head. But enough to kill? Rebecca had never professed her love to James. But she would have, he reminded himself, given time. Time was all she had needed. He had seen her ride off with the Northerner. A step, two steps, closer now to the man at the rear of the alley. James tightened his grip on the knife. Sweat beaded his forehead, stung his eyes, streamed down his cheeks. *Hurry. Hurry before the white man turns.* He wiped his forehead on his shirt sleeve and realized he had lost his hat again. Strange to be worried about a hat now, at a moment like this. He was almost within arm's reach. *No. This is wrong. I cannot.* James paused, the realization of what he was about to do seeping at last into full-blown perspective. Kill a man, like this? No! He retreated, confused but unable, no, unwilling to murder. A shard of glass from a discarded bottle cracked underfoot as a cloud scudding free of the moon momentarily flooded the alley with bone-colored light. Tom swung around at the sound and saw the Indian standing directly behind him, the knife held away from his body, and to Tom's thinking, poised to strike.

"God in heaven!" the youth gasped, and reached for his saber.

"No, white man," James hissed. But Tom Bragg had already caught the hilt at his side and the long curved blade gleamed wickedly as it slid from its scabbard with a rasp of metal.

"Murdering bastard," Tom snarled. The blade of his saber caught, he jerked it loose and slashed awkwardly at the Southern Cheyenne, who leaped inside the saber's reach and tried to shove the youth back against the wall. Both men, unsteady on their feet, tumbled against the rain barrel. Tom fell backward and with his free hand on the Indian's throat dragged James Broken Knife over on top of him. Both men landed heavily, the white man underneath. Tom gasped as James worked loose of his grasp. The brave crawled out of reach of the saber. Tom groaned and pulled himself to his feet. In the bone-white glare James could see a knife hilt protruding from the Easterner's chest. The Indian stared dumbly down at his own empty hands.

"He's killed me. He's killed me!" Tom shouted, and staggered toward the side door of the Babylon. "Someone . . . help!"

"No. I didn't mean . . ." James crawled to his feet, panic welling in his breath, and ran as the youth collapsed. The side door of the Babylon opened and noise spilled into the alley. Two men in the uniform of Bragg's Militia froze as they spied Tom Bragg's sprawled body. James Broken Knife collided with the men at a dead run and knocked them aside. He cleared the mouth of the alley as the men behind him began to cry out an alarm. They had glimpsed enough of their assailant to know him for an Indian. That and the sight of one of their own lying dead in the alley were enough to sober them.

Once in the street, James acted on instinct. There was a hitching rail nearby with half a dozen horses tethered before a water trough. He crossed the distance in seconds and leaped into the saddle of the closest horse as one of the men he had collided with emerged from the alley, gun in hand.

"Hold it, you red devil," the soldier called out. James tore the reins free and swung the animal around. A revolver roared, a lead slug burned the Indian's neck as it whined past. James whipped the startled gelding into a gallop down the street. Gunshots rippled on the night air, but James didn't turn to see. He kept himself low in the saddle, his cheeks whipped by the plunging mane of the brown gelding he had stolen. Other white men stumbled into the street at the sound of all the commotion. Lighted windows, startled faces, barely heard voices—all rushed past as in a nightmare. Horse and rider approached the end of Commerce, and James drove his heels into the gelding's flanks, urging the animal to even greater effort. Figures darted from a side street leading over to Main. A pack of boys on a nightly excursion had come running at the first sound of gunplay. The youths held up at the sight of the madly fleeing Indian on horseback. But one boy of ten years, quicker than the others, tried to leap across the path of the galloping horseman. The toe of his boot caught in the churned earth and the boy tumbled beneath the plunging hooves. James felt the collision; the gelding lost stride and nearly fell before regaining its balance. James heard the screams of the boys, then nothing but the rushing wind, as the town of Castle Rock slipped past. Ahead lay a long night's ride.

No one had caught a long enough look at him to

identify him as the soldier's assailant. And the knife would fix the blame on Panther Burn.

May 17, 1865.

Tomorrow I will lead my men back south. Tom really hasn't had time to enjoy the comforts Denver has to offer. I am excited by the prospect of bringing him into business. He is a bright lad, well-educated. Bragg Bros. Freighting. I like the sound. Bragg Land and Title. And then there is our interest in a railroad linking Denver City to the Union Pacific in Cheyenne. Tom has studied engineering and though he found bookwork and the life of a student not to his liking, my partners and I shall certainly make use of his knowledge on the subject, which is certainly superior to my own or for that matter to any of the gentlemen in the consortium. I am happy—

Jubal leaned back from the desk in his hotel room. The gunshots distracted him. No doubt some wild celebration. He hoped it wasn't his men. But then, again, they were hard men who did a hard job. The townspeople of Castle Rock would simply have to put up with a little noise and one more sleepless night. It was a small price to pay for the safety of their loved ones. And it certainly had been a successful if relatively bloodless campaign. Jubal decided he would have to add a bit more drama to his account when he reported on his latest exploits to Bill Byers at the *Rocky Mountain News*. Jubal enjoyed seeing his name in print, and as Byers told him, the militia made good copy for the Denver paper. Jubal listened, noted that even as the gunfire ceased, there continued a good deal of disturbance. In fact, it seemed to be on the increase. He studied his journal a moment, tried to recapture his thoughts, then sighed and patted the leather-bound diary, and reaching out, took a final sip of brandy. Obviously his men were getting too carried away.

"I better put in an appearance," he said aloud, and

pushed away from the desk. He stood, patted the wrinkles out of his trousers, donned his blue coat, and fastened the shiny brass buttons. He placed his plumed hat on his head and adjusted the brim so it sat at a rakish angle, and thus properly attired, left his room. His footsteps were muffled by the carpeted hallway. He reached the stairway and started down. The lobby of the Hippolyte was empty, for the hour was late and the hotel's residents had either retired for the night or were celebrating in one of the establishments along Commerce. Only the night clerk, Andrew Jackson Goyne, stood at the window staring out at the town. Padded wooden benches lined the walls; couches and overstuffed Windsor chairs, though a bit on the tattered side, lent an aura of elegance to the lobby. Smoke trailed from a pipe firmly clasped in the night clerk's mouth. And the smell of tobacco and cherry bark mingled with the scent of leather and polished wood. The clerk took notice of the footsteps on the stairs. Goyne turned, revealing a pinned-up left sleeve, legacy of the charge at Chattanooga when Federal troops had swept the Rebels from Missionary Ridge. The clerk saluted, out of habit. Any uniform and every uniform he saluted, as long as it belonged to an officer and as long as it was blue.

"My men are a little on the wild side tonight." Jubal chuckled, returning the salute.

" 'Tain't celebratin', Colonel Bragg. Appears to be trouble of some kind. Cod Tatum come by lookin' for Dr. Schaefer. Me and the doctor have us a game of chess now and then. He don't sleep much and the game helps to keep me awake. Before Schaefer took off, Cod said how some Injun's gone and stabbed one of your boys, stole a horse, and skedaddled. Rode down one of Widow Kierby's boys, little Alfie, scarcely ten years old. Broke his neck. Of course that's Cod talking, and so who knows. I mean, Henry Schaefer's the doctor." Goyne inhaled, then blew a pungent cloud of tobacco that hid his features as he resumed his vigil at the hotel window. "Somebody's coming."

Jubal headed straight for the front doors. He felt a

tightness in his chest and suddenly his mouth turned dry as dust; it seemed every pore on his face was opening, becoming desiccated by the wind that struck the colonel as he walked out onto the broad front porch. He stood in the shadow of the false-front structure; the sign "HIPPOLYTE" creaked from its supports overhead. A group of men headed toward him. Several held lanterns, others carried torches held aloft. His soldiers, townspeople, ranch hands, and farmers mingled with a familiarity they seldom experienced in normal times. But this was not a normal time and tragedy had brought them together, and as word spread from house to house, other men and women, many half-clothed, streamed toward the throng that converged on the Hippolyte Hotel. A woman was sobbing. The sound of her broken-hearted cry rang piteously on the night wind. A broad-shouldered farmer walked at her side, in his arms the lifeless form of a young boy. Other men supported the woman, walking to either side of her and holding her up. Now and then her voice rose shrill and she shouted, "Oh God . . . oh God . . . oh God!", repeating herself over and over until her voice would break and subside back to the soul-racked sobbing. Jubal waited at the top of the steps. He could make out the boy's features as the soldiers and townsfolk came to a halt in front of the porch. Not a word was said. Only the desperate sound of the widow. Then the crowd melted back and allowed Big Marley through.

He carried the blood-soaked corpse of Tom Bragg.

Jubal shivered as the cold hand of recognition clasped his spine. He reached out and supported himself against a nearby whitewashed pillar. Marley's eyes were red-rimmed as he looked up at the colonel.

"He just stepped outside for a minute. I swear I wasn't away from him but just for . . . a minute." He glanced down at the young man in his arms, the blood-stained shirt, and where the knife had been, the rent in the fabric just under the heart. Marley laid the body of Tom Bragg down on the bottom step and backed away. Jubal seemed to stare at the corpse as if denying it. As if trying to wake from a dream. Then he numbly moved forward down the steps and knelt at his brother's side.

"We have the knife. It's got markings, it belongs to the Northern Cheyenne," Marley said. Another man worked his way through the crowd to stand alongside Marley. Sabbath McKean held out the knife.

"It's got the markings, all right, but that doesn't mean a damn thing," he said.

"He took my horse," a voice shouted from the crowd.

"And rode this young'un down," the farmer holding the dead boy added. The widow began to wail "Oh God" again.

"He was headin' east. Probably back to the Warbonnet," another townsman interjected.

"White Bull's village," Marley said. "I guess he thinks he'll be safe there."

Jubal reached out and touched his brother's face. Just a boy, just the . . . last . . . link . . . with another time. He stood and looked from the widow's son to Tom's drawn blood-drained features frozen in a mask of pain.

"Assemble the men," he said to Marley. "I think I shall pay these Cheyenne a visit."

"Maybe some of us could ride along with you, Colonel," the farmer holding the dead child said. His offer hung on the air for a grim moment, unsupported.

"Us too." Several ranch hands in faded denims and sweatstained hats stepped forward, adjusting their gunbelts and checking their revolvers. They reeked of whiskey but their movements were steady enough.

"Count me in," said A. J. Goyne. The clerk glanced about to see if he echoed the sentiments of the townsfolk. "I see you, Cod Tatum. Go fetch your brothers and tell them to bring their shotguns."

"This is madness," Sabbath blurted out. "The knife could be anyone's." He searched the faces of the crowd, hoping to find reason. "This is a matter for the law."

Jubal pointed at the scout. "Marley, if that man speaks again, kill him." Marley pulled his Colt Dragoon from its holster and leveled it at McKean. Jubal continued up the steps and disappeared into the hotel.

Marley called over to Hec Knowles. "Hec, you and a couple of men carry Tom here into the lobby and then get the coroner." He glanced over at the farmer who held the widow's dead son. "Put the boy in there too."

"I'll take him to his house," the farmer replied. "We will grieve in our own way." The crowd parted to let the widow and the farmer pass through. The wind rose and flames streamed like fiery banners from the torches. Weeks of fear had come to fruition this night. The ugly mood spread like wildfire as more townspeople found their way to the Hippolyte to discover for themselves the nature of these most recent tragedies.

"A bad time for Sheriff Yarbrough to be in Denver," a portly old gentleman observed. He wore a black frock coat and carried a doctor's bag. He stood watching the soldiers bear Tom's corpse up the steps and into the lobby. "Or a good time, depending on one's persuasion."

"No matter, Doc Schaefer," said Sabbath McKean, daring a bullet, "Colonel Bragg's Militia is a law unto itself. They look after their own." He did not try to hide the sarcasm in his voice.

"You're damn right," Marley growled. He slapped his revolver up alongside McKean's head. The scout groaned and sank to his knees, a bloody lump forming at his temple.

"Blast you, Marley," he said in a thick voice. "I'll remember that."

"Then remember I didn't kill you like Bragg told me to. I figured I owed you for the drinks." The sergeant cocked the revolver. "Now, squaw man, we're even."

Jubal Bragg stood before the mirror in his hotel room. With slow, deliberate motions he buckled his gunbelt around his waist beneath his knee-length blue coat. The button-down flap holster rested on his left, the revolver butt-forward. He stared at himself in the mirror but what he saw was the image of the Northern Cheyenne. Tom had braced the savage at Foot o' the Mountains and now the red heathen had exacted his revenge.

Panther Burn, that was the name. Panther Burn. He saw him standing over Tom's crumpled form, the crimson blade held aloft. Jubal reeled away from the reflection that his tortured mind had conjured. He stumbled to the desk and reached for the bottle of brandy, but his hand paused, as Jubal's gaze dropped to his journal and the unfinished entry. His dreams for a life with his brother, for a future, once more had been stolen from him by a murdering savage. *I am happy—*

The scrawled entry seemed to taunt him. *I am happy. I am happy.* He read it in silence over and over until his knuckles whitened as his fingers dug into the desktop and blood trickled from beneath his fingernails. *I am happy. I am happy.* The cry began deep in his throat, a cry from his soul that continued like a wounded animal's, a cry of anguish, as if his very heart were being ripped from his chest. *"Aaaaaahhhhhhhhhh!"* It rose in pitch and in volume until it reverberated into the hall, until it tore at his vocal cords. *"Aaaaaaaaaahhhhhhhhhhh!"*

A cry of pain that died in a whimper; with it died mercy.

Sabbath McKean grimaced as Esther Bird Hat Madison dabbed at his bruised scalp. With trembling hands she washed the blood away while the scout recounted the events of an hour ago to Reverends Holstead and Madison. Sam's features were bunched with concern and his cheeks had paled.

"I watched them ride out," Sabbath concluded. "Bragg's Militia and most of the menfolk in town. It's bad. Real bad. They wouldn't listen to me and I didn't try to press them. After all, maybe the Northern Cheyenne is guilty. Oh hell, I can't see that. But I wanted to keep from getting shot. So I just held my head together and waited for them to leave." Sabbath's eyes bored into Sam's. "It is not going to be a good time to be an Indian in these parts. Or to be thought of as an Indian lover."

Sam's color returned as his whole lanky body tensed.

"No need to raise your hackles," Sabbath said. "I weren't meaning no insult. I had me a Sioux wife for a spell. Prettiest little thing, too."

"Oh dear oh dear oh dear," Reverend Holstead muttered. He began to pace in his nightshirt and black woolen pants. He still wore his nightcap with a long tassel that hung down his back. "I suppose we're lucky that savage did not slit our throats while we slept."

"None of this makes sense," Sabbath said. "That young buck had the bark still on, right enough. And Tom had braced him. I was there. But to kill Bragg . . ." Sabbath glanced about the room. "Panther Burn wasn't the only other Cheyenne in town?" He waved Esther away. She had done all she could. The lump would hurt and there was nothing to be done but endure it.

"Rebecca Blue Thrush and James Broken Knife also came with us to town," Samuel explained.

"And where are they?" Sabbath asked. Sam looked at his wife a moment, then back to the scout. "Rebecca left with the Northern Cheyenne. And we cannot find James. We don't know where he is."

"Maybe the Northerner has done something to Rebecca as well," Esther exclaimed. She bit her lip and reached out to take Samuel's hand.

"Come first light, I'll see what tracks I can pick up," Sabbath offered. He stood and gingerly placed his broad-brimmed hat on his head, grimacing as he did so. He brushed a shock of red hair out of his face. "People been scared so long, makes 'em kind of loco. Hell, I ain't never been much of a talker," Sabbath continued, studying Sam. "But you got the gift, Reverend. I'm sure Parson Holstead would loan you a fresh team to hitch to your carriage. I got a feeling Simon White Bull may need some help. 'Cause the little army that just left was in a mighty dangerous mood."

"Of course, I'll leave right now," Sam said. He had not been to bed and was still dressed. All he needed was a hat and coat.

"I got a bad feeling about this," Sabbath added. "I'd

stay here if I was you, Mrs. Madison. Should there be trouble . . ."

"I go with my husband," Esther said with such conviction that Sabbath could only shrug. His gaze switched to Sam Madison.

"Fetch your coat, Reverend," said the scout. "I'll harness the team."

The horses were not only fresh and well fed but eager to run, and Sam Madison lost no time in applying the whip, driving the team of Tennessee bay mares at a gallop through town. He wanted to avoid confrontation, and the fear that gripped his stomach in a vise did not ease its hold the entire length of Main. Only with Castle Rock a half-mile behind did he begin to breathe easier. A crossroads ahead beckoned in the moonlight. Here the trails diverged, heading north toward the Wyoming Territory, or east to Simon White Bull's village, where the trail was churned from the passage of almost two hundred horses, or south toward Denver. Holstead's advice returned, tantalizing, and now making so much more sense. They could be in Denver by midmorning. Sam pulled back on the reins and the carriage slowed as the bays responded to his command. Sam tugged the reins in his right fist and the carriage swung around onto the wheel-rutted road that led south to Denver, to St. Louis, to Washington, and safety for them both.

"My husband . . . what are you doing?" Esther said. "This is not the way to our home."

"Our home is in Washington. Or at least it will be," Sam replied. His wife stared at him, incomprehension blanking her delicate features. "Listen to me, Esther. When I was a boy, I caught a bird in the woods behind my father's house. It was a fragile creature with a broken wing. A robin. I set its wing, fed it, kept it alive, tamed it to my call. My pretty robin grew healthy and I built it a large cage and kept it in my room near a window. That simple creature provided me precious moments of happiness in a stern, unhappy house. Eight years passed. And then it died." Sam's voice grew soft but the ungainly lines of his face took on a hard edge. "When it died, I went crazy. I struck out at anything and everything. Such rage, and all for a bird, a silly, dear bird." He looked at Esther. "If I could know madness over the death of a robin, what would a man like Jubal Bragg be capable of over the murder of his brother? Or the townspeople, at the brutal killing of a child?" He cracked the whip in the air above the manes and the carriage lurched forward. "Your life is all that matters and I will do anything to save it."

"No, my husband, we cannot!" Esther clawed for the reins.

Sam shoved her away. "You will obey me, wife. Do you understand, you will obey me!" Esther shrank against the back of the carriage seat. She loved him. She loved her people. "To love, honor, and obey"—the words formed in her mind. "Obey."

"We'll come back," Sam said, trying to sound reasonable above the drumming hooves and the rattle of the axle. "After things have calmed down. We'll come back. Right now there's nothing I can do but risk losing you. And I will not do that. But I promise, we will come back!" Esther had nothing to say. He was her husband. And she would obey.

Moonlight showed the way. The trail ahead was paved with a ghostly glare. Sam allowed the twin bays to settle into a mile-eating trot. He kept his eyes fixed on the road, unable to meet his wife's defeated gaze and lacking the courage to glance over his shoulder, toward the east, toward the Warbonnet. I am doing this for her, he thought. His eyes began to tear. It was from grit kicked up from the horses' hooves, nothing more, he lied to himself. Esther was all the love in his life and for her he would sacrifice anything, his pride, his honor if need be.

And even his God.

7

Rebecca bolted upright and wiped the sleep out of her eyes. She was alone on the buffalo robe. Stomach tightening, Star's daughter glanced around and was relieved to find the pinto grazing contentedly twenty yards away. The day was awash with a feeble glare as a lowering cloud pack held the sun at bay and dimmed the brightness of the world below, where even the evergreens seemed lusterless and dull. Rebecca started to call out, then hesitated as an inner sense cautioned her against raising her voice. Suddenly the full realization of her situation and the time of day burst into her mind.

Esther was leaving this morning! And Rebecca had promised to spend this last evening with her friend. Esther would not only be hurt but she had probably raised an alarm when Rebecca failed to return after an hour. Sam and Rebecca would be leaving on the southbound stage to Denver. They may even have already left. No. On the contrary, Esther was probably delaying their departure until she learned of Rebecca's fate. *We have to leave now! The least I can do is return to Castle Rock to ease Esther's fears and say good-bye.* Rebecca looked down at the robe, still warm from the bodies that had rested upon it. The warmth eased her guilt. For something was happening in her life so important as to make even the glow of friendship grow pale in comparison. Still, if she and Panther Burn left now, they might just reach Castle Rock in time for Esther and Sam to make their morning departure.

But where was Panther Burn? Rebecca crawled to her feet and began to methodically circle their cold camp, searching the ground for some sign of the Northerner's departure. But the carpet of pine needles covering the earth revealed no trace of Panther Burn. Fifteen minutes passed. Rebecca sighed in exasperation and widened her perimeter, all the while resisting the urge to quicken her pace. Haste only meant missing the sign. A mourning dove sounded its melancholy call— coo-ah, coo, coo—the notes rising in pitch, both lovely and sad. Just as hope faded, Rebecca found a moccasin track indicating Panther Burn had crept off through the ponderosas and down the hill. Why? Suddenly she glanced back over her shoulder at the buffalo robe and blankets. The rifle was gone! She returned her attention to the heavily wooded slope. Nothing stirred. Not a sound now. A false peace? Only one way to find out. She started down the hill.

Panther Burn waited for Sabbath McKean to ride clear of a dense cluster of lodgepole pines before stepping out from behind the outcropping of granite he had chosen for his own concealment. McKean was so intent on following the trail left the night before, he was caught completely off guard as Panther Burn leaped into view a stone's throw away.

"*Ha-hey*, McKean!"

The scout reared back in the saddle. His gelding danced to one side, bucked and kicked as Sabbath shouted "Whoa" and clung to the animal's back. The gelding finally settled down after a brief violent struggle.

"Damnation!" Sabbath gagged and spat a stream of

tobacco juice. He coughed, dug the chaw out of his mouth, and coughed the last of the leaf out of his throat. "I been too long in the wind to let a mere younker like yourself spook me into swallowin' my tobac." McKean held up both of his hands to show he held no weapon. Then he reined his mount closer to the Northern Cheyenne. Sabbath adjusted his battered felt hat, then reached back into his saddlebag and retrieved the knife he had brought from town. Panther Burn eyed the man suspiciously. He respected Sabbath and yet knew that white men in general were a mercurial lot. Panther Burn waited in peace but kept his Hawken cocked. McKean fixed a shrewd stare on Panther Burn and tossed the knife into the dirt at the Northern Cheyenne's feet.

"Recognize that, laddie?" The scout began idly to twist the tips of his flowing red mustache, a habitual gesture of which the frontiersman was totally oblivious. Panther Burn scooped up the knife and slid it into the sheath sewn inside his calf-high moccasins.

"I am in your debt, McKean. This was given to me by my father. I did not think I would ever find it . . . again." The brave glanced up to find that the man on horseback now brandished a short-barreled Navy Colt. Sabbath had palmed it after distracting the Northern Cheyenne with the knife.

"Sorry, younker, but this helps me save face for the way you caught me." He gestured at the rifle. "Now, just toss that bear-killer aside." Panther Burn remained motionless. "I know you savvy me, laddie, so do what I told you. I get nervous with these belly guns with their hair triggers and all. I'd never forgive myself if it was to go off."

Another few yards beyond the Northern Cheyenne, Rebecca cleared the shadows of the timber and froze at the sight of the men with their guns leveled at each other. Sabbath caught sight of her as she emerged from the trees. He was distracted for just a second, but long enough for Panther Burn to hurl his rifle at the scout. The Hawken landed on the rocks beneath the white man's gelding. The rifle belched flame and thundered. Sabbath's skittish horse bolted straight up, pawing air as the frightened mare neighed in terror, then took off at a dead run. The scout, still airborne, squeezed off a shot from his Navy Colt. The world turned upside down, then righted itself with a jarring thud. Sabbath landed flat on his back, the air exploded from his lungs, and his head bounced off the table rock. His last thought: Getting my skull cracked twice in two days is too damn much.

Sabbath opened his eyes. Vision blurred, shimmered as if he were swimming from the depths of a pond to the surface with his eyes open. When he broke clear, the shock of his aching skull helped him to see with renewed clarity. Nothing like pain to remind you that you're alive, he thought. He located the gelding where the horse grazed in a clearing a few yards from the pinto. He remembered being puzzled that the horse he was following carried double. He turned as Rebecca knelt at his side. The young woman had soaked his bandanna in an icy spring. Cradling the scout's head, she gingerly applied the cloth to Sabbath's skull. He yelped, but the cold soon numbed the pain. Sabbath craned his head to the left, where Panther Burn sat cross-legged, his rifle loaded and cocked in his right hand, in his left, the Navy Coat.

"Now tell me, *ve-ho-e*. Why do you follow me?"

Sabbath's tongue felt like leather. He mumbled something unintelligible, groaned, tried again. "Seeing as I'm still alive . . . and you're riding double . . . and no offense, ma'am, but I get the feeling you two have spent the night here in keeping one another company . . . uh . . ." He sat upright. Simon White Bull's village! Sam Madison must be having his hands full this very minute. The scout shuddered as the pain once more knifed through his head. Catching his breath, he looked over at Panther Burn, and studying the Northerner's eyes, Sabbath asked one question. "Did you kill

Tom Bragg, the colonel's brother?" He heard Rebecca gasp to his right, but continued, "He was found with your knife in his chest."

Panther Burn shifted his gaze to Rebecca, then back to the white man.

"Hear me, *ve-ho-e*. I walk in truth. It is the warrior's path. What guilt I have is for all to see." He held out his maimed left hand, three fingers and a thumb. "But it is a private sorrow for my heart alone to bear. As for the one you name, I know nothing of the matter. You have returned a knife that was lost last night. Who has held it between your hand and mine I do not know." Panther Burn leaned forward and placed McKean's Navy Colt in front of the scout, who took the weapon in his callused hand. It was still loaded save for the shot he had accidentally fired. "I have spoken," said Panther Burn. His gaze did not waver for an instant. Sabbath tucked the pistol back in the pocket of his wool-lined denim coat. He nodded, satisfied.

"Younker, I hope you're up to riding, 'cause we got to race the rabbits. Bragg's taken a whole army to the Warbonnet to have a reckoning with White Bull's village. They say they're lookin' for you but I got a feeling any fight will do. Sam Madison's gone on to try to talk some sense into them. You and I are gonna have to risk our skins to clear up this mess. Help me to my feet." He looked over at Rebecca. "Best we leave you at Reverend Holstead's, lass. Things could get a mite fractious before we settle this."

Images, phrases of a conversation, a jumble of memory. Rebecca felt her flesh grow cold as she remembered a sign of great and terrible change. A wolf demon rising from medicine fire. *Star! All-Father keep her safe!*

"My place . . . is with . . . my people," Rebecca haltingly replied. Sabbath started to protest. "My place is with my people!" Rebecca's gaze bore into Panther Burn. They were not the eyes of the woman he had held in his arms. She seemed frightened of him, and more, full of unspoken accusation. "I will ride with you until we find a horse for me." The tone of her voice brooked no argument.

"Blue Thrush," he tenderly called to her. But she was already hurrying toward the pinto stallion. Driven by a terrible premonition, suddenly she had no time for gentleness . . . or love.

8

A soot-blackened sky had drawn the three at a gallop over the last few miles. Now Rebecca sat motionless on the horse Sabbath had "borrowed" on the way, from an outlying farm, as she struggled to comprehend what lay before her. Panther Burn and the white man, McKean, were like statues set upon the crest of the hill that rolled gently to the banks of the Warbonnet.

"My God," Sabbath managed at last to mutter. Not that his brief prayer changed anything. God seemed far indeed from this place of destruction. No cabin, tipi, or lodge remained untouched. Even the split-rail fencing that protected the garden littered the earth like so many burned husks. Smoldering logs and planking marked former homesites and tendrils of smoke trailed into the sky from the charred skeletons of collapsed cabins. And strewn like so many toy dolls among the gutted remnants of the village were the people themselves, Southern Cheyenne men, women, and children, most burned beyond recognition by the flames that had spread from cabin to cabin, igniting the meadow grasses underfoot, until the earth lay scorched to the river's edge. The waters of the Warbonnet were tinged a sickly rust color and bloated, bullet-riddled bodies were sprawled in the shallows. A carrion horde circled lazily through the smoky residue that darkened an already somber sky. On the ground, vultures feasted in packs of half a dozen or more upon mortal remains. They filled the air with their caustic cries as the carrion brood quarreled and fought over a particular chunk of meat. Greedy birds; there was plenty to go around. For the villagers had died in their sleep, died as they staggered from cabins set ablaze, died as the braves attempted to fight off the attackers with guns and farm tools, died as mothers gathered their children and pleaded for mercy in the face of men driven to savage slaughter by righteous anger and blood lust. Women, children, and babes had died where they huddled, died as they ran toward the safety of the forest, died with the men in their newly plowed fields, watering the crops with their blood; died with their cattle, the tame buffalo of the whites; died fighting or kneeling in prayers and supplication to *Jay-ho-vah*. The stench of the butchery, of day-old blood and charred corpses, assailed the slope as the wind shifted. Rebecca doubled over and vomited. She slid from horseback and fell to her knees until the spasms ceased and she managed shakily to stand. She started forward then, with numbed steps, down the incline. She did not feel the gentle caress of the wind as it stirred the dust underfoot. Behind her Sabbath McKean raised his voice. "In the name of heaven, what have you done, Jubal Bragg? What have you gone and done?" Panther Burn ignored the man. He searched out the approximate location of Joshua Beartusk's cabin and nudged his pinto into a trot, then as the ground leveled, a gallop, leaving Rebecca and McKean in his dust. As he rode into the ruins of the village the Northern Cheyenne loosed a wild, high-pitched war cry, and raising his Hawken, fired the rifle into the air. Back up on the rise, Sabbath dragged his Spencer from its scabbard and levered off another three rounds. The reports echoed over the budding prairie land, washed to the line of trees hiding the pond, and reverberated back to its source. As the rifle shots sounded, Panther Burn continued his cry, and grabbing a blanket, waved it overhead, whipping the air as he voiced a piercing war cry. Turkey vultures, some with wingspans greater than a man was tall, rose in a chorus of shrill protests, a hundred wings drumming the air like thunder and billowing, swirling skyward in alarm, some with grisly morsels of flesh jutting from their hooked beaks. Rebecca raised her hand as if to ward them off and stumbled and fell. Tears streamed down her cheeks, blurred her vision. Grit stung her eyes. But she pressed onward past children who even in death appeared to cower by their mothers, past the gas-bloated corpses of those she had known, of childhood friends she had played with in a time of innocence. And the men, those unburned, she recognized as well, blasted and bullet-riddled, scarred by saber thrust and the talons of the carrion birds. Rebecca stumbled on, through the landscape of a nightmare.

"*Na-hko-eehe* . . . Mother . . . *Na-hko-eehe!*" she called, knowing there would be no answer. With leaden footsteps she approached the blackened rubble that had been the house of Star, medicine woman of the Southern Cheyenne. Rebecca paused on the scorched threshold, and using every ounce of strength, it seemed, she raised her head. "My mother?" Nothing. Perhaps Star had escaped. The young woman's gaze shifted to the chimney and down to the hearth, and there poking through the crumbled wreckage of the north wall a blistered, seared forearm and hand jutted upward in death as if Star had grasped at the vast battlements of clouds above, even as the fiery timber had come crashing down, crushing and killing the medicine woman. Rebecca's whole body shuddered, her shoulders bowed forward. But not a whimper escaped her, for silent is the song of sorrow, whose lament no throat can capture, no heart contain.

*　　*　　*

The pinto stallion pawed at the earth, knocked a board loose, and danced back, skittish in the presence of so much death. Panther Burn finished searching the gutted ruins of his uncle's house but found nothing, which did not necessarily mean Joshua Beartusk was alive. Panther Burn glanced past the wreckage toward the pasture. Judging by the line of corpses, it appeared a number of the villagers had made a break toward the forest. Quite possibly some of them had reached the pines and escaped. He remounted and walked the stallion away from the village. The first bodies were two boys and a girl. He thought he recognized them but couldn't be certain, nor did it matter. It was enough that they had been children of the Morning Star. Panther Burn rubbed the wetness from his eyes and was glad he was alone here on the fringe of what had once been the village. Grimly he forced his pony into a trot, unable to linger too long by the children sprawled upon the gentle bosom of the earth in the late afternoon. He tried to give the other corpses only the most perfunctory appraisal, checking for Joshua Beartusk or young Zachariah Scalpcane. However, the sprawled lifeless form of one other brave attracted his attention beyond the others and Panther Burn altered his course and reined to a halt alongside Simon White Bull. The chief of the Southern Cheyenne lay on his back, his dead stare focused accusingly heavenward. He was minus a boot. His stiffened hands held the American flag that had wafted over the village. Perhaps the chief had taken it down, in the furor, as if its presence might stop the attackers. It covered Simon like a shroud. There were several bullet holes in the material and bloodstains the color of rust marred the bars of red and white. For some reason the vultures had not yet found the chief. Perhaps the flag frightened them away: a corner of the fabric flapped in the breeze. Panther Burn jumped down, and kneeling by the dead man, closed Simon's eyes.

"You tried the way of *ve-ho-e* but it was not to be. They killed you anyway, Simon White Bull. But they are wrong to think it ends here. There are still Cheyenne in this world." Panther Burn heard an approaching horse, and standing, turned to find Sabbath McKean close at hand. The scout appeared to be in shock; his face was devoid of expression, his jaw hung slack, his very pallor a sickly white.

"I think there is nothing more you can do here, *ve-ho-e.* You had better go while I still call you friend," Panther Burn said bitterly.

"Now, just you wait a minute, younker." McKean's face reddened to the color of his bristling beard, for Panther Burn's words had struck home. "I've seen the handiwork of your kind, before. So don't you shift this on me. God damn you. God double damn you! It's all of us. Each and every one. We got the beast in us, lad. The beast! And sometimes we let it out and it claws and kills like the mad thing it is. And when it's sated we put the monster back and close the doors and try to forget we loosed it in the first place. Red man or white, we call ourselves something better than we are and try to forget." Sabbath arched his back and looked toward the faint white rays of sunlight fanning out from behind a barrier of clouds to the west. "Sam Madison! Where were you!" The outcry seemed to sap the frontiersman's strength and he bowed forward over the pommel of his saddle. Panther Burn swung astride his pinto and sat still, struggling with his feelings and with the words of McKean. At last he nodded.

"We will ride together," the Northern Cheyenne said. He started off toward the forest. Sabbath read the brave's intentions and angled off to the side about twenty feet from the pinto. The scout could see for himself, the tracks showed that many people had broken for the woods, more than could be accounted for by the dead. The two men reached the forest about the same time and entered the shadows. Pine needles muffled the sound of their horses. Here the rich dark loam was scored with tracks that plainly revealed the path the fugitives had chosen in their panic. The forest was as silent and funereal as the devastated land beyond the trees. Panther Burn steeled himself against the sight of more butchery.

"Not a bird, animal, nothing," Sabbath said, studying the branches. He scratched at his whiskers and shook his head. "It makes me as nervous as a mud dauber in a drought."

"This is a place of death. Even the spirits have left," Panther Burn replied.

Off to the left, beyond a thick stand of sentinel pines, a baby started to cry and was quickly hushed. Both men turned toward the sound, then glanced at one another as if not daring to hope. They headed for the river, cutting upstream and winding through the lengthening shadows, seeking . . . What? Ghosts? Or survivors? Panther Burn recognized a fallen log, a lightning-split pine, the tops of the willows. He had his bearing now. The pond and surrounding glade was a natural place to hide! At last Panther Burn and McKean emerged into a clearing where the soft sandy bank led down to the hidden glade and the pond where the Northern Cheyenne had first caught sight of Rebecca. Now a place of single sweet memory had become a sanctuary for two dozen men, women, and children.

"Thank God," Sabbath whispered.

Panther Burn could not speak. But his heart soared with gratitude as the frightened remnants of the Southern Cheyenne turned toward these newest arrivals. A ripple of panic swept over the gathering, then became relief as the Northerner was recognized. Panther Burn heard his name called out and from the survivors a bruised, brave little warrior of eight years stepped away from the knot of battered villagers. He held a rawhide tether on the end of which an old blind warrior gamely stumbled after. Panther Burn leaped from horseback and raced across the sand, a cry of thanks on his lips as he ran to embrace Uncle Joshua and the young boy who had saved him.

*　　*　　*

They spoke of death, these people of the Morning Star. And each had a separate nightmare to recount, how friends and loved ones died in the village by the Warbonnet. Fragments of a tragedy placed together like pieces of a grisly puzzle formed a picture of horror none would ever forget. As the last of the survivors, Hope Moon Basket sobbed out her account of the attack, Sabbath McKean plundered his saddlebags for the food stored in them. Sabbath had brought enough provisions for himself and had intended them to last a couple of weeks. When shared among the survivors of the massacre, his stores were depleted on this first night. He had visited the village before and had counted Simon White Bull among his friends. Though McKean had always been regarded as a friend, many a suspicious glance was cast in his direction, even as the survivors ate his food. He couldn't blame them. The scout ladled out the last of the salt pork, fried bread, and beans onto a little girl's improvised plate, a broad strip of bark, and watched her hurry away from him in fear once she had some food. The scout sighed to himself and returned to Zachariah and Joshua's campfire. Panther Burn sat in the warmth by the dancing flames and listened as Zachariah told his story. The boy's voice trembled as he spoke; from time to time he would dig in the sand with the tomahawk Joshua had given him.

"My mother was gathering roots with three others, I cannot say who, I could not see their faces. The soldiers charged them. I thought they were trying to frighten the women. There was much shooting, much smoke. I saw a man in a blue coat ride into my mother. His horse kicked her. Then a second man rode past where she lay and he fired down at her. The other women were also trampled. I started to run to her. Many guns were firing. White men with long knives rode by but did not see me. The men of our village attacked with the rakes, the hoes, what guns they could find. But the soldiers killed them. I remembered then I was to look after Joshua." Panther Burn's uncle snorted in disgust as if appalled that anyone should think him incapable of taking care of himself. "I led him here." Zachariah finished without elaboration, as if an eight-year-old boy leading a blind man to safety through the heart of a raging battle happened every day of the week. "After the white soldiers left, I went to find my mother." Zachariah's gaze lowered, his head dropped forward. Joshua reached out and placed his leathery old hand on the boy's shoulder. Zachariah choked back his sob.

"He found her," Joshua said, finishing the boy's tale.

Panther Burn took one of the eagle feathers from his braid, and leaning over to the boy, solemnly and with great authority placed the feather in Zachariah's lap. The boy straightened and looked up at Panther Burn. What passed between them remained unspoken but Zachariah's hand closed around the symbol of his bravery and he wiped the tears from his eyes. Warriors did not cry.

Sabbath's shadow fell across them. The white man squatted by the campfire and held out his hands to the flames. An almost palpable hatred radiated from Zachariah. Sabbath tried to ignore the boy and turned his attention to Panther Burn. He noticed the untouched plate of food by the Northerner.

"Rebecca hasn't come in yet." Panther Burn shook his head "no."

"You tell her where we are?" Panther Burn nodded. "What'd she say?"

"She did not speak to me," said the Northern Cheyenne.

"Well, we better have a talk," the scout said, "you and me, laddie." Sabbath glanced about, then lowered his voice. "It ain't over. Not yet. Not by a long shot."

Panther Burn frowned at Sabbath. "I do not understand what you are saying."

"Then listen. What happened today was a terrible wrong. The soldiers, the townsfolk, everyone—by now they're starting to realize if the truth of this attack ever gets out, the Army will enforce the law and round up each and every one of them. Bragg sure as hell ain't about to sit still for that. He's gonna start thinking. And

145

the thoughts ain't gonna be pretty. There's only one way to keep the truth from being told—make sure nobody is alive to tell it."

"He will be back," Panther Burn softly concluded. He glanced across the leaping flames at the broken, frightened remnants of the Southern Cheyenne huddled by their fires. They were a lost and leaderless people. Slowly he stood, knowing what must be done, wondering if he had the wisdom or courage to do it. "Hear me, my brothers and sisters!" Faces turned toward him, dark, haunted features waited for him to continue. "Tomorrow we will leave this place of sorrow and death. We will head north, to Spirit Mountain and the hunting grounds of the Northern Cheyenne. My father shall be your father; my mother, your mother; my people, your people."

"Our place is here," Hope Moon Basket cried out.

"If you would die here when the soldiers return, yes, your place is here. But if you would live, then you must head north. And you must leave with the rising of the sun."

"Spirit Mountain is far away. Who will lead us on such a long journey?" an old woman asked in a frail, fearful voice.

Panther Burn did not hesitate. "I will lead you," he said.

Rebecca knelt by the ruins of her mother's house. She had settled back on her heels, and with the fading light, lost sight of the outstretched arm amid the ruins. She did not need to see, in fact the darkness was more merciful, for it allowed her to form an image in her mind of Star, radiant and alive.

"Our Father . . . who art in heaven . . ." said the young woman, speaking the prayer of the one God in whom Rebecca had learned to place her trust. Sam Madison had taught her the prayer. He said the words were powerful. Rebecca needed power this day. So she prayed and as she recited the words for the hundredth time her fingers stole up to clasp the medicine bag hung around her throat and other words came to mind. The primitive and the Christian prayer, mingling, became one. ". . . who art in heaven, hallowed be thy name . . . All-Father. Thy name . . . kingdom come . . . The All-Father calls us by our secret name, calls us home to his lodge . . . thy will be done, on earth . . . The All-Father calls us and we must go. And it is good . . . as it is in heaven."

Two prayers, one heart, one soul divided between the old and the new. *Oh, my mother, you knew, and yet you sent me away. Why?*

"Rebecca," Panther Burn said.

The young woman gasped, startled, rose and spun to face the Northern Cheyenne intruder. The air was cool and heavy with rain. Yet the clouds that had driven the moon from the sky and blanketed the stars refused to loose their burden upon the thirsty earth.

"Rebecca, come to the fire," said Panther Burn. "There is food. And you will need it. We start north tomorrow. To Spirit Mountain." Rebecca did not answer. "Come, I will walk with you," said Panther Burn, and he reached out to her, drawing closer in the process. Rebecca slapped his hand away where it brushed her arm.

"You brought this," she hissed. "It is your doing. My mother knew. She said you were the one. A man from the north bringing terrible changes. And if you had not come, then none of this would have happened. My mother and her people would still be alive!"

"Rebecca, no . . ." Panther Burn tried to catch her flailing arms. The wind rushed past, in a sudden furious gust, moaning like the spirits of the dead, a chorus of accusation. Rebecca slapped the Northerner across the face, her fists pummeled his chest and shoulders. He endured blow after blow and made no move to defend himself. She bruised his ribs and drew blood as she raked his cheek. At last, her strength spent, Rebecca sank to her knees in the ashes of the buffalo grass and with the dying of the wind wept for her people, for her mother, and for herself. "I . . . wish . . . you . . . had never . . . come to our village. I wish you had been . . . killed . . . on the way."

The sight of her was more than Panther Burn could bear. Perhaps she was right. It wouldn't be the first time he had caused a death. He touched his scarred left hand, an awful realization welling in his soul. *All-Father, am I to blame? Not again, please not again.* He had almost buried the pain in his heart, the terrible burden that had driven him in shame from his father's lodge. Now it returned full-blown and awesome in the presence of yet more death, more suffering. But to pursue the thought was madness. And a madman was of no use to the few survivors. So he forced himself not to think, not to feel at all. "Woman, we leave at sunrise," he said in a hard, emotionless voice. "You are coming with us if I have to tie you to your horse. Say your prayers, but do not forget to save your life." He turned on his heels and walked back toward the woods. His footsteps receded in the darkness, leaving Rebecca alone once more. She started to call out to him, to tell him she did not really wish he had died, but the words melted in her breast, remained unspoken. She hated him as she hated the gods who had used him. *And yet, Mother forgive me,* she silently prayed, *I cannot cut the love from my heart. But I will learn to. I must learn. I must.*

The western horizon shimmered with distant lightning, followed by a drum of thunder, ominously nearer than the night before.

9

A day's ride north from the valley of the Warbonnet, from the place of vultures and ashes and rain-washed bones, Jubal Bragg left the encampment where thirty of his men huddled in their tents. For three days it had rained steadily. Twenty yards up the nearest slope the orderly row of canvas tents was indistinguishable against the downpour's gray backdrop. A cold camp, cold biscuits and beans, rainwater to drink unless some weather-beaten soldier built a lean-to to keep his fire dry long enough to brew coffee. Yes, there would be coffee, Bragg thought to himself. He had every confidence in the abilities of his men.

However, they couldn't catch ghosts. And ghosts were what they were chasing, now that the three days of rain had washed out the tracks of the survivors and made following them well nigh impossible. Bragg climbed to the top of the hill. The muddy slope sucked at his boots until he gained a shelf of granite, then the way became slick and threatening. Bragg didn't slip. Not once. And when he reached the summit he stood, huddled in the sodden wool folds of his greatcoat, and turned his burning eyes toward the north. Water dripped from the hard flat brim of his hat with its sad soaked plume drooping off the back and plastered to the caped coat. Jubal stared down at the pool of water forming in his cupped hands. No wind stirred. The rain fell in straight thick sheets; slackening, a tantalizing ruse as nature sought to raise a man's hopes, then increasing again.

Jubal listened. Had he heard his name called? Tom, poor dead younger brother, dead dream, dead future, Tom called to him, where he wandered restless in the gray gloom, a spirit in the wet afternoon, crying, "Jubal . . . Jubal . . . avenge me, avenge . . . !"

How, dammit? *I returned to finish the job and found where the bloody murderers had escaped and made their camp by the pond in the heart of the forest. And I pursued them until the rain, the cursed rain . . .* Jubal poured the water from his hand and made a fist and raised it heavenward.

"First my parents. Now Tom. I am alone. What more do you want? I have served you. I have been a scourge to the heathen. Yet you send armies against me, sickness and rain. And yet do I say: If God is for me, who can prevail? I fight on!" The rain cooled his haggard, unshaven features. He no longer looked the gentleman. The death of his brother had stripped away the civility and revealed the dangerous man Jubal was. And always had been.

"Colonel."

Jubal gasped and spun around, thinking at last to confront the ghost of his brother. But the rider in the rain was far too big for Tom. Still, Jubal shivered though he recognized Big Marley. The sergeant dismounted and climbed the few remaining yards to stride the hill alongside the man to whom he had pledged his loyalty, long ago.

"I told you not to come back. I ordered you to take six good men and press on." Jubal Bragg turned away in disgust. "I thought I could count on you."

"Colonel, I heard you. And I ain't never let you down," Marley said. "Beggin' your pardon, Colonel . . ." Marley wiped the water from his eyes and tugged his short-brimmed cap low over his eyes. Even Pa, dumb as a bedbug, knew enough to come in out of the rain, the big sergeant said to himself, taking care not to accidentally voice his thoughts. "Sir, we know them Cheyenne are headin' north. Like you said, they probably figure to join up with the Northern tribes. But there's a dozen passes over the mountains if there's one. And plenty of hard ground that don't take to tracks."

"So you gave up, old friend," Jubal said. He couldn't see the next hill beyond the rain curtain, but he searched all the same. It was better than trying to sleep. It was better than the lonely madness of his tent.

"Give up, hell. I turned back the way we come," Marley snorted. "The back a' my neck's been crawlin' all day. So I figured to scratch the itch. Circled my men, and damn if we didn't catch us a rabbit. A Cheyenne rabbit. Seems he got himself drunk, lost his horse, and slept off the cheap whiskey back in the woods. He come to after we rode back to Castle Rock. He thought maybe some gods had come down and killed off his people. He hung around and watched the murderin' dogs we missed hightail it out of the valley."

"Why didn't he join them?"

"Seems they were bein' led by a brave he don't rightly have use for. That Northern Cheyenne, the one who murdered Tom." Marley noticed Bragg stiffen, then slowly turn toward the sergeant. "Yeah," Marley added. "Panther Burn. And get this, McKean was with them."

Jubal slammed a fist against his thigh. "What else did the buck say before you killed him?" he asked in the shaky voice of a man struggling to maintain control in the face of overpowering frustration.

Marley shook his head. "He ain't dead. He's here, Colonel. I let him have a horse and brought him here." Marley glanced back toward his horse as another rider materialized out of the downpour. The figure remained on horseback, waiting, a strange and somber silhouette. Jubal muttered a curse and drew the revolver from inside his coat. He covered the distance to the Cheyenne in half a dozen strides and raised the barrel, thumbing the hammer on his Colt as he sighted squarely on the man's heart.

"I know the way the Northerner will go," the brave said. "I have been to the village of his people. Many years ago. But I still remember. The rain will not stop you. The rocks where horses and man leave no tracks will not stop you. I know the passes they will use. And I will lead you."

Jubal stared at the mounted figure above him. The colonel's finger hesitated on the trigger. An ounce of pressure and the Cheyenne would die, leaving Jubal Bragg another corpse but nothing more. His thirst for revenge would remain unslaked. Only one death had the power to fulfill such a desperate need.

The revolver lowered.

"In return for what?" he asked.

"My life. And gold. A hundred dollars. It means little to you, white man, but much to a farmer."

Bragg nodded and holstered his gun. The rain continued, just as hard, just as incessant. And Jubal laughed. After all, it didn't matter now. Marley listened, felt his flesh crawl at the sound. The brave, however, who was alive, and who intended to stay that way whatever the cost, remained unconcerned.

Jubal Bragg started down the slope, thought better of slogging through the mud, and mounted Marley's horse. The colonel, eye to eye with the brave, drew close.

"Do not try to trick me." Bragg's tone as he uttered the warning was rife with unmentionable consequences. "Do you have a name, dog that hunts dogs?"

The brave glanced aside as if casting away the last remnant of his honor to the storm. "I am called . . ." His voice failed, then finished, "James Broken Knife."

10

Into the Wind River Mountains fled the remnants of a people, a dispirited band of children and old men and women. Two wounded braves were confined to travois, makeshift litters pulled by the horses Panther Burn had managed to round up the morning of departure. Two weeks of hard travel on a diet of roots, berries, and small game brought the survivors of Rebecca's village to a place where the Big Horn River cut a gash through thickly forested hills and craggy cliffs, a primal valley, narrowing, doubling back then widening with nature's typical and capricious disregard for the necessities of man.

Home to the Absarokas, home to Montana. What would his father say, seeing the son who had brought shame to his lodge? More and more, Panther Burn began to relive the pain of his previous trek—the lonely journey that had brought him to the Warbonnet Creek where first he had caught sight of Rebecca Blue Thrush, where first his heart had called to hers in a secret song the young never fully understand, the old never completely forget. Now Rebecca kept apart from him, from all of them. Perhaps behind the walls of her indifference, her wounds mended and the horror dimmed. Panther Burn resolved to wait. He had been taught a lesson in patience months ago and carried the scar to prove it. On the fifteenth day of their arduous journey, all thoughts of Rebecca and songs of the heart were swept away by the news Sabbath brought on returning to camp late one night. He had backtrailed all afternoon and made a chilling discovery: Jubal Bragg had made camp with more than thirty troopers not more than two miles, as the crow flies, from the Southern Cheyenne's own fires.

Sabbath had called Panther Burn aside and wisely spoke in lowered tones so as not to alarm the others. Come morning, Panther Burn announced that he and the white man, McKean, were going to hunt. The old ones were grateful for the chance at some extra sleep. They had no way of guessing the object of the hunt, the nature of game, not until a smattering of gunfire reverberated from the cliffs, to echo the length and breadth of the valley. Not one shot, or two, but several.

Too many for a hunt.

The boom of a Hawken and the sharp crack of a Spencer carbine were followed by the whine of slugs caroming off a stone outcrop, tearing chunks of bark from the ponderosas and spattering the blue-coated soldiers with splinters. Bragg's column of men scattered from the trail as the rifle fire from their unseen assailants burned the air. Several of the soldiers opened fire toward the distant forest line, but without a target their shots only seemed to panic already skittish mounts. As the men on horseback broke for cover, low-hanging branches seemed to reach out and slap the soldiers out of their saddles. Rocks crumbled away, crippled hooves; horses neighed in agony and tumbled down the slope toward the river a hundred yards below.

Bragg shouted for his men to regain their order. Marley, an expert horseman when it came to mountain riding, charged back into the heart of the confusion, bellowing orders right and left and regaining control before it completely crumbled away.

"Hold there! That's it, lads, watch yourselves. Hec Knowles, you son of a whore, keep them lads with you in line. You there, head up the slope and clear the ridge above. What are you, wet-nosed whelps, bitch-suckled babes is it? And I thought I rode with fighting men. Fighting men, you hear! Well, that's what you be, so look tight. Look tight or lose scalp!"

Jubal Bragg guided his own mount behind a granite ledge, and dismounting, waited for Marley to bring order out of chaos. When he deemed his men able to pay proper attention, Bragg stepped out from conceal-ment and walked briskly into their midst. He kept as much in the clear as possible, inviting the attention of unseen snipers. Authority was in every stride. A slug ricocheted from table rock, fanned his cheek and bur-ied itself in the trunk of a nearby pine. He continued on to the front of the column, his presence bringing calm to the militia. Reaching the forefront, he came to a halt, and facing the hills in their shroud of shifting shadows, removed his plumed hat. A bullet plowed the earth before him. He kicked the dirt from his boots and bowed, then replaced the hat on his head, and turning, walked back through the ranks of his men, who raised rifles and hats in salute and cheered him. Jubal Bragg drew close to Marley, whose own expression revealed his pride and affection for the colonel.

"Sergeant, bring the Indian to me," Bragg said. "And send half a dozen men out on point. Clear the trail ahead. I suspect this is no more than a couple of rifles trying to slow us up. Still, it pays to be cautious."

"Yes sir," Marley said, raising a beefy hand to his forehead in a grave salute.

A few minutes later James Broken Knife made his way down through the stand of ponderosas where the soldiers were making their cold camp now that the gunfire had slacked and the point riders had been dispatched. From time to time the Southern Cheyenne lifted his eyes to the northern reaches of the valley, his muscles tense, ready to propel him behind the nearest tree at the crack of a rifle. He made his way to Jubal Bragg where the self-styled officer squatted over a hastily built campfire, nursing the contents of a blue metal coffeepot to a slow boil. Bragg didn't bother to stand. He looked up as the Indian's shadow fell across him.

"I'm thinking of having Sergeant Marley put a bullet in your head," he said. "We've followed this trail for two weeks, seen neither hide nor hair, now we've come under fire. Maybe you're trying to see how many of us you can lead into gun sights."

"You pay me to help you find a panther, not to cage it. Now, when the panther shows his claws, you blame me," James Broken Knife replied, with a forlorn wag of his head.

"The Northerner isn't alone. Your people are with him."

James Broken Knife glanced toward the threatening hills beyond them, in the west, snow-covered precipices, partly hidden in the mist. Dead. All dead, his life ended too, in the valley of the Warbonnet. And yet he walked, breathed air, hungered, knew thirst. He survived. James Broken Knife had found a way to live again. But there was a price to pay.

"I have no people," he said.

Rebecca was dreaming of a hand rising from ashes. In her mind's eye she relived the horror of the sight of that hand, the death it symbolized, the aloneness. The guilt too for being alive when so many had perished. And what was left for her . . . what solace for a bitter heart? *Mother, I am confused and frightened and alone.* It was the cry of a child, no matter what race or creed, age or wealth.

Tears glistened at the corners of her closed eyes. She saw the outstretched hand, the ashes of her mother's house, smelled again the stench of carnage, in her dream, looked upward, a prayer, muted in the silence, then saw, in the blackness coming toward her, glowing

. . . glowing . . . in her dream saw what had not been before . . . the eyes of the wolf. Wolf of the sacred fire. Spirit-wolf. Its fur was blacker than the night, its eyes like twin coals, pulsing fire. Here was the *maiyun* Star had conjured. Rebecca could see it more clearly than ever before . . . this great spirit-wolf prowling through the night of Rebecca's dreams, dusting ashes from its bristling coat, fire eyes gently mocking. Against her breast, the medicine pouch Star had hung about her daughter's throat grew warmer until it seemed to sear her flesh, burn with a life of its own, like the eyes of the spirit-wolf. Rebecca gasped at the pain, but endured. Quite suddenly, as quickly as it had begun, the pain ended, leaving exultation in its place. And a sense of . . . completeness.

Rebecca wasn't alone anymore.

Hope Moon Basket shook her awake. Rebecca bolted upright at her friend's touch. The round-faced young woman looked close to panic. Then she noticed something in Rebecca's eyes and backed away.

"What is it? What is happening?" Rebecca glanced across the clearing at the other survivors of the village. Mothers gathered their children, the old ones began to moan in their fear. The wounded were dragged to the travois and roughly laid upon the crudely woven pallets lashed behind the horses. Zachariah led Joshua Beartusk over to Rebecca.

"The soldiers come." Hope wailed. "They come with their many-times-firing rifles and their long knives." She reached out and grabbed Rebecca by the arm. "We must hurry!"

"We heard shots," Zachariah said by way of explanation. The boy had woven the eagle feather into his braided hair, his expression was grim and determined. It seemed to Rebecca that Zachariah had grown up during these past two weeks, that he had matured as they trekked from the dark and bloody ground of the Southern Cheyenne village up into the high passes of the Wind River range.

"Panther Burn and McKean left to hunt. It is right to

hear shots. We will fill our bellies tonight," Rebecca said.

"Too many shots," Joshua said. He placed a leathery hand upon the boy's shoulder, his sightless eyes facing down the valley as if he could capture an image the rest of his people had missed. He wrinkled his nose and sniffed the still air. "Trouble coming." He nodded. "A storm . . . but whether it is of man or *nonoma-e*, the heaven shaker, I cannot tell."

"Aiiieee! We must hurry," Hope yelled, charging back into the clearing, startling the horses and causing the children to cry. Her panic was infectious. "Run before it is too late for us." Others took up her cry as blankets were gathered, dirt tossed on campfires, and the evidence of their camp hurriedly destroyed. Little ones wept and called out to their mothers. One old woman, Mary Fox, began to wail her death chant.

"We must scatter like the leaves before the wind!"

"Hide from the long knives."

"We are lost. We are lost!"

"No!" Rebecca walked into the center of the clearing. Two of the older boys had started to lead the horses away. She grabbed the reins from their hands and tethered the animals to the branches of a white fir. "Have we become rabbits that we must scatter at the distant baying of a wolf?"

Rebecca's voice cut through their fear. Young and old alike turned to see who had spoken in such a manner and they were surprised to find Rebecca. She had kept to herself during the long journey into Wyoming Territory, opening herself to no one, keeping her sorrow locked deep within, unwilling to display her emotions to the others. Now she stood before them, strangely different, almost defiant. Hope rushed up to confront her friend. "What do you say to us? Shall we wait to be slaughtered like our families? Run. We must run! Run while we have the chance!" Rebecca slapped her across the face. Hope stepped back, startled, then with her cheek reddening she buried her face in her hands and sobbed.

"Run where?" Rebecca asked in a calming tone. "We must wait for Panther Burn."

"He is dead. The white men have killed him," said a voice from the crowd of frightened faces.

"We are old men and women, we are mothers and children. We have no warriors to protect us," another voice bemoaned.

"Then we must protect ourselves," Rebecca said.

"How?"

"By being Cheyenne, not rabbits." Joshua was making his way toward Rebecca, following the sound of her voice. She turned as he approached to stand beside her. "Someone hand me a branch. I shall crack the skull of a *ve-ho-e* before I face the All-Father."

"And I am not a rabbit," Zachariah exclaimed, brandishing his tomahawk as he took his place alongside Joshua.

Mary Fox stepped forward, her gray hair trailing down across her bowed shoulders, her care-worn features creased as she spoke.

"I know you, Rebecca Blue Thrush. At least I once did. But you are not as you once were," she said in a cracked voice. She continued to peer intently at Rebecca.

"None of us is that. Nor will we ever be again."

"And you would have us wait. How long?"

"Until Panther Burn returns to us."

"And if he is dead?" said Mary Fox, speaking for the others and the terror they harbored in their hearts.

"He is not dead," Rebecca stated. "I would know if he was." She met the stares of her people, the fearful frightened stares that threatened even her own newly won resolve. She called to mind the dream, the spirit-wolf, the source of her mother's power. And now hers.

Panic faded, dissipated like an early-morning mist. Hope managed to stifle the last of her sobs. Rebecca leaned forward and helped her friend to stand, and spoke to her in a soothing, gentle tone.

"Take some of the others and see if you can find some berries, roots, anything we can carry with us for food."

Hope nodded, wiped a forearm across her tear-streaked face.

"I will help," Mary Fox said with a shrug. "I'm too old to run anyway." The old woman toddled off after Hope. The rest of the Cheyenne returned to their earlier places of rest in the clearing. Children gathered about their mothers. Eight of the children, about Zachariah's age or older, left to help in the search for food. Others of the group sat slumped forward in attitudes of defeat, beaten remnants of a proud people, awaiting the will of the All-Father in the forest's gray-green gloom.

Rebecca, who had kept to the fringe of the camps the survivors had made, now chose a new place for herself. She knelt in the center of the clearing, sat back on her heels, closed her eyes, and began to sing in a soft voice. The words came haltingly at first, a song of courage, one of the last medicine songs Star had ever taught her. The song flowed out from Rebecca and seemed to fill the clearing, causing those who listened to take heart.

> All-Father, hear your sorrowing children.
> Send us your strength. Heal us.
> Then who can stand against us?

Minutes passed, almost an hour. At last, sensing another's presence, Rebecca opened her eyes and spied Panther Burn standing in the shadow of the ponderosas. Only then did she end her song.

For three days the small party of Cheyenne played cat and mouse with Bragg's Militia. Whenever an opportunity presented itself, Sabbath or Panther Burn would double back to scatter their pursuers with a few well-placed shots. Bragg's response was predictable. Fearing an entrapment, each time he held his force in reserve and sent out a small detachment of soldiers to scour the terrain and clear the ridges and forest groves of the bothersome snipers, unaware that Panther Burn had already fled. And all the while, Rebecca's people kept to a grueling pace, fear spurring them onward long after muscles had fatigued. Still, their fragile lead couldn't hold forever. Panther Burn knew it and so did the others.

On the night of the third day the hunted camped beneath the towering rim of a narrow high mountain valley. All day, the sky had hung black and foreboding. Now, apportioning the food, Rebecca took charge in arranging the night camp, seeing to the needs of the wounded, encouraging the old, delighting the children with tales of the Thunderbird and how this sacred creator of thunder and lightning was returning from the warm countries. "The Thunderbird leads the way for the Sun," said Rebecca in a grave tone. "And sometimes the Thunderbird shoots an arrow and strikes a person dead but of course the arrows are invisible." The children clutched one another in mock terror, knowing well the game, that the tale teller must build apprehension until the moment comes to leap upon someone in the audience, shouting and striking the person with the Thunderbird's "invisible arrow." Rebecca played the children well and chose the least suspecting to playfully attack. There were screams and laughter among the young.

Panther Burn watched, amazed and hopelessly puzzled by Rebecca's sudden transformation. What strange occurrence had rescued her from her grief? She seemed more uncomfortable than hostile when near him now. Perhaps the recent tragedy had opened her to the crazy spirit and the *masanee* had possessed her. He forced himself not to dwell on Rebecca's strange transformation. His head reeled before the many thoughts that assailed him—the decisions he must make, the responsibilities he had taken on. Panther Burn sighed and looked across the dancing flames of the campfire where his uncle, Joshua, Zachariah, and Sabbath McKean eased the chill of the mountain country from their bones.

"This pass seems like a good place to hold them up," the white man said, gnawing a twig and staring at the coals. His voice sounded no more hopeful than the proposition.

"I will wait for them tomorrow," Panther Burn said. Sabbath nodded, rolled the twig around to the other side of his mouth, stretched out the kink in his left leg.

"Suit yourself. What worries me is, I think ol' Bragg's wise to us. He might just come full steam ahead. So keep your horse handy. Jubal is one curly wolf who would love to get his paws on you more than just about anything else I can think of."

"The rabbit can outrun the wolf when it has to," Panther Burn absently replied. He was thinking of James Broken Knife. Panther Burn had recognized Bragg's scout but kept the knowledge to himself. He wasn't even sure why.

"I can fire a rifle," Zachariah spoke up. "I am not afraid of the soldiers." He rose and tried to stand as tall as an eight-year-old could manage. Panther Burn reached down and tossed the Hawken rifle to the boy. The heavy-barreled percussion rifle dropped into the boy's out-stretched hands and promptly bore him to the ground. The youth struggled to his feet again and with all his strength managed to raise the weapon, though the big gun wavered in his grasp. Zachariah realized his inadequacy and lowered the gun. He dropped the weapon, spun around, and walked away from the fire to nurse his wounded pride in the shadows.

"You shamed him," Joshua muttered disapprovingly.

"He will live," Panther Burn said. "He would have tried to stay behind without our knowing. I have seen enough dead children, Uncle." Panther Burn rose from the campfire, and glancing up, met Rebecca's gaze. She was watching him. Why? He tried to read the feelings hidden in her eyes but she looked away before he could track the course of her heart. The night was oppressively warm; even the air, thick and hard to breathe, gave one the feeling of being in a state of quiet panic. Panther Burn gave vent to his restlessness and ambled out of the circle of light, disappearing into the dark embrace of the forest.

No sound. Only the night. Only a man in the night, leaving the camp far behind. He walked in prayer, his heart lifted to his god.

"*Taa-e*," Panther Burn's voice drifted on the thickening air. "Mother Night, bring my prayers to the All-Father."

The Northern Cheyenne lifted his gaze to the starless heavens where latent storm clouds blanketed the light from the sky and left the world below in gloom. He continued on through the trees until the forest thinned and he could see in the stygian reaches of the valley behind him a collection of flickering lights he recognized as distant campfires.

"Jubal Bragg," said Panther Burn. Too close now. Delaying the militia would do no good. They would have to be stopped. Panther Burn glanced over his shoulder at the sound of a snapping twig. Nothing moved. Overhead a screech owl soared on its nightly hunt. The rush of wings reminded Panther Burn of another time, of a hawk. Around him, the shadows took form. Figures standing in the night. "Little Coyote," Panther Burn called out. "High Walker . . . my pride took your life. A fault I cannot escape." More shadows, sentient brooding shapes, fueled by a weary imagination, seemed to spring from the rich earth and surround the Northern Cheyenne. Panther Burn pictured the faces of the dead, the butchered innocents, Rebecca's people. Bragg has come looking for me, Panther Burn thought to himself. Right or wrong, if I had never come to the Warbonnet, then the killings would never have happened. He closed his eyes.

"All-Father," he whispered. "What must I do?" He outstretched his arms, his face tilted upward toward an obscure sky. "Speak to your unhappy child, All-Father. Hear my plea. Your words are sacred. Teach me. Tell me what to do."

No branch stirred. Yet he did not move, but remained,

still and supplicant, waiting for the sacred wind, for an answer that did not come.

But he did not stand alone, for another had followed him into the forest, though she had remained at a discreet distance. Rebecca paused, peering through the spiny branches of a fir at the man in the clearing. She wanted to go to him, to tell him her words of blame had come from her grief, from her desperate sense of loss. She wanted to tell him she held no blame and to ask his forgiveness. Rebecca kept a quiet vigil and in her heart prayed with this Northern Cheyenne, with this man she loved and had hurt. Loath to interrupt him, she backed away, choosing her steps with care so as not to break another twig and alert him to her presence.

Tomorrow . . . tomorrow she would tell him.

Panther Burn lowered his arms and looked again toward the twinkling glow of the distant campfires and sighed. How long had he stood here on the hillside? Long enough for his arms to ache, long enough for the *maiyun* to have spoken to him, to have shown him the way. *Well, I must make my own way*, Panther Burn thought. "Little Coyote, High Walker, we will hunt together again in the land of our grandfather, let your courage be with me, my friends." The shadows became trees once more, the ghosts returning to their far country. "Soon I will join you," the Northern Cheyenne softly called to the departing spirits. Sabbath McKean had unwittingly planted the seeds of an idea, hours earlier. Jubal Bragg wanted Panther Burn more than anything, even the remnants of Rebecca's people. "Let him find me," the warrior said aloud as he stared toward the distant fires of the encamped soldiers. "And we will end this. Jubal Bragg," he promised quietly, "it will end tomorrow."

11

Zachariah, leading Joshua Beartusk by a length of leather rope, followed his people out of the valley. The trail Sabbath found had been rough going, a narrow serpentine path that zigzagged up the face of a steep ridge. The horses balked from time to time, and the elderly, needing rest, paused continually throughout the climb. But the young were there to help them along. At last, with what seemed one mighty and communal effort, the band of Southern Cheyenne reached the summit of the ridge and skylined themselves along the granite spine to peer back the way they had come. It was an L-shaped valley and even from the ridge, the place where they had made camp the night before was well out of sight, hidden behind ponderosa-covered hills and granite battlements. Black clouds boiled overhead, an ominous turbulence loomed all the way to the horizon. In the distance, lightning lashed the mountains as the storm crossed the divide and unleashed its violence. Zachariah thought of Panther Burn, waiting in the valley below, the valley so pristine and still and directly in the path of the storm. He should have been allowed to stay behind. He had proved himself and won his eagle feather.

He was no longer a boy but a warrior. He should have stayed behind and killed many soldiers.

"Who would be my eyes, then, young Zachariah?" asked Joshua, reading the boy's thoughts. The old man sensed the tension in the youth. It was obvious he still chafed from Panther Burn's rebuke the night before.

"I cannot always be your eyes, old one," Zachariah snapped.

"Nor can I always be your common sense," Joshua chuckled. "Come, my young warrior, life has many battles and you will have your fair share." The blind man tugged on the length of rawhide, pulling the boy away from the trail's edge.

"Sometimes I wonder just who is leading who," Zachariah muttered.

Sabbath McKean sauntered back through the weary ranks of the Cheyenne. He noted the people had reluctantly grown to accept him, which was all he asked. He did not care to have a knife sunk in his back by the very folks he was trying to help. He cradled his Spencer in the crook of his arm and walked slowly among the band, encouraging the weary, checking on the condition of the travois with their burden of wounded. McKean was troubled, and uncertain of exactly why. Everything seemed in order and the old ones were none the worse for their exertions. Not that I should be troubled, he mused, standing here among a bunch of red heathens who would probably just as soon toss me off this hill and leave me for Bragg and his lads to slit my gizzard. If a man could count his greatness by the number of enemies he had, Sabbath decided he must be king of the world. He stopped in front of Joshua Beartusk. Zachariah stared coolly at the white man and waited to one side.

"How are you, old-timer?" Sabbath asked, placing his hand on the blind one's shoulder.

"Sometimes it is easier not to see how far we have come. I do not know enough to be tired." Perspiration beaded Joshua's forehead, his leathery features glistened with sweat. The very air around them seemed to shake as the heavens growled thunder.

"We better get off this stony-back before that storm hits," Sabbath said, taking note of the glowering thunderheads sweeping toward them out of the northwest. The air lay still and heavy on the land and smelled of ozone. "I wish that storm would miss us and just keep Bragg busy."

"Maybe the medicine woman could help," Joshua suggested. "There are many spirit songs. Even one for storms."

"What medicine woman?" Sabbath said.

"Rebecca. Star's daughter. She who must walk in her mother's path."

"Damn. That's it!" Sabbath swung around toward the other Cheyenne resting amid the rock-strewn summit. Some of the youngsters had started down the gradual grass-covered slope that led to the forest a hundred yards away. "I knew it. I knew it but just didn't . . . see it." Sabbath searched the faces of those on the ridge, then took count of the youngsters on the slope, then turned to face the valley again and the treacherous way they had come. "Where in hell is Rebecca?" he said in a low voice. It carried, though. And soon, Joshua and Zachariah and Hope Moon Basket and all the others roused themselves from their rest to stand along the ridge, faces turned toward the coming storm, their hearts echoing Sabbath's question. Where indeed was Rebecca?

Dark clouds churning. A sky like a witches' brew. Thunder in the hills. A place for killing. And being killed.

Panther Burn had chosen a broad open grassy expanse of ground near a clear running creek whose black water mirrored the grim heavens. With the sun hidden, an unsettling illumination bathed the valley, hiding the distant mountains, hills, trees, creek, and meadow trapped in twilight. Ignoring the elements, Panther Burn finished his preparations. In a circle around him, he placed a spear made from a strong young pine sapling, a war club, a tomahawk, and ammunition for the Hawken, powder and shot. Two knives he kept on his person, one in a sheath sewn on the inside of his calf-high moccasins, the other scabbarded at his waist. His chest was naked save for a quill breastplate, and muscles rippled beneath his coppery flesh. One last item he drew from his belongings, a ten-foot length of rope with a loop at one end and a four-inch wooden spike at the other. He slid the loop over his head and tightened it around his waist, then walked into the center of the circle and drove the spike into the ground.

"I regret, All-Father, I do not have a proper *ho-tam-tsit*. This dog rope is of my own making and will have to do." Using a rock for a hammer, he struck the spike one last time. "This stick will sooner leave than I."

"No!"

Panther Burn whirled around to see Rebecca standing a few yards away.

"Woman, you have no place here," he said gruffly, hoping to hide the way his heart leaped into his throat. She threatened his courage. It had been easier to think of dying without her around.

Rebecca refused to be put off by his hostile front. "I dreamt, last night, and saw you bind yourself with the dog rope. Only another born to the Morning Star can free one who binds himself with the dog rope." Rebecca started across the circle. Panther Burn moved to block her path, his hands outstretched to stop her.

"You must leave this place. The soldiers will be here soon."

"I cannot let you do this," Rebecca said. Was it because of her? Because of her accusations spoken in her moment of pain?

She lunged for the stake. Panther Burn was too quick for her. His hands closed about her and spun her into his arms. It was neither the time nor the place for such an embrace, but as they closed with one another, their bodies pressed like hands joined in prayer. The tears from her eyes moistened his jaw and neck.

"You are not a Dog Soldier," she said in a trembling voice.

"Before the night falls, I will be." He tilted her head, the better to lose himself in the earth-brown depths of her eyes. "*Aatome*. Listen to me. The soldiers think I killed the brother of Jubal Bragg. I am the reason they burned your village. And I am the reason they continue to follow you and the others. Once Jubal Bragg finds—"

"My words were like . . . . a blind man shooting arrows. I did not care who I wounded," Rebecca said, her voice muted against his shoulder. Too much had happened. Being alone with him, wanting to give her love to him, to join her life to his, then hurting and hating and striking out at him. And now, holding Panther Burn once more and feeling his strength, sensing his own undiscovered depths of bravery and caring. And Panther Burn, fearing the nearness of her would rob him of resolve, discovered quite the opposite. He loved her. And what better use for his life than saving hers?

"Go now," said the Northern Cheyenne, holding her away from him. "Do as I say."

"I can help."

Panther Burn abruptly laughed.

"You will see," Rebecca blurted out. An idea flashed like gunfire in her thoughts. Suddenly she dared to hope. She started back toward the timbered slope. Choosing a place beneath a granite ledge that protruded like a massive pink-grained table out of the hillside, Rebecca knelt and gathered together a small pyre of twigs and dry grass and pine needles. Panther Burn realized she was staying. He started toward her.

"Follow the others!" he shouted. "You must not stay. *Ta-na-estse!*"

"No!" Rebecca called back.

"Then I will . . ." Panther Burn reached the end of his tether. The dog rope sprang taut, the noose tightened around his waist. ". . . make you." She had tricked him. He could not reach her without pulling up the ground pin, and to do that meant offending the All-Father and all the spirits of the dead who had worn the dog rope into battle. He grabbed a stone and threw it at her. Then another. And missed with both. He shook his head and sagged in defeat. Panther Burn watched as she struck flint and lit the pyre, gently blew upon the tendril of smoke until a flickering pinprick of light danced atop the twigs.

Rebecca nursed a single flame into a fire. She fed more twigs to the blaze. The heat bathed her face. Perspiration beaded her forehead, stung her eyes. She continued to add wood, ranging out now for larger limbs. The blaze danced upward, lapping at the granite table rock. Rebecca stood back and stared at the fire. She needed pine cones now and needles for smoke. There were plenty nearby, and ignoring Panther Burn, she gathered an armful of dry debris and returned to the fire. She closed her eyes and visualized her mother. Star had taught her the prayer-song long ago. Maybe too long ago. It had been in a time before Reverend Madison and the new ways and *Jay-ho-vah*. The memory faded. Rebecca began to despair. For she couldn't remember the song. The medicine woman's daughter lowered the dry needles onto the flames, all but snuffing out the fire. White smoke blotted out the pyre and billowed over the table rock to rise in a thick coruscating column, a gash of brightness against a backdrop of somber greenish-black clouds.

The song . . . the song . . . Rebecca tried to remember. No, it was lost to her. Lost! Coals exploded, ruby-red embers shot upward. Rebecca backed away, startled, then gazed in awe and reverence, for two of the embers seemed to linger in the smoke, like smoldering eyes staring at her from beyond some distant and terrible vale, a place of incomprehensible power, a realm of spirit. She trembled before that fearful glowing gaze. Then a warmth filled Rebecca as if Star's own soul had passed through her daughter's.

"Mother . . . my mother," Rebecca whispered, and a voice within her mind hushed her and told her to sing.

Then in a voice thick with emotion, Rebecca found the words where they had been all along, locked within her heart, and she sang. And she knew that Star, somehow . . . somewhere . . . sang with her.

Thunderbird, lord of storm, of wind.
I call you to me.
Earth-shaker hear me.
Follow the trail I have made.
Send *Oh-ho-ta* to split trees, to fire the grass
and scatter my enemies that they may learn to
    fear you.

Rebecca's voice carried over the meadow to Panther Burn. She repeated the song, like a litany; her invocation was hypnotic. This song-prayer was no game, rather the way of powerful medicine. But she wasn't Star. Only Rebecca. What chance did she have of—

The trees upon the hillside shuddered. As quickly, a guest of wind had returned. The breeze rushed headlong down the valley and Panther Burn spread wide his arms as if to embrace the invisible force of nature. The All-Father was here with him now. The spirits flowed around him. Panther Burn tossed back his head and loosed a wild war cry. Thunder answered him. Rebecca continued to sing, her body swaying as if in a trance, while the column of smoke no longer rose directly in the air but flowed down the valley, streaming white in the wind.

And Panther Burn's heart leaped with joy.

He returned to his circle of weapons. The Northern Cheyenne lifted his eyes to the oncoming storm and saw, arranged in a single line across the valley floor, the soldiers.

For like the Thunderbird, Jubal Bragg had also seen and followed the spirit smoke to its source.

*   *   *

North wind rising. A whisper of violence in the wind. And a warning. But Jubal Bragg had long since ceased to listen to the spirits.

The soldiers held their file, thirty men strong, in an unsteady blue line, for the horses smelled the coming storm. The wind that buffeted their backs sent manes and long flowing tails streaming like banners, frightened the animals, and left them skittish and difficult to control.

"I don't like this," Marley said to the officer beside him as a single fat drop of rain spattered off his shoulder and others began to strike the earth; they sounded like hoofbeats, and where they struck, geysers of dust shot upward. "Colonel Bragg, sir . . . I don't like this." The colonel ignored his trusted sergeant and continued to study the long figure at the other end of the valley. Bragg squinted through his spyglass, twisting the brass casing until the image of the Northern Cheyenne swam into focus. Then he shifted the glass and studied the forested slopes and craggy hillsides rising to either side, walling them in. He returned his attention to the brave. As near as he could tell, the man was alone. Still, it could be a trap. What better bait than the man who killed Tom Bragg?

"James Broken Knife," Bragg said to the Cheyenne on his right. "You take a look." He passed the spyglass to the Southern Cheyenne, who took it, fumbled with the instrument a minute, then hesitantly peered through the scope. He studied the figure at the end of the valley and then passed the spyglass back to the colonel.

"It is him . . . Panther Burn."

"I know that," Bragg said testily. "But what is he doing?"

"Waiting for you," said James, steadying his horse.

"I don't like it," Marley repeated for the third time, with the same effect. He cast an apprehensive eye toward the rumbling heavens. The soldiers donned their ponchos as the fat round drops continued to fall, pummeling the earth and bruising flesh. The hills trembled with thunder. James Broken Knife looked to the north and remembered stories about the Thunderbird and shivered despite himself. He had not been a Christian long enough to forget.

"Waiting for me? Is it a trap? Speak plain, you red bastard," Bragg said. Tom was dead. Half of Jubal's own life was gone, cut from him. He was alone now, truly alone. And all because of the man at the other end of the valley. The Cheyenne's voice carried to the soldiers. Panther Burn was singing. Then he shouted something unintelligible, at least no one could understand the words; the tone and gestures were another matter.

"He's taunting us," Hec Knowles blurted out from down the line. "The son of a bitch is daring us to come for him."

"He wants you," James said, glancing at Jubal.

Murdered my parents, my brother . . . my parents, my brother. Jubal wiped the perspiration from his features as his mind raged with an unspoken litany. "So be it," Bragg said beneath his breath. "So be it."

Marley sensed the madness rising to the surface. Lucid, the colonel might be able to hold his own with the brave. But not like this, Marley thought.

Bragg drew the saber at his side. And as the black clouds spilled toward them and thunder shook the hills, Bragg stood in his stirrups and howled above the wind.

"So be it!"

Suddenly Big Marley lunged across and snatched the saber out of the colonel's grasp and tore the officer's rein from his hand. Marley drove his heels into the flanks of his own mount, a big prairie-bred roan, and the animal charged forward out of the formation of soldiers. Loosing his own wild yell, Marley swung the saber in an arc overhead as he raced down the valley, offering himself in battle in the place of Jubal Bragg. The colonel shouted for him to come back. Marley ignored him. In truth, he could no longer hear anything but the rushing wind and his own savage cry as his heart leaped with the prospect of battle.

Panther Burn saw the man burst from the safety of his companions. The brave shouted for him to come and meet his death. He raised the Hawken and sighted through the rain and sighted the trigger just as a clap of thunder shattered his concentration. Black smoke belched from the barrel, to be swept away by the wind. Marley came on. From beneath the ledge, Rebecca watched, a prayer-song on her trembling lips.

Fifty yards. Panther Burn reached for his powder horn. Forty. Poured a charge down the barrel. *All-Father, hear me. Send the thunder spirit.* Thirty yards. Panther Burn tapped the charge, rammed ball and patch down the barrel. Twenty. *All-Father, I have made the magic fire.* Ten. Panther Burn searched the pouch at his side for a percussion cap. Rebecca sang into the flames and in the coals saw the eyes of the spirit-wolf. Five yards. Panther Burn fit the cap over the nipple, aimed, and squeezed the trigger. The hammer struck the cap. And nothing happened. Marley yelled in triumph.

"I have you now!"

The saber sliced down as Panther Burn leaped in front of the roan. The brave's momentum carried him to the end of his tether and the rawhide rope fastened to the ground pin pulled taut, tripping the roan in its headlong charge. Panther Burn cried out as the rope bit into his waist. The horse buckled and went down, hurling Marley head over heels. Panther Burn landed on his back, rolled to his feet as the full force of the storm hit and a wall of clouds rolled down the valley. The unusually warm, humid air clashing with the cold created a violent wind. Panther Burn could make out the roan on its back rolling over and pawing the air with its broken legs. The Northern Cheyenne heard a shriek of pain and through the ever-thickening sheets of rain glimpsed Big Marley pulling himself along the ground, a length of steel blade protruding from his thigh where he had landed on the saber and shattered the blade, skewering himself. Picking up the Hawken, he replaced the defective cap. He had been freed from his dog pin, but resolved to drive it in again. He staggered out toward the circle but had taken only a few steps when a chunk of ice the size of his fist plowed into the earth, followed by another the size of his skull. Rebecca shouted his name, hoping he heard her above the din. She could see only a few feet into the downpour as day became night before the unleashed fury of the freak storm. Caught in a monstrous updraft, the hail continued to gain in mass before breaking free of the wind's centrifugal force, jettisoned with the velocity of an artillery shell. Round chunks, flat sheet ice, irregular and lethal fragments with glazed jagged surfaces shattered branches, exploded against granite boulders, drummed a deafening cadence upon the earth. Rebecca covered her ears and called out once more, losing heart. Then, without warning, triumph. Panther Burn leaped out of the storm's deadly grasp and rolled across the coals into Rebecca's arms. The Thunderbird had spared him. Not so the men of Bragg's Militia. The hailstorm struck just as the colonel ordered his bugler to sound the charge. A chunk of ice caved in the man's skull, cutting short his bugle's cry. Another hailstone fractured Jubal's collarbone and knocked him out of the saddle. He caught the stirrup of his horse and hung on as the animal followed the others to the safety of the trees. The soldiers, their discipline broken by nature's awesome attack, wheeled their mounts toward the forested hillside nearest them. Riders toppled from horseback, horses reared, pawing the air, neighed in terror. Horses fell screaming to earth, literally beaten to death, leaving their battered and wounded riders to burrow beneath the dead or crippled animals. Shocked and suffering, Jubal Bragg's troops surrendered to pandemonium.

The storm had lost it fury and become a steady hard downpour through which Jubal Bragg stumbled as he made his way up the valley. His numbed mind assessed the damage to his command—what was left of it. The valley floor was littered with dead and wounded soldiers and their mounts. The colonel gasped as the pain from his broken collarbone knifed the length of his

weary frame. He recognized the dead, each by name
. . . Hec Knowles, young Rutledge, and others. He
stumbled past them. A soldier called out to him in a
voice thick with pain. Then the shadow of a horseman
fell across him in the watery gray light.

"I am leaving, *ve-ho-e*," James Broken Knife said.
Blood trickled down from a nasty bruise on his temple.
The skin was beginning to crack and swell. "The *maiyun*
have spoken this day. And I have heard enough." Bragg
did not answer but continued past the Cheyenne renegade. He ignored the sound of fading hoofbeats as the
brave rode off into the downpour. Bragg drew his revolver, and reaching the opposite end of the valley,
spied the rained-out remnants of the medicine fire.
Bragg thumbed a shot into the shadows beneath the
granite outcropping. The revolver's recoil caused a fresh
onslaught of white-hot pain to course through his body.
He grimaced in agony and emptied his revolver. The
gunshots echoed down the hills.

"They're gone, Colonel," a weak voice said from behind him. Bragg spun around as Marley crawled toward
him across the mud, a length of steel still jutting from
his thigh.

"I thought you were dead," Bragg said, stumbling
toward the sergeant. Bragg holstered his Colt revolver
and with his one good arm dragged Big Marley to the
shelter of the granite ledge. Both men rested, out of
the rain now, their backs against stone, legs splayed
upon the sheltered earth.

"Bad enough you steal my saber, then you had to go
and break it," Bragg said.

"Yes sir," Marley gasped. "Sorry." He stared at his
butchered flesh and the bloodstain spreading across his
trouser leg. "What now? We can't go on—" Marley
sucked in his breath as the pain seared him. "Is it
over?" he asked.

Bragg chuckled. It was a mirthless sound, full of
pain, but not defeat.

Another time.

Another place.

He could wait.

"It has only begun, my friend," said Jubal Bragg. He closed his eyes and listened to the rain, to the distant, taunting wind. "Only begun."

"I thought you were dead. Both of you," said Sabbath McKean as he held out his hand to take the reins from Rebecca as she walked her newfound mount up the last few yards of hillside. Panther Burn, leading his own horse, followed about half a dozen yards back. "Never seen a storm like that. Heard tell of 'em. Never seen one." The buckskin-clad scout helped Rebecca over the rise. The storm had passed, leaving in its wake recurring showers as the north wind sent the gray clouds rushing overhead. The ground was slick and much too treacherous for a man to risk his neck on horseback. Panther Burn gained the summit and walked along the ridge toward the others he had risked his life for. They seemed to take heart on seeing him. No longer did they mistrust the Northerner. He had become their salvation. They might be frightened, but the people from the Warbonnet would follow him, wherever he might lead. Zachariah led Joshua Beartusk over to his nephew. The blind man reached up and touched Panther Burn's face. Then Joshua put his arms around the younger man and hugged him. Rebecca drew close, as if loath to be any farther from Panther Burn's side. Joshua turned his blind eyes toward her, a knowing expression on his face.

"You are indeed your mother's daughter," he said, nodding.

She reached out and placed her hand on his arm.

"We better get a move on," Sabbath called out. "Bragg will be—"

"It is finished. At least for now," Panther Burn replied.

"I don't understand," Sabbath said, scratching at his bearded jawline.

"You have been a friend, Sabbath McKean. But you are still a *ve-ho-e*. You will never understand." Panther

Burn glanced at Rebecca, his expression tender, yet gravely respectful. Then he smiled and turned toward the north. His confidence was infectious. Many of the Southern Cheyenne rose with their faces to the wind. Children could be heard playing in the meadow below.

"The thunder spirit has scattered the soldiers like leaves in the wind. We need fear them no longer," Panther Burn said, his words carrying to one and all. "Your new people sit and sing by their cookfires in the shadow of Spirit Mountain. They wait for us. For you. What has been lost will be found. What has been wronged will be avenged. What has been hurt will be healed. And the weary shall find rest." He raised his arms and lifted his gaze to the storm-swept heavens. "I will bring you home!" The word reverberated among the hills, echoing in beauty a most beautiful word.

Home . . . home . . . home . . .

12

February 1866
Montana Territory

In fire, in flames, are memories captured. Images of mind and soul are all we have and all we will be, from frightened hearts to hearts that are free. Memories are the warmth against a winter's tale of chill winds and frost-laden trees and days of meager provisions, when the wood burns low. Memories warm the soul. Love is never beyond reach, as long as a flame burns, as long as memory lives.

In the time of *ho-koneneheso-esehe*, "the little hard-face moon," Rebecca turned her features to the camp-fire burning close at hand. She was too sore and too happy to sleep. She nestled deep beneath the buffalo robe, felt her day-old son stir where he lay sleeping upon her breast. She grew still, fearing to wake him, yet wanting to rouse him too, for her breasts were full and had begun to ache. Yes, she would have to wake him soon. But not now, not in this quiet time of memory.

She closed her eyes and saw again—this time in an overview, as if she had become a mourning dove circling the camp in the azure sky above—the arrival of the Southern Cheyenne as the bone-weary handful of survivors entered the great circle of lodges and tipis that made up the village of the Morning Star people. Looming over the village, casting its reflection upon the Yellowstone River, Spirit Mountain, wreathed in its tendrils of mist, echoed the cries of welcome as the newcomers were recognized and brought into the center of the village. The voice of Joshua Beartusk rang out and filled the air with his tale of tragedy and triumph. The Southern Cheyenne were no more. But these few still lived. The people of the Warbonnet were destroyed, yet a few lived and had been led out of the fields of despair by Panther Burn . . . the very same Panther Burn, Yellow Eagle's son, who had left in dishonor. And Yellow Eagle was there along with the other elders of the tribe, the chiefs of the Dog Soldier, the Red Shield, the Fox, and the Bowstring societies. Men, women, and children came from the furthermost reaches of the Great Circle to hear the tale, to share the sorrow, to rejoice that not all had been lost, that the one who once was shamed had redeemed himself by the grace of the All-Father. And after Joshua finished, silence reigned over the village as everyone turned toward the hill to the south to watch as Panther Burn, alone now, erect and proud, walked his mountain pony along the banks of the Yellowstone and entered the Circle. His long black hair hung down his back and the afternoon sunlight bathed him in its golden glow. He looked neither left nor right, but kept his eyes fixed on the older braves gathered at the ceremonial fire which was always kept burning in the center of the village. His father was there, and others he recognized: Crow Killer, Three Coups, Lone Bear, and Tall Dancer, father of Little Coyote and High Walker, friends long dead.

Panther Burn paused alongside Rebecca, who waited on horseback, and for the first time shifted his gaze. She was ready. He needed no words. She followed him. The two rode together past the Southern Cheyenne, past Joshua and Zachariah, who looked as though he wanted to follow more than anything in the world. Only Joshua's hand on the boy's shoulder held him back.

Panther Burn and Rebecca dismounted before his father. Their horses, made nervous by the crowd, pawed the earth and shook their manes. The elders waited for Panther Burn to speak. Though Yellow Eagle remained as silent as the other chiefs, he could not conceal the pride he felt for what his son had accomplished, bringing the surviving Southern Cheyenne from the gutted remains of their village to safety here by the Yellowstone. His son, the dishonored one, had done this. Panther Burn glanced around, studying the Cheyenne who gathered with increasing number as young women returned from root gathering, the children from the fields, young braves from tending horses. At last, Panther Burn discovered the face he had been seeking. Crescent Moon worked her way through the crowd of Cheyenne. A mother's love radiated from her. Panther Burn returned his attention to the tribal elders as the father of Little Coyote and High Walker stepped forward.

"We pray that the All-Father might find us worthy to use," Tall Dancer said. He spoke softly, yet the tones of his eloquence carried over the gathering. "My sons are dead. For this I blamed you, Panther Burn. For this, in my grief, would I have driven you from the village. I was glad when you left us." Tall Dancer paused, cleared his throat. He brushed his long unadorned black hair away from his face. Other than his unusual height, he seemed rather unexceptional in his greasy buckskins and worn leggings. But all held him in reverence. He was the chief arrowmaker of the village and it was said his shafts never missed their mark, so true did they fly. "Now you have brought us our brothers and sisters from the south, from the shadows of death you have brought them life. You have walked the great circle. Truly the All-Father has brought you back to us. I welcome you, Panther Burn, son of Yellow Eagle." Tall Dancer drew closer and embraced Panther Burn. The crowd of Northern Cheyenne cried out in approval and as the ceremonial drums began to toll rhythmically for

the massacred men, women, and children by the Warbonnet, in contrast, cries of jubilation erupted as the
surviving Southern Cheyenne were swept away by Northern families eager to take these homeless ones into their
lodges. Only Panther Burn and Rebecca, Joshua,
Zachariah, and Sabbath McKean remained in the center of the village.

"You have done well," Yellow Eagle said, when his
throat had relaxed enough that he could speak. While
Panther Burn's father strove to hold his emotions in
check, Crescent Moon had no such reservations. She
ran to embrace her son, sobbing as she wrapped her
arms around his shoulders. At last Panther Burn freed
himself long enough to bring her to Joshua. Crescent
Moon began crying all over again. Zachariah started
backing away, looking suddenly lost and very alone.
Panther Burn took notice and separated brother and
sister to bring Crescent Moon over to the young boy.

"Mother," Panther Burn said, "I have brought you
another son." Zachariah blinked in amazement. He
looked bewilderedly past the woman as Crescent Moon
swept him into her arms. Panther Burn returned to his
father as Yellow Eagle concluded a word of welcome to
McKean.

"You will always have a place at our campfire," the
chief of the Dog Soldiers said. He took a leather pouch
adorned with the Morning Star from his side and handed
it to Sabbath. "Keep this with you so that all will see it
and remember. I would be grieved to have one of our
young braves forget what you have done and kill you for
revenge."

Sabbath scratched at his shaggy red beard and spat
on the ground. "That'd plumb grieve me too."

Yellow Eagle turned to Rebecca, who had remained
silent and watchful, feeling more than a little lost herself. "Where is Star?" said the Dog Soldier. He saw
Rebecca's surprise and nodded. "I know you, girl."

"My mother is dead."

He studied her for a long moment and saw—what?
Perhaps something of a wolf, of magic. "We will build

you a medicine lodge that you may live among us. I think we will have need of you, Star's daughter, in the days to come," Yellow Eagle concluded in a somber, worried tone, a mood his son was determined to lighten.

"Then build the lodge tall and wide, Father, for she will share it with your son." Panther Burn reached out and took Rebecca's hand in his. "We are called together."

Crescent Moon, hearing the pronouncement, rushed to her son's side. She glanced over at Rebecca, who smiled sheepishly beneath the older woman's scrutiny. Crescent Moon gave a soft cry and gathered Rebecca into her happy embrace.

"I am your mother now. I call you *na-htona* from this day forth. *Na-htona* . . . daughter."

The flap to the tipi was pulled aside and Rebecca's heart leaped with the vain hope it might be Panther Burn, unexpectedly returned from the south country. Instead Crescent Moon ducked through the opening and crawled as silently as she could over to her daughter-in-law's side. An icy gust of wind followed the older woman into the tipi. Rebecca shivered and dug deeper beneath her buffalo robes. Seeing the kindly, weather-worn features of her mother-in-law reminded Rebecca of how Crescent Moon had organized her friends so that within a mere week all the provisions and tools and the clothes necessary to begin one's married life had been gathered. Under Crescent Moon's guidance, twenty-six buffalo hides had been used to make a dwelling place for the young couple. Rebecca wanted to snuggle in the warm robes and think back on the ceremony, but Crescent Moon's bustling attentions interrupted her dreamy memories. The older woman smelled of wood smoke and crushed chokecherries, fragrant and sweet, and carried a clay bowl filled with cakes made from dried berries mixed with cornmeal and honey; Crescent Moon was determined her son's wife not perish from lack of food. She placed a tin of hot cherrybark tea by the circle of glowing coals in the center of the lodge.

"*Na-htona*," the woman cooed, brushing a lock of hair from Rebecca's forehead. "The child?" she asked in a whisper; Rebecca nodded. "My own was born on such a cold day as this. And my brother took far too long waiting for his vision to tell him what my little one was to be called."

Rebecca understood, for it was the custom of the Southern Cheyenne as well as the Northern that a child's revered uncle choose his name. In this case, Joshua Beartusk had secluded himself in his tipi and smoked the medicine pipe that the *maiyun* might speak to him the name of the child, Panther Burn's son. Crescent Moon glanced wistfully over at the war shield leaning against the hide wall. It was a circle cut of hide stretched upon a rack of young sapling and adorned with the Morning Star symbol, a design painted coal black. "Yellow Eagle, my husband, has told me not to worry. That my son will be well. The All-Father protects him. But I fear he was too young to lead such a raid. And our allies the Sioux are a troublesome and headstrong lot. Will they follow Panther Burn?" Crescent Moon looked down, ashamed she might be causing Rebecca even more concern. "He is fine."

She patted Rebecca on the shoulder and ducked through the opening in the tipi, choosing to leave rather than stay and cause Rebecca any further anxiety. A mother's fears are a solitary burden. Rebecca closed her eyes, picturing Panther Burn . . . alive.

"All-Father, hear me. Watch over your son, the Dog Soldier Panther Burn, my husband. . . ." She listened to snow settling over the land. In the distance, a pup barked in protest. A voice called out, one brave to another. Several footsteps . . . children running past. Then echoing down from the white-capped reaches of the Absarokas, the faint heart-stopping cry of a hunting cat. A panther stalked Spirit Mountain. Rebecca allowed her mind to drift again into memory, as if holding Panther Burn safe in her mind would guard him in the waking world. She saw again the great ceremonial fire, where she and Panther Burn had stood before Yellow Eagle and Tall Dancer. It seemed but a heartbeat ago, a time so close she could reach out and embrace it. . . .

The chiefs spoke eloquently of the goodness found in the Cheyenne way of life. They spoke of the Great Circle of life, of the many colors found in the ceremonial robes—blue for youth, red for the middle years, yellow for the days of wisdom, black for death becoming life once more. Then Yellow Eagle and Tall Dancer stepped forward and loosely bound the wrists of the couple to show that they had chosen to be bound one to the other throughout their lives. The ceremonial robe, of finely brushed soft buckskin, was draped across their shoulders, signaling for Crescent Moon and half a dozen other women to lead the couple to the lodge the women had built a week earlier. Rebecca was filled with a mixture of fear and expectation, wondering what would happen; how would she behave? She had no experience as a lover. Crescent Moon had done her best to impart what wisdom she had gleaned from her years as a wife and mother. At this moment, stepping into the tipi, Rebecca could not remember a single word her mother-in-law had said.

A small fire burned in the center of the tipi. Flames leaped up, coals glimmered and pulsed as if alive and mirroring the desire that coursed like fire through her veins now that she was alone with Panther Burn.

Rebecca opened her eyes. Something . . . a sound . . . she glanced about, saw that she was still alone. The baby continued to sleep. Rebecca yawned. Listened for the cry of the mountain cat, heard only the stillness of the snowfall. She closed her eyes and surrendered to her dreams. She had surrendered that night as well. And never done so more willingly once Panther Burn's kisses had roused in her a wanton courage that cast off all fears. Come now, a memory of brief pain, of savage ecstasy, of sweet fire, all-consuming. Come now, memories of love.

Firelight on flesh. All that we have is here now, she thought to herself, all we will ever be. After the first brief pain, there was no other. Only pleasure, more than she had ever known, and the same for Panther Burn.

"Now now now . . ." The scream began in her mind, through lips drawn back as the pleasure exploded in the first release. Rebecca dug her nails into Panther Burn's back, drew furrows of blood as her whole being tried to draw him in. Two called together became one in the dearest of acts, in the greatest of trusts, in complete surrender. Two called together were made one in the violent rush of seed, in the onrush of breathlessness and tightened muscles as hands transformed into talons raked flesh. Pleasure burst the bonds of innocence and the two made one loosed a heartrending cry as flesh and bones strived to merge one beloved with the other. They cried their names in the night. Such is the yearning-thankful-satiated song of love.

Rebecca tightened her hold, her legs wrapped around his waist. Panther Burn buried his face in the crook of her neck and repeated her name in a litany that seemed without end. Rebecca sighed, then caught her breath, surprised as he spasmed again, feeling within her an unexpected wave of warmth. She pressed him into her and whispered endearments in his ear and kissed his earlobe. And Panther Burn chuckled softly. "Again I have counted coup."

"*Saaa!*" Rebecca exclaimed, and rolled him onto his side. He laughed and feigned resistance as Rebecca reached down to cup his softened manhood. "See who has surrendered," she exclaimed, daring him to challenge her. Her small breasts were round and taut from lovemaking. She covered them with a flick of long black hair. Panther Burn found her demure pose arousing.

Her hands traced a line across his moist manhood. Once it had reared fierce and warlike. Poor proud stallion, she thought, playfully wicked, a romp in her fertile fields had gentled him. She traced a swollen blue vein that ran the length of his manhood to the black ringlets covering his groin. He gasped at her explorations. She looked at him, stretched out before her, muscles cording his powerful physique, latent power in his supine form. And yet, as he lay open to her, vulnerable beneath her, she loved him for that vulnerability. Her hands continued to play until the life returned to his once spent muscles and he pulled her down to him. Their forms entwined anew.

Their rhythm was as timeless as the wind in the branches of the ponderosas. Limbs shiver in the gentlest of breezes. Then sway as the breeze becomes a storm. And in the unleashed fury of the tempest, the tree shudders to its roots. . . .

A sudden icy gust roused Rebecca Blue Thrush from her heated recollections. She started, disoriented for a moment, felt her baby stir and grope hungrily toward her left breast. Memories of passion faded. The infant demanded immediate attention and Rebecca readjusted her position accordingly, rising up to prop herself against a willow backrest. The infant's lips closed around his mother's nipple and the strong mouth began to suck greedily. Rebecca cooed to her baby and softly sang a mother's song.

> Little one, little one,
> grow strong, grow brave,
> be true and generous,
> be wise with the sacred wind.
> Little one, little one,
> may the All-Father bless you
> and guide you
> along the path of the Great Circle.
> Little one, my little one.

She glanced up, remembering in an instant the icy breath that had roused her from sleep. Someone had entered. In the dead of night with the campfire but a mound of pulsing red coals, it took several long anxious moments for Rebecca's eyes to adjust to the light. At last she spied Joshua Beartusk huddled in the shadows, his back against the buffalo-hide wall of the tipi.

"I did not mean to wake you," the old man said. "For a moment I was uncertain if I had entered the right lodge. The snow . . . confused me. I could not find Zachariah. He broods and keeps to himself, angry that Panther Burn did not allow him to join the raid. It is more important to him to avenge his parents than to help this poor blind one." A note of self-pity crept into Joshua's tone. The old man sounded tired. He cleared his throat, coughed, bent double, and sent a stream of spittle into the coals. "The winter will kill me. See, already it has counted coup. This will be my last season of snows." He sighed, lost in his own reverie of remorse.

"Uncle . . ." Rebecca began. The urgency in her voice brought him back from grim speculations on the nature of his life and death. He laughed softly to himself. Feeling his way, he crawled forward until his fingertips touched the circle of coals, then drew back a moment. His seamed face loomed close to hers; he reached out and gently stroked the infant's cheek. The baby never paused, but continued to nurse, his priorities firmly established.

"Yes, I have heard the boy's name. The *maiyun* have told me, the fire in my lodge has whispered in my ear." He eased back and smiled. "He will have two names, this one, a *ve-ho-e* name, a Cheyenne name."

"My husband will be displeased," Rebecca said. "Two names. What manner of visions were these? Why?"

"Panther Burn will accept what I have said. He has no choice unless he wishes to walk beyond the Circle. The child will be called Michael. And he will be called *Mahta-ho-nehe*, Spirit Wolf. Michael Spirit Wolf. He will walk the world of the Cheyenne and that of the world to come, the world of the white man."

Spirit Wolf! Eyes of fire. The strange and wondrous visions Rebecca had experienced. It was a good sign.

"Michael Spirit Wolf. A child of the old ways, he shall walk in the new," said Joshua Beartusk. "He will walk the path of *ve-ho-e*, the straight path that leads only to death, to nothing. And he will not be lost, for the Circle will be within him and the Morning Star will sing to him. And one day he will lead our people as his father does now. But it will not be down a trail of war, but a path of peace."

Joshua rose, steadied himself, and started out of the tent.

"Uncle, stay awhile. There is tea," Rebecca called to him. "Stay and warm yourself."

"Crescent Moon, my sister, has cooked a nice fat rabbit for me. Anyway, it is best I find my sister and tell her that her grandson has a name. She waits to hear of my dream. And she can be impatient, such a one. I would rather face a she-grizzly than her wrath."

"But the storm?"

"The snowfall only blinds those who can see. For me, it is all the same . . . sunlight or night. And as long as I keep among the Dog Soldiers, I will not become too lost. I have taught myself the way." He smiled, then doubled over as another spasm of coughing shook his thin frame. "Funny . . . the *maiyun* . . . the *maiyun* spoke with your mother's voice." He vanished into the night. Rebecca spied the downy white flakes drifting against night's black backdrop before the flap settled into place, hiding the outside world, secluding Rebecca Blue Thrush once again with her child, the two of them snug in their own private world.

"Michael Spirit Wolf," she gently said. She glanced at the coals, her heart aching for her husband. At last she could bear her silent longing no longer. It welled in her breast and sought release. Then Rebecca cried out in the long winter's eve of her soul. Her voice trembled with yearning and terrible need. "Panther Burn! My husband. You have a son! You have a son!"

A coal cracked, exploded, sending a coruscating col-

umn of sparks churning upward in the air. And among
the pulsing embers, a single flame sprang forth and
bloomed among the ashes like a flower of the night.

Castle Rock was burning. Main and Commerce were
narrow avenues through a sea of flame. Fiery tides
leaped upward and seemed to lap against the stars. Castle
Rock was burning, from the caved-in remnants of the
Hippolyte Hotel to the smoldering wreckage of the
Church of Good Hope to the ruins of the Babylon
Saloon. Flames spread outward from the town, ravaged
dugouts and cabins. The livery shop, the general store,
a dress shop, the barber's, Doc Schaefer's office, and
the proud bastion of Castle Rock's first and only bank,
blazed out of control and crumbled in on themselves.
Panther Burn walked his mount down Main Street. A
solitary figure, he rode past the fallen twisted bodies
littering the porches and alleyways. It had been a brief,
bitter battle. Panther Burn had led better than a hundred young Cheyenne braves down from the north
country, and joining with a war party of Lakota Sioux
and a force of Walking Coyote's Ute, had attacked the
town of Castle Rock in the wee hours of a winter's
morning, scattering the inhabitants out onto the plains.
Some resisted, determined not to leave their homes.
And so red men and white fought and died among the
burning buildings. A raging conflagration coursed from
one false-front structure to the next. Once the flames
had died and the wind scattered the ashes away, the
town of Castle Rock would cease to be, just like the
Southern Cheyenne village by the Warbonnet. Gunshots erupted on the edge of town, somewhere beyond
the fiery barrier. Doomed resistance, nothing more.
The victory this day had been complete. Panther Burn
sighed, his mind full of misgivings, uncertainties brought
about in part by Sabbath McKean's words of warning.
The scout had decried the Northern Cheyenne's quest
for vengeance and spoken against the raid.

The pony neighed and backstepped. Panther Burn

thumbed the hammer on his Hawken and raised his war shield. He glanced to either side, searching for whatever had spooked his horse. The lurid light only heightened his war-painted features, a streak of black across his eyes and yellow slashes on his cheeks. The north wind gusted, scattered the soot-blackened smoke from the wreckage of an assay office. A man, barely distinguishable in the night, materialized out of the smoke. He walked directly toward the Northern Cheyenne, who leveled his rifle but held his fire. The white man was barefoot. This portly, middle-aged clerk, clad in gray trousers, a white shirt, and brown silk vest torn in front where a bullet had ripped the garment on its deadly passage, loomed like a specter of defeat. A crimson stain spread across his belly. As the man drew near, Panther Burn spied a cap-and-ball revolver dangling from the man's left hand. The clerk did not speak or even seem to be aware of the Cheyenne warrior on horseback. Dying with every step, the wounded man seemed to fix his gaze on some point not of this world. The man continued past. Panther Burn did not try to stop him. Timbers cracked and the roof of the assay office came crashing down. The pinto danced sideways in reaction. Panther Burn brought the animal under control and continued down the street; the stench of gunsmoke and blood-drenched ground sickened him. Yet it was what he had come for. Revenge. He urged the pinto into a gallop and left the burning town behind him.

The survivors of the town had arranged themselves in a circle out on the prairie, women and children toward the center, every man still able to fire a gun guarding the perimeter. None of them held any illusions. The war party far outnumbered the survivors of the ravaged town. And so the women began to wail and scream and call for those they had left behind to come and help them, refusing to realize that Castle Rock was a haunt for the dead and nothing more.

Cheyenne and Ute and Sioux milled in a heavily armed cluster, each brave anxious to have done with the task at hand. One charge would sweep over the *ve-ho-e* and finish the matter once and for all. Walking Coyote saw no need to wait for the one who had planned the attack. The Ute war chief was loudly asserting his own authority when Panther Burn rode up behind him. Walking Coyote turned to face the Northern Cheyenne and fell silent. The Sioux, accepting Panther Burn as the leader of the raid, waited with the young men of the Spirit Mountain Cheyenne for his instructions.

"Their courage is broken. The white-eyes wait to die," Walking Coyote exclaimed with a sweep of his hand, indicating the cluster of townspeople just out of rifle range. Bathed in moonlight, the survivors were a pathetic island of humanity all but lost on the reaches of a prairie as limitless as the sea. Panther Burn walked his horse through the midst of his warriors until he reached the forefront of the war party. There he found Sabbath McKean, who had taken no part in the attack on Castle Rock. The short, burly frontiersman sat astride his horse, impervious to the hostile baiting of the handful of Ute braves. McKean rested a Spencer rifle in the crook of his arm. His back was ramrod straight but an aura of tension radiated from him. His expression brightened as Panther Burn arrived.

"There's a powerful lot of innocent folks out yonder," he said, and spat a stream of tabacco at one of the Ute braves nearby. A second stream spattered the snow-patched ground underfoot. Away from the fire-swept streets, the chill air bit deep into the bones. The breaths of horses and men cast silver clouds upon the darkness.

"And innocent ones at the Warbonnet as well," Panther Burn säid, sensing the Ute war chief, Walking Coyote, moving up from behind, the better to hear.

"All the deaths in the world ain't gonna make that right," McKean replied. "War's one thing. I done my share of killing. But I ain't never played the butcher. Couldn't live with myself if I did. I don't think you could either."

"Do you know me so well, white man?"

"I only know we part company here. I'd like a minute

so's I can ride over and join them folks yonder." The frontiersman scratched at his red beard, grimaced. "Them's mostly women and kids. Panther Burn . . . I'd like to think I been riding with a better man than Jubal Bragg."

Panther Burn adjusted his hold on the Hawken. As yet, he had not fired a shot. He had been too busy directing the threefold attack that reduced Castle Rock to so much rubble. He closed his eyes and listened to the fearful cries of those out on the flatlands. He heard in his mind other cries, other voices, those of Cheyenne women and children, ghost voices weeping in the dark dead past. He could add more voices to the atrocities of a year ago, but at what cost? He was a Cheyenne warrior—that was his dignity and his truth. He would not spit on his life nor needlessly soak his conscience in blood.

"Go to your people," he said to Sabbath. "Tell them I give them their lives. But if the town is rebuilt, I will return and burn it again."

"No! We must be avenged," Walking Coyote said. "The earth must flow with rivers of blood. Only then will the ghosts of our people sleep!"

"My people! Not yours!" Panther Burn corrected him, his eyes narrowing.

"Shall a woman lead us? If you have lost your stomach for battle, then another will replace you. Let those who would be braves follow me." Walking Coyote glanced around for support. His face was streaked with red war paint and glistened like a mask of blood. He held up his iron-tipped spear and raised up on horseback. "Who among you are still warriors, hear me."

"They will not hear you," Panther Burn said.

"Why not? My lance is hung with fresh scalps. You have none. I am Walking Coyote, war chief of the Ute. Who is there to still my voice?"

Panther Burn swung the Hawken rifle in an arc and brought the heavy barrel up alongside Walking Coyote's head with a resounding smack. The war chief, knocked from his mount, landed facedown on the frozen ground. The Ute braves stared in shocked amazement. By the time they recovered, the other warriors had already demonstrated their allegiance and gathered behind Panther Burn. The Ute braves could do little more than dismount and gather up their fallen chief and drape his unconscious form over his horse. They were too few in number to risk attacking the townspeople. Without a word the Ute turned their backs on Panther Burn and rode off into the night, heading west toward the mountain passes.

Panther Burn nodded. It was done. For now. He doubted the *ve-ho-e* would ever forget. Well, then, let them send their armies against him. Let them send Jubal Bragg. He glanced over at McKean. "One day, *ve-ho-e*, we may meet in battle, perhaps you with the longknives and I with my people. We will meet and fight and one of us may kill the other. But today, let it be said we parted as friends." He held up his hand, palm out. "*E-peva-e.*"

And Sabbath repeated, "It is good. Fare thee well, Panther Burn." The scout nudged his heels against the flank of his horse and the mountain pony trotted off toward the circle of survivors. Sabbath called out to them in English, telling them to hold their fire.

Panther Burn turned his own mount toward the north. He called out for the rest of the braves to follow him.

And to a man, they did.

In spring, in the time of the Muddy-faced Moon, Rebecca Blue Thrush took her son up the slope of Spirit Mountain. She climbed the broad spacious hillside where the bitterroot was just beginning to dot the golden grass with pink buds. Little Michael Spirit Wolf squirmed and fidgeted and fought the constraints of his carryboard. His protests echoed down the hill, spooking the nearby horses where they grazed. Zachariah ran ahead, for spring had even thawed his moodiness. He raced his shadow and called for Rebecca to hurry along. Rebecca was determined not to alter her pace. An hour's climb carried them into the forest, where they followed a deer trail to a sun-dappled brook nestled in the heart of the forest and fed by an underground stream that poured in a lovely waterfall from the granite battlements above. Here in the shade of ponderosa and lodgepole pine and red fir, the world seemed awash with an emerald light. Here Rebecca found peace, a timeless balm to soothe her fears for Panther Burn. For try as she might to trust in her dreams, in the spiritual bond that linked her to her husband, she was only human, with human frailties and fears. When misgivings threatened to overwhelm her, she would flee to the mountain, to the brook, to this place of peace.

She freed Michael from his constraints and placed him on his back among the boughs. The infant seemed to be drinking in all the world at a single glance. He cooed and gurgled and filled the tranquil setting with his happy sounds. Zachariah ran off into the forest. Rebecca heard him playing as if he were in the thick of battle. She looked down at her child and wondered if Michael too would be a warrior. She did not want to think of him being hurt. Or hurting. Maybe by then men might have learned to live in peace.

"Don't worry, Rebecca," Zachariah's voice echoed in the forest. "Panther Burn will return to us. And he will have many scalps."

Rebecca closed her eyes and placed her hand upon her child, who wrapped his nut-colored arms around her wrist. The brook, a dozen yards away, lulled her to sleep. She dreamed of peace. And of her husband. . .

A moment became an hour. She might have slept longer, but Michael's full-voiced bellow of hunger roused her. Rebecca opened her eyes. Michael kicked and complained next to her. And on the other side of the boy lay Panther Burn. His expression was haggard. Yet his eyes radiated the joy he felt. For he had found his son. How long he had been beside Rebecca, watching her sleep and holding Michael, she could not tell. The medicine woman stared, unmoving, fearful of reaching out to touch him. If this were a vision, she wanted to keep it whole. Panther Burn put an end to her fears. He placed the infant against her breast, and rolling over, gathered mother and child in his arms.

Alone in the shadows, hidden behind a fir, Zachariah watched, a frown darkening his face. He heard the baby cry and Panther Burn laugh aloud and call out to his new little son. Zachariah scowled and darted away, hoping to outrace the sound that seemed to taunt him.

For Rebecca, her fears were vanquished and a completeness filled her being. Panther Burn was alive. He was with her. Souls soared; hearts nearly burst with an excess of love unspoken. No words were needed. Between Rebecca and Panther Burn, touching was enough. And sweet silence a song, eternal.

After the silence, after the moments when love must reign supreme and no thought be given other than to love, Panther Burn rolled free of his family's embrace and crawled over to the pool of spring water. He stared down at his reflection; his long black hair almost obscured his features, like a black cowl covering his head. He brushed his fingers across the glassy surface of the water and the Panther Burn he saw disappeared. When it formed again he saw his wife and son behind him.

"My husband, come with me to our lodge. Our people will have a great feast now that you have returned."

He reached around and grabbed her naked calf where her buckskin dress failed to cover. He turned and buried his face in the soft brushed folds of her dress. She could feel his heat all the way through the buckskin and her belly grew warm from his kneeling embrace. She dropped a hand to his head and stroked his hair. "And later I will spread a feast of a different sort," she said in a voice hoarse from her aroused passion. Panther Burn drew back and looked up at her.

"It is a feast at which I can never have my fill," he said.

"*Saaavaaaa!* You take me for a maiden whose fancies can be turned this way and that with words." Rebecca playfully pushed him aside. Panther Burn stood and looked back toward the spring, where for a moment he had a vision of his own. Rebecca sensed this and said, "My husband?" She was suddenly worried for him.

"I have punished those responsible for the deaths of our people. I have gained a victory over the soldiers," he said.

"One of many," Rebecca added. "I have heard it in the wind."

"Sabbath McKean tells me the white man is a river that cannot be dammed. Try and it will overflow its banks and cover all the land. Stand before it and it will drown us. I have gained my victory but I cannot win. We can never win and one day I will be forced to give up my weapons and wash the war paint from my face and be a tame Indian or die."

"McKean is a white man," Rebecca offered.

"He is also our friend."

"A friend, yes, but no medicine man gifted by the All-Father with spirit dreams. What does McKean know?"

Panther Burn held her close. His son struggled and yanked at him and the warrior tried to surrender to the joy of homecoming. He gazed with love upon the shadows in the forest, and beyond them, in his mind, he saw the mountains . . . his mountains. What does McKean know? she had asked.

"The truth," said Panther Burn, turning away from the spring. He carried his son in his arms; Rebecca walked at his side. He could have run, and even considered such a course for a brief moment. Why not run, and hide deep in the heart of the mountains where the wind blew free, where he could escape the fate he had glimpsed in the pool's icy mirror? But the moment passed and Panther Burn started down the hill, returning to his people, and his destiny.

A thousand miles away and more, another world away and more, in a town house in Philadelphia, Esther Bird Hat Madison screamed with all her life, with all her strength as the pain seemed to split her in half. She stared past the physician's face toward the flower pattern on the canopy over her bed. The doctor, his face as sweaty as hers, leaned forward. "Push. You've got to push."

The room seemed to spin and the doctor blurred, became one with the face of a maid and the mahogany posts of the bed and the austere landscapes hung upon the walls. She hurt, she wept, she wanted to die and gain peace and end this suffering. And like so many women before her, Esther curled upward and pushed and bit through the twist of leather she held clamped between her jaws. She pushed and brought a child, her child, into the world. Esther sank back upon the goosedown pillows as the pain suddenly loosed its hold. She closed her eyes and heard the white medicine man tell one of the maids to go and fetch Mr. Madison. Rebecca shook her head no but could not speak and the doctor failed to understand. He worked with the infant a moment, then wrapped the child in soft white blankets and placed the wrinkled, struggling morsel of life against Esther's breast.

"Mrs. Madison, you have a fine daughter," the doctor said. His lined face swam into focus. She stared at the silvery goatee hiding his chin. How strange were the customs of the *ve-ho-e*. Perhaps in such a way were the medicine men set apart, by the strange hair coverings upon their faces. The door to the bedroom creaked open and the physician stepped away, gesturing for the maids to leave with him. He leaned forward and whispered to Sam and then patted the younger man on the arm and walked out the door and closed it after him. Esther watched as Sam approached. He smiled nervously, then leaned down to look upon his daughter.

"Katherine was my mother's name. It is a good name," he said, kissing Esther on the forehead. "Little Katherine Madison," he repeated aloud. "Kate." He stroked the infant's forehead. The baby peeked out at the world through slitted lids and squalled until she found her mother's nipple. Nature's pattern triggered within and the child began to suck.

"Are you in much pain?" Sam asked. Esther shook her head no.

"You bore it well, all those hours," Sam said. "I prayed that God would give you strength."

Prayed? He no longer even wore a collar. But then, his father's businesses were all-consuming.

"Not your Jay-ho-vah," Esther said. "My strength was here." She opened a clenched fist, revealed a crumpled yellow paper in her hand. Sam frowned, puzzled by her words. He reached out and took the paper and patted it open. It was a portion of a newspaper page, seven months old, a page from the St. Louis *Dispatch* describing the attack on a village of Southern Cheyenne. The headline read, "NO SURVIVORS. COUNTRYSIDE FEARS REPRISALS." Sam had seen this before, for they had bought the paper in St. Louis during their flight from the battleground of Colorado.

"You see, here is one"—Esther wearily glanced down at her daughter—"that you did not betray. I will tell her of how you left her people to be murdered. All the while in my pain, I knew I must not give in, I must bring this child into the world, so after I am dead, there will still be one of my people who will hate you. And you will never be able to forget what you have done, how you abandoned those who trusted you. Our daughter will hate you as much as I!"

Sam staggered back from the bed, recoiling as if struck. He stumbled over an end table and knocked a china basin to the floor. A pool of bloody water spread across the throw rug and seeped past the embroidered edges into the polished wood; the crimson smear spread outward, trapping Sam as he retreated from his wife's horrible pronouncement. He charged across the room and hurled the door open and sent it crashing against the cloth-covered wall. Esther stared at the empty doorway and then glanced down at the trail he had left in his wake, a pattern of bloody footprints that led across the room and out the door, following Sam Madison wherever he might run, the legacy of his horror. And his guilt.

Esther Bird Hat Madison cuddled her newborn child. And smiled. . . .

BOOK TWO

PLAINDEALER TELEGRAPH
Sidney, Nebraska
July 1, 1876

DEBACLE ON THE LITTLE BIG HORN

News has reached us of a terrible tragedy. General Armstrong Custer with a force of over two hundred men was massacred by an overwhelming horde of bloodthirsty savages on the afternoon of June 25. The astonishing rapidity with which the gallant soldiers of the Seventh Cavalry were overcome can only be attributed to the vast numbers of Sioux and Cheyenne savages assembled on the plains of Montana Territory. Our correspondents report that several notorious war chiefs have banded together for the first time, just to bring their combined might against the man they called Yellowhair. Most notable among the chiefs, we are told, were Sitting Bull, a Sioux medicine man; Crazy Horse, another Sioux; Chief Gall of the Hunkpapa Dakota; and Panther Burn, the Northern Cheyenne war chief also known as the Butcher of Castle Rock. . . .

BASIN CITY HERALD
September 7, 1877

Two days ago within the walls of Fort Robinson in the Dakotas, Chief Crazy Horse was at last punished for the massacre at the Little Big Horn. During a scuffle with troopers escorting the Sioux chief to the stockade after his surrender, Crazy Horse was summarily dispatched and bayoneted to death. It is difficult to condemn the passions that led to such an act. In truth, Crazy Horse brought about his own demise. Those others responsible for the Custer debacle have scattered to the wind. It is rumored Sitting Bull has sought sanctuary in Canada. Panther Burn has taken to the mountains up along the border. Despite the few followers he has with him, it appears he continues to defy the forces sent against him. . . .

VIRGINIA CITY DAILY UNION
October 18, 1880

The bodies of six prospectors, among them Will Gusser and th Pyle brothers of this town, were discovered this day up on Bear Paw Creek; the men evidently put up quite a struggle, for a number of rifle shells littered the ground. Nance Pyle lived long enough to identify his attackers as Cheyenne. This account is more than likely true, as Panther Burn is rumored to be heading south through the passes. All men are advised to keep their powder dry until this wily renegade is apprehended.

ST. JOSEPH GAZETTE
July 23, 1881

SITTING BULL SURRENDERS

Custer's murderer laid down his weapons on July 19 at Fort Buford in the Dakotas. With the surrender of Gall and the killing of American Horse of the Cheyenne, only one other war chief of notoriety remains at large: Panther Burn. The fate of Sitting Bull remains to be seen, but decent citizens everywhere can breathe a sigh of relief. It is our trust that justice will be served.

SAN FRANCISCO HERALD
September 10, 1883

Two soldiers were killed and four more wounded in a skirmish with Cheyenne renegades holed up in the Wind River range. Despite such a setback, General Nelson Miles is confident of success and told this correspondent that time and winter are on the side of the United States Army.

ROCKY MOUNTAIN NEWS
Denver, Colorado
December 24, 1883

THE BUTCHER OF CASTLE ROCK APPREHENDED AT LAST!

Residents of northern Colorado have no reason to fear. They have received a marvelous Christmas present in the form of wonderful news. Panther Burn, the last of the war chiefs and the renegade responsible for the atrocity at Castle Rock, was forced to come down from his mountain hideout and hand over his weapons to the soldiers who had been besieging his paltry band of renegade Cheyenne. Panther Burn was immediately restrained and we are informed he will be confined at Fort Dodge, Kansas. It is presumed the remainder of his followers will be shipped north to Montana Territory. What better describes this paper's elation than to simply conclude . . . MERRY CHRISTMAS.

13

⤳

July 4, 1889
Montana: The Northern Cheyenne
Indian Reservation

The son should be the image of the father, Rebecca
Blue Thrush thought as she watched her son stroll down
from the cedar-trimmed hill behind their cabin. But
Michael Spirit Wolf was taller than his father and his
shoulders were heavier with muscle, for the duties of
ranch life required more strength than litheness. There
were bales of hay to be hoisted to the loft and stored
against the inevitable harsh winters. Calves to be rescued from the springs and wallows and full-grown cattle
to drive from the high meadows and crops . . . yes . . .
crops to be planted and worked and harvested. Michael
did have his father's eyes, pieces of flint waiting to
strike fire. And a laugh like Panther Burn's, only more
reckless and coming easy to his lips. But then Michael
had only seen some of the sorrow and the past was
yesterday's labor, repairing the corral fence or weeding
the garden which caused him no more anguish than a
sore back.

Rebecca stood beside the buckboard and made no
move to climb up onto the bench seat. Michael crossed
around in front of the bay mares he had hitched to the
singletree and held out his hand to his mother. At

twenty-three years of age he appreciated a good time as much as any young man and more than most. At forty-four, Rebecca could care less, especially if she thought that such a good time was at the expense of her people. Time had left her coppery skin remarkably free of wrinkles. Her long black hair shone with the luster it had in youth. Though many a brave considered her a beauty to be admired, none sought her favor. She was still Panther Burn's woman whether he bedded her or not. Michael wiped his dusty palm on the thighs of his Levi's and offered his hand a second time, and a second time his mother refused.

"You still aren't coming with me?" the young man asked, obviously disappointed. "It will do you good."

"What will? To celebrate the sacred day of the white man's freedom when my husband is denied his?"

"I do not think of the white man. Only of the free food, the beer, the fiddlers, and the pretty girls who will have no one to dance with them if I do not go." Michael chuckled and ran a hand through his thick but close-cropped black hair and adjusted his freshly brushed gray hat. He straightened and tucked in his plaid shirt. At his waist, sunlight gleamed off the polished belt buckle he had won bronc riding in last year's rodeo up in Miles City. It was a shiny chunk of brass pounded into a flat smooth square with a horse's head etched in the center by a local artisan.

Rebecca turned from her son and walked away from the house Michael had built with the help of Father Lee Hillary in Lame Deer. It was a four-room structure with two rooms to a side and divided by a dogtrot nine feet wide that ran the length of the house and opened onto porches in the front and rear. The dogtrot, a hallway to catch the cool breezes in summer, could be sealed off with buffalo robes in the winter. Here and there a wood shingle on the roof needed replacing, but the walls wore a fresh coat of white paint and bitterroot bloomed in the front yard and lined the walk from the hitching rail twenty feet from the porch. The rolling countryside was bedecked in garments of pink and white bitterroot that unfurled in beauty to golden hills splashed with emerald cedars. Two dozen head of cattle lazily grazed upon the sun-dappled slope. Cloud shadows swept across the earth like ghostly barkentines bound in silent passage toward unknown destinations. Rebecca watched the shadows, longing to board one of those spectral ships and sail from the heaviness that darkened her spirit, that never left. She turned as her son approached. Michael reached out and put his hands on her shoulders. A breeze tugged at a lock of hair curled over his forehead.

Rebecca caught her breath. For a second Panther Burn seemed to peer out at her through the face of his only child.

"What is it?" Michael asked, seeing his mother grow pale.

"Nothing," she said. Sometimes the visions were a curse. She ached for her husband. Memories were like red-hot daggers in her breast.

"Are you hurt?" Michael said.

"Always," Rebecca answered, and patted his arm. The vision was gone and in its place was left a "tame" Indian, Michael Spirit Wolf.

"Come with me," he repeated. "Uncle Joshua will be there. You always enjoy seeing him. And Hope Moon Basket and her children. The little ones are anxious to show you their newborn colt. It's only a week old. And the men will be wrestling for fifty dollars— Think of it! Fifty dollars cash prize, and you could watch me win."

"And patch you up afterward," Rebecca scoffed, and reached up to stroke his cheek. He would always be her baby, her child. Michael took her hand, his strong callused fingers closed around her slim smooth wrist.

"Mother . . . don't stay here. Laugh with me, live with me. You mourn as if Father was dead."

She did not surrender to despair and say, "He might well be." She pulled free of his grasp. "And you laugh as if you had no father at all." Even as she spoke, she knew the words cut Michael to the quick and she cursed her own thoughtlessness. Rebecca heard him turn and start back to the wagon. She heard the springs creak as he climbed aboard, then the crack of leather as he freed the reins.

"Wait!" Rebecca looked at her son and read his feelings; in this way he was not like Panther Burn, for Michael had never mastered the art of masking his emotions. The hurt was evident in his eyes and Rebecca knew but one salve to heal, to undo the harm her rashly spoken reply had done. "Wait . . . please. I will go with you." Michael lifted his eyes to the hills and spied a pair of coyotes loping along the skyline. Beyond, the sun climbed higher to catch the scudding clouds. It wasn't that he did not miss his father. But Michael still had hope, and this hope in its own way eased the ache of separation. Today was going to be a very important day. He felt it in his bones. Maybe some of his mother's medicine had worked off on him. Now if only he could use it to shoe horses or drive the cattle to market or feed them during the bitter winters. He smiled and looked at his mother and held out his hand to her.

In 1884, the government of the United States in its wisdom set aside fifty-eight square miles of land in southeastern Montana for the Northern Cheyenne to use as their home. A haven in the midst of the nation's westward expansion. In return the Cheyenne nation agreed to live in peace as wards of the government. To a people whose numbers had been ravaged by war, this was the only way to survive. But there were those who dreamed of the past, when the buffalo thundered over the plains and the people of the Morning Star ranged far and wide and free, from the Dakotas to the Rockies. Some said the past was dead. Perhaps so. But not all the warriors were dead, not all were tame. An hour from the ranch, Michael Spirit Wolf guided the buckboard around a grove of aspen and down a sandy bank to ford the pebble-strewn shallows of Lame Deer Creek. Lame Deer Valley opened before them, and the hills seemed to draw aside, revealing a broad green grassy meadow in whose center the tides of civilization had pooled to form the settlement of Lame Deer. Here the Bureau of Indian Affairs chose to build their agency headquarters. Here the Cheyenne families gathered every Friday to receive the rations issued to them from the government. Time passed and many of the Indians moved in from the outlying countryside to form a community around the agency. Camp Merritt was established and garrisoned with a detachment of soldiers out of Fort Keogh, forty miles to the north. The soldiers acted in support of James Broken Knife's Indian police and ensured order on the reservation. The Capuchin fathers had arrived a few years later and built a church in hopes of ministering to the needs of the tribe. Log cabins and hide lodges and whitewashed government housing littered the slopes and spread out along the valley floor. As they approached the settlement, Rebecca remembered her husband's words of long ago when describing her own people. Now his too had lost the Circle.

Gunfire shattered her reverie and Michael nudged her and pointed toward a cluster of horsemen charging out from a throng of people crowded around the red-white-and-blue-festooned Bureau of Indian Affairs headquarters. "The race has started," Michael said, angling the wagon off the wheel-rutted road as the horsemen bore down on them. "Knows His Gun, Black Owl, John Timber, I can't see the others," he added. He stood up in the wagon, shouted, and waved his hat over his head as the riders swept past. There were fourteen riders in all, mostly Cheyenne with a sprinkling of soldiers and cowpunchers from off the reservation, all riding hard. The course ran the length of the valley from the springs to the south and back to the settlement. The finish line was located directly in front of St. Theresa's Catholic Church, where Father Hillary would proclaim the winner. A cloud of dust billowed back over the wagon and Rebecca closed her eyes against the grit. Michael started the team forward at a brisk trot. His eyes were lit with excitement as he took note of the gaily decorated buildings. Ribbons hung from the flour mill, general store, the agency, even the low stockade around the military camp. Stalls painted red, white, and blue dispensed beer and lemonade, cookies and pies, fry bread and pudding and slabs of barbecued beef to a crowd of Indians and whites gathered to celebrate the Fourth of July. Slabs of beef and whole freshly butchered hogs hung from spits over cookfires ringed with rocks to control the flames. Grease sizzled on the coals and the mouth-watering aroma of ribs and beef steak drifted through the crowd. Michael could not find a free hitching post and so ground-tethered his team and stepped around to help his mother down. And as usual Rebecca did not wait for him but brushed her buckskin dress away from her legs and leaped down of her own accord. She heard someone call to her and thought she spied Hope Moon Basket in the mass of men and women gathered around the cookfires. Then the ever-shifting sea of faces blocked her view. At another stand half a dozen blue-clad soldiers were busy drawing beer from wooden barrels stacked high on the back of a flatbed wagon. Several of the soldiers were tipsy and a number of braves had already passed out in the shade of the nearby aspens. A wooden deck for dancing had been erected alongside the church but the fiddlers would not make their appearance until later in the afternoon. Rebecca noted that several families had come in from the surrounding ranches. The white homesteaders used the general store in Lame Deer as a source of supplies, as it was closer than making the trek to Forsythe, especially in the winter. A shadow fell across Rebecca. James Broken Knife walked up to stand before her. He was dressed in soldier blue and buckskin breeches, the uniform he had worn as a scout for General Crook down on the Rosebud. As a reward for his service, James had been appointed chief of the tribal police without regard to the fact that he wasn't of the Northern Cheyenne. His square solid features drew back in a grin.

"Glad you came in, Rebecca. Come find me when the fiddlers strike up a tune." He touched the brim of his campaign hat. His hard eyes revealed only contempt. She had spurned him once and run off with Panther Burn. Well . . . where was her high-and-mighty husband now? Rotting in jail down in Kansas. Rebecca lowered her eyes to the star pinned to his shirt. His name was etched in the center of the polished metal.

"Agent Gude has put the wrong name there," Rebecca replied, causing James to glance down at the badge. "It should be 'White Man Runs Him.' " The tribal policeman's countenance darkened and he turned on his heels and retreated back into the crowd. Michael arrived to stand by his mother's side and for a moment the humor left his face as he watched James walk away.

"What did he want?" Michael asked, glowering.

"Nothing. Only to dance." Rebecca did not want her son at odds with a man like James Broken Knife. He was the law and had the trust of the soldiers, while Michael was a warrior's son, the offspring of the last Cheyenne chief to surrender. She forced herself to smile and defused Michael's anger and tugged at his arm. "Your friend Father Hillary has saved a place for you on the steps of the church. Go to him. I will find Hope Moon Basket and help her with her children. I saw her husband among the riders in the race."

"I would have a better view of the finish," Michael agreed, hesitant to abandon his mother. But she gave him a shove.

"And from the porch you will be able to find the prettiest girl to ask to come with you to the dance."

Michael blushed and grinned despite himself. "But I am leaving the prettiest girl here," he said. Half a dozen children scurried past, almost knocking mother and son down.

"Saaa! You lie no better than your father," Rebecca said, darting aside as another herd of children rushed by in pursuit of the first, screaming and yelling at one another, chunks of freshly baked sweet-potato pie clutched in their fists.

"Father Hillary might need help calling the race," Michael conceded, an excuse more for his own benefit.

He patted his mother's arm and started off toward the church.

Father Hillary was a broad-shouldered congenial man of forty-seven, whose priestly robes hid a physique better suited to a laborer than a cleric. In truth he performed less of his ministries within the walls of St. Theresa's and more at hard labor among his flock. Before becoming a priest, Lee Hillary had been a carpenter. And so whenever there was a barn-raising or a hog shed to be built or a family needing a new cabin to replace a home lost in a fire, Father Lee Hillary could be found hammer in hand, pitching in to help. The priest, his scalp sunburned beneath his thinning hair, his square-jawed features flush with excitement, waved to Michael and gestured for him to come up on the porch.

"Didn't think you'd make it," he called as Michael bounded up the last few steps to the church porch. Behind Father Hillary's hulking frame a familiar figure scooted his chair closer to the railing as if to catch a better glimpse of the race. A futile gesture indeed.

"Uncle Joshua," Michael called out, and after shaking Father Hillary's hand stepped over to embrace his uncle, who pushed him away, embarrassed by such affection. The blind old leather-faced brave had not died during the winter of '66 nor during any of the subsequent winters, although he had declared each to be his last. Father Hillary had hired Joshua to help around the church. The old warrior's favorite duty was ringing the bell rope on ration Fridays and Sunday mornings. Over the years the blind man had memorized his way about the church and its grounds. He slept in a single-room cabin back of the rectory. Too proud to accept Michael's charity, Joshua had refused to live at the ranch, preferring to earn his keep at the church.

"You're late, Michael. The race has already started," Joshua complained. "Now, stay close. You said you'd tell me who won. I think Sits at Night lied to me the last race and took my money when he should have been paying me. I don't intend to let it happen again. Where is Rebecca? Does she not have a hug for this old one? And I am so close to death. This winter will be my last. The owl has called me by name." Joshua shook his head in mourning for himself. A cheer rose up from the crowd. "Who won?" Joshua gripped the porch railing. "Will no one tell me? Was it John Timber? I have wagered money on him. Who won?"

"The race has not ended," Father Hillary answered in a deep soothing tone of voice. He patted the old man's bony shoulder. "The troopers have raised the money pouch to the top of the lodgepole there in the circle where the young men will try their best to reach it. The crowd has cheered them, nothing more." Father Hillary glanced over at Michael. "And see you take care, Michael, for I have learned James Broken Knife will be among the wrestlers and he has no love for you . . . I am told." Father Hillary glanced at Joshua to see that the old man was nodding his agreement.

"He does not frighten me," Michael said.

"He should," Joshua replied.

Father Hillary shaded his eyes and stared up toward the northern end of the valley. A column of dust signaled the arrival of oncoming horsemen. "That ought to be Tyrell Gude. He'll be glad to have made it back in time to see the finish of the race."

"He's been gone?" Michael inquired, looking in the same direction.

"Up to Miles City to welcome the new doctor and escort him down to the 'Res,' and also the new captain assigned to Camp Merritt. A young fellow just arrived at Fort Keogh but a couple of weeks ago. Captain Henry Morbitzer by name. An ambitious lad, or so I am told." Father Hillary blessed himself with the sign of the cross. "Saints preserve us from ambitious men."

"A doctor . . ." Michael softly said. "Mother isn't going to like that." The Bureau of Indian Affairs had adopted a policy of subtle suppression when it came to the subject of medicine men and women among the tribes in its care. People like Rebecca Blue Thrush were said to exert undue influence on the reservations.

If trouble were ever to arise, it would begin with the medicine makers, the holy ones, keepers of the old ways and living symbols of a vanishing way of life. Michael knew his mother cared for her people. Herbs and prayers had cured many an ill child. Rebecca Blue Thrush had no use for doctors. And neither did her son.

Rebecca managed to spy one of Hope's children and followed the youngster's lead toward a table laden with fry bread and chokecherry pudding and steaming fresh apple and sweet-potato pies. She exchanged greetings and waved hello and at last made her way over to the table where Hope Moon Basket greeted her with a hug and a cry of pleasure. Three boys, twelve, seven, and five, emerged from behind Hope's voluminous cotton dress. Jim, Jason, and Francis Timber considered Rebecca part of the family. In truth, Panther Burn's woman would have it no other way. She loved the boys as if they were her own.

"Did you see John?" Hope asked around a mouthful of fry bread. Time had not dulled her round cheery features, only added fullness to her cheeks and another twenty pounds to her already round frame.

"He nearly ran us down." Rebecca nodded. She started as a fusillade of firecrackers exploded above the din and in response a soldier cranked off a dozen rounds from the Hotchkiss gun, a hand-crank-operated five-barreled rapid-firing weapon drawn up before the military encampment at the rear of the agency building. Several of the braves over among the aspens loosed wild cries and a few even managed to climb to their feet at the roar of the gun. Rebecca recognized Zachariah Scalpcane standing unsteadily with the others. He raised a brown jug high in the air and tilted it up to his lips. He lowered it after several fiery swallows and his gaze met Rebecca's. Thirty-one years old, wiry, with deep-set eyes, Zachariah had fought his battles in a cause that was lost before it was even started. Panther Burn's surrender six years ago had taken the heart out of him and left him bitter, with an emptiness inside he tried to fill with whiskey. Zachariah had become a warrior without a war. He took a shuffled step forward. His jeans were brown with mud and hung loose around his narrow waist. His denim shirt hung out, unbuttoned, revealing a hollow-looking belly above his belt. He lifted the keg as if toasting Rebecca's health, a pathetic gesture in the light of his own condition. As he turned to rejoin his friends, Rebecca caught a glimpse of the eagle feather braided in Zachariah's unkempt stringy black hair. It was a worn and battered emblem of another, happier time. Still, as long as it remained, perhaps Zachariah Scalpcane was not entirely lost. Rebecca looked past the aspens down the north road as Gude's carriage entered the settlement. A breeze swept the dust away, and Rebecca saw the agent wasn't alone.

A chorus of cheers erupted from the exuberant crowd as the horsemen raced into view at the bend in the valley. Men hurried to place last-minute bets as mothers chased their children from the street in front of the church in an effort to clear the finish line.

"I see him. I see him!" Hope blurted out. "Rebecca . . . Oh, Rebecca, he's in the lead. I think John's in front." Hope glanced at Rebecca, who remained with her back to the race, forsaking the outcome to stare down the road to Miles City. Behind the carriage, a dozen soldiers from K Company stationed in Forsythe rode in columns of two and headed straight for the agency office. There was nothing unusual about such an event. Troops were continually passing through the reservation. But the carriage demanded attention. It belonged to Tyrell Gude, the Bureau of Indian Affairs' agent for the reservation. The column angled past the aspens where Zachariah and his companions held rude court. They could see what Rebecca now noticed, that Agent Gude had a companion seated beside him on the carriage seat, a very pretty young woman dressed in a long gray woolen skirt and jacket, her black hair gathered in a bun at the back of her neck. Though they rode in sunlight, the young woman seemed bathed in shadow.

Rebecca realized with a start that the woman in gray was Indian. Now the magic worked, the awareness Rebecca had inherited from Star. Her flesh grew cold as the soldiers angled off to either side of the crowd, who were oblivious of their presence. All eyes were fixed on the race save those of the medicine woman, who saw not only with her eyes but her spirit as well. The procession halted to allow the race its completion. Rebecca ignored Hope's exhortations, ignored the pandemonium as Cheyenne and soldiers and cowhands cheered on their favorites. The earth trembled with the riders' wild approach, each man galloping at breakneck speed. But Rebecca took a step toward the carriage, drawn onward by a sense of destiny, a link with this stranger. Tyrell Gude noticed Rebecca and waved to her. The Indian agent was a rarity among his kind. The short, rotund, bald little man also happened to be honest. He dabbed at his sweat-shiny skull and wiped his kerchief beneath his double chin. The horses smelled of sweat, the carriage of leather and dust. Gude stood in the carriage as the horsemen crossed the finish line to a mixture of cheers and groans. The Indian agent's cheeks were red with sunburn.

"Well done," Gude shouted, slapping a soft fist into his cupped hand. "I knew John Timber's horse was the fastest on the res." Rebecca drew closer to study the young woman, who appeared uncomfortable beneath such scrutiny. Gude noticed Rebecca's interest and nervously cleared his throat. He had hoped to avoid a confrontation. "Father Hillary promised the race would be later in the day." Gude sighed, hoping to ease any tension. "I suppose even a priest can be allowed to stretch the truth from time to time."

"I am sorry if I ruined your celebration," the woman beside him replied. She looked to be in her early twenties. Her skin was as dark as Rebecca's but her eyes were a piercing sky blue set in delicate fragile features, a gently upturned nose, high cheekbones, a slim-bodied, willowy frame that stiffened in her white woman's trappings. She carried herself with an authority

217

that belied her appearance. *The face so familiar, no, it could not be.* . . .

"Ruined? Hardly. Can't help train schedules. Anyway, the company of a beautiful young woman is nothing an old man like me ever regrets," Tyrell Gude exclaimed. He climbed down from the carriage and handed the reins to the young woman, then swung about to greet Rebecca.

"Why, Rebecca, how fine you look today. Wonderful day, simply wonderful. Ahh. I have been thinking of nothing but that chokecherry pudding all the way in from Forsythe. Our nation's birthday. Grand thing. Grand thing." He turned to wave to a blond-haired officer, who saluted in return. "Thank you, Captain Morbitzer."

"My pleasure, sir," the officer replied. He ducked forward so as to present himself to the woman in the carriage. "Allow me to escort you to your house, ma'am."

"Thank you, Captain," the woman said.

"Henry, ma'am. Please call me Henry." The captain walked his horse in a tight circle and gave his orders to his sergeant, who in turn bellowed them to the troopers. The soldiers of K Company broke ranks and walked their mounts across the street, each man making his way through the crowd as best he could and more than one passing a food table and requisitioning a platter of ribs or a mug of beer as he passed.

The woman in the carriage looked over at Rebecca. Tyrell Gude, ever alert to the proprieties, stepped up to the two women.

"Your pardon, Rebecca, I plumb forgot my manners. You two ought to have a great deal in common, at least in spirit. Katherine, this is Rebecca Blue Thrush. She is a medicine woman. And all these poor people have had to rely on the past years except for an occasional visit by the surgeon over at the post in Fort Keogh. Things will be a lot better now for all of us. Rebecca . . . the agency has sent us a doctor. In fact the way I heard it, Miss Madison pulled some strings to get here. She's Cheyenne too—think of it, Cheyenne!—and a doctor.

Rebecca, this is Katherine Madison, come all the way from back East."

"Rebecca Blue Thrush . . ." repeated Kate. "Why . . . you knew my mother. She often spoke—"

Rebecca spun around and darted off into the crowd. Only now, noticing Rebecca's flight, did they turn to stare with curiosity at the stranger in their midst, at this Indian dressed as a grand white woman. Kate, her words left hanging, looked down at her outstretched empty hand.

"Medicine woman . . . madwoman if you ask me," Henry Morbitzer said in an imperial tone of voice. "Don't worry, Miss Madison, I am told these medicine makers are a trifle odd is all. That one's obviously been sifting through bones too much and talking to the wind. And I daresay folks about have need of something more than her witchcraft."

"I hope so," Kate replied in a worried tone.

"Will someone tell me who won?" Joshua asked, still sitting on the top step of the porch in front of the church. Father Lee Hillary had left to present the twenty-five-dollar purse to John Timber, the husband of Hope Moon Basket. Only Michael remained on the porch and to his nephew Joshua directed himself. He reached out in hopes of catching hold of Michael's trouser leg, but Rebecca's son had crossed over to the railing and was standing just beyond the blind man's grasp. "Who won? Who won? *Saaaavaaaaheeeey*. Answer me. Does Lone Bull owe me money? Am I abandoned? Father Hillary, Nephew . . . who won?"

"Beautiful . . ." Michael said softly. Standing above the crowd, he had a clear field of vision as he studied the woman in the carriage. The news had spread through the crowd. This woman was part Cheyenne. And a doctor. A real doctor. Michael smiled, a wicked light in his eyes. Suddenly he had a use for doctors. Especially pretty ones.

"Who? Who?" Joshua slapped his hands on his bony

knees and then doubled his fists and shook them in the air. *"Who!"* But unfortunately for Uncle Joshua, a horse race had suddenly become the farthest thing from Michael Spirit Wolf's mind.

14

Captain Henry Morbitzer pulled the cover sheet off the last article of furniture in the parlor while Kate Madison finished inspecting the house. Everything was just as Tyrell Gude had described it to her during the three-day ride from Miles City. This had been Tyrell Gude's house. He had lived here with his wife for the better part of a year. Then after his wife took sick and died, Gude had moved over into the more austere bachelor quarters at the agency. A parlor and dining room and kitchen downstairs, and two bedrooms upstairs, and every inch haunted by memories of the woman he had loved, the woman who had kept house for him, been friend and lover for twenty-one years. Kate emerged from the stairway and glanced down the hallway toward the back door. She had left it open to clear out the stuffiness. She walked back into the parlor, and smiling at the captain, continued on to the spacious, sunlit dining room, which ran almost the length of the house. Mrs. Gude had liked to entertain and loved dancing. Move the dining table out and arrange the chairs along the wall and the space would be ideal for physical assessments and surgery. The extra bedroom upstairs

221

could be used for patients needing intensive care and hospitalization. Yes, the house would do nicely as a clinic. The front door banged open and a Cheyenne man in his early twenties entered staggering under the weight of both her trunks. He was a brawny fellow, handsome in a rough-hewn sort of way. Certainly nothing like the men she had known back East. The Cheyenne stumbled and dropped one of her trunks, thankfully not the one with her medical instruments and the supplies she had purchased from a pharmacy in St. Louis. However, several of her personal items spilled from her dropped trunk and Henry Morbitzer scowled as he came to the rescue.

"You clumsy oaf," the officer muttered, righting the trunk. The lid hung ajar on its broken leather latch. Michael Spirit Wolf gingerly set the other trunk down in the middle of the floor and removed his gray broad-brimmed hat and lowered his head in an attitude of subservience.

"Sorry, Miss . . ."

"And a knock would have been proper," Morbitzer added.

"Then he would have dropped both trunks," said Kate. She turned to Michael. "No harm done. Dresses can't break. Thank you." She held out her hand. "I am Dr. Katherine Madison." A second fusillade of fireworks erupted in the street, followed by a howl of approval from the crowd.

"Excuse me, Captain, but Agent Gude sent me to tell you he needs to see you. Over in the agency building, his office there." Michael smiled and his eyes were innocent, his shoulders slightly bowed forward.

"Blast it all," Morbitzer exclaimed, and slapped his hat against his trouser leg. Then he shrugged. After all, he was in charge of the government's military command on this reservation and the responsibility of rank was ever a burden willingly accepted. "Well then, come along. I beg your pardon, Kate . . . may I call you Kate . . . I intend for us to be friends. Good friends. If you ever need me in any way, just come right on over to the camp. You can count on my support."

"I am sure I can," Kate replied, removing her hat and dabbing her upper lip with a silk kerchief.

"Come along," the captain said, directing his command to Michael.

"Agent Gude sent for you. Not me."

"See here, whoever you are . . ."

"I am Michael Spirit Wolf."

"Oh . . . Well, I have heard of you. A troublemaker according to the briefing I received at Fort Keogh. Your father, Panther Burn, was a notorious troublemaker too."

"He was a warrior chief, the last to surrender. He has killed many soldiers in battle. Yes, Captain Morbitzer . . . you could call him a troublemaker. He has turned many boy-soldiers into men."

Morbitzer reddened. "Just what the devil do you mean by that."

"Captain Morbitzer, I believe Mr. Gude is waiting," Kate said, hoping to defuse an increasingly uncomfortable situation. Henry Morbitzer glanced toward the front door. "Quite so. But I don't like leaving you . . ."

"I am certain Mr. Spirit Wolf means me no harm."

"I hurt my arm," Michael said. "That why I dropped the trunk." He started rolling up his shirt sleeve. "Maybe you will take a look."

Captain Morbitzer knew when he had lost a skirmish. After all, she was a doctor. He nodded and headed toward the door, withdrawing as gracefully as possible. "We'll talk later," he said, donning his hat and bowing to Kate. "Until then." He stepped out into the noise of celebration, the aroma of pies and meat broiling, into the heat of the day and the reservation dust that had discolored his once immaculate blue uniform.

Michael walked across the room and took a seat on the newly uncovered couch. The cushions were too soft for him, and like the whole house, needed airing. Kate followed him to the couch. Michael gingerly lifted his arm for inspection. A subtle grin brightened his features as Kate leaned over, close enough for him to catch the scent of perfume and sweat. "It hurts real bad," he said, as his eyes ranged approvingly over her long neck and to her wine-red lips. Kate placed a hand on his arm and he groaned and scooted across the couch to be closer to her. She frowned, muttered something beneath her breath, and then crossed back to a black leather bag and removed a wicked-looking bone saw; its jagged metal teeth gleamed in the shadows as if it possessed a malevolent life of its own.

"I am afraid it will have to come off," she solemnly said. "I haven't unpacked the opium yet but I do have a drop of sherry if that will help, although I am afraid the amputation will hurt like hell." The woman doctor advanced on Michael, whose eyes widened in disbelief at first. As Kate bore down on him, he looked with actual panic from the saw to his arm and back to the dreadful apparatus used for shredding flesh and bone. "Just rest your elbow on the back of the couch and hold on. I can have it off and the stump cauterized in a matter of minutes."

Michael jumped off the couch. "Wait!" He tripped over the end table and fell sprawling. Kate loosed a hearty laugh and stared down at the young rancher who lay flat on his back.

"What a fine physician I am. See, your arm is healed already." She tossed the saw aside and placed her hands on her hips. "I hope you have learned your lesson, Michael Spirit Wolf."

"Oh," Michael groaned. He tried to prop himself up but fell against the wall and cradled his right wrist. "Oh . . ." His features were bunched in pain. Kate's expression changed from one of triumph to concern. She crossed over and knelt by him. He *had* taken a nasty fall. It appeared her prank had backfired.

"Let me examine your wrist. You may have a fracture. How foolish of you. That's what you get for carrying on so. I—" Suddenly the wounded wing came to life and closed around her shoulders and drew her into his kiss. She was the dove snared by the hawk, too surprised to struggle at first and lost to this bird of prey, though pride would teach her to strive against his strength. His kiss was hard and fierce and filled her with streams of fire coursing all the way to her heart. Then, just as she began to struggle, he freed her, as if Michael wanted the kiss to end on his terms. Kate staggered to her feet and backed away, nearly losing her balance as her heel caught on the hem of her charcoal-gray dress. She steadied herself, wiped the perspiration from her forehead. "How dare you?" she said.

"You are very beautiful. So . . ."—he shrugged—"it was the easiest decision I ever had to make," Michael said. He got to his feet. She backed away from him. "Tell me you have been kissed like that before. I haven't. A little bird told me you were Cheyenne. I wanted to find out for myself. You are."

"I am half Cheyenne," Kate blurted out. She was used to being in control. After all, she was a physician. Now she was at a loss and didn't like it.

"Cheyenne is Cheyenne, part or whole. Didn't you learn that among the whites?" He saw his words had struck home.

"Don't ever . . ." she said, and flustered, lost her train of thought.

He cut her off. "Maybe the next time you will come to me on your own."

"There won't be a next time," Kate said. She wondered if she sounded as uncertain as she felt. Judging by the conceited grin on his face, she most certainly did. He clambered to his feet and patted the creases out of his jeans. "I think you had better leave," she added. He nodded, placed his hat on his head, then something among the clothes in her trunk caught his eye and he reached down and picked up a Beadle dime novel. Kate took a step forward on reflex, but it was too late. Michael began to real aloud.

" 'Guns on the Graybull—being an account of the pursuit and capture of Panther Burn, notorious war chief of the Northern Cheyenne, the bloodthirsty Butcher

of Castle Rock. The innocent avenged, justice at last.' "
Michael glanced up at Kate, who blushed and folded
her hands in front of her.

"I wanted to learn as much as I could about the place
and the people I was coming to serve," the physician
defensively said. She held out her hand but Michael
ignored her and stared down at the book.

"So you have read this?" he asked. She nodded.
"Does it tell of how the village of Simon White Bull was
attacked by the militia from Castle Rock and almost all
my mother's people, men, women, and children,
murdered? Does it tell of how my father surrendered
because he could not bear to see his people starve, of
how he entered the camp of General Miles under a flag
of truce to negotiate terms for his followers, and was
arrested, chained like a mad dog, and shipped off to
prison in Kansas?" Michael dropped the dime novel
onto the folded clothes. He noticed other penny
dreadfuls, exploits of Indian fighters and Indian chiefs
and lurid accounts of famous battles and massacres, as
well as tomes about various and sundry lives lived among
the savages. He looked up at Kate.

"Take down your hair, Doctor Kate," Michael said
with a sigh, his temper fading. "And come outside
with the 'savages.' " Michael started toward the door—
spun around and headed for the door at the rear
of the house. "I'd better stay out of sight for a
while," he explained. "Until Captain Morbitzer cools
off."

"I don't understand. He wasn't angry when he left to
meet with Agent Gude. Unless you lied about Tyrell
wanting to see him." She sucked in her breath at the
realization and stared at his already departing figure
and then shook her head in disbelief. There had never
been anyone like *him* at medical school. She touched
her lips, for the warmth of his kiss lingered. There had
never been anyone like him . . . anywhere.

*   *   *

Unpacking was the hardest part of settling into her new home, not for the work but for the memories. After the dresses and high-topped shoes, after the tins and bottles of medicines, Kate carefully unwrapped a photograph mounted in a silver frame from its oilcloth package and cleared a space for it over the mantel among the pewter mugs and china plates Corinthia Gude had so laboriously collected. The photograph was of a small-statured delicate Cheyenne woman dressed in what appeared to be a black skirt (Kate remembered it was dark brown, the color of chocolate) and a white silk blouse with tiny pearl buttons that fastened from the waist to the throat. The girl, eight-year-old Katherine, was as dark as her mother and she wore a white flowery dress and white pantaloons and high-buttoned black shoes. Mother and child were standing in front of a flat painted to look like the entrance to a magnificent garden, though unfortunately, the sky had been torn and covered with sailcloth, ruining the illusion. Sunlight streamed through the western windows and a single golden beam fell across the photograph. She had strewn the contents of the trunks about the house, some in their proper places, others simply stacked upon the nearest available chair or table in her haste to find the picture of her mother. The photograph had been tucked safely away in the center of the clothes trunk, protected by woolen dresses and waistcoats. Music from a trio of fiddlers drifted in through the open windows. Kate began to hum along with their merry melody. A knock sounded at the door and Kate steeled herself, for she expected the return of an irate Captain Henry Morbitzer. She opened the door, blinked in disbelief, and finally stood aside as three Cheyenne children stepped into her living room, the oldest a boy of seven with dirty cheeks. A girl not more than five and another girl, just a toddler, held hands and waited just inside the room. The noise of celebration drifted in through the doorway, flowing over the children and filling the parlor.

"We come to visit you," the boy announced. The five-year-old nodded in accord and the toddler simply stared wide-eyed. The girls wore homespun dresses, the boy seemed lost in a pair of baggy Levi's with the cuffs rolled up to form a thick band of denim around his ankle.

"Won't you sit down," Kate invited. The three walked over to the couch and sat down and looked at her. And said nothing. Just sat, watching and waiting.

"Well . . ." Kate began lamely, searching for a topic. She clasped her hands, sat in a cushioned easy chair opposite them. "Well . . . how nice." She told them her name. She told them she was a doctor. The children giggled and laughed and continued to study her. Kate asked them their names and they told her . . . Jonah Yellow Leg and Susan and Sara Pretty on Top. Sara was the youngest. They offered nothing further than their names. They sat and they smiled and continued to giggle nervously from time to time. And then Kate remembered the peppermints she had bought from a general store in Miles City. She dropped a couple into each child's outstretched hand. The children, contentedly munching their gifts, promptly concluded their visit. The three left, telling her good-bye. When Kate invited them to come and see her again, the children laughed among themselves as if sharing some private joke that only a child could understand, most certainly not an adult. Kate smiled and watched the children scamper off and then lifted her gaze to the couples dancing on the platform by the agency, and she thought she spied Michael Spirit Wolf. For a moment she felt drawn toward the dancers. But necessity won out over desire; she had too much to do, too much settling in yet. In truth, she was afraid. After all, she was a stranger. A priest looking like a great raven flapping his broad black wings strode into the center of the platform, waving his arms and shouting that the wrestlers were gathered at the lodgepole near Camp Merritt. Kate closed the door as the dancers hurried off the platform, following the fiddlers who had bolted from their stage, instruments in hand. Kate had no

interest in wrestlers. She returned to the mantel and
the photograph.

"I'm here, Mother. As you wanted. As I wanted
too. . . . At least I think so." Yet, who had planted the
seed of her yearning? "Whose idea, Mother? Yours or
mine alone?" Alone. Kate had always been alone except
for Esther. Alone as a child. Alone as a young woman,
although blessed with an education. She closed her
eyes and tried to picture her mother alive. But all she
re-created was a headstone rising out of the Pennsylvania countryside, a burial plot in the rich farmland near
Haverford, the Madison ancestral home. A month ago
seemed like a century now. Yet only a month. It had
been the last day for Kate and she had come to say good-
bye. . . .

Esther Madison
b. 1846 d. March 9, 1889
Forgive

Through lazy days of golden sunshine and gentle
silvery showers, the land grew lush with the blossoms
of spring. Green buds thrust through their blankets of
earth, yawning tendrils awakening from winter's sleep.
The landscape was a tapestry of rebirth promising a
summer of abundance, of flourishing crops, the earthly
riches to be won from the land. Nowhere was the
advent of summer more evident than among the crop-
lands and meadows of the Madison farm. Five miles out
from Haverford, a bustling village of pristine cottages
and well-stocked stores, of whitewashed fences and sober freshly painted Congregational churches, simple
and direct in appointment, much like the residents of
the area themselves. Sam Madison's forebears had settled here, ten miles from Philadelphia, back in the
days when the Delaware and Algonquin carried out
their raids. Madisons had fought and died to keep the
land they claimed as their own. Madison iron had armed
the Continental Army in exchange for vast acreage grants
up in the Piedmont country, Madison iron had cast

cannon in the War of 1812, and Madison forges in Philadelphia had helped to arm the Grand Army of the Union during the Civil War. Sam Madison could count the fourth President of the United States among the branches of his illustrious family tree.

Kate had learned the lineage of her father's people by heart. Learned and forgotten now, or at least was determined to forget. She was twenty-three years old, no longer a half-breed girl growing up in a household of wealth where even servants looked upon her as more of a curiosity than the daughter of Samuel Madison. None of it mattered now.

Kate saw herself leaning to run her fingers along the letters etched in granite. Her lips silently formed her mother's name. In the room, in her mind, the name that was conspicuously absent from the headstone . . . Esther *Bird Hat* Madison. Now a breeze set the branches of a nearby willow atremble and ruffled the hem of her skirt, where she stood at her mother's grave as her memories reenacted the past. . . .

"Mother . . ." Kate knelt to touch the mounded earth. Images . . . memories . . . of her mother's tender voice, of her mother's hidden pain, of guilt, of hatred and love, the mixture of emotions that had bound her to her husband and yet separated them in the same house. Esther Madison had learned of the massacre at the Warbonnet from an Eastern newspaper, hard, bitter reading that had sealed her fate. She could never go back now. Her people were gone—murdered. And worse, it might have been prevented. Sam should have tried, no matter the risk. Family . . . friends . . . all dead. Later she had read that some of the Southern Cheyenne had survived and joined the Northern Cheyenne and a war chief by the name of Panther Burn in a raid upon the town of Castle Rock, an occurrence that sadly seemed to silence any public outcry concerning the destruction of Simon White Bull's peaceful village. That same winter Kate had been born. And while Sam slowly abandoned his ministerial calling for the duties of his family's business, Esther undertook the rearing of their daughter. Sam's Cheyenne bride changed, became bitter and increasingly morose. Meanwhile Sam found himself continually preoccupied with his father's legacy. The ironworks needed new contracts and Sam resolved to get them. That involved repeated visits to Washington. Then the shipping interests needed attention, not to mention a variety of land speculations in South America. Life in the nation's capital and in Philadelphia where the Madisons kept a town house was furious-paced and impossible for Esther to fathom. Overwhelmed by her husband's world, Esther retreated to the ancestral farm near Haverford and concerned herself with her daughter's education, arranging for tutors to visit from Philadelphia. Esther was determined to see to it that Kate had the skills to survive in a world utterly alien to the Cheyenne. Kate endured her isolation. And as she matured, she begged her mother for stories of Esther's past and of the Cheyenne way. In her aloneness, Kate began finally to feel a sense of belonging. A bright, well-read young woman, she left home at nineteen to enter the School of Medicine at Syracuse. That she was the only woman in her class, and part Indian at that, mattered little to Kate Madison. Her father's name and prestige smoothed her entry. But a keen mind coupled with plain old-fashioned stubbornness helped her through the rigorous three years of training. Now she had come to say good-bye, knowing in her heart it was forever. A shadow fell across the grave. Poor Mother. Pennsylvania had finished the task Jubal Bragg had begun twenty-three years before. Another Cheyenne was dead.

"Father is expecting me to meet him in New York," Kate said. "He has secured a teaching position for me at the Women's School of Medicine. I think he takes personal pleasure in guiding my success. Maybe it helps him sleep at night." Kate glanced around at the horse and carriage tethered by the wrought-iron fence that bordered the family cemetery plot. So many Madisons buried here. Did they care that an Indian lay among them? "Forgive me, Mother, but I can't hate Father. I know you wanted me to, but I cannot. But neither can I live with him. You made me a stranger as much as the color of my skin ever did. You left me hungry for more than the lonely world of Samuel Madison." She lifted her eyes to the elegant spacious farmhouse but a hundred yards away and imagined the servants watching her from the windows, trying to guess her intentions. Oh, they knew she was leaving, but to go where? New York, to be with Mr. Samuel, the cook might say and the upstairs maid agree. *No . . . not New York.* "Good-bye, Mother. Sleep well."

Images melted like snow in May. Reflections of the past became a still life, a single picture, yesterday merged with today. She leaned forward and kissed her fingertips and placed them against the image of Esther Bird Hat Madison. *Sleep well.* By now Samuel Madison probably knew the whereabouts of his daughter, but what would he do? She had not joined him in New York, but fled westward from his wealth and position, from loneliness itself, to Montana, to this reservation, to the people of the Morning Star.

Her people now . . . she hoped.

15

Michael stood on the edge of his garden and examined with pride the long green stalks of corn. Arrayed like soldiers on parade, he thought, then frowned, remembering soldiers, his father in battle. It had been years ago but Michael could still see Panther Burn leading his Dog Soldiers through the ranks of a company of troopers he had ambushed out among the badlands. He could still hear the clamor of battle as the blue-coats panicked and tried to fight their way out of the Cheyenne encirclement. Panther Burn dared their bullets and led his men in wave after wave that crushed the soldiers' resistance. The war chief took no prisoners but fought to the death. And when the last trooper fell, spitted on Zachariah's war lance, then the silence returned. Panther Burn wheeled his horse among the corpses and rode back to where the women and children watched from a ridge. Michael remembered how his father's arms were soaked to the elbows with blood. Oh, how the women had cheered his victory, yet Panther Burn seemed unmoved. Rebecca guided her son to his father. The stench of death clung to the air.

"You have done well, my husband. Again you have saved your people."

"There will be more soldiers, always more. As numberless as raindrops," Panther Burn said. "We have won today but in the days to come . . ." The war chief sighed. The dead Cheyenne were irreplaceable.

"If we cannot win, why fight?" Michael blurted out loud. The sound of his own voice brought him back to the present. He stared at the stalks of corn and glanced around, embarrassed. Yet he had said the same thing then, a mere slip of a boy speaking out of turn and enduring the withering look of his father. Now, as then, Michael's question remained unanswered. He shaded his eyes and studied the rolling thunderheads springing up in the west. Michael tested a single ear with his fingertips, reaching in among the husk's gossamer strands to feel the hard golden kernels. He glanced at his mother on her knees among the tomato plants. She was dutifully lining the bottom of a basket with orange-red fruits.

"If we get some of that rain the corn will ripen early. Though I staggered the planting, it looks as if it all will make at the same time," Michael called to her. "And all need to be picked at once."

"If the rain comes this far," Rebecca said. She plucked the last tomatoes; the rest were green and she preferred to have them ripening on the vine. She hoisted the basket under her arm and started toward the house, ignoring the squash and cucumbers and peppers that needed harvesting right at her feet. Michael wagged his head in dismay. He left the garden and caught up to his mother and grabbed the basket out of her hands.

"I'll finish," he said. She looked around and realized what she had left.

"No, you tend to the cattle," she said. "And I the garden. I wasn't thinking."

"Oh yes, you were," Michael replied. "Of her."

"*Saaaa!* What are you saying?" Rebecca snatched the basket out of his hands and started back to the garden.

"I am saying the daughter of Esther Bird Hat, your

friend of long ago." Michael fell into step with her. Kate had been on his mind too, though in an entirely different way. She knew it and said nothing. Rebecca continued on to the garden and began again to fill the vegetable basket in a determined effort to keep from discussing the matter further. Her feelings were her own and she wanted to keep it that way. She was perturbed that her son did not share her animosity toward the new doctor on the reservation. He was blind to the machinations of the Bureau of Indian Affairs, how the *ve-ho-e* were determined to destroy the sacred beliefs, determined to shatter the Great Circle. She closed her eyes and placed her hand on the warm dirt and solemnly, silently prayed, "Not while I live. Not while I live." She lifted her heart not to Jay-ho-vah, the white man's God, but to *Ma-heo-o*, the All-Father of the Morning Star people, for he would hear her words and understand.

The jingle of reins and the drum of hoofbeats on the road out from Lame Deer alerted Rebecca and Michael, who had just saddled his horse. Rebecca's prayer faded from her mind as she recognized the carriage belonging to Kate Madison rolling toward them at a crisp pace. Michael led his roan gelding out of the corral, swung into the saddle, and waited by the gate as the carriage continued toward them, leaving a spiral of dust in its wake. Kate guided the mare off the road and toward the ranch house. She seemed a bit surprised at finding Michael and his mother, and with a sharp tug on the reins brought the mare to a stop a few feet from the man by the corral. Michael lowered his head until the dust drifted past.

"Good morning," he called. When he raised his head Kate noticed a nasty bruise just below his left eye.

"You're hurt," she said.

"James Broken Knife doesn't wrestle fair," Michael replied with a wry grin. He reached in his back pocket and brought out a roll of bills, fifty dollars in all. "Then again, neither do I."

"Sergeant Broken Knife has a broken nose," Kate

said. "One of his tribal policemen summoned me over to their headquarters last night. I had to cauterize it to stop the blood."

"I hope you didn't come all the way out here to tell me about a nose." Michael moved closer to the carriage. His shirt was unbuttoned to the waist and a bead of sweat rolled down from his neck and left a glistening path across his hard coppery flesh all the way to his stomach. He noticed her gaze left him to study the neatly arranged yard, the rough-hewn but well-constructed ranch house and outbuildings.

"You expected the son of the Butcher of Castle Rock to live in a buffalo-hide shelter and eat raw dog."

"Maybe," Kate said. "I suppose I did." Michael nodded. He liked her honesty. He leaned in under the shade of the folding top.

"Well, I expected the doctor to be an old man with a long white beard. Not someone like you," Michael said with a mischievous gleam in his eyes.

"I am trying to visit as many families as I can, to let them know who I am and why I am here," Kate said. She spied Rebecca on her knees in the garden. "But then, as you both seem to know me, I had better be on my way."

"The reservation is a big place. Not every house is as easy to find. You ought to have a guide with you. Someone who really knows the area. Many families have made their homes well off the road and are not so easy to find as we are."

"And where would I find such a guide?"

"I am at your service," Michael said with a sweep of his hat and a gracious bow.

"I thought so," Kate said, smiling despite herself.

"And not just a guide. Think of me as protection as well."

"From what?"

"Wild Indians."

Kate pursed her lips, reflected for a moment on his proposition. She wondered if he was daring her to accept, sensed he was. She could use his knowledge.

And as for the dare, she did not doubt in the slightest her ability to handle herself in any situation. "Very well."

"I'll saddle a horse for you," Michael said. He started back into the corral, then stopped. "There are some places a buggy won't go. As I said, well off the road and back in the hills toward the Divide."

"The Divide?"

"You'll see. And then you'll understand." Michael paused a moment and searched in his saddlebags. He brought out a pair of faded dungarees. "The dress won't do. Change in the house."

"Now, see here . . ." Kate started to protest.

"You won't look any stranger than you do right now. And you cannot ride in that dress." Michael left her there by the gate. Kate tried to think of a better protest, but nothing came to mind. The problem was, he made sense. So she shrugged. Her woolen gray dress would have to go.

Kate tethered the mare to the corral fence and walked across the dusty yard to the ranch house. She paused by the picket fence where the bitterroot bloomed and called toward the garden, "Good morning, Rebecca."

Rebecca did not answer. She had seen her son all but fall over himself for this "white" Cheyenne. Well, Rebecca Blue Thrush would put such a one in her place. She ignored Kate, who continued around the house to the garden.

"I said—"

"I heard you," Rebecca snapped.

"What is the matter with you? I have only come here to help."

"You come to destroy. But maybe," Rebecca's voice deepened in tone, becoming ominous, ". . . maybe I will not let you."

"Once my mother was your closest friend." Kate remembered conversations of long ago. "It is as my mother knew it would be. You blame my mother and father for what happened on the Warbonnet."

"No. For not trying to stop it. I will talk no more.

Except this: it were better if Esther Bird Hat had died with the rest of her people."

"What makes you think she didn't?" Kate retorted, bridling at the older woman's accusations. "I buried my mother this spring. But I tell you this. Her heart was buried long ago."

Kate spun on her heels and started back to the house. She wiped the moisture from her eyes and cursed her weakness. No one but Esther had ever seen her cry, and she resolved no one would now. Tears were for the weak. Kate climbed the steps to the dogtrot and stepped into the cool interior of what she took to be a living room. Hand-woven blankets, parfleche war shields, and tanned hides brightly painted with depictions of Indian villages and braves in battle were hung from the walls. Sturdy-looking hand-built chairs and a broad oaken table and—to her surprise—bookshelves filled the room. She recognized several titles on closer examination, Gibbon's *Decline and Fall of the Roman Empire*, Blackstone's *Commentaries*, *The Collected Works of Shakespeare*. Many of the books wre battered and worn, their spines crinkled and titles obscured. But she had seen enough to cause her to reevaluate her opinion of Michael Spirit Wolf. She checked the window and saw Rebecca standing near the barn.

Kate took a deep breath and willed herself to be calm. *Rebecca Blue Thrush . . . I am here to stay. I refuse to let you drive me off. This is my home and these my people, no matter what you say. I am here to stay.* Her eyes were dry now, her composure returned. She began to change clothes. Time was wasting and she wanted to meet as many of her people as possible. Not that her feelings were wholly samaritan. She was intrigued by Michael. And a little frightened of him . . . or perhaps frightened of herself.

"My prizes."

"Oh." Kate jumped, turned around. Her shadow fell across the rows of books neatly sandwiched between the shelves. Michael stepped into the room as she finished buttoning her shirt.

"You have found me out, Doctor Kate," Michael gently chided. He walked past her to the bookshelves, placed his hand upon the creased spines.

" 'That time of year thou mayst in me behold/ When yellow leaves, or none, or few, do hang/ Upon those boughs which shake against the cold,/ Bare ruined choirs, where late the sweet birds sang.' " He turned to look at her, the distance softening between them. He sighed, shrugged. "Not bad for an ignorant Indian." He had committed the Shakespearean sonnet to memory.

"I never implied anything of the sort," Kate replied, angered at what she read behind his words. "Maybe I will find my way alone, after all." She started toward the door.

"You and I are much alike, Kate," Michael said in a soothing tone. "We are used to doing alone. Even among our people, we are, in a way, alone." He drew close to her. The smell of earth and honest toil clung to him. He seemed to her incapable of subterfuge. And she would not lie.

"You read me like one of your books. You must have had a great deal of practice," Kate said. Michael leaned upon the doorsill. The muscles rippled along his forearm.

"Books," he said. "Such a thing, to put thoughts, and feelings, the heart, yes, down on paper for all to read. And to understand. To laugh as I laugh, pray as I pray, weep as I weep." His brown eyes took on a faraway look and sunlight washed over his clean direct features. His breath warmed her cheek like a kiss. "One day I will try, when my heart can no longer hold what it feels." Kate moved toward him as if drawn to his warmth. And as quickly, Michael broke the moment, sensing Rebecca watching from the barn's interior. He stepped through the doorway and onto the porch.

"I have saddled the bay for you, it is docile as a kitten. Come and I will show you the lands of Morning Star."

Kate wondered if she was being toyed with, suspected

as much. But she followed anyway, unaware of the stirrings in her heart that overruled propriety and, in truth, left her no choice.

"What do you think of it?" Michael reined his roan gelding to a halt on the edge of an outcropping of pink granite and looked back at Kate to see if she would follow him onto the precipitous overhang. Kate had ridden often while growing up on the Madison farm. But the rolling countryside around Haverford was no match for the winding deer trails, the switchback path that climbed sheer walls, the steep ascents through slopes so choked with timber she almost swooned from the claustrophobic effect, only to be dazzled as the forest suddenly cleared, revealing vista after vista. But she was game if anything and proud enough not to let Michael Spirit Wolf best her. She urged her bay forward. "The Divide," Michael said with a grand sweep of his arm as the sun broke from behind a cloud to bathe them in its golden light. More than a thousand feet above the rolling hillsides just to the west around Lame Deer, the cool air defied the warmth of afternoon's golden embrace. Peak after rugged peak formed an unbroken chain north to south as far as Kate could see, a stretch of jagged wilderness sixty miles long and fifteen wide that cut the reservation in half. It was a high and lonesome place, a place primeval, that left her awed. Its beauty lifted the gloom from her heart, for the morning had been one of awkward introductions to families who stared at her as if she had come from another world and listened politely if skeptically as she explained she was a healer. Names ran together in her mind, Buster Long Wing and his family of eight, Adam Red Dancer and his young pregnant wife, and Tobias Buffalo Head's children whom she had amazed with the anatomy chart that she had thought to roll up and place in her black bag. She had lanced a sore and dabbed it with iodine for Mrs. Buffalo Head—Kate had forgotten the woman's first name. Others too, all had listened and stared as if amused by some secret joke. She doubted if anyone outside of the community around Lame Deer would ever seek her out. As she watched the shadows shift and re-form upon the mountains, she followed from her vantage point the progress of a distant thunderstorm as it drifted down the narrow valley. Lightning stabbed earthward and a ponderosa pine split apart and ten seconds later the sound reached them, while above them against the cloud-bedecked sky a hawk seemed suspended in space as if it too had glimpsed for just a moment its place in nature's wondrous scheme. The problems of a country doctor, even a woman country doctor trying to make a place for herself, became minute before such grandeur, before life's unspoken meaning. Stillness, distant violent beauty, staggered sounds and more quiet, a herd of whitetail deer pausing—oh, she had just spied them—it was as if the world were a still life, Kate and Michael were held bound by the plan of God: the wind, still caught among the branches of the pines, the doves hesitating in their full-throated call. For an instant, time stood still, then life returned with the rolling thunder from far off. The hawk soared out of sight.

"We notice what we are," Michael whispered, "and break free."

16

⌒⌒

"Three weeks," said Rebecca Blue Thrush. She slammed a blue metal coffeepot down on the kitchen table for emphasis. Michael scooted back in his chair to keep from being splashed by the scalding-hot liquid. "Three weeks that you ignore your work. The barn roof leaks. The cow may calf any day. And still you disgrace me by leaving for Lame Deer to see the half-breed doctor."

Michael slid over to his plate once more. He rested his forearms on the table, sighed, and shook his head. "I promised Father Hillary I would help him build benches today for the church. He has worked with me often enough."

"White man's church. White man's God. Once I too followed the way of Jay-ho-vah. Reverend Sam Madison spoke of how we were all brothers, that with the God of the white man we could live in peace." Rebecca brought an iron skillet over to the table and ladled out half a dozen rashers of thick-sliced bacon for her son. "Peace," she contemptuously repeated. She placed the sizzling strips of meat atop a two-inch-thick slab of fry bread in the center of Michael's plate and then returned the skillet to the stove. She reached up and opened a shuttered window. A cataract of brilliant gold flooded the kitchen, bathing the Cheyenne woman in its iridescent stream. She lifted her hands to the source of such brilliance and offered silent thanks to the All-Father for the beauty of the morning, for the glory of life. Michael watched. His thoughts were on beauty too, for he had never seen his mother more lovely, with her long hair so black and lustrous in the shimmering light. Dressed in a buckskin smock and calf-high moccasins, in her simplicity she seemed endowed with a grandeur no queen could match. And he knew then why his father had loved her so much, and why he always returned after all the battles, after the long lonely hunts. He always returned.

"I have more memories of you waiting for Father to come back . . ."

"It has ever been so. Panther Burn is a warrior. And I am a warrior's woman." She turned from the window, and forsaking the golden raiment of the sun, resumed a mortal mantle, the garb her longing heart demanded she wear.

"Mother?"

She ignored her son and left the kitchen for the room they used as a parlor. Michael, his appetite gone, shoved the plate of food away and rose from the table. He walked to the doorway and looked in at Rebecca, who stood facing his books.

"Oh, all right. I am going to Lame Deer for more than Father Hillary. I want to see her. Is that so terrible? Have you forgotten the way a heart can sing just by being near one who . . ." Michael shook his head. He was no poet. His education had been a solitary struggle as he worked his way through the books Tyrell Gude had given him, that and the frequently interrupted lessons when Corinthia Gude had been alive. She had taught him to read. But the thirst for knowledge, the yearning to broaden the scope of his experience, was beyond any teacher's power to instill. It could only have come from the All-Father.

Rebecca knew this also. But she found it difficult to

accept. For it meant that her son, like all the other Northern Cheyenne, no longer walked in the way of the Circle. He was lost.

"Nothing I can say will touch your heart . . . will make you hear me."

"Everything you say," Michael replied, "touches me. I am your son."

"Are you? Then do not see this doctor woman again." Rebecca turned and fixed him with her unwavering stare. Michael met her gaze. His eyes were wide, unflinching, and touched with a sorrow, as though he knew he would betray her despite his intentions.

"*Saaaaa-vaaaaa*," Rebecca hissed. She stalked from the room, out onto the porch, down the steps. She walked hard and fast, leaving the house behind her, leaving her ungrateful son. The ground rose gradually, became steeper, required more exertion. She never slowed but left a plume of dust in her wake. And when she gained the top of the hill, only then did she stop, to turn her face to the morning sky where the sun hung like the eye of God, impossible to behold. Yet it mellowed as the minutes passed, and through heaven's ancient alchemy, this amber star bathed Rebecca's face and turned her tears to precious jewels. . . .

Behind the woman on the hill, to the west, a line of thunderheads crept across the Absarokas, the vanguard of a coming storm.

A gust of wind swept into the room, scattering a mound of twigs and frightening off a fieldmouse that scampered across the hardwood floor to cringe behind the iron stove against the north wall. James Broken Knife looked up from his desk where he had been sleeping, bent double, his head upon a short stack of requisition forms he had to complete before morning. A rumble of distant thunder, then a vicious explosion reverberated among the nearby hills. The flame in the oil lamp flickered as if startled. The man in the doorway paled for a second but held himself in check. It was the door opening, not the storm that had roused Sergeant Broken Knife from his slumber. He blinked the sleep out of his eyes, angry at the intruder for having disturbed him and caught him dozing. The man wore a brown wide-brimmed hat and long rain-shiny brown slicker that hid most of his physique. But James sensed an aura of authority about the man. He was a tall, reed-thin individual with his face all but obscured by the upturned collar of his slicker. His hat was pulled low as if to further disguise his identity. The stranger took in the office at a glance. In truth, there wasn't much to see. It was a spacious room, built to accommodate James and his two subordinates, Ezra Yellowhand and Julius Bear, both of whom were home with their families. Behind James's desk a door stood ajar and two cells were faintly visible in the lamplight. A couple of crudely built chairs, a cot that served as a couch when needed, and a square heavy-looking table were set around an iron stove. On the wall behind James, just off to his right, hung a map of the reservation. The map and a risqué sketch of a Barbary Coast prostitute, whose faded likeness had been snipped from a police gazette, were the room's only wall decorations unless one counted the rifle rack on the wall off to the left.

"You have print on your face," the man in the doorway observed. Rain spilled past his boots as the wind continued to gust through the doorway. The tribal policeman placed a knife on the papers before him, to keep the requisition orders from blowing away, then started to make a rude retort, when he noticed the stranger's pale white hands as the man in the doorway stripped off his gloves. The sergeant assumed an attitude of deference out of habit. It was the only way to deal with whites. He never knew what official from Washington might be passing through. Agent Gude had a number of friends in President Harrison's administration, at least that was what everyone said. James bit his tongue, swallowed his pride, and wiped the ink off his cheek. Blue eyes bore into him from under the water-soaked brim of the stranger's hat.

"I want to see the doctor. Which building?"

"You hurt?" James asked.

"Which building?" the stranger repeated. Water dripped from his brown slicker and formed a puddle on the floor that the wind slowly worked into the room.

"White-painted house down the street," James said. Something about the stranger . . . "But she probably ain't in. I heard one of the men at Camp Merritt broke his leg. And she's gone to set it. Some say the boy broke it on purpose just so he could meet her." James waved a hand toward the coffeepot resting on one of the burners of the stove. "You can wait here. Coffee's hot."

"Not now," said the stranger.

"Well"—James shrugged—"suit yourself. If you need me, I am Sergeant—"

"James Broken Knife," the stranger finished in a weary voice. He stepped back out in the lurid glare of the storm. Rain beat down the brim of his hat and battered his long-limbed frame. But in the frantic light, a horse and buggy waited only a few yards from the headquarters door. A sudden shift in the wind's direction sucked the air from the room and slammed the front door shut. James felt the hackles rise on the back of his neck. Who was this late-night visitor? And how did he know James? The tribal policeman stood and stepped around his desk and walked over to the cabinet beneath the gun rack where he kept a jug of home-brewed whiskey bought from the cook at Camp Merritt and a couple of stoneware cups for when he had company. Tonight he ignored the cups and lifted the jug to his lips and downed a burning bellyful of courage.

Lightning flashed, illuminating the shuttered windows of the church and rattling the glass windowpanes. Father Hillary jumped and blessed himself. *Here I am a man of God and still afraid of the thunder*, he chided himself. But then he had never heard thunder so loud, so awesome as here in Lame Deer valley. It sounded as if the soldiers at Camp Merritt had placed cannon on either side of the church and were busily firing round after round into the night. Father Hillary continued on down the aisle between the sections of pews until he reached the front door of the church, where he checked the bolt. It shamed him to lock the door but he knew no other way of keeping the local troublemakers and drunks from vandalizing St. Theresa's. Twice he had confronted the likes of Zachariah Scalpcane and his cronies and ordered them from the premises with threats of passing their names to the soldiers. He did not want to make trouble for them. In fact he pitied Zachariah for his brokenness, a man in the prime of his days but so lost. Father Hillary was loath to add to the man's misery. Neither was he going to let some rowdy burn St. Theresa's to the ground. Oh, what was built by man could be rebuilt by man right enough, but an act of destruction would return martial law to the reservation and bring a resumption of the heavy-handed military policies of bygone years. The tribal police force, for all its faults, was at least a body of Cheyenne enforcing the reservation laws to other Cheyenne. Whereas men like Captain Henry Morbitzer were just itching to play more than a supportive role to James Broken Knife and his men. Standing in the background was no place to win glory. Glory. Father Hillary hated the word. It had caused too much suffering throughout history. It was the drug of heroes and fools. The priest checked the bolt and stood to one side to peer out the window at the street. In a shimmer of light he glimpsed Kate making her way along the rain-spattered boardwalk spanning the churned mud of the street. The folds of her dress lifted as the wind tore at her slicker and lifted the yellow cloth. She stumbled in a puddle. A faintly voiced curse carried on the wind. The priest smiled, not blaming her, and continued to watch as she regained her balance and pressed on to her house. The woman was plucky. She was a survivor, all right. At first, Father Hillary had given her a couple of days at best, but she had fooled him. She not only had lasted into her third week but gave him the impression of having far more strength, maturity, and determination than her youthful beauty indicated.

"Well, it wouldn't be the first time I've been wrong," the priest muttered aloud. Seeing her safely home, Hillary abandoned his vigil and retraced his steps down the aisle and out back of the altar to the two-room apartment at the rear of the church that served as the rectory. A bedroom and kitchen were enough for the Capuchin priest. An oil lamp burned in the kitchen and there by the wooden stove sat Joshua Beartusk and Michael. The old man, in his rocker, creaked back and forth as he waited for his nephew to play. Michael sat on a three-legged stool across from his uncle; a checkerboard on an overturned barrel rested between them. Joshua turned in the direction of the priest, hearing the man's boots scrape on the wood floor.

"I'll check the front door," Joshua said, starting to rise.

"I already did."

"That's my job." Joshua sank back into the rocker.

"I didn't want to interrupt your game." The priest crossed over to the stove, and wrapping a cloth around his hand, poured himself a cup of coffee from the blue metal pot. He winced at a particularly nasty thunderclap.

"Your move," Michael said. The old man reached out and walked his fingers across the checkers on the board. Father Hillary had notched the tops of the red checkers with his pocketknife so Joshua could tell them from the black. Tonight the notched red ones were his. "Your move," Michael repeated, hoping to goad his uncle into a mistake.

"No, yours," Father Hillary said. "I saw Kate on her way home. Looks like she's finished setting that trooper's broken leg over at Camp Merritt." He noticed Michael brighten up considerably. The young brave glanced down at the checkerboard. He was losing by a piece. But then, his mind wasn't on the game. "I'll take over," the priest said.

"Well . . . I suppose it is getting late. And the rain will hound me all the way home as it is."

"Go on. Go on with you. If you're too moon-eyed to keep your uncle company," Joshua complained. "When I was young . . ."

"You got moon-eyed too." Father Hillary chuckled, sliding into Michael's seat. Michael Spirit Wolf looked away, embarrassed.

"All the same, I am his uncle. And he won't have me around much longer. This winter'll be my last. The Great Snow Spirit will carry me to the All-Father. And then who will my nephew go to for wisdom and counsel? These are bad days, when the young do not heed the old." Joshua wagged his head and stroked his bony chin and addressed his new opponent. "Mind you, we start where we left off and you are one behind. So you owe me two bits. And it's my move."

Father Hillary gave Michael a blank look. Michael shrugged, feigned innocence, and pulling on his coat, started out the back door. "Two bits for each piece?" the priest asked, in the tone of a man who has just stepped into a bad arrangement. After a couple of years of playing, Joshua, despite his blindness, had gotten quite good. Too good.

"There," Joshua exclaimed, and began jumping one of his red pieces over three black.

"Hey!" Father Hillary whirled about. Too late. Michael had vanished into the storm. The back door slammed shut.

"Let's see," Joshua cackled. "That makes—"

"Have I ever shown you my chess set?" interrupted the priest.

Kate stood in the front room, in the dark. She stared down the hall, then searched the blackness around her. She wasn't alone in the room. She heard the back door slam, swing open in the wind, slam again. She could not remember bolting the door on her way out. She remained still, her breathing shallow.

"Who is here?" she asked. No answer, but she heard someone slowly exhale, as if just coming awake. Kate reached blindly out to the wall and located the brass receptacle just inside, a few inches from the doorsill beneath an oil lamp hung from the wall. Her fingers fumbled over and removed a match. Three steps to her right she knew she would find a lamp on the table near the arm of the couch. She struck the match and lit the lamp, lowering the smoked glass shade down over the flue, and turned, gasped, straightened upright. The medical bag fell from her grasp.

"No cry of love, no outstretched arms and a few quick steps to embrace, no delight, but a look of horror. Then perhaps you thought I would still be waiting at Penn Station after all these weeks," said Sam Madison. His long legs were stretched out, his lanky body collapsed in the easy chair. In his rumpled coat and vest, the rain-soaked slicker in a pile at his feet, he looked every bit the worn and weary traveler.

"How did you find me?" Kate said. She realized how silly her question sounded. She had left him a note explaining her actions and that she had taken a position with the Bureau of Indian Affairs. It must have been quite simple for him to track her down. Of course, she had also begged him not to follow her, that her departure was for the best.

"It was easy," Sam said, leaving his explanation at that. He sat up in the chair, noticed the slamming door. "Sorry. I mustn't have shut it all the way. I will now." He rose, steadied himself. "Must have fallen asleep. It was so damn dark in here." He walked out of the living room and down the hall to the kitchen. He hit his knee against a chair and muttered an oath. Kate picked up her medical bag and brought it into the dining room, which was still in the process of being converted into an office, thanks to the skill of Father Hillary. Not to mention the hard work of the troopers Kate had been able to cajole Captain Morbitzer into lending her. The men seemed actually grateful to be spared the captain's afternoon close-order drill. The soldiers of Camp Merritt were bored. Nothing ever happened on the reservation. Kate wished for a little boredom herself. She was tired. She had worked the better part of two hours setting the broken leg and fixing the limb in a proper splint. Finding him had certainly jolted her awake. She couldn't remember anything but confrontations with her father, at least not for the last few years. When she was a child, yes, he had tried to be a loving parent. But at his every attempt her mother would interject some cutting remark a child could never understand, something said to drive him away. Not that he hadn't helped her from afar. Indeed, her years in medical school had been filled with very few difficulties, thanks to the reputation of the Madison name and Sam's always timely bank drafts.

A light blossomed in the kitchen. She heard Sam stoke the coal in the wood stove and hand-pump water into a coffeepot. Kate hung her rain-soaked slicker on a peg by the front door and wandered down the hall to the kitchen. She watched as Sam poured a cup of coffee for himself and one for his daughter.

"I took the liberty of helping myself. Then I forgot all about the coffee. I was so tired from the ride I went in and sat down and dozed off." He took a sip, grimaced. "I let too much of the water boil away. Soon as what I added starts to boil, we can freshen our cups. It's been a long time since I made coffee for myself, much less slept out on the road. I should have hired a driver with the carriage." Kate, still at a loss for words, sat at the kitchen table and continued to study her father as he made small talk about the weather and his discomfort. In his late forties now, Sam Madison had matured gracefully, thanks to the wealth inherited from his father. His hair was thinning fast now but was impeccably trimmed, his suit was of the finest cut. He was developing a slight paunch, all the more noticeable on his otherwise bony frame. His cold blue eyes were deep-set and shadowed, the eyes of a man who did not sleep well at night. He turned and stared out the back window at the cedar-and-pine-covered hills, visible for a moment in a flash of lightning. The darkness returned and where he had looked out at the storm, he now saw his own countenance reflected in the glass. His breath clouded the windowpane. He shifted his gaze to the reflected image of his daughter seated behind him at the table and thought for a moment she was the incarnation of Esther. *Why could you not forgive me? It was all for you, I feared for you.* He rubbed his eyes, wiped his face on the sleeve of his coat, and willed the ghosts away.

"I can save us both a lot of pain," Kate said. She took a swallow of coffee and almost gagged on the thick bitter brew. She set the cup aside. She stood and walked across to her father and stared out at the storm, their reflections almost merging in the window.

"I never thought I would come back. Not among these people. I am told the survivors from the Warbonnet are among the Northern Cheyenne here."

"I am not going back," Kate said. She placed a hand on her father's shoulder. "Go home, Father. You don't belong here."

"And you do?" Sam replied with a voice thick with sarcasm. "You think the pigment of your skin makes a difference, that it makes you Indian. Kate, you aren't a savage. You are a Madison, my daughter, a civilized human being, for heaven's sake."

"I am needed here," Kate said. She turned and walked back into the hall.

"I said that very same thing once to my father," Sam said. "But times changed. I grew up, I suppose."

"Yes," said Kate. "And you forgot." She looked back at her father. "But Mother didn't."

"No. Your mother did not forget," Sam bitterly agreed. "Nor did she forgive."

"And yet you stayed married to her. Despite your absences, you always returned to her. But you could have sent her away if she made you so unhappy," said Kate.

Sam sighed softly and set the coffee cup aside, walked over to the table and sat down. He leaned his elbows on the table and folded his hands beneath his chin in a prayerful gesture. "I loved her." He glanced up at his daughter. "And I know it is hard to believe, but I love you. Oh, at first, when you furthered your education and entered medical school, I was glad to send money, to help in any way the Madison name could, but only because I knew what people thought of you and your mother. And me too. Sam Madison's squaw. Sam Madison's little red-skinned daughter, poor dear savage. I wanted to prove to them how exceptional you were. I wanted to shove your success down their throats. I wanted you to triumph for me. Me! And then, much later, I began to have such a feeling of pride for you and in you. And when you graduated I didn't care anymore about opinions and how I could hold you up to my associates . . . oh, the things a vain man is heir to . . . I was happy for you. I envisioned us together. Because I knew you would not only survive but . . . but continue to triumph in the city, in this culture your mother never understood, in civilization. I had lost Esther but I had you. She hardened your heart against me, I know. But if you only give me a chance, if you will just come back with me and let me show you how good life can be for us. Let me be your father. I am going to sell off the shipping interests. I am pulling out of South America. We'll make time to get to know each other, to see the world. And after a long rest, why, I know I can get you appointed to the medical college in New York." Sam brightened as his vision of the future unfolded before him, in this humble kitchen on an Indian reservation in south-central Montana. "*See* the world? By God we can *have* the world!" Caught up in his own dreams, he had not noticed Kate rise from the table. Now he heard her footsteps in the hall. Alarmed, Sam followed his daughter back into the front room.

"Don't you see?" he said. "Try to understand."

"No. You try!" Kate snapped. She crossed over to her medical bag and took out a black-leather-bound journal. "This is private. But I will let you see it. Now I am going up to change clothes. Here, take it." She placed the journal in his hands and disappeared up the stairway to her room above. Sam walked over to the couch and sat down near the oil lamp. He opened the journal and began to read.

July 3, 1889. Our last night on the road from Miles City. Agent Gude and the young Captain Morbitzer have been very kind. They have tried to make me as comfortable as possible. But I am filled with apprehension. And the same burning question I have asked myself since leaving Philadelphia: Am I doing the right thing?

July 5, 1889. It is morning. I have time to reflect on the night before. A tremendous celebration here for Independence Day. All looked as though they were enjoying themselves. I should have joined in but felt too much a stranger. And I felt so alone. As I did in my father's house. Am I a frightened girl again? Where is my sense of purpose that has sustained me for so long? Dig deep, Dr. Madison, and find it. First things first, then. The people won't come to me unless I come to them. So be it. I met an interesting man yesterday, about my age. Although his manners left something to be desired, I found him . . . interesting. I am told he has a small ranch. Perhaps I shall begin at his place. I am sure the Indian agent will give me directions.

Michael Spirit Wolf stared at the two-story house. He noticed the light appear in the upstairs window. Kate was obviously home. But he made no move toward the house, for he had also noticed the buggy and mare tethered out behind the house in the cover of a woodshed. Michael sloshed across the mud toward this unidentified carriage. The mare craned its head around as Michael stepped in under the roof. He noticed the mare's lead reins had been wrapped around one of the logs in the woodpile at the rear of the narrow shed. The carriage stood just out of the rain. As Michael entered the shed's meager protection, a figure loomed up on the other side of the carriage and backed away, as startled as Michael. Lightning flashed and Michael recognized James Broken Knife.

"You're too late," James chuckled. "She has a visitor tonight. A white man." The tribal policeman's features were flushed from his efforts. His eyes were black smears lost beneath his furrowed brows and thick jowls. He looked as mean and hard as he was, and Michael knew enough to be wary of the man. He smelled the alcohol on the sergeant's breath. "Nothing here tells me who he is. Damn rented carriage. Must have brought his clothes into the house." James leaned on the buggy. Its iron springs creaked beneath his weight. "Reckon he plans to stay the night. He has good taste, huh?"

"Why don't you shut the hell up?" Michael answered.

James chuckled. "Very brave. Like your father. I was there, remember? The mighty Panther Burn, war chief of the Cheyenne, leading his people into General Miles's camp. I saw them arrest him and lead him away in chains. The panther . . . . chained." James lifted the jug to his lips, took a swallow, lowered it, and replaced the cork. He sloshed the contents and judged how much he had left. The hell with the stranger, the carriage, and Michael Spirit Wolf too.

"I remember. Everyone remembers," said Michael Spirit Wolf in an ominous tone. But James would not be baited. He had the law. And the law was power.

"One day maybe I'll get the chance," James said. He sighted along the jug. "Bang! Bang! And Panther Burn dies. Or maybe the son of Panther Burn." James aimed the jug at Michael. "Bang!" Then the tribal policeman walked unsteadily off toward the street. He was already drenched to the skin. A little more rain wouldn't matter at all. Michael looked at the windows of Kate's house. An amber glow filtered out through the black of night from the kitchen window, from the bedroom window upstairs. Michael thought of his mother, of Rebecca's first meeting with Panther Burn and how she knew in her heart they were called together from the very first time they stood alone in the wind. Michael and Kate had stood together in the wind and watched the storm rage upon the earth and heard the wind call them by name. Michael dug his hands into his coat pockets and decided to wait a bit, at least until the downpour eased. And then, by heaven, he would come calling. He could care less as to this other visitor. He felt a little foolish and grinned to think of what Uncle Joshua would say. Foolish or no . . . Michael kept his vigil in the rain.

July 20, 1889. I delivered a baby son to the family of Lester Old Mouse. It was a hard birth. I thought I might be forced to cut on the mother but happily the baby corrected itself with a little help from me. I did not have long to enjoy my triumph, however, as Lester's youngest daughter, Sarah, took to coughing and all but lost consciousness. She had gotten a kernel of corn caught in her throat. I managed to extract it with a twig and some hairpins but I shouldn't like to try again. Checked on Mr. Hollowbreast. The fractured femur is mending nicely. I should set all my breaks with a flatiron and rope. Have covered many miles today. Michael accompanied me on my way into town. Rebecca Blue Thrush will have nothing to do with me but at least she keeps to herself whenever I come out to the ranch. The hurt runs deep in her. How I wish there was a cure for the heart's pain. Setbacks . . . victories . . . my life is full. I am needed here. And slowly I am making a place for myself. Had to promise I would attend an officers' party at Fort Keogh with Henry Morbitzer. At least I said I would meet him there. The things I must do to keep him helping me with the renovations of my house into a hospital. Tired. Tired. Tired.

July 21, 1889. Children visited again today. Ate the last of the peppermints. However, a fresh supply should arrive with my shipment of pharmaceuticals from Miles City. The children are so sweet. They love to look at the bottles of medicines and all the liquids and powders and pills in my medical bag. Oh, I am not accepted by all, not yet. But I belong here.

Sam Madison closed the journal and sat quietly, listening to the storm abate. He closed his eyes and pictured Kate as a child, pictured Esther dead, pictured himself forever running from the truth about himself. He read the journal of his own heart, entry after entry he had written by simply being alive. He had cast aside his missionary zeal because he had found that part of himself false. In a moment of blind panic he had set the course for his life and Esther's. He bunched his eyes shut and tried to fight the overwhelming tide of guilt that threatened to engulf him and to destroy what remained of his life. He lost all sense of time, a tear spilled down his cheek. A hand wiped it away. He looked up at Kate. She wore a simple dressing gown and a coarse cotton robe. Her hair hung long and lustrous black.

"Father . . ."

"How can I help? I mean . . . here . . . where you belong?" He stammered, cleared his throat.

"I do have a favor to ask," she said, sitting beside him on the couch and placing her hands in his. "Something I think only you can do, with your influence and reputation. Something only a Madison can accomplish, I think."

Sam nodded. He wanted to feel like a father again. "What do you need?" he asked.

"A favor," she said.

"For you?"

"For him," Kate said, looking past her father. Sam turned.

Michael Spirit Wolf stood in the doorway.

17

Sunlight drifted in through a hole in the curtains behind the couch and roused Michael from dreams of vast herds of cattle covering verdant hills and he and his mother sitting on the porch of the grand ranch house he intended one day to build. The sun was shining too, in this dreamscape, and he was at peace with the world. He stood on the porch and breathed in the warm summer air. He glanced to his right and Kate was standing there with her hair hanging down and the sun in her eyes and her beauty rivaled the world itself, for the breeze pressed her dressing gown to her body outlining the contours of her legs and hips as she turned to smile at Michael. In silence there was nothing to say they knew one another, and what they had shared was the stuff of dreams, of eternity itself. Michael grudgingly looked away and saw his mother beside him, stand. Rebecca pointed toward the hills. Michael lifted his eyes to the skyline and glimpsed his father standing on the rim of the valley. He saw Panther Burn start down, his hand raised in greeting, his voice ringing with a jubilant cry. Together now, his parents, and Kate nearby, and a sprawling ranch before him ... Michael felt complete. He was whole. And he was ... dreaming.

He woke and worked a kink out of his back as he sat up, his fingers kneading the small of his back. He ran a hand through his hair and swallowed to clear his throat. The house was quiet. The chair across from him empty. He wondered if Mr. Madison had returned. Michael had told his father's story to the white man. Sam listened and even seemed sympathetic. Panther Burn's actions were no less barbaric than those of the townspeople and militiamen who had massacred a peaceful village of Southern Cheyenne. Yet Panther Burn had been betrayed, singled out and handed over to be punished, taken to prison at Fort Dodge down in Kansas. By the time Michael had finished his tale and the rain ceased falling Sam was ready to be alone. He left by the back door, walked off into the darkness. Kate gave Michael a blanket and offered him the couch for the night. He remembered now the way she had looked in her dressing gown and robe, her hair unbound and lying in luxuriant folds about her shoulders.

He crawled out of his makeshift bed, listened to the quiet, pulled on his boots, buttoned his shirt and tucked it in at his waist. His gaze drifted to the stairway; the shadows at the top of the stairs beckoned him. He started forward, drawn by a spark of desire that burned within him, that he dared to kindle into flame.

He waited in the hallway; the windows at either end were shuttered and left the upstairs in darkness. One bedroom door was open and Michael could see the bed within had not been slept in. He looked around at the door on his left, stepped toward it, grimaced as the wood floor creaked underfoot. He reached out and placed the flat of his hand against the door and felt it give beneath the pressure. The door swung open and Michael stepped into Kate's bedroom. She was turned on her side, one arm along her thigh, the other lost in the folds of her pillow. Quietly, on the balls of his feet, Michael crossed the room to her side and looked down at her. A sheet covered her legs and waist. She sighed, rolled over on her back. Her hair like a sleepy storm, her lips as red as chokecherries against her smooth, tawny features. Nipples dark as blood pressed upward like twin delicate buds against her cotton bodice. And her eyes, blue as the sky at dusk. She was awake . . . she glanced toward the open bedroom door. He seemed to read her thoughts.

"What on earth . . ."

"Your father has not come in yet. I think he looks for answers among the clouds." Michael smiled and shrugged. "I can think of worse places."

"What on earth are you doing, Michael?" Kate asked, finally finding her voice. Odd, she wasn't alarmed. Surprised, but unafraid.

"Ahhhh. Dreaming, I suppose." Michael leaned forward. The mattress shuddered beneath his weight. "Thank you for trying to help me. For trying to help my father."

Kate pulled the sheet up to her neck. "Really, Mr. Spirit Wolf, couldn't that wait until morning? I mean until I was up and about."

"My thanks could, but not this." Michael pressed his lips to hers. His kiss hinted of desire, yet he did not try to take more than she would give. The kiss was ended prematurely by a sudden knocking at the front door. The rapid hammering sounded urgent. Michael straightened and then turned and walked out of the room. Kate gasped and hurriedly wrapped herself in a robe and hurried out into the hall and managed to catch Michael at the top of the stairs.

"Wait, for heaven's sake. That may not be my father. What will people think to find you coming out of my house at such an hour?"

"They will think what a lucky man is Michael Spirit Wolf."

"Michael, do you know what the word 'brazen' means?"

Michael furrowed his brow. He wasn't sure of the meaning. Tyrell Gude had given Michael all the books he owned. As of yet he had only worked his way through part of them, mostly the Shakespeare. And a copy of Malory's *Mort d'Arthur* of which he was especially fond. But "brazen"? "No," he said.

"Well, you ought to look it up. I think the dictionaries invented it for you." And with that, Kate brushed past him, and tying her robe at her waist, hurried down the stairs to the front door. She slid the bolt free and yanked it open. Father Lee Hillary stood on the other side of the screen door. His shoes were caked with mud from slogging across the street to the clinic. Mud discolored the hem of his black robes. Kate tried to remain unperturbed but her reaction was one of horror. Why a priest, with Michael having spent the night under her roof. Of course, he need never know.

"Why, Father Hillary. What is it? Are you ill?"

"I must speak with Michael. It is urgent. Forgive me if I am interrupting any-uh-thing." Hillary coughed nervously.

Kate blushed. So much for reputation. "You are not interrupting anything!" she said pointedly and stood back to allow the priest to enter. He spied Michael sitting in the middle of the stairway with a somewhat bemused expression on his face. Whatever humor he had found in Kate's predicament faded as he saw the expression of grave concern on the priest's face.

"I have some bad news. It came while I was having morning coffee with Tyrell. A telegram . . ." Father Hillary glanced around at Kate, who also had forgotten about her embarrassment, then he looked back at Michael. "I stole it. Tyrell's probably already looking for me." He held out a wrinkled page to the young Cheyenne rancher. Michael took the dispatch and began to read.

Sam Madison watched the mist that coiled on the valley below, writhed like some tormented spirit, denizen of an earthly hell invisible to the eyes of men. He had left his coat behind and stood his ground, looking every inch the citified stranger in his wrinkled finery. He glanced down at his mud-caked shoes and the brown-spattered hem of his trousers. If the men at the club could see him now. He lifted his gaze to the horizon, where the sun's golden fire washed over the land and scoured the haunted hills, chasing the vapors of the night, banishing the mist.

"It has been a long time," Sam said aloud. It was difficult to see the sunrise in the cities of the north. It was dark and then it was light. So then, here was the sun. He waited out the night. And what of answers? To use his influence to gain Panther Burn's release might spell trouble for Sam later on. It certainly would not help his reputation and might even cost him some of his business contracts with men who felt the wild savages of the West got exactly what they deserved, especially savages like the "Butcher of Castle Rock." The sun warmed his stubbled features. Sam ran a hand across his jaw. I must look like the most desperate vagrant, he thought to himself. In truth, he had acted out of desperation. Why not let Kate run out of his life if that was what she wanted? Why follow her these thousands of miles from the comfort of hearth and home, to return to the frontier, which he had sworn never to do? Somewhere, Esther must be laughing at him. *No, not laughing . . . oh God, not weeping, though, please. Esther, forgive me. I do not understand. What broke me long ago and caused me to flee, to abandon everything I held dear? Now it is too late. At least for us, but perhaps not for my darling daughter. You see, I still love her, always have, as I loved you although I could no longer tell you because you could no longer hear me.* He had failed his wife long ago, had feared to take a risk. Well, by heaven and hell and all that was holy in this world or the next, he would not fail his daughter.

Sam spun around on his heels and marched down from the hilltop back to the winding road leading out of town. He slogged through the mud but paid it no mind. It would wash off. In truth he needed a good hot bath and a fresh change of clothes if he was going to confront the local Indian agent with his intentions. Then a courtesy call at Major Halliwell's in Fort Keogh to present his case to the officer in charge of the military presence in this part of the country. And last but not least, a wire to the Secretary of State, who owed Sam Madison any number of favors for the financial support Sam had given to the campaign of Benjamin Harrison. Whatever the current temperament of Congress, money could generate a veritable torrent of sympathy for Panther Burn. And who knew, perhaps Sam Madison might come off being regarded as a humanitarian.

Sam touched his throat. He had worn a white collar once, but the worldly had warred with the saintly and won. It was impossible to recall the past. Sam Madison/humanitarian, or Sam Madison/Indian lover—none of it mattered. Whatever the outcome, Kate had presented him with a second chance, the opportunity to atone in at least one small way. And he might just win his daughter's love in the process. He cared for nothing more and hoped for nothing less.

He worked his way through the last few remaining yards of mud and paused on the back porch, looking back at his tracks. He could see a line of men heading for the mill at the edge of town. Some rode horses, others crowded into a wagon, and a number were afoot, preparing to climb atop the stacked timber and work the remains of once mighty ponderosas into the voracious iron jaws of the mill's rip saws. Sam had a task of his own to attend to. He kicked off his shoes and stepped into the kitchen, and spying Kate at the other end of the hall, hurried toward the parlor.

"Kate, I am glad you are up. I'll see it through. I will not rest until Panther Burn is . . . free . . ." He stopped, seeing the priest and, near him, Michael, still sitting on the stairway.

"This is my father, Sam Madison," Kate said. The priest nodded. The tension was almost palpable. The Seth Thomas clock, nestled in between the medical books over the mantel, chimed once, tolling the half-hour.

"What's happened?"

Michael handed over the telegram he had just read aloud to Kate. Sam unfolded the piece of paper.

TO TYRELL GUDE, INDIAN AGENT:
INFORMING YOU THAT AS OF YESTERDAY JULY 24, 1889, PAN-
THER BURN A WAR CHIEF OF THE NORTHERN CHEYENNE
ESCAPED A WORK DETAIL OUT OF FORT DODGE STOP KILLED
ONE SOLDIER WOUNDED ANOTHER STOP BELIEVED HEAD-
ING FOR RESERVATION IN MONTANA STOP PLEASE INFORM
CAPTAIN MORBITZER STOP SEE THE SOLDIERS STATIONED
AT CAMP MERRITT ARE ALERTED STOP A UNITED STATES MAR-
SHAL WILL BE DISPATCHED TO HELP IN THE APPREHEN-
SION SHOULD THIS RENEGADE ELUDE CAPTURE IN THE
SOUTH AND REACH THE RESERVATION STOP EXERCISE EX-
TREME CAUTION STOP PANTHER BURN IS TO BE TAKEN
DEAD OR ALIVE STOP.

"I am grateful for your good intentions," Michael said. "But you are too late. My father is already free. And he is coming home." Michael looked up at Kate, hurt in his eyes, his voice trembling. "He is coming home."

BOOK THREE

18

September 1, 1889

Here on the border between Montana and Wyoming, Marshal Sabbath McKean really couldn't tell where one state began and the other ended. He peered at the tendril of smoke spiraling upward against the backdrop of amber hills and figured that was Wyoming. He looked north, the way he ought to be heading, and then turned his horse to backtrack his own trail. Someone was following him and had been since Sheridan. Sabbath had a sneaking suspicion just who it might be. Not Panther Burn—the Cheyenne would never reveal his whereabouts with such a fire. No. This was a white man's fire.

With the sun a ruby-red ball balanced on the rim of the hills to his right, Sabbath McKean walked his buckskin gelding around the twisted stump of a lightning-shattered cedar and continued straight into the night camp of the two men whose fire he had glimpsed from afar. A massive, granite-fisted hunk of beef and bone stood and raised his Winchester 76 about waist-high and levered a shell into the rifle's chamber. The second man was slight of build, thin-limbed, birdlike in appearance, what with his bony frame and black coat and trousers. His face was angular and pale and his hair, a

267

startling white, hung to his shoulders. He held a broad-brimmed felt black hat in his hands and he waved it toward Sabbath, inviting him into the camp. Sabbath recognized both men and noted with self-satisfaction that being forty-seven had not dimmed his intuition—even if he needed specs to read sign now. Yes, Sabbath McKean's once hawklike vision was trapped behind round wire-rimmed lenses. He was not the kind of man, though, to count the wrinkles in his own reflection. Sabbath measured his life on how well he did his job. On the down side of forty, Marshal Sabbath McKean could still track a fly across piled coal. Bald, clean-shaven save for an enormous carrot-red mustache that curled at the tips like twin fishhooks, he wore faded Levi's and a trail-worn buckskin shirt with an elegantly polished U.S. marshal's badge pinned to his sheepskin coat. Short, broad-shouldered, solid as stone, Sabbath looked every inch what he was.

The law.

He tethered his horse with the other two geldings grazing near the camp and let the aroma of bubbling hot coffee lead him over to the fire. Night was falling, the land was gradually losing its store of warmth. A good hot campfire always felt good out on the trail. He nodded to the man towering over him. "You've put on a gut, Marley," said Sabbath. He looked around at the bird man. "Hello, Bragg."

"Marshal McKean . . . welcome," Jubal purred.

"Been a long time, Jubal. Thought you might have retired on your laurels," Sabbath said. He noticed the Winchester lying across Jubal's saddle and a brace of Smith and Wesson revolvers belted at the man's waist.

"Looks like you're fixing to do some hunting," McKean said.

"It appears we all are. And no doubt we are tracking the same game. I see little reason for subterfuge, Marshal McKean. I have always taken you for a man who appreciates honesty." Jubal brought a silver-filigreed flask out from underneath his coat, unscrewed the shiny silver cap, and tilted the flask to his lips. He sucked greedily on the tea-colored brandy, spilling a trace down his chin. He lowered the flask and sighed. "A renegade like Panther Burn is fair game for any man. And we are all hunters, one and the same."

"I am the law, Bragg. That is the difference between us."

"Granted, my dear fellow. Marley and I are only here to help the law along. Nothing more."

"There ain't no law agin the colonel and me bein' here." Marley squatted by the fire and hung a couple of rabbits on a spit over the flames. A pair of bloody pelts lay among his gear.

"I guess you are right," Sabbath replied. He shrugged and walked back to his gelding and unsaddled the animal. He carried his own gear over to the fire and tossed his bedroll down opposite Marley and Bragg. "In fact I'll even go you one better. You ride with me. We'll take him together." He grinned and helped himself to the coffee. He made a point of averting his face from the colonel's scrutiny. Bragg did have a way of seeing into a man. Sabbath knew that Jubal Bragg would hunt Panther Burn despite Sabbath's objections. Keeping Bragg and Marley close by might just save the Cheyenne's life. Sabbath intended to take the warrior alive if at all possible, even if it meant bracing these two.

"An interesting proposition." Bragg helped himself to the brandy, swallowed, sucked in a draft of the cooling air.

"I trust you as much as I trust a rattler to kiss and not bite. Which ain't much," Marley growled, glaring over the dancing flames. "Well, you just mark this, McKean. Me and the colonel are coming after that buck and we don't intend to let him slip away. Do we, Colonel?"

"Of course not. I have a score to settle with Panther Burn. I have waited a long time. A long time." He brought a crumpled sheet of newspaper out from his coat pocket. "Since the moment I read of his escape I have thought of nothing else. In truth I believe God willed his escape that I might settle accounts with Panther Burn." Jubal stared at the headlines again beneath

the banner *The Denver Republican*: "BUTCHER OF CAS-
TLE ROCK ESCAPES. HEADING NORTH!" He placed the page
on the ground and lifted his flask in salute. Sabbath was
up to something, but never mind. Jubal wanted to be
around in case McKean took it in his head to let the
renegade go free. Despite the past, or because of it,
McKean just might.

"We shall be honored to accompany you, Marshal
McKean. After all, we are only interested in justice
being served." Jubal patted the newspaper page smooth.
"You will not escape me this time, you red devil. I
swear it on the memory of my brother."

"Hell, Panther Burn isn't trying to escape," Sabbath
said. "I get the feeling he knows we'll be coming. I've
followed him across Colorado and Wyoming and think I
read his sign pretty well. It's like he's calling us on, and
looking for a place to make his stand." Sabbath finished
his cup of coffee and leaned against his saddle and
stared up at the evening sky, a deep blue ceiling hung
with clouds like chandeliers. "He's waiting for us."

Marley stared up at the northern ridges looming dark
and suddenly foreboding, twenty miles ahead. He
lowered his gaze to the meat hanging over the fire and
tore loose a chunk of seared flesh. He tossed the leg
bone from hand to hand until it cooled. Then he began
to eat, trying to dispel a feeling of doom that had
settled on him as silently as dusk upon the land.

Jubal Bragg chuckled and patted his Winchester, so
close at hand. "I wouldn't have it any other way."

The dream rose with the wind on this September
night. It swept aside the peaceful fabric of sleep and
revealed a circle of leaping flames to Rebecca. She
writhed and tried to turn away but the flames reached
toward her, as if to consume her flesh and spirit. And
beyond the walls of the house the two soldiers stationed
to keep watch buttoned their collars and turned their
backs to the wind and to the man coming out of the
wind, riding at a gallop in the night, his body low in the

saddle. The hooves of his stallion were muffled by the buffalo grass that covered the valley floor. Yes, a man came riding as Rebecca dreamed.

The flames were dancing madly, spirits of crimson, children of a mad devil writhing violently and parting now. Eyes watched her. Eyes peered at her from across the flames. She saw now the panther in the fire, a beast of rage, at bay but unvanquished. She knew the panther, she would have dared the flames to come to him. But with a savage roar he leaped . . .

Rebecca bolted upright in bed. The wind howled, the night came alive with spirit voices.

Outside the soldiers exchanged glances and shuddered, though the wind held no chill. Fowler was a name, Denny another. They were both mere privates. Fowler was hardly more than a boy, his cheeks were covered with downy soft fuzz. Soon he would experience his first shave. Private Denny was a strapping, corn-fed lad from Kansas, no older than Fowler but physically more intimidating. The cuffs of his blue woolen coat were two inches shy of his wrists.

"Better check on the one in the barn," Denny said. Size carried rank. Fowler nodded and started across the yard. "Hey!" Fowler exclaimed. The wind snatched his hat away. The boy soldier leaped for it and missed.

"Damn!" the boy soldier shouted, and ran out toward the garden in pursuit.

"Forget the hat, dumbass!" Denny shouted. He started from the porch and thought better of it. "You left your carbine here!" Denny scowled, cradled his own Springfield breechloader in the crook of his arm, and stepped back out of the wind. "What a stupid . . ." He glanced up at Rebecca standing in the doorway. She was dressed in her buckskin smock and overshirt and a tanned leather pouch dangled from her shoulder. Her hair hung long about her shoulders and fell to her waist. The wind smelled of pine and tasted of earth. Denny caught the scent of wild roses as Rebecca bolted past him. At first he thought she was going to join her son in the barn, for a cow was in labor this night and Michael had decided to sleep close by. Denny entertained notions of how grateful this squaw might become if he gave her a bit more free rein about the place. She had no use for soldiers now, but Private Denny reckoned he could change her mind with half a chance. His thoughts were still cluttered with fantasy when he heard Fowler scream, a high-pitched shriek of terror borne on the wind and cut short.

In the barn, Michael lifted his bloody hands from the newborn calf he had just helped bring into the world. His naked torso glistened with sweat. Yellow slivers of straw stuck to his knees as he staggered out of the stall at the scream. The calf began to bawl. It took a hesitant step toward its mama; the calf's spindly brown legs barely supported the weight of its ungainly brown-and-white-patched body. Mama turned a broad brown face and mooed reassuringly.

Michael hurried down the alley, then inexplicably veered and climbed the wooden ladder to the loft, raking his palm with splinters in his haste. He might not share Rebecca's visions but he was his mother's son all the same. Though he was bone-tired from the birthing, Fowler's cry had sent a surge of adrenaline coursing through Michael. He reached the loading window and braced himself against the frame as the moon reared from behind a battlement of clouds, like the shimmering marble walls of some ethereal city founded among stars.

He saw his mother and the horseman charging toward her as if to bury her beneath his galloping mount.

"Mother!"

Rebecca had seen him in the fiery furnace of her dreams, the wind called his name and it howled in her heart and filled her with impossible joy, an overpowering happiness she had never truly abandoned. Time rolled back, became in an instant another night, when long ago he had stolen her away. Now, as then, the stallion flashed fire where the iron-shod hooves struck stone. Now, as then, Panther Burn loosed a cry of triumph and leaned forward over the plunging neck, his features buried in the animal's lashing mane.

Hands outstretched, caught one another, the momentum propelled Rebecca up behind her husband. Her arms wrapped around his chest.

Poor Private Fowler staggered toward them, his coat and trousers torn and smeared with dirt.

"Denny. He run his horse over me. It's him!"

Private Denny already suspected as much. He leaped from the porch and ran in front of Panther Burn. The soldier raised his rifle, squeezed the trigger, the weapon sprouted a deadly blossom of fire. The figure on horseback seemed more an intangible demon of the night than some mere mortal. The stallion reared at the rifle shot and the man blocking its path. Denny dropped his Springfield and fumbled at his holster flap, and tried to free his Army-issue Colt revolver. A Winchester roared in his face. The muzzle flash blinded him. The force of the bullet knocked him backward. He hit hard, rolled on his side, and curled up.

Young Fowler leveled his own revolver. The boy soldier gripped his gun with both hands and sighted at the couple on horseback. Michael acted on instinct and leaped from the loft. Fowler buckled beneath the rancher's unexpected attack. The Colt blasted a hole in the dirt. Michael took the weapon out of the unconscious man's fist. Panther Burn wheeled at the shot and saw his son standing over the fallen trooper and reined his stallion over toward him. The wind ebbed, at least enough for them to hear each other. In the dark, the two men were barely distinguishable.

"My boy has become a man," said the man on horseback. "Come with me. Together we will ride the path of war."

The cavalry mounts pulled free of the hitching post in front of the house. The geldings stared out at the dark as if uncertain which way to flee. They seemed to be waiting for Panther Burn's mount to take the lead. "Come with me," the brave repeated.

"No," said Michael. "My place is here." He lifted the Army service revolver in his hand and stared down at the weapon. His hands were stained from the bloody birth of a calf. It had been a breach birth, hard going, but he had saved both mother and calf.

His were the hands of a life-giver. The gun seemed out of place. It belonged in another's grasp.

A hand swept down and snatched up the revolver. "My son," hissed the brave, looming above Michael now. Panther Burn's voice was thick with contempt. Suddenly the stallion reared, pawing the air. Rebecca screamed, "No!" Michael dodged the flailing hooves and slammed up against the barn. The stallion leaped away and vanished in the night, the two cavalry mounts trailing after at a gallop.

Michael swallowed. His throat felt dry as crushed rock and his limbs were weak. His own father had tried to kill him! His own father . . .

A groan cut through his panic and Michael remembered the poor youth lying at his feet. Another moan drifted toward the barn, coming from the trooper lying among the bitterroot.

"Help me. Help me. I am killed," Denny cried out in a trembling voice. Young Fowler rose up on his hands and knees, then began to rub his shoulder and neck. He glanced over in Denny's direction, then up at Michael, who leaned over to help the trooper stand.

"I think I busted my arm," Fowler gasped. He peered at the Cheyenne through eyes clouded with fear and a single knifing pain that took his breath away. "I could have had him if it weren't for you. Had him cold. You got any notion of what you've done?"

Michael slapped the trooper's crumpled hat against the barn and placed the battered article on Fowler's head.

"Yes, I saved your life," said Michael. He looked out at the night. "And maybe lost my own."

19

After love, after the warm entanglements and sweet words, the giving and receiving, after the passion, the triumphant storm and savage surrender, comes the stillness. The longing remains for lovers. It never leaves even in the quiet moments. The longing remains despite the wondrous sense of completeness. Love heals the broken, it shatters then mends, one can never have enough. In giving is the precious gift received, such is love's sublime irony.

Afternoon. The sun, balanced between the distant cliffs, hovered like a golden bird suspended delicately between sky and earth. Moments earlier Panther Burn had eased himself from the sleepy embrace of his wife and emerged from the lodge to check the valley sweeping out before him. Nothing stirred save the branches of the pines down by the creek bed. The meadow was empty except for a pair of gray squirrels chasing each other through the buffalo grass. He glanced back at the simple lodge hidden among the trees. Rebecca, with Michael's help, had built it more than a year ago. Her dreams had told her to. She seemed to know that one day Panther Burn would come for her. And she was right. He needed a refuge, a place to plan his next move. Lost among the pines, the single-room lodge was all but invisible to anyone downhill, on the edge of the pines. The air was cool here and felt good against his nakedness. This lodge was a good place too. He padded across the dark earth, burnt-umber pine needles cushioning each step. He had a mountain at his back, granite battlements ranged to either side. He was satisfied. The warrior stepped from the safety of the pines, raised his hands, and cried out in a voice that echoed down the hills.

"All-Father, you have brought me to this place. I have seen enough of my people and heard enough to know they have lost the way. Their feet no longer tread the one path. They are divided in themselves. They have abandoned the Circle. They no longer walk from life to life but take the straight road of *ve-ho-e* that only leads to death. What must I do, All-Father? Where are the warriors I may lead in battle? I do not think I will find any. Now I am alone. My father was killed by the Long Knives when we destroyed Custer Yellowhair and sent him under. So many of my people died in the battles we fought after that. You know their names. Now I am alone. How can I fight the Long Knives? Show me, All-Father."

His words faded, each reverberation fainter than the last, until the world was silent again. He stared at the chain scars on his wrists. And he remembered the betrayal of a friend. A hand upon his naked back lessened his gloom. Rebecca stood at his side.

"My husband," she said. Her voice was sweeter than the wind. When he turned to hold her close, the warmth of their naked flesh roused his desire. His fire was hers. She opened herself to him, became an instrument for his caress, for every kiss to play upon her lithe form. They clung to one another in the warmth of the sun, with the earth for their bed. They loved, and together, discovered every answer, every truth.

*　　*　　*

While Panther Burn slept, Rebecca brought water from the spring and washed her lover. His features were peaceful now, the deep lines softened. His hair was thick but close-cropped and threaded with silver. His eyes deep-set above prominent cheekbones. Gentle her hands upon his rock-hard shoulders. In the light of day she saw how the twin ordeals of war and imprisonment had marked him. Jagged furrows of scar tissue ridged his back and thighs—here the puckered flesh of a bullet wound, there the mark of a lash. Now her fingers traced a slim white line on his side where a saber had just missed its mark. This was a legacy of the Battle of the Little Big Horn when the Cheyenne and Sioux nations rose up and destroyed Custer and his soldiers. That had marked the beginning of the end. She touched the roughened skin circling his wrists, and her thoughts reached back to another day, when his flesh had yet to wear the mark of the white man's chains. A day in winter . . .

Winter 1883. There were guns on the Graybull. Amid the frosty peaks that rose like jagged spear points against a gray sky the panther had been brought to bay at last. A dozen Cheyenne braves, fifteen women, as many children, all reed-thin, all desperate but proud. Cliffs circled them on every side. Only one way into the valley and from the cave high up on the rocky slope Rebecca could see the campfires of the soldiers where better than two hundred troopers blocked the valley. The soldiers had tried two sorties against the Cheyenne and had lost seven men killed and thirteen wounded in the process, convincing General Miles to decide against another attack, in favor of reason. He had a plan and the man to carry it out, a man the general knew Panther Burn trusted.

The braves sat in a half-circle around the white man, listening to his words. Zachariah and a few of the other younger men were for shooting the man outright, but Panther Burn would not hear of it. Sabbath McKean had come under a flag of truce.

"The way I see it, you got two options," said McKean.

He looked like a diminutive bear in his fur robes that dusted the icy floor of the cave as he paced the frozen granite, his worn boots slipping on the glaze.

"Why listen to this man who admits he has ridden against us? He has killed our warriors," Zachariah said. At twenty-six he was in the prime of life, a man of reckless courage with a score to settle and memories of his murdered mother to fuel his hatred.

"I have killed in battle. As have you, laddie." Sabbath turned and stabbed a finger at Panther Burn. "And you." Sabbath blew a vaporous cloud of air from his nostrils as he sighed. "I do what I think I must do. We have fought, yes, and yet I come without weapons now to speak of peace."

The scout's voice rang out and echoed off the back of the cave. A baby began to cry in its hunger, a plaintive sound to move the hardest heart.

"What words does your General Miles have for us?" Panther Burn said at last, looking out toward the mouth of the valley and the smoke from the soldiers' cookfires curling upward in the frozen air. He was trapped. That much was obvious.

"Well, for one thing, January ain't no time to be fighting a war," said Sabbath. He turned his back on the other braves to concentrate on Panther Burn. "Miles is offering you food and medicine for all men, women, and children. And a place at Fort Keogh up in Montana Territory with the rest of your people. Word is there'll be a reservation, over between the forks of the Big Horn and the Tongue. Panther Burn . . . life can be mighty good there. Sure it ain't Spirit Mountain. But neither is this damn cold cave."

"And what must I do to enjoy such a good life, old friend?"

"Lay down your guns. Come with me to camp. Now."

"Saaaaa!" Zachariah exploded. He spat at the white man's feet. "We will never do such a thing. We are not women to cower before the soldiers." He stalked out of the cave and stood on the lip of the sharp incline up which the Long Knives had charged and died. Blood

still smeared the rocks, blue-clad bodies twisted in attitudes of death. Sabbath glanced warily at Zachariah, then drew closer to Panther Burn, who stepped out in the sun that no longer warmed him.

"You got a chance to get out of this alive. And to bring your family out alive as well. The boy ain't gettin' any better." Sabbath nodded toward the rear of the cave, where Panther Burn's own son lay with the other ill and wounded. Michael was unconscious, his breathing ragged, his flesh feverish, so hot to the touch, and yet the boy shivered beneath the buffalo robe Rebecca had spread across him. Panther Burn walked back to Rebecca. She had no answer for him. But her eyes were pools of sympathy. Her heart was a wellspring of strength. He had been at war for sixteen years. A war impossible to win. For every victory, Cheyenne had died and there were none to take the place of the fallen, while the soldiers seemed as numberless as the stars.

"They got cannon now. Two field pieces. The lads were just setting them up when I started out. You know what them long guns can do. If you ain't starved out, you'll be blasted out. The end will be the same. But we can save something if we act now." Sabbath reached into his pocket and drew forth a watch on a gold chain and checked the time. "The general give me fifteen minutes. I gotta start back. Don't let it end like this. All the other bands have surrendered. The Red Shields. The Otter Creek band. All of them. You're the last."

"The last . . ." Panther Burn repeated with a sigh. He looked at the gaunt faces of his people, those who had followed him in his war against the white-eyes. They trusted him. He could lead them into death. But . . . for what? He no longer knew. Death or life. It was indeed up to him. He reached down and took Rebecca's hand and held it a moment. Then he turned and walked back over to Sabbath McKean and held out his carbine to the scout.

"Nooo!" Zachariah roared and charged into the cave. He jerked his rifle up to bear on Sabbath. Panther Burn stepped in front of the white man and snatched *the gun out of Zachariah's grasp and threw the rifle out the mouth of the cave. It crashed on the rocks below. Zachariah backed away, stunned. He stared at Panther Burn and shook his head. He scowled, reached up and tore loose the eagle feather Panther Burn had given him so many years ago. He ripped it from a single braid, crushed the feather in his hand, and dropped the remnant at Panther Burn's feet. A light extinguished in his eyes and, when he at last looked up at Panther Burn, the expression on Zachariah's face was utterly bleak. "I would have died with you," he said in a trembling voice. He turned away in defeat as the other braves set aside their weapons and moved to rejoin their families. For the Northern Cheyenne, the war was over. . . .*

Rebecca cradled her husband's hand in her lap and lifted his wrist to her lips. Everyone had been saved that day, long ago, except Panther Burn, who was dragged from her side at gunpoint the minute he entered camp. Unarmed, there was nothing anyone could do. The Butcher of Castle Rock was to be made an example of. Sabbath McKean had protested but to no avail. Panther Burn struggled, tried to break free, to get his hands on Sabbath. He was knocked unconscious. The chains were hammered into place. He was taken to a separate wagon and placed under armed guard. That was the last Rebecca had seen of Panther Burn until now.

"You are back, my husband," she whispered. "And I will never let you leave me again."

But Panther Burn was sleeping. And he did not hear.

Michael stood at the iron door of the stockade. His new home consisted of a single room with a hard cot and a barred window. It was a jail cell for misfits and miscreants that the soldiers had built in the heart of Camp Merritt.

"Whatever happened to gratitude?" Michael yelled. He had brought Fowler and Denny back to Lame Deer and been promptly arrested for aiding and abetting a criminal—his father. There were no guards stationed at the stockade. A heavy chain and padlock secured the door. The soldiers were busily outfitting themselves in preparation for a long day's search of the reservation. Captain Morbitzer was determined to bring in Panther Burn. The few troopers ordered to remain in camp were either asleep or on duty protecting the Indian agent, while James Broken Knife's tribal police patrolled the town and outlying hills.

"Pssst."

Michael turned and stared at the narrow window at the back of his cell. A hand patted the bars. "Hey!" came the whispered cry. Michael crossed the cell and peered out the window. Zachariah Scalpcane stepped back into the sunlight. He shielded his eyes and peeked past the corner of the stockade, then returned to the window. His breath reeked of cheap whiskey but his motions were steady.

"What do you want?" Michael asked.

"I want to know. I heard the soldiers talking. Has he . . . has Panther Burn come back?" Zachariah sniffed, spat on the ground. His voice was hoarse and he looked as if he were about to be sick. Michael studied the Southern Cheyenne; his expression grew guarded. "You'd better get away from here. The soldiers may find you. Then we will have to share this cell."

"I want to know. You tell me," Zachariah exclaimed, his voice louder, his red-rimmed eyes burning with intensity as he drew closer to the window. Then he slowly nodded as Michael cautiously retreated, an inner sense warning him about this man.

"He has returned," Zachariah said. Tears formed in the corners of his eyes. "Too late, Panther Burn. Too late. Your people are gone. You abandoned them and they are no more. Your son is no more."

"Zachariah . . ."

"No," Zachariah hissed. "I was his son, before you. Then you came." The brave shook his head and staggered back. "I loved him. All of us who followed him . . . loved him. But he handed us over to the soldiers. Now

we die as old women. We could have died as men, as
warriors, as Cheyenne." Zachariah stared down at his
shaking hands. He dug inside his dirty vest and took
out a brown bottle, uncorked it, and lifted the bottle to
his lips. He paused, shook his head, and hurled the
bottle against the wall of the stockade. The bottle exploded, leaving a tea-colored smear spreading over the
rock walls. Zachariah lost his balance and fell to his
knees.

"What the hell is going on here?" A beefy-looking
trooper rounded the corner. He spied Zachariah Scalpcane on his knees. "Oh shit, it's one of you drunks.
Get up. Go on. Git." The trooper nudged the brave
with the barrel of his rifle. Zachariah ignored the prodding, and bracing himself against the wall, struggled to
his feet. His lifeless features filled the barred window.

"I will make him pay," Zachariah whispered. He
coughed and wiped a dirty forearm across his face.

"Hey! I said move out," the trooper ordered. He gave
the brave a violent shove that propelled him unsteadily
across the trampled earth toward Lame Deer.

"Zachariah Scalpcane!" Michael shouted. "If you are
broken it is because you were brittle to begin with! The
fault is your own!" Michael clung to the bars until the
brave was out of sight, then crossed to the barred door
and picked up the soldier and Cheyenne once more.
"He never forgot you were his son. You did! Do you
hear me? You forgot!"

Zachariah turned and waved. It was a meaningless
gesture. Michael cursed and slammed his hand against
the bars.

"Let me out of here!"

No one seemed to be listening. He pushed against the
barred door with all his strength, he tore at the blackened
links of chain until his fingernails were bloody. At last
he slumped against the wall and slid down to the floor.
Three horsemen walked their mounts through the makeshift entrance to Camp Merritt. The soldier who had
chased off Zachariah Scalpcane stepped in front of the
trio and held up his hand to signal them to stop. Michael

caught a glint of metal on the lead horseman's chest. He was a small-statured, broad-shouldered man who exchanged a few remarks with the guard. The trooper stood aside and the horsemen rode their mounts into the camp and over to Captain Morbitzer's cabin. Michael frowned, trying to remember something—yes, he knew the lead horseman. He was certain of it. But the name . . . McKean. Sabbath McKean. It was Marshal McKean now, or so Michael had heard once. Probably here to arrest me for helping Fowler and Denny make it back to the camp. The son of Panther Burn closed his eyes. A fly landed on his hand, then, as if taunting the prisoner, flew through the bars and vanished.

"Whatever happened to gratitude?" Michael wearily repeated. It was a question that had no answer.

20

Kate Madison paced the length of the hallway, and sick from the repetition, altered her course for an already worn path between the parlor and what had been the dining room. She was sick with worry, the tension like an acid eating at her reserve. A knock at the door caused her to explode into action. She hurled it open, expecting Michael, and found Father Hillary.

"Oh," Kate said, spirits sagging.

"Hum, I have had more cheerful greetings," the priest replied. "But then, I suppose the early Christians had worse."

"I'm sorry. I thought you were Michael."

"Hoped, you mean."

"Yes," Kate said. Hillary's honesty was infectious. She stood aside as the priest entered, toolbox in hand.

"You're worried about him. So am I," Father Hillary said.

"I feel so helpless."

"You brought the letter to Gude. You've done all you could. They brought Michael over and are talking to him now."

"How . . . ?"

"I've been building a planter box for Tyrell, which happens to be outside an open office window." Hillary brought a single cutting in a clay pot out of his toolbox. His broad square features brightened with mischief. "Now, if someone were to take this cutting over and plant it in the planter box, that someone would hear what was going on."

Kate grabbed the clay pot, hugged the priest, and darted for the door, stopped and turned to the priest.

"I forgot. Some of the children were coming over today. Probably Susan and little Sara . . ."

"I'll tell them to wait for you." Hillary smiled. "Just show me where you keep the candy."

Washington, D.C.
August 20, 1889

My dearest Katherine,

Wonderful news. As of my meeting with Charles Dolph, the director of the Bureau of Indian Affairs, I have been personally assured that if Panther Burn surrenders himself to the authorities, his case will be given all due consideration and if no life has been lost due to his escape, he will be subsequently discharged to the confines of the Northern Cheyenne reservation with the understanding that he may not leave the reservation. To do so would be to jeopardize his freedom once and for all.

I daresay this decision has cost me plenty. But not nearly so much as a "decision" of my own lost these many years ago.

Trust you will present this letter to Agent Gude, who no doubt will instruct the garrison there.

God bless you, my dear daughter. And please know, I love you.

Sincerely,
Sam Madison

Michael glanced up from the letter. Seated across from him, at his office desk, Tyrell Gude studied Michael over the edge of his teacup. Next to him stood Sabbath McKean, shoulder against the back wall, slouched forward, sheepskin coat unbuttoned, a star pinned to his gray vest, his gaze unwavering. To Michael's right sat Bragg and Marley. Both men appeared uncomfortable, as if they wanted no part of deeds done in bright daylight. James Broken Knife sat on a narrow bench by the front door. His eyes darted from Michael to Bragg and Marley. It was obvious he wanted to be out of the room in the worst way. As for the others . . .

"What do you want?" Michael said. A day in the stockade had left him in a mood to be direct.

"Well . . . uh . . ." said Gude, looking to the others for support. He took a clay pipe from the humidor rack on his desk, filled it with the tobacco, and struck a match. He touched flame to the brim of the bowl and puffed a gauze cloud of aromatic smoke.

"I want you to help me find your father," McKean said.

"Go to hell."

"Probably," said McKean, tucking a wad of tobacco in his cheek. "And more than likely I'll see a few of you boys there. No help for it, though. It's plumb out of my hands. But here, in this old world, I can do something. I'm told no one knows the res as good as you. Might be you have an idea where he's holed up. Take me to him and save his life." He leaned forward and spat a brown stream into the spittoon on the floor near Gude's filing cabinet. Bragg and Marley shifted uncomfortably in their black frock coats. Bragg endured. Playing along with McKean was a means to an end. "You tried to save his life once before," Michael sneered. He ran a hand through his dirty hair. The manacles James had put on his wrist scraped a patch of flesh from his forehead. "Get these darn things off me or take me back to the stockade."

Gude looked to McKean, who nodded. James hesitated. "Do it," said McKean. James Broken Knife stood and brought over the key. He unfastened the cuffs and walked back to his bench. The iron cuffs and chain dropped with a clank to the hardwood floor. McKean pushed off from the wall and sat on the corner of Gude's desk. Michael massaged his wrists and continued to study the lawman.

"I was lied to, same as Panther Burn," McKean said. "I wasn't in charge then. I am now."

"The letter says if no lives have been lost," Michael replied. He started to pass the letter over to McKean, then decided to return it to Kate in person and tucked it in his shirt pocket.

"Denny will have a sore belly, nothing more. The bullet hit him square in the buckle between the U and S," Gude spoke up. His gaze shifted to McKean. "And the marshal tells me that the reports of your father's escape were exaggerated. A guard was hurt, yes. But he will recover."

Michael looked questioningly at McKean.

"It's true, lad. I wouldn't lie. Believe me or no, but I've nothing against your pa. I rode with him and agin him and never had anything but respect for Panther Burn. I am trying to help him now. Be truthful, lad. Can you find him?"

"I can find him," Michael slowly said, his gaze lifted to the map of the United States on the wall behind Gude. Such a mighty country with civilization stretching from coast to coast. Was there a place in all that United States for a man like Panther Burn?

"Will you?" McKean asked.

"I have to think on it," Michael said.

"You'll help or else," Marley warned. McKean straightened and fixed him in a murderous glare. Marley began to study the throw rug underfoot. Michael rose from his chair and headed for the door.

"Where are you going?" James muttered.

"Stretch my legs. I'll take this letter back. Then I'll give you my answer."

"Let him go," McKean snapped. James slumped down on his bench. Michael sauntered past him and out the door. He rubbed his wrists and started down the street to the clinic. A breeze stirred the dust underfoot and carried the cool heady fragrance of the pines. He was grateful to be free again and he wondered how Panther Burn could have endured so many years in prison and not gone mad. But then, perhaps he had.

"Going my way?" asked Kate, moving up alongside him.

Michael glanced around, surprised. "Where did you come from?"

"I was listening at the window," Kate explained. "Well, after all, it was my letter."

"Watch out, you might wind up in jail with me."

"Oh, would that be so bad?" Kate laughed. Shadows drifted across the valley floor as heavy white clouds lumbered through sunlight. Kate reached out and took his hand.

"Be careful," Michael warned. "I hear Henry Morbitzer is a jealous man."

"He has nothing to be jealous of, except what he has imagined," said Kate.

"It is all the same to some men."

"Are you really worried?" Kate looked sharply at him now.

"No. But then, he left this morning to try to catch my father." Michael grinned. He looked at the clinic and tugged at her arm. "Come with me." Kate nodded, unsure of what he meant. In truth, her own heart was a mystery to her. She was drawn to Michael by emotions beyond her understanding, much less control. Perhaps she recognized a kindred spirit in him, for they were very much alike in one important way, as he had said: they were both a part of, yet strangers among their own people—Kate because of birth and the legacy of her father's wealth and the education it had provided, Michael through his desire to rise above his situation. He was drawn by a dream that the reservation, rather than being the end of his people, could also be the beginning.

They walked together in the warmth of the afternoon, through the shifting shadows, out from the settlement, past a cabin where two women scrubbed clothes on a washboard in an iron tub, past the sawmill where half a dozen men labored at a steam-driven ripper, turning fresh-cut timber into one-by-twelves to be sold at Forsythe, where there was a ready market for prime building material.

They followed a deer trail up into the hills until they reached the rounded summit of a hill overlooking the settlement. Kate spread her shawl on the ground and sat, spreading her gray skirt out over the yellow grass. Michael knelt beside her. He looked at her pinned-up black hair.

"I will make you some braid holders one day, then you will have to let down your hair and become an Indian." He laughed softly and lay back on the ground. He plucked a reed of Russian thistle and stuck it in his mouth.

"Father Hillary is worried about you. We all are."

"All two of you?"

"All three. Don't forget Uncle Joshua." Kate watched the patches of light and darkness play upon the land. "Three people who worry for you and care what happens to you is three more than most have." *How like life this ever-changing pattern on the valley floor. Each of us stands in sunlight, knowing where we are and what we must do, then in shadow, when we are lost, with no clear direction or course of action. Yet we hope for the light and it always returns.*

"What will you do?" Kate asked.

"Maybe I will take you in my arms," Michael said. "The stockade was a cold hard place. What would you do, Kate Madison, Doctor Kate, if I took you in my arms and—" Michael turned toward her. Kate's eyes widened, yet she held her ground. Michael reached for her. "Maybe all the answers I seek are in your arms, Doctor Kate." Suddenly he stopped and looked past her, his hand frozen in midair. Kate was thoroughly confused and turned to see what had caused him to stop. Three children sat on the ground ten feet behind them. Kate recognized them, for they had become frequent visitors to her house along with all the other children in the settlement as word of her miraculous jar of peppermints spread from child to child. But these three were the first who had ever come calling, and they had a special place in her heart.

"Jonah Yellow Leg, what on earth?"

Jonah glanced at the two little girls beside him. Susan and Sara Pretty on Top brightened into broad grins. "We come to visit you," said the boy. All three of the children laughed and stood and walked over to the couple. Michael was profoundly grateful he had only reached out to Kate, and nothing more. Jonah sat beside him.

"I seen your pony once. You have a little gray pony."

"Yes."

"Where is your pretty pony?" Susan asked. She wiped a patch of red clay from her cheek and managed to smear it down to her neck.

"Pony!" Sara echoed, her eyes large and lovely and full of innocence.

"He is running the high meadows with his mama. But when I bring him down to the lowlands I will make a wagon and hitch him to it and the three of you can ride up and down the valley. Would you like that?"

"Yes!" the children said as one.

"Will the soldiers not take us away?" Jonah asked. Michael looked at Kate, a frown on his face.

"Why should the soldiers take you away?" Kate asked, putting her arms around Sara and Susan.

"My papa said that now Panther Burn is back there will be trouble and people will get hurt and the soldiers will become angry and take us away from our valley and put us all in jail."

"They will take our mountains away forever," Jonah added, his voice thick with alarm.

"No one is going to take you away," Michael said, patting Jonah's arm.

"Can we stay with you? It's pretty here," Susan replied, her fears easily allayed.

"Bring candy?" Sara asked hopefully.

"No," Kate said, smiling. She hugged the little girl. "No candy."

"I wish." Sara sighed.

"It's all right. We can go home with her and visit there too," Susan explained to her little sister.

"I sure would like to ride that gray pony," Jonah wistfully added.

"You will," said Michael determinedly. And Kate could tell by his tone of voice, in the way his eyes ranged the valley floor, that there among the shifting patterns of his own life Michael had seen the path he must take.

21

Rebecca awoke at sunrise. Panther Burn lay sleeping. In his stillness, he seemed carved of wood, an idol depiction of primitive strength and indomitable will. He and Rebecca had made love by moonlight. Hours ago, at morning's earliest moment, when the world slips past midnight and desire becomes an unquenchable thirst, their silvery limbs were entwined in passion. Now Rebecca waited alone by the medicine fire she had built, with only the sun-kissed peaks and vast reaches of a lonely sky for comfort. She waited and watched as the last of the stars winked out.

Now. The magic time. When the *maiyun* were trapped between dreams and dawn. Her hand closed around the pouch she wore at her throat, the medicine bag given to her by Star more than twenty years ago. Then she set fire to the sweet grass she had gathered the day before and soon had a merry blaze. Behind her, Panther Burn emerged from the lodge and stood for a moment watching the sunrise. He wore breechcloth and leggings and moccasins. A bandolier of rifle cartridges hung across his naked chest.

"Will you eat?" she asked.

"First I must check the passes."

"No one knows of this place."

"My son does. You said so yourself," Panther Burn repied.

"He is still your son whether he walks the Great Circle or not. Michael would never betray you," Rebecca said.

"Still I will ride to the passes," Panther Burn replied, squatting down in front of her. "My shoulder . . ." The tone of his voice was more a request. Muscles rippled beneath the white scar tissue that crisscrossed his dark flesh. Rebecca took a bowl of medicine herbs and sprinkled a few dried leaves into another bowl that contained a paste made of deer fat. She blended the mixture and covered her hands with it and then held them over the fire until they were warm. Then she placed both hands on his shoulder and kneaded the muscles. Panther Burn winced, then sighed softly as the pain eased. They had not spoken of prison. Some memories Panther Burn would not share. And Rebecca respected his wish.

Panther Burn turned around and held her, brushing the hair away from her cheek as he talked softly of his love for her. She lowered her eyes as a maiden might, to hear such a one open his heart.

"Little Bird. You are next to my heart. My spirit has no home except when you are with me."

"I shall pray here by my fire and listen to the secrets in the wind. And will ask the *maiyun* to show me the paths that lie ahead. And while I pray, no harm can befall you." Rebecca pressed her cheek close to his, and when it came time for him to leave, she grudgingly let him stand. Panther Burn took up his rifle and walked to the horses. Rebecca found a raven feather from among her belongings and gently fanned the flames, which leaped up like tongues of fire. Coals grew ruby red and pulsed with life. She began to sing as Panther Burn rode away, and closing her eyes, she envisioned a panther at bay, its back against a cliff, with no place left to run. The image saddened her. And in her mind she saw the wild dogs approach, in a hunting pack, fangs bared, froth dripping from their muzzles. Nowhere to run, to hide. No escape. The panther made its stand. *No. I have no use for such a vision. Leave me. This is an evil spirit.* Her song droned on, a chant of protection and courage. She sang and the sun climbed higher in the sky, until at last her mind was freed from the grip of the troubling visions. The panther faded then, but the hounds remained, and leading them, a wolf. The wolf became a man.

Her son.

Michael Spirit Wolf walked his gelding up into the left fork of a narrow creek bed. A crystal-clear ribbon of water flowed underfoot in lazy undulations that would carry it down toward the forest below. The wind gave a cool kiss to his cheek and he paused to let his horse drink its fill. He dismounted, stepping clear of the creek, and with his left hand caught hold of a wind-eroded pocket in the stone walls and worked his way up the wall of the ravine until he gained an unobstructed view of the valley he had just crossed. Golden meadow dappled with cloud shadows, purple mountains distant, a swatch of forest land wrapping the slopes, everything as it should be. Michael nodded, satisfied. It was the second time in the past hour he had checked his back trail and the twelfth time since starting out from Lame Deer. He had told Marshal McKean that the son of Panther Burn would not lead an armed posse to his father's lair. But Michael offered to go alone and present Sabbath's case to Panther Burn. And Sabbath, after due consideration, had agreed.

Michael eased himself down the wall and leaped onto his mountain-bred gelding. The Cheyenne pulled a denim jacket from its ties on his saddlebag and tugged it on. He ran a hand through his thick black hair, and shielding his eyes, glanced up at the sky and thought to himself how blue were the eyes of Katherine Madison. He wondered what Panther Burn would do when he saw his son again. Their first meeting had been brief but certainly to the point, if attempted murder could be called that. *Of course, Father may have only been trying to trample me partly to death,* Michael consoled himself. He patted the gelding's nut-brown neck and nudged the animal's flanks.

Half an hour later the walls of the ravine leveled and Michael rode at an easy gait out across another valley floor that rose sharply through a stand of ponderosas. When he cleared these, a smaller meadow waited to be ridden through. Beyond it, in a grove of lodgepole pines mingled with the more stately sentinel ponderosas, Michael had helped Rebecca build a cabin, as if she had known all along she would need it someday, this place where even a panther might live in peace.

"There it is. By damn, there it is," Bragg said, craning his neck over the rotted trunk of a fallen pine. He stretched out alongside McKean on the needle-carpeted earth. Here on the forest's fringe the two men watched as Michael walked his gelding directly toward another stand of timber higher up; the direction Michael took inadvertently pinpointed the cabin with its camouflage of dead gray limbs and underbrush.

"Now what?" Bragg said. "I'll bring the others. We can rush him. We'll nail that red devil's hide—"

"Shut up," said McKean. "Ease on back. Keep flat to the ground." He started back the way they had crawled up, easing their way under deadfalls, deeper into the forested barrier intersecting the valley. Only when the hillside was completely lost to sight did Sabbath permit them to stand and run the rest of the way to the clearing where they had left Marley and James Broken Knife.

The tribal policeman sat cross-legged in the shade of a fir with his back to a mule-sized chunk of granite. He was whittling on a slab of jerky and hungrily devouring the shavings. Marley, stretched out on the ground, was nursing on his canteen. He sat upright when Sabbath and Jubal entered the clearing.

"Well?" the big man growled.

"The younker is a good trailsman. But I'm better," McKean said. He held back and let Jubal Bragg get ahead of him. Then he tugged his Colt revolver out from under his jacket and leveled it at the two white men. Bragg, seeing the look of surprise on Marley's face, turned and stared slack-jawed at the marshal.

"What in blazes are you doing?" he asked, his voice soft, almost a purr.

"I am taking your guns. Now!" Sabbath glanced over at James, who stared at the lawman in astonishment. "Go take their guns," Sabbath ordered. James pointed to himself with his beef jerky. "Hurry up, lad."

James stood, set aside his food and knife, and hooked his thumbs in his suspenders. He looked from Marley to Bragg, then after reflection, liked the idea of disarming Jubal Bragg. He sauntered over and took Bragg's matched set of Smith and Wessons and Marley's Army Colt. He tossed them over to Sabbath, who nodded in approval.

"Bragg . . . have a seat with your man there," said Sabbath.

"Son of a bitch," Marley spat. "Low-down son of a . . ."

Sabbath shoved Bragg forward onto the ground and stepped over him and slapped Marley across the face with the barrel of his revolver, opening a gash from the man's mouth to just below his left ear. Big Marley rolled over and crawled to his knees. "You're lucky you got that gun," he spat, wiping the blood from his cheek. Sabbath holstered the revolver. Marley charged, rising up like some primordial beast to lunge at the man who had hurt him. Sabbath hurt him some more. The marshal waited for Marley to straighten. Then he kicked him in the crotch. Marley grunted, doubled over, and Sabbath clubbed down on the big man's unprotected neck. Marley dropped facedown in the earth. Sabbath drew his gun and knelt by the fallen man and leaned forward so that Marley could not help but hear him.

"You've gotten old, Marley. Old and soft." He stood and glanced around at Jubal. "And you, Bragg. You're still like blued steel inside. But you're apt to find out there's a hell of a lot of difference between hiring your killings and having to do them yourself. All I know is I don't want you tracking around and messing things up. It has been a lot easier to know just exactly where you were."

"He killed my brother," Jubal said. His eyes lowered in defeat, his expression downcast, his voice bitter. He seemed to sag in on himself as if crushed by the weight of his memories and dreams.

"We've all got things to answer for, Bragg . . . Panther Burn, me, and you. Maybe you most of all, for what you started long ago, back on the Warbonnet. Look to yourself, Jubal Bragg, 'cause one day they'll come for you, all those poor dead ones you left behind. How can you stand such an army of ghosts—the slaughtered men and women and children? Look to yourself, Bragg. But stay the hell out of my way. I have work to do." Sabbath looked around at James Broken Knife. "Watch them. If they move, shoot. That is an order, Sergeant."

The tribal officer drew his service revolver and cocked the weapon. "I understand," he said.

Sabbath holstered his revolver and hurried over to his horse. He led the animal from its grazing out of the clearing.

"What if you don't come back?" James asked.

"Give them their guns and ride like the devil, 'cause you won't be any match for Panther Burn. None of you will." Sabbath vanished on horseback into the emerald shadows of the forest. When he was lost from sight, Jubal straightened. His mask of despair seemed to melt away as he crawled to his feet and dusted himself off, appearing to take no notice of the tribal policeman. It was fortunate that McKean had no knowledge of James Broken Knife's prior association with Jubal Bragg. The colonel hurried over toward the Smith and Wessons lying in the dust. James Broken Knife intercepted him, brandishing his own Army-issue Colt.

"Oh, come on, man, I doubt you have any love for

Panther Burn," said Jubal. Behind him, Marley sat up and struggled to stand, groaning and cursing with the effort.

"I have no love for you either, *ve-ho-e*." James sneered.

"But you have a love for this," Jubal said, and reaching inside his shirt, he withdrew a small leather pouch. He untied the pouch and shook out a half-dozen shiny gold coins, which he tossed in the air. They sparkled, spinning in flight, and landed at the feet of James Broken Knife. The Cheyenne stooped and picked them up.

"I'll double the amount if yours is the bullet that drops Panther Burn," Jubal said as he picked up his guns. He turned and looked around at Marley, who had moved over to his horse and stood leaning on the saddle, his hand on the stock of his Winchester. Bragg holstered his matched pistols, one at his belt and the other in a pocket in his black frock coat. He walked over to the ex-sergeant and stood in the man's shadow.

"Are you all right, Marley?"

Marley dabbed at his face where the blood had already begun to coagulate along his swollen, bruised cheek. He sighed, his great weight sagging against the horse. Big Marley looked aside at Bragg. "One moment I'm ready to ride hell-bent for leather. The next, Sabbath McKean leaves me facedown in the dust and it gets me thinking, Colonel. What the hell are we doing here? You ain't fired a gun in years. And me, I'm thinking the war was a long time ago. Once I could have taken the likes of McKean. I got no doubt of that. But once ain't now." The big man shrugged. "I'm thinking, and it's piss poor timing, I know, but . . . well, dammit, Colonel, a fella chases his nightmares long enough, he's apt to catch 'em. And then what? Katy bar the door, I warrant."

"Get your rifle and come on," Bragg said. He glanced over his shoulder and saw James Broken Knife disappear down the deer path Sabbath had taken. Bragg fixed Marley in a steely-eyed glare. "Sergeant . . . that's an order."

Marley stiffened. The military tone worked. Reflex

made him obey the voice that had led him in the past. He reached for the rifle before he realized exactly what he was doing. Then his hands froze on the stock a moment more. They had come this far. What else was there to do? "Did I ever tell you about my brothers?" said Big Marley with a weak grin lighting his battered homely features. "Lord but they were dumb. They wanted to come out west, only they couldn't figure out where it was." Jubal was too close to the end of a lifelong hunt to enjoy his old friend's comfortable retort. Instead he turned and hurried out of the clearing.

And Marley, despite the first clear premonition he had ever known, took up his rifle and followed.

The places set, in the golden glory of the day, the deadly act unfolded. Michael Spirit Wolf reined his gelding to a stop a few yards from the cabin. His mother sat before a medicine fire, soft brown features hidden behind a coruscating curtain of smoke. Michael checked the woods around the cabin, then glanced at the empty doorway as if expecting his father to emerge. He looked to his mother, shifted in the saddle, but found it difficult to make her out.

"I have come to speak with Father. He must talk to me. He must listen to what I have to say."

Rebecca raised a hand and cut through the smoke with the raven feather she held. The smoke parted and when she waved her hand twice more through the smoke, a breeze stirred and swept the curtain away. "My son. He will not listen and the time for talk is ended. I have seen the trail he must take written here in the fire and heard it whispered in the wind. But why have you chosen to stand against him?"

"I love him," Michael said.

"Then why did you bring the *ve-ho-e*?"

Michael stared in surprise. "I came alone," he said, anger rising in him. "Where is Father?"

"Gone to hunt those you brought to hunt him."

"I came alone," Michael protested again. "I brought

no one . . ." The words died in his throat as the realization hit. McKean! And the others! What a fool he had
been to trust the marshal. They had tracked him from
Lame Deer. Michael darkened with fury and he wheeled
his horse about and savagely dug his heels into the
animal's flanks. In the medicine fire a coal cracked apart
and its fiery center poured out like blood. Rebecca
gasped in horror and stared after her son.

"Michael! No!" Too late. He could not hear. Rebecca
scrambled to her feet and ran toward the horses tethered
in back of the cabin. She had to stop him. She had to
save her son.

A forest at peace. A world held in the still and fragile
grip of a September afternoon. In emerald shadows,
through slanted barriers of golden light, the hunters
came and Panther Burn waited for the one he wanted
more than the others, the one he had recognized from a
distance when first the Cheyenne had spied the strangers entering his valley. Panther Burn was one with the
breathless quiet, one with the shimmering sliding light,
as patient as time itself. And he was rewarded at last as
Jubal Bragg stepped around a grove of fir trees and
started up the wooded slope directly toward Panther
Burn. The Cheyenne thumbed the hammer back on his
rifle and silent as his namesake padded past the ponderosa
he had used for cover. Jubal did not see him. At least
not at first. Then he stumbled, regained his balance,
kicked a pine cone out from underfoot, and looked up.
The colonel froze as he beheld his death.

"Did you really think you could stalk the panther in
his lair, Jubal Bragg?" said Panther Burn. His finger
tightened on the trigger of his Winchester. Jubal Bragg's
mouth fell open. This was only a man, yes, but a man
transformed into the living fabric of nightmare. Jubal
looked into eyes as nakedly savage as a beast's. And his
courage failed. The revolver in his hand suddenly
weighed a ton. Jubal could not lift his arm. And he
would have died right then, if not for Big Marley, who

charged out of the grove like a wounded buffalo. Marley
shouted his challenge and fired his rifle. The shot went
wild but distracted Panther Burn. The Cheyenne swung
around and fired, levered another shell into the chamber, and turned to see Jubal Bragg roll backward down
the slope and scramble under the firs. Panther Burn
loosed a yell and charged. Marley moved to block his
path. The big man roared out, Panther Burn fired again
and saw Marley stagger and fall. Panther Burn ignored
him. He wanted Bragg. With a wild war cry ringing from
his lips, the Cheyenne burst through the cluster of firs.
The ground fell away in a sharp five-foot drop. Panther
Burn momentarily lost his balance, landed on his feet
and rolled forward, and glimpsed movement out of the
corner of his eye. He whirled and brought his rifle to
bear and squeezed the trigger. The Winchester bucked
in his grip. He saw a flash of blue uniform, then James
Broken Knife broke from cover, firing his revolver
with every erratic step. He slammed headlong into a
ponderosa and wrapped an arm around the trunk. He
clung to the rough bark and worked back to catch a
glimpse of Panther Burn, who was already running
after Bragg. James glanced down at the Army Colt he
had dropped. His hand crawled across his stomach and
down, reaching for the grip of his revolver. He caught
hold, raised it as he straightened, and sighted on Panther
Burn's departing figure. James felt no pain, only a
numbness in his chest and a pressure as if he were
being crushed beneath a terrible weight. The moment
was lost and he slid down the trunk until he was seated
against it. He stared at his empty hands and wondered
where his gun was. He fumbled in his coat pocket and
brought out the five gold coins Bragg had given him.
James leaned to the right and scooped a hole in the
earth, dropped the coins in the ground, and covered
them over with a fistful of dark loam. He remembered
an alley in Castle Rock and Tom Bragg lying dead at his
feet. *If only . . .* He fell over on his side and died with
his left hand covering the mounded earth as a man

might sleep alongside his beloved, his hand upon her breast. But this was a dreamless sleep and his last thoughts were not of love, but of choices. *If only . . .*

Horses in their panic reared in terror as Bragg burst among them in his headlong flight and tore the reins free on the first animal he could reach. He swung into the saddle as Panther Burn emerged at a dead run along the path and dug in his heels as he raised his rifle to his shoulder.

"Jubal Bragg!" he roared, bringing the colonel under his gun. His finger tightened on the trigger just as two hundred and eighty-five pounds of behemoth crashed into his back. The rifle went flying and Panther Burn after it. A massive weight bore him to the ground, crushing the breath out of him. The Cheyenne drew up his legs and kicked out and rolled free, gasping. Every bone in his body ached from the jarring impact. The world spun before his eyes, a blur of shadow and light, of trees and underbrush and looming darkness. He willed the world into place and the patch of darkness became Big Marley, bloody, battered, and still very much alive. He brandished a broad-bladed knife, fifteen inches of razor-sharp steel glinting in sunlight. "I'll carve you once and for all, you red demon of hell!" Marley growled. He towered over the Cheyenne. Needles clung to his ravaged face, bloodstains spread over the front of his coat. Big Marley lunged. Panther Burn darted out of harm's way and landed with feline grace by his rifle. He swung the barrel and knocked the knife out of Marley's grip. Big Marley closed in and caught the Cheyenne in a choke; the huge man's beefy fingers formed an ironlike grip encircling Panther Burn's throat. He lifted Panther Burn off the ground.

"You've haunted us too damn long," Marley hissed, raising the Cheyenne till his legs dangled in the air.

Panther Burn rammed the muzzle of his Winchester against Marley's throat and squeezed the trigger. An explosion, smoke stung his nostrils, blood spewed in a grisly arc and spattered the ground behind Marley as the huge man hurled Panther Burn aside and toppled forward. Panther Burn struggled and kicked away as Big Marley, although nearly decapitated, reached for the Cheyenne's ankle, missed, and with his fading effort caught a pine cone, crushed it, and died. Panther Burn coughed and crawled to his feet. He staggered toward the horses. Bragg was gone, but he could still be caught. Wood splintered. Branches tore away as a horseman rode at a gallop out of a thicket to Panther Burn's left. The war chief spun and fired on instinct, and through the gunsmoke saw the rider topple and roll down the incline almost to Panther Burn's feet.

It was Michael.

Panther Burn lowered his Winchester, dropped it, and sank to his knees.

"No." The war chief's voice was a whisper. No, he hadn't meant to . . . he thought it was . . . no . . . "No!" Michael's face was a mask of red. Part of his scalp was puckered and ripped loose, welling blood. His breathing was shallow and weak. Then a woman wailed and he heard Rebecca as she rode into the clearing, dismounted, and ran to her son. Panther Burn looked at her and shook his head, his unspoken entreaty, that he had not recognized Michael. Rebecca looked down at her only child and cradled him, a chant of anguish in her throat. Another shadow fell across them and Panther Burn snatched up his Winchester as Sabbath McKean led his horse toward them. The marshal held his own rifle in one hand, the hammer back, ready to fire from the hip if necessary. He came to a halt a few yards from where mother and father gathered about their wounded son. Sabbath stared at Panther Burn. The silence of the forest descended on them, but in this place of death, the beauty of the earth was tarnished, almost mocking.

"Now, we can kill each other or we can try to save that lad," McKean said.

Panther Burn looked down at his son, then across at Rebecca, confusion and helplessness in his eyes.

"There is . . . a doctor . . . in Lame Deer," Rebecca said.

22

Two women by lamplight, both healers in their own way. Both loving the same man, in different ways. Kate snipped the last of the sutures and examined her handiwork once more. The slug had peeled the scalp down to bone and butchered flesh as it glanced off his skull. The result was a nasty wound that by the grace of heaven, or the All-Father, hadn't killed. At least, not yet.

> My son, my child,
> my little one,
> be strong
> as your father is strong.

Throughout the long ride down from the Divide, Rebecca had watched over Michael and sung her healing prayer. And as she sang, perhaps deep in his wounded sleep he heard and breathed and refused to let go of life.

> My son, my child,
> my little one,
> be healed
> as you are loved.

Rebecca sat to one side of the bed, her eyes fixed on her son, her whole body tense as Kate bathed away the blood, cleaned the wound with alcohol, and stitched him back together. She covered his head with a gauze bandage, keeping the pressure firm but unrestrictive. And when she had finished, Kate slipped into a nearby chair across from Rebecca on the other side of the bed. Michael lay between them. They were in the upstairs bedroom that Kate used for a hospital room, where a patient might receive more intensive care. She folded her hands across her chest and leaned back in the leather-backed chair. Her robe was smeared with Michael's blood. She sighed and looked over at Rebecca, reading the silent pleading in the medicine woman's expression. Her song was ended, the All-Father must listen to her anguished heart now.

"He lost a great deal of blood," Kate said, remembering midnight, two hours earlier, when she had answered the knock at her back door and discovered Rebecca, Panther Burn, and Sabbath McKean with Michael stretched on a litter looking like a corpse. Only Kate's professionalism had kept her from crying out in horror at the sight of the wounded burden being carried into her house.

Kate lowered her gaze to his strong yet gentle face, still unmoving as death. A tear spilled down her cheek, tracing an erratic path to her jawline.

"You love him too," Rebecca quietly said.

Kate looked up and nodded. "I love him," she admitted.

Rebecca nodded. "The wolf spoke your name," she replied, knowing Kate would not understand. It was impossible to explain the old ways. They had to be lived. She rose from her chair and stood by the bed. Michael's once powerful physique seemed shrunken and drawn in.

"His color is bad," said Kate, "but his breathing is at least even and regular even if it's a bit shallow. I like to think these are positive indications."

"He will live," Rebecca said. "I know this now. But I hurt because he hurts."

"Such a blow to the head can lead to extremely negative complications . . . blindness . . . even speech problems. But if we are lucky, and infection doesn't set in . . ."

"My son will live," Rebecca matter-of-factly repeated. She glanced over at Kate. "Thank you."

Kate seemed surprised. Rebecca read her thoughts; it wasn't difficult.

"I saw my son, dying. And I asked why. Why had he risked his life so for a father who walked a different path? Then I remembered something your father told my people, long ago. Blessed are the peacemakers." She placed her hand on Michael's. "I knew him then. My son was no longer a stranger to me. Panther Burn, my husband, is a warrior. He can never be anything else. His day is ending. My son is the peacemaker. He can never be anything else. His day has just begun!"

"And between sunset and morning?" Kate asked, caught up in the medicine woman's spell.

"Are the women who love them. You and I," Rebecca softly answered. She looked down at Michael. "Stay with him, daughter of my long-ago friend. Your place is here." Rebecca turned to leave. Her footsteps were muffled by the throw rug spread across the hardwood floor. The medicine woman paused, her hand upon the doorsill.

"Perhaps, one day, you will teach me some . . . of what you do here."

"Yes," said Kate. "If you will teach me . . . to . . . to 'sing.'"

Rebecca smiled. Her heart grew warm, and when she turned toward Kate, a smile lit her face, erasing her hurt and her fears. "*E-pave-e.* It is good," she said. And seeing Kate draw near to Michael, added encouragement. "He will live."

"I hope so," Kate whispered.

"Not hope. You must believe," said Rebecca Blue Thrush.

Kate nodded and wearily scooted her chair closer to Michael's bed and leaned forward, resting her head on the down mattress. The top of her head pressed against his outer thigh. She used her left forearm for a pillow, her right hand bunched into a fist on the sheet. Kate closed her eyes and told herself she had done all she could. Nothing left now, but to—*yes, Rebecca, I will*—believe.

She closed her eyes a moment, heard a whisper of motion. A hand touched her head and clumsily caressed her hair. Rebecca saw, and froze in the doorway. Kate sat up, clutching at the hand. Michael was awake and watching her, a fragile smile upon his face despite his pain. "So, woman, I finally found a way into your bed."

Moonlight soft on shuttered windows, curtains drawn, oil lamps burning low, faint light for fearful hearts. Sabbath McKean walked to the front window, and lifting a curtain, opened the shutters no more than an inch and peered out at a column of soldiers threading their way through the settlement past darkened houses and the shuttered buildings strewn along either side of what passed for Main Street. Captain Morbitzer, in the lead, sagged forward in the saddle, head nodding, jerking up as he caught himself falling asleep. Sabbath thanked his lucky stars that he and Panther Burn, Rebecca, and Michael had arrived unnoticed. Panther Burn sat on the stairs, a rifle across his lap. He seemed lost in thought, his eyes fixed on a still point far from the turning torturous world of the present. Sabbath continued to watch the troopers file past. He gave a start as the moon cleared the clouds, for among the soldiers rode Jubal Bragg. He must have stumbled into them by accident. Sabbath quickly closed the shutter and eased the curtain back. He picked up a cup of coffee from a nearby table and took a sip and grimaced. "Worse than old man Wister's at Foot o' the Mountains," he said to himself. He had never learned to make good coffee. Cooking was the least of his vocations. He glanced over at Panther Burn. "He'll be all right. It ain't your fault. I mean. You didn't know it was the lad."

"I thought it was you," Panther Burn said. "I wish it had been."

"Hope you understand if I don't share your sentiments." Sabbath walked over and stood in front of the Cheyenne. "I want you to know something. Michael agreed to come and talk with you. I trailed him. It seemed a good idea at the time . . . keeping Bragg at bay until I had a chance to reason with you." Sabbath tugged at his long mustache. His stomach growled. He took out his pocket watch. "Three in the morning." He sighed, shook his head and started toward the kitchen, and paused as Rebecca appeared at the top of the stairs. Panther Burn looked over his shoulder and saw her and stood. She motioned to him.

"Your son would speak with you."

Panther Burn hurried up the stairs and down the brief hallway to Michael's room. Kate stood aside, for the first time realizing that this was the terrible Panther Burn, scourge of the penny dreadfuls—just a man, average in height, a trifle too thin. Yet there was indeed an aura about him, and she had the feeling his kind would not come again. Panther Burn stepped quietly to the bed, and when his shadow fell across his son, Michael opened his eyes again.

"Father."

"Yes, I am," said Panther Burn. "I forgot that, in my anger at seeing how my people have lost the Circle. And how you have lost the Circle. You have lost the way."

"No, Father." Michael winced as pain cut through him like a surgeon's scalpel, shattering his resolve. He gasped, regained control for a moment. "I walk the Great Circle of life and death and life with the All-Father, I follow the Cheyenne way only by another trail. There is more than one trail through the forest."

"Perhaps," Panther Burn said. "I will think on this. Yet I grieve for my people. If it is true that they must walk in the new ways, what will keep them Cheyenne?

Who will teach them to hear the wind? They must have something to remember. Something . . . ." Suddenly Panther Burn's expression changed as he discovered an answer in himself.

"Father?" Michael tried to rise but Panther Burn pushed him back.

"We have never known each other," Panther Burn said, drawing close. "There was no time. But you have always been my son and you will always be."

"What are you going to do?"

"You will know—when you hear the thunder in the hills." Panther Burn placed his hand upon Michael's shoulder and patted once, then turned and left the room. He hesitated a moment by Kate, looked back at Michael and then to her again. A smile touched the corners of his mouth as if he sensed the growing bond between them. He continued past her, took up his rifle, and descended the stairs to the floor below, where Sabbath waited in the parlor.

Kate stepped inside the room again and resumed her vigil at Michael's bedside. His concern was evident. He looked at her.

"I don't think I will see him again," Michael said. He reached for her. Kate placed her hand in his.

"I love you, Michael Spirit Wolf." There. It was said. Time was spinning away from them. Pride had no place. She wondered what her own father would say and thought he just might approve. Now. She leaned forward and kissed him. And in her kiss, in her warmth, was life. Michael closed his eyes and drifted into sleep, remembering when first he kissed her and how shocked she had been. "I told you," he said in a drowsy voice. "The next time you would come to me."

Kate remembered, and throwing caution out with pride, kissed him again.

"How is the lad?"

"He will do well," said Panther Burn. He leveled his rifle at Sabbath, who was caught unawares, and started to reach for the pistol holstered at his waist. Panther Burn shook his head. "I would not like to kill you now. There is no hatred in my heart."

"Fire that gun and you'll alert the soldiers."

"You will still be dead."

"That I will." Sabbath sighed. He raised his hands and Panther Burn disarmed him. "I guess I never really wanted to bring you in. But the soldiers are another story. The Army will never stop looking for you. Stay around these parts and they'll make your people suffer so much they'll turn on you like a pack of—"

"Dogs," Rebecca said from the stairway. She walked down to be by her husband's side.

"Sabbath McKean, I trust you. You carry my words to the soldiers. Friday is the ration day?" he asked, glancing at Rebecca.

"Three days from now." She nodded.

"On that day, when the sun clears the Divide, let the soldiers wait for me in the valley to the north at the place called Squaw Hill. For I shall ride against them."

"Are you crazy? You won't stand a chance. They'll kill you."

"Then let the soldiers see how a Cheyenne warrior can die. But tell the Long Knives I shall ride through them. And I will count coup on them. Let the soldiers stop me if they can."

Panther Burn started down the hallway toward the back door. Rebecca remained behind, keeping Sabbath covered with his own gun. Her expression remained unchanged, though Panther Burn's pronouncement had been like a white-hot dagger plunged into her breast. His words had filled her with horror. She wanted to run to her husband and beg him to reconsider. Instead, like the warrior's woman she was, Rebecca Blue Thrush continued to hold Sabbath at bay long after she heard the back door close.

Outside, in the night, Panther Burn clung to the shadows as best he could as he crossed the backyard and worked his way to the carriage shed where the horses were tethered. He had just gained safety when he heard the hammer of a rifle being cocked. The war chief stopped in his tracks, one hand outstretched, fingers reaching for the rawhide reins. Slowly he lowered his arms and turned around. In the faint silvery glow of moonlight a man aimed a Hawken rifle at Panther Burn's midsection. The war chief unconsciously tightened the muscles in his abdomen. He sniffed the air, detected the reek of whiskey. Yet the rifle was steady in the man's grip. Long stringy hair, a thin half-naked body clothed in ragged overalls and battered worn-out boots—here was a broken Cheyenne. Panther Burn drew closer and recognized the Hawken, for it had once been his. Starlight glinted on a design, a Morning Star outlined in brass tacks on the rifle stock.

"Zachariah . . . ?" whispered Panther Burn, scarcely believing his eyes. Could this scarecrow of a man really be Zachariah Scalpcane? He received no answer, but he chanced death, and ignoring the rifle, stepped closer until the muzzle pressed against his chest. Zachariah looked up at him. Tears streaked his face.

"You should not have returned." He tried to squeeze the trigger. The rifle wavered. "You betrayed me." His voice rasped like the dull teeth of a saw blade scraped across metal.

Panther Burn remembered what Michael had said, his words of reconciliation. Panther Burn had also felt betrayed. Now Zachariah accused him. So many paths through the forest . . .

"I never meant to," said Panther Burn. "I think maybe you have betrayed yourself as well." The war chief placed his hand on Zachariah's shoulder. "Are we Cheyenne, or dogs whom the white man has set one upon the other?"

Slowly the rifle lowered. Zachariah no longer understood. His shoulders bowed forward. "I am lost," he said, his voice trembling.

"I know a path. It will not be easy, but you can walk it with me, if you want." Panther Burn swung around, padded over to his horse. He cut the leather tracings of the crude travois strapped to another of the Army horses, and freeing the animal, led it over to Zachariah. Panther Burn mounted his own and waited. The moon drifted behind clouds like gauze strips draped upon the sky. An owl screeched and swooped down from a nearby cottonwood by the creek. It lost its prey and rose aloft, complaining to the night. The cry of a coyote lingered in mournful echo, filtering down from the hills.

"A path . . ." stammered Zachariah. He pulled himself into the saddle, gasped, and steadied himself. "Does it lead far? What must we bring?"

The last war chief of the Cheyenne looked at Zachariah, leaning close and remembering the daring of a small boy. And oh, the wild glory that shone in the eyes of Panther Burn as he answered, "Courage."

23

Thursday.

A lead slug tore a fistful of wood out of a fencepost on the edge of Lame Deer. The gunshot echoed down the hills. Captain Henry Morbitzer sighted down the length of the Smith and Wesson, thumbed the hammer back, and squeezed off a second round. Splinters flew from the post.

"Shoots good," he said.

"Sixty dollars' worth," Jubal Bragg replied.

"Nice balance," Morbitzer added. He heard the creak of axles, and turning, spied another pair of wagons heading into town. Both buckboards were crowded with Cheyenne families, men, women, and children in from farms and hardscrabble ranches coming early for their rations. Henry Morbitzer knew the reason why.

"More of them," Jubal noted. "The town's already crowded with the likes of these red devils."

"It is their town, after all," the captain remarked. "I expected as much. The troop from Fort Keogh ought to be arriving sometime this afternoon." Morbitzer was obviously pleased at the way he was handling this emergency. "I have assured Tyrell Gude the situation is under control. No need for alarm."

Bragg brought out a brandy flask and lifted it in salute. "I commend you, Captain," he said, and tilted the flask to his lips, only to pause with the pungent fragrance clinging to his nostrils as he watched a horseman come riding out of the hills. The figure on horseback seemed poised on the polished surface of the flask. Bragg lowered the shiny silver bottle and tucked it back inside his coat pocket. He had the unsettling notion he recognized the man in the distance. The colonel could make out another couple of horses or mules strung out behind the rider.

"Hmm," the captain muttered, staring in the same direction as Bragg.

"Ought to be McKean. Bringing in Sergeant Broken Knife and your man . . uh . . . Muly?"

"Marley. Big Marley," said Jubal Bragg.

"Queer sort of name."

"It fit," Jubal replied. He watched the rider in the distance increase in size as he angled toward them across the valley floor. Jubal recognized Sabbath by his short broad build and the flame-orange mustache that obscured the lower half of the man's face.

Sabbath led two mules on a length of rope looped through their bridles. A tiny brass bell hung from each of the bits and jangled with every step of the plodding beasts. Two blanket-wrapped corpses were slung facedown over the mules. Jubal felt a pain gnaw at his gut at the sight of Marley's long legs dangling from under the brown blanket; then he willed the discomfort away, protecting himself from grief. Sabbath headed straight for the two men. A half-dozen Indian children charged toward him. A rabbit darted from under a patch of dry thistle. The mules tried to fight the rope as the rabbit scrambled beneath their hooves. Sabbath shouted and cursed and brought the skittish animals under control. The rabbit leaped to safety. Its respite was brief, for the six fearless hunters in pursuit brandished their bows and arrows, ignored the mules with their burden of death, and gave chase. They scampered past the mules without so much as a backward glance, so immersed were they in a ritual of life. Sabbath brought the contrary beasts under control and continued toward the captain and Bragg. The expression of displeasure on Sabbath's face made clear how he felt about seeing Jubal still on the reservation. He noticed the bullet-scarred fencepost, then gazed over at Camp Merritt. Men sat before their cabins, cleaning rifles, sharpening sabers, polishing boots. The place was a flurry of activity as soldiers prepared themselves for war.

Sabbath looked down at Jubal and then tossed him the end of the rope. "Bragg, you left something up on the Divide." Sabbath turned toward the captain. "Maybe you ought to have the other one brought over to Gude's."

"Leave them here. I'll assign a man to it," Morbitzer said.

"Obliged," Sabbath said. He glanced around at Jubal. "I ought to arrest you."

"For what? Defending myself? Panther Burn attacked *us*." Jubal hooked his thumbs in his vest pockets. He returned Sabbath's glare, measure for measure. He was a man well aware of his rights.

"Just look at all these soldier boys. They can't wait to get at it. They don't even know they're working for you. How does it feel, Jubal, to have your killing done for you?"

"It feels good," Jubal replied, a thin smile on his lips. He refused to be baited by the lawman.

"That is quite enough, Marshal McKean," the captain added, stepping between the two men. "Mr. Bragg has recounted his story to me, of the personal tragedies he has suffered at the hands of these hostiles, especially Panther Burn. I cannot blame him in the least for wanting to see such a renegade apprehended. And as for your opinions, sir, I will have you know the cavalry works for no one but the government of these United States."

"Spoken like a patriot, Captain Morbitzer. Spoken like a patriot. I don't suppose the government could

316

just back down on this? You know, turn around and ride away and ignore this whole business? Kill Panther Burn, and you'll create a martyr. Ah, hell . . . don't bother. I already know your answer." Sabbath touched the brim of his hat and walked his mount off toward St. Theresa's Catholic Church. McKean rode up to the front of the church, where Father Hillary was sweeping the front steps. The priest looked up, paused to catch his breath; his hands propped on the broom handle, the very picture of calm. But appearances were deceiving. Father Hillary dreaded the day to come.

"Good afternoon to you, Marshal McKean," he said, tightness in his voice.

"Afraid I left you some work over at Camp Merritt, Father."

"Oh?"

"Two funerals," Sabbath said, stabbing a thumb in the direction he had come from. The soldiers were leading both mules over to the Indian agent's house. "I reckon ol' Marley might have use for a minister about now, at least to read some words over him."

"Oh my," Father Hillary gasped. He tossed aside his broom and hurried down the steps. Sabbath dismounted and blocked the priest's path.

"They ain't going no place, Father. You offered to share a bottle of good Kentucky whiskey with me the other night. Does it still stand?"

"In the kitchen, just inside the pantry, top shelf," Father Hillary said.

"Will you join me?" Sabbath asked as Father Hillary brushed past.

"Good heavens, man. No. It's too early for me," the priest called over his shoulder as he broke toward Tyrell Gude's house at a dead run. Sabbath lifted his gaze toward Squaw Hill north of town where Panther Burn would ride down to make war against the government of the United States. Too early, the priest had said.

"And too late for the rest of us," Sabbath muttered to

317

himself. He climbed the steps to the church and entered, seeking the solace to be found not at the altar but the pantry . . . holy spirits.

The ashes of the spirit fire danced above the flames. The coals glowed baleful yellow and crimson; shapes unfathomable to all but the medicine woman billowed and leaped in mad gyrations above the embers. Rebecca sang and sprinkled a mixture of crushed antelope horn, the pulverized roots of wild strawberries, and dried sagebrush onto the fire. Firelight made vivid her buckskin dress and braided hair. She held a small wooden flute adorned with beading and brass buttons and when she had finished her prayer-song she lifted the flute to her lips and blew a piercing note, blew softly and the note grew mellow, harder again and the note rose in pitch, becoming like the scream of a wounded animal. She reached in her pouch of badger hide and brought out the large silky feather of a great blue heron and fanned the fire three times, then set the feather aside. In a second, another figure had stepped forward. Panther Burn brandished a war lance and warily approached the medicine fire, where he waited for Rebecca to give him the sign. Her eyes were on the flames. The wind rose here on the hill crest and the flames became streamers of light. Rebecca sounded another piercing note on the flute and placed the heron feather into the heart of the coals. As it burst into flame she nodded to Panther Burn, who loosed a wild cry of his own and drove the point of his war lance down into the fire, where he skewered the remains of the sacred feather. Sparks flew upward, exploding in his face. Motes of pulsing fire clung to his naked torso, blistering his flesh. The wind stole his cry and carried it down the hills to the town of Lame Deer in the valley below, and there were men who heard that cry and trembled.

Rebecca moved quickly now. She took up the war shield she had made for Panther Burn, and as the war chief stepped back from the fire, Rebecca clamped the shield over the flames with a single sudden motion that smothered them out. When she lifted the shield, only a thick column of gray-black smoke spiraled upward toward the night sky. She held the rawhide shield aloft then so the moonlight shone upon the Morning Star she had painted on the surface. Panther Burn stretched out his arms and she placed the shield in his hands and said softly, *"Hena-haanehe,"* which means "It is ended." Panther Burn turned and walked back to the ridge, where he could better watch the village below. The valley floor was dotted with campfires. Zachariah was seated on a stump, Panther Burn's Winchester and his own Hawken at his feet. He had cleaned and loaded both weapons and sat slumped forward, the picture of depression and fear.

"Our people have been coming into the valley all day. I think they have come to watch us do battle with the soldiers . . ."

"Good," said Panther Burn.

"I do not think they will help us."

"Good," Panther Burn repeated, staring out at the night. The townspeople had no place during such an action on the morrow. He glanced down at Zachariah.

Somewhere behind his weary eyes, the little boy Zachariah Scalpcane had once been still lived. Panther Burn could see the fear in the younger man's expression. He did not blame him. Tomorrow would not be easy.

Zachariah sighed. "I wish Joshua were here with me. I would like him to know how we faced the soldiers together."

"The story will be sung around the campfires and he will hear and feel proud." Panther Burn reached forward and patted Zachariah on the shoulder. "The All-Father has blessed me. For I have two sons and both have made me proud." He noticed how the younger warrior's shoulders straightened with pride at such an admission. "The many-times-firing gun is yours," Panther Burn added. "Carry it with you tomorrow."

Zachariah sucked in his breath, then took up the rifle

319

and gingerly caressed the tempered metal and worn but solid stock. Bravado conquered fear as he sighted along the barrel. Such a fine weapon this was.

"I wish Uncle Joshua were here too," admitted Panther Burn. He walked back the way he had come. Above him, the sky was draped with clouds like bridal veils strewn upon obsidian seas. And windrift was the world below, where the branches of the pines rustled, weeds trembled, and the creek was a diamond-studded ribbon uncoiled through the valley. Half a dozen wild ducks erupted from a cluster of scrub brush, the rush of their beating wings like tearing silk. Beauty was in the night and Panther Burn's heart was glad. Glad, too, that Rebecca waited for him by the still-warm embers of the sacred fire. Panther Burn sat next to her and took her hands in his.

"I journeyed many miles to reach this place. I have seen the towns of the white man, I have seen the way he lives. I have cut his fences and eaten his tame food and drunk from his dead water. I have seen things I do not understand. Yet I know this, I do not belong. I am saying this because I want you to understand."

"Saaa. I know who I love. Do you think you are a mystery to me?" Rebecca answered. She remembered lovemaking, and secret words; she remembered his rashness, his incorruptible will. He had been born to ride to war. He had been born for the morning about to come; a panther cannot be tamed. "You are of your father's blood, a warrior." She placed the palm of her hand upon his chest. "My heart and yours are one and the same." She lay back and pulled him to her, and although her eyes glistened in the night, her voice was strong and there was magic in her embrace. "One and the same . . . always."

The night lay soft and quiet and seemed to fill the bedroom with the promise of fall. Michael sat propped against the pillows, an open notebook upon his lap, a few lines of prose scrawled upon the pages. He studied himself in the vanity mirror on the wall opposite the bed. His wound had indeed looked far worse than it was. The bullet had struck at a peculiar angle and glanced off his skull, saving his life by a fraction of an inch. Ignoring a savage headache, he had spent a few hours Wednesday on his feet. Today the dizziness had decreased and he had spent most of the afternoon out of bed. Kate had been away. The ever-increasing number of Cheyenne arriving in Lame Deer for ration Friday always meant an opportunity for Kate to recruit new patients. There were always young women whose term of pregnancy needed to be assessed and children with a gamut of cuts and bruises, some of which needed treatment. He could hear her downstairs. She was working in the kitchen, softly humming as she prepared an evening meal for them. He stared at the notebook before him and wrote a line, frowned, marked it out, tried another line, and decided it would do. He had never tried this before . . . writing, putting his own thoughts and emotions down on paper, his penmanship a struggling scrawl. It pleased him, even more than reading. Footsteps sounded on the stairway and a moment later Kate appeared in the room. She carried a tray and brought it over to the bed. Michael smelled eggs and bacon and fry bread, and Kate had added a clay bowl of chokecherry pudding to dip the bread in. She noticed the notebook and looked over at his open saddlebags and realized it was his. She had never seen it before. Then she remembered his desire to write when his heart could no longer contain his feelings.

Michael put the notebook aside, seemingly embarrassed at her discovery. Kate placed the tray alongside the bed. He glanced at the food and wondered if his father was hungry on what was probably the last day of his life. He reached down and took the tray and placed it on a table near the bed.

"You need to eat," Kate said.

"Maybe later." The curtains on the window fluttered inward, roused by the gentle kiss of an autumnal breeze. Kate walked to the window and looked out at the dark

and silent hills. She understood the reasons for his lack
of appetite. "Perhaps Rebecca will talk him out of it."

"She loves him too much to try," Michael said.

Kate looked around at him. "I do not understand
such a kind of love."

"Who can?" Michael said. Then he lowered his gaze
to the notebook. "Not I," he went on. Then he
brightened again. "Tell me. Did you heal many Cheyenne today?"

"Not many," Kate said. She heard the note of sorrow
in his voice. He dreaded the morning. She did not
blame him. She yearned to comfort him and yet when
she felt he needed her, Kate could not escape her own
professionalism. He was her patient. And what she was
feeling was most unethical.

"Come here," he said, cutting through the silence, his
voice guttural and thick with emotion. Humor, sadness,
and a fierce and abiding appreciation for life, balanced
on the knife edge of a passion too long restrained. It
hurt too deeply to hide. Kate had changed from the
woolen dress she wore as a uniform—somehow, the
more formal her attire, the more respect she received
from the skeptical families that lived back toward the
Divide. A coarse cotton nightgown covered her from
neck to ankle and a brown robe covered the nightgown.
Tonight her hair hung loose and free, flowing over her
shoulders and down her back. She stepped back from
the window. His soft brown eyes wore a haunted look.
His finely chiseled features revealed his pain. The bandage on his forehead showed starkly white against his
coppery flesh. His hands opened, to hold her.

"Be with me." He sighed.

She walked to him, her mind full of arguments, her
heart full of surrender. "Your wound . . ."

"If I get dizzy you can take over." He rose up from
the bed, the covers falling away from his naked flesh. In
one brief motion he extinguished the lamp. Moonlight
through the windows flooded into the room; a beam of
silvery light crept across the rug, vanquishing the darkness. Michael's arms entwined with Kate's embrace as

she came to him, needing him as desperately as he needed her. Robe and gown were swept aside. Lips joined in a fevered kiss, then flesh in fiery union. A cry of momentary pain. A moan of unimagined pleasure. Quick breaths, sudden ecstasy in oneness . . . peace. Darkness dispelled, two called together slept upon the tousled sheets, two lovers, lying close, loving and loved, but at last, asleep. In the trembling glow of a solitary candle, the journal lay open to the place where Michael had set his thoughts, in art, upon the page:

Kate—

Love me still for the weariness I hold
thrown round me like a robe of sorrow.
I step helpless on a path so cold.
In the lonely dark, be light, my love aglow.

24

Ration Friday, September 27, 1889

In late September, in *tonoove-he-ese*, which is the fall-moon, summer ends and the world welcomes the dying of the year. The cycle of renewal begins, the past is discarded for the promise of the future. Leaves curl, shudder in the cool wind's embrace, leaves run riotous red or turn the color of raw gold shining in a pool of melted ice. The world in *tonoove-he-ese* dons warpaint so all men may witness what they are about to lose. And gain. The world wears a mantle of glory in autumn, and grieves not the coming of winter, for it has heard the promise whispered in the sacred wind, that nothing is forever except the Great Circle. Out of loss comes gain, out of death . . . life.

Panther Burn dabbed his fingers in a shallow cup of clay dyed with crushed berries. He placed two fingers on his forehead and slashed down, leaving twin trails of crimson across his eyes and cheeks. He glanced up at the sky. The far horizons wore morning's first blush. Zachariah busily applied a mask of black clay over forehead and chin. He wasted little time in his preparations, fearing to tarry lest he lose heart. He mounted and sat motionless, cradling his Winchester in the crook of his arm. Zachariah kept a respectful distance from Panther Burn and Rebecca. And there was a touch of sadness in his heart, for he had no one to bid farewell or hand him a war shield as he rode out to do battle. He thought of his mother and of Warbonnet Creek. So many years ago, so many deaths ago. The memories were painful to relive, but he clung to them for courage. Hate was all he had now. It was all he had ever had.

Rebecca had lived with the knowledge of this moment. Now, it had finally come. . . .

"Woman, it is good you do not weep," Panther Burn said, finishing his own preparations.

"Am I not a warrior's woman? I cried my tears long ago," she said. "My heart has grown used to the sadness I feel. And used to the joy." Rebecca frowned, trying to put her feelings into words; she tried to speak them now, for fear she might never get the chance to say them to him again. Panther Burn looked toward the horizon where the clouds billowed upward, shaping and reshaping themselves. There a winged horse, an eagle's talon, a waterfall, a mountainous realm for the All-Father. Panther Burn lowered his gaze to Rebecca. He was drawn to her eyes, for they were the windows of her love.

"Listen for the bells," she said. "It will be Uncle Joshua." And swallowing through the tightness in her throat, Rebecca handed him the war shield she had made magic over. He took it from her and walked over to his horse and swung up on its back. She studied him as if committing to memory every detail. His moccasins and fringed leggings, the porcupine-quill breastplate, the raven feather he had fixed into a headdress to hide the shame of his close-cropped hair. He carried the war shield in his right hand and the war lance in his left. The spear was ten feet of pine sapling tipped with a sharpened stone point and trimmed with raven feathers below the tip and just above his fist. He had smeared war paint upon the horse's flanks to better hide the cavalry brand and painted white circles around the animal's eyes that it might frighten his enemies in battle. He walked the mount toward Rebecca.

"One day I will come riding, you will hear me call you by name. I will carry you away, Rebecca Blue Thrush. And on that day, there will be no leaving . . . ever again." He leaned forward and his eyes blazed with fire and his voice rang with a truth, impossible to deny.

"There will be no leaving," Rebecca said, her voice firm. The wind blew the strands of her black hair across her features and concealed the moistness she had been unable to hold back. She reached down and scooped up the ashes from her medicine fire and placed her handprint in the center of the shield, in the heart of the Morning Star. At that gesture Panther Burn reared his horse and whirled around and cried out because he could no longer contain the feelings that filled him with both a sense of loss and yet such wild joy. He rode at a gallop back to the crest of the hill where Zachariah waited, where they could watch the sun rise and listen for Joshua Beartusk to summon them down into the valley.

A hundred soldiers representing K, and C troop on loan from Fort Keogh, were formed in a double row across the north end of the valley about a quarter of a mile out of the settlement. The two lines were staggered so that each trooper might bring his carbine to bear. Directly behind the soldiers but flanked to either side were better than six hundred Cheyenne men, women, and children. They had gathered in the early-morning hours, in darkness, singing and praying: they had come to see the last warrior and the last battle. Michael Spirit Wolf was there, standing in the bed of Father Hillary's buckboard. He too had come to be with the father he had never really been allowed to know. The Cheyenne families around him watched him closely as if expecting him to ride to his father's side. But he knew his place, he knew where his battles must be fought and won. His were the days to come. And if his people did not understand now, one day they would. He waited and looked to the hill where two lonely figures watched and kept vigil with the sun as it poked above the hilltops, sending a silent shimmering of light rushing down the hillside flooding the valley, warming the dew-laden ground. Kate stood next to Michael and when she spied the two men on the bluff her hand tightened in his. Three men rode up behind the wagon and Michael glanced over his shoulder at Captain Henry Morbitzer, Sabbath McKean, and Jubal Bragg. Behind the three, Tyrell Gude waited nervously in the shadows of his canvas-covered buggy. He was anticipating the worst possible scenario, that the Cheyenne would rise up in support of Panther Burn and attack the soldiers. But the young captain had assured him everything was under control. He had more than enough men to handle any emergency.

Morbitzer nodded and tipped his hat as he rode past Kate Madison.

"Good morning, Captain. May I have a word with you?" she called out.

"Hardly the proper time, madam. I am about to engage the enemy in battle."

"One man?" Kate asked, incredulous.

"One man who has boasted he will ride through our ranks," the captain replied. He removed his hat and wiped the perspiration from his face. "He has offered an insult we cannot let pass." Morbitzer shrugged. "I wouldn't worry, Doctor Madison. I doubt any of this will come off. He's up there and he can plainly see the force I have arrayed against him." He looked at Michael, fixing the wounded man in a steely stare. "No doubt we will have to ride up there and flush him out. Only a fool would attack us. A fool or a madman, and I doubt he is either of those." Morbitzer turned to Jubal Bragg. "I'd keep well back, Mr. Bragg. This is government business, after all."

"I have come to bear witness to the final act, Captain

Morbitzer, and wish to take no part in the play." Jubal Bragg shaded his eyes and peered at the distant hill. "He's up on the top, all right." He touched the brim of his hat and nodded to Kate and the captain, ignored Michael and Sabbath McKean. He rode at a trot over to a place well away from the crowd of Cheyenne and between them and the troopers. Sabbath noticed as Bragg checked the loads on his matched revolvers.

"He may not take a part but he sure has had more than his share in the writing of the script," said McKean.

"Marshal, you can take your place with my command in the center of the line," Morbitzer suggested.

"Not hardly," said Sabbath. "I came to say good-bye to the younker here."

"But you are sworn to uphold the law!" Morbitzer's tone betrayed his nervousness. He had counted on keeping the old Indian fighter nearby, just in case.

"And murder ain't my idea of upholding law. Henry, I cannot stop you, 'cause you got your heart set on being a big hero today. But I sure don't intend to see you through it." He turned his back on the unnerved young officer and leaned over to shake Michael's hand. He kissed Kate's in a gesture of time-honored gallantry.

"McKean, you are a United States marshal and by the authority of the badge you wear it is your duty . . ." Sabbath swung his horse around. A look from McKean and the captain's voice faded. The marshal's horse danced skittishly, clouds of dust drifted up from beneath the pawing hooves. Sabbath ripped the badge from his coat and tossed it on the ground in front of the startled captain. That was his answer to the officer. Then Sabbath looked back at Michael.

"Should have done that long ago. Mighty heavy for such a tiny piece of metal. Somewhere . . ." He lifted his eyes to the horizon, his right hand absentmindedly tugging on the curled tips of his mustache. Now his expression grew dreamy as he spoke. "Somewhere I think I will find me a mountain I ain't seen the other side of yet." He sighed in satisfaction.

"Good luck, Sabbath McKean," said Michael. And Kate said, "Godspeed."

"I only wish I could tell your pa that I . . ." Sabbath's voice trailed off. "Ah hell, I reckon he knows." The ex-marshal looked over at Captain Morbitzer. "Tell me, bucko, you know what counting coup is?"

Morbitzer shook his head no.

Sabbath grinned. "I got a feeling you're about to find out." He touched his heels to his gelding's flanks and rode off toward the west, toward the dimly visible peaks of the snow-tipped Absarokas. Not once did he look back.

"Soon," Michael whispered to himself. Golden was the valley and azure the sky. A morning mist rose with coming warmth, diaphanous waves spread out from Lame Deer Creek to lap against the base of the hills, turning the soldiers into ranks of disembodied specters and all but obscuring the throng of Indian and white spectators gathered at the north end of the valley. Michael etched the moment in his memory, locking the scene away in his heart and mind, creating for himself a reservoir of inspiration upon which he would later draw.

He memorized the silence; for all the formidable numbers gathered in the valley, hardly a sound could be heard as the mist rose unannounced, dampening what sound there was, horses cropping the earth, the jingle of traces and creak of leather harness.

"He expected the mist to rise. That's what he's been waiting for. My father might even have a chance now," Michael said, reaching for Kate, who drew closer to him.

"I wish it could be stopped," she said, staring at the columns of soldiers, their carbines drawn. The tension from so many inexperienced troopers was infectious. Kate felt her flesh grow icy, she could count each beat of her heart.

"Oh, Michael, is there nothing you can do?"

"Only watch. Here is the father I have known, this

one who waits to ride into battle. Now I know him. And I think I understand him. And these are his children. All of us. He has always fought . . . for us."

"And now we do not need him anymore, the Morning Star people have no more use for warriors," Kate said, realizing what was about to happen, that Panther Burn was leaving his legacy indelibly etched in the minds of the onlookers. The Cheyenne had come to see Panther Burn, last of the war chiefs. And he intended to give them something to remember. Beside her, Michael straightened, his body hardened; he reached out to steady himself on her shoulder. And when he spoke, his voice was for her ears only.

"Now!" came his sharp whisper.

In the church, Father Hillary knelt in the pew closest to the altar. The hardwood kneeler bruised his knees but he ignored the discomfort. He prayed for the Cheyenne, for the soldiers gathered to do what they must, he prayed for peace . . . and for justice. At the back of the church blind old Joshua Beartusk stood by the bell rope, listening to the silence. Though he could not see, his hand found the rope, for he had memorized the steps to the bells. He always rang them on ration Friday to signal the families of the Cheyenne to come into the settlement to receive their allotted portion of staples from the United States government. Today he summoned them for another reason. He closed his fists around the rope and gave a mighty tug, grunting from the exertion as he pulled down. And with each tolling of the bell, his heart broke, little by little. And yet, in a way, his was a selfish sorrow. Joshua Beartusk wished that just for today the All-Father had returned an old man's sight so that he could ride with his nephew to glory.

Panther Burn lifted his eyes skyward. A tiny speck of shadow flashed across the sun, swirled lower, became a hawk. A gust of wind rushed up from the valley, the grasses on the hillside bowed in its passing. The hawk, the wind, the mist below were good signs. It was time.

Panther Burn stood in the rawhide stirrups and raised his spear and shield aloft as he loosed a wild cry that rang out over the valley. Zachariah added his voice to the war chief's and then the Cheyenne gathered in the valley took up the cry, for they had listened and heard with their hearts and remembered when the earth trembled beneath the great herds of buffalo, remembered when the Cheyenne were the lords of the plains, roaming at will from the Badlands to the Continental Divide, remembered a past that would never come again except in this one last instant when a man called Panther Burn, who had refused to live "tame," rode the warpath for them all.

The soldiers in the valley looked around nervously and realized how outnumbered they really were. Tyrell Gude eased back in his carriage and muttered to himself, "Lord help us." Jubal Bragg drew one of his Smith and Wessons. Come what may, he resolved to stand his ground. He would not run again.

A soldier in the front column loosed a shot from his carbine and young Captain Morbitzer drew erect in the saddle to spy the culprit. But a number of the soldiers followed suit. They levered shot after shot despite the fact that the men on the hill were out of range.

"Hold your fire," Morbitzer shouted, but his voice was drowned out by yet another fusillade as more of the troopers, sparked into action by the first gunshot, opened up with their Winchesters. Then a chorus of war yells erupted on every side and the captain turned in time to see the two braves on Squaw Hill, three hundred yards away, start down.

Panther Burn and Zachariah rode at a gallop, risking broken necks as they covered the slope, their horses slipping, regaining their stances, and always guided by the riders' excellent horsemanship. The animals leaped the final few yards into the mist that layered the valley floor. The water droplets caught the sunlight until all the world wore a golden mantle of blinding brilliance. Henry Morbitzer ceased trying to issue orders. He yanked his Colt revolver from his holster and opened fire into the mist with his men. Carbines emptied. Troopers clawed at their belts for cartridges and thumbed the shells into their carbines and opened fire again, working the levers of their guns as quickly as they could. And back within the reaches of the forest, Rebecca paused in her prayer-song where she sat in the shade of the pines and listened to the roaring guns like thunder in the hills. She closed her eyes, and both hands clasped around the pouch dangling from her throat, she resumed her song asking of the All-Father not that Panther Burn be spared but that he accomplish what he needed to, even if it cost him his life.

Panther Burn knew Rebecca was with him and as he rode at a gallop through the mist his heart burned with pride and the sound of the guns did not frighten him and in that moment he feared neither life nor death because he was one with the Circle now, he had heard his name whispered in the Sacred Wind, and who was there to stand against him?

The mist closed around him, shifted blindingly. But Panther Burn knew there was only one direction to ride, to the thunder of the guns and the destiny that awaited him. Bullets sliced the air around him, burned flesh; something slammed into his side. Ignore it. Something battered his shield, shattered his knee. Ignore it. No pain, his eyes ablaze, his soul on fire, what was pain to such a man? Three hundred yards. Two hundred. A hundred. Scream defiance. Kill me if you can, *ve-ho-e*. Zachariah's horse stumbled and collapsed and Zachariah went sprawling head over heels. He rolled to his feet and emptied his rifle at the troops. Another five slugs lifted him into the air and slammed him backward. He cried out to Panther Burn, who heard but could not stop. Nor did Zachariah want him to. Dying, the Cheyenne brave forced himself upright, wiped the blood from his eyes, and watched as Panther Burn charged headlong into the gunfire. No one could stand against such firepower. No man. But perhaps a legend. Then Zachariah shuddered as bullets continued to pelt him. He tried to endure, to cling to life. "*Hena-haanehe*," he groaned. *This is the end*. And died, sitting upright, legs outstretched, facing the ranks of troopers who had killed him.

The mist parted fifty yards from the soldiers. Panther Burn jabbed his spear point into the flanks of his war horse and the animal lunged to even greater speed. The acrid smoke from the rifles of the soldiers stung the warrior's nostrils but the gunfire lessened as the troopers struggled to reload. Several of the troopers in their haste had jammed their carbines and now had to dig the cartridges out of the blocked breeches. Forty yards, thirty, twenty—reach their lines and the men would have to fire at themselves. Blood was in his mouth. He spat it out. *All-Father, give me the strength*. Ten yards and then the panther was among them. Panther Burn loosed a shrill, bone-chilling shriek like a man possessed and the soldiers massed before him threw down their weapons and spurred their horses out of the way, wanting no part of this demon warrior. Captain Henry Morbitzer all by his lonesome in the middle of his vanishing ranks of men crammed a couple of shells into the cylinder of his revolver and looked up as Panther Burn bore down on him. The spear tip loomed like the scythe of death itself. The captain tugged sharply on his reins, his horse reared and tossed the young captain off. Henry Morbitzer landed on a rock the size of a melon and knocked the breath out of himself. He struggled to retrieve the gun he had dropped. The troopers to either side held their fire for fear of hitting their commanding officer. A shadow fell across Morbitzer and he looked up to see the Cheyenne war chief about to impale him.

"Sweet Jesus!" the young officer shouted, and tried to dodge. But it was Panther Burn who saved him. At the last possible second the Cheyenne warrior reversed his spear and tapped the captain on the head and galloped past, counting coup. Two soldiers spurred their horses to block the Cheyenne, but Panther Burn burst through their midst batting one aside with his shield and counting coup on the other with the shaft of his spear. He struck the trooper hard enough to stun the man and sent him tumbling from the saddle. No one remained to stop him. Panther Burn roared in triumph as he cleared the line of soldiers, riding through them as he had promised he would do. A cheer rose up to either side, a cry of triumph that grew louder than all the gunfire. But Panther Burn never allowed his horse to break stride. A tug and the painted gelding, itself bleeding from half a dozen wounds, bore down on the man who had waited behind these hundred soldiers, who had come to see his nightmares destroyed forever.

"Bragg!" Panther Burn shouted as he charged. He was dying, his strength had begun to fade. But he had to hold on. "Braaaaggg!"

Jubal Bragg grew pale. The troopers were no help now, for they would have to fire directly at both men to stop the Cheyenne. But in his last desperate moments, Jubal Bragg had found his courage.

"I'll kill you. By my hand, I swear it, you will die!" he yelled and aimed his Smith and Wesson .45.

Bragg fired. Panther Burn drew closer, trailing blood.

Bragg fired again. And Panther Burn lowered the point of the lance. Closer came the lance with its tip of sharpened stone.

Fired. Again. Again. Again to no avail. Panther Burn's will to live was stronger than death.

"Die!" Jubal shrieked. He raised his hands, dropping his empty gun, his palms outstretched, reaching out for the mercy he had never shown, the very quality hatred had leached from him long ago. The stone spear point took the colonel chest-high, shattering his sternum, ripping through lungs, crushing his spine as the shaft splintered and broke. The cry from the lips of the impaled man was inhuman, a hideous wail of terror, the wail of a doomed soul plunging into never-ending nightmare. Jubal clawed at the length of wood jutting from his chest. Flung backward off his horse, he hit the ground, and pain exploded on impact. Bragg wriggled and moaned and gibbered as the pain engulfed him. He no longer understood what had happened. He knew only pain, and one thing more, the faces of the dead, the innocents of Warbonnet Creek who in his mind's eye had come to circle him, to watch him die. And to harry him along on his way to hell.

Silence again. Captain Henry Morbitzer stood and dusted himself off and wondered why the war chief had spared him, and in the same thought process realized Panther Burn had never intended to take the lives of any of the soldiers. He had not come to kill. But to die. Henry Morbitzer held up a hand, ordering his men to stand ready. But now that he had the attention again of his troopers and the war chief was no more than fifty feet away astride a bloodied, winded horse, the captain could not bring himself to issue the order to open fire. Suddenly the taste of battle was bitter in his mouth. Panther Burn had ridden through them. He had killed the last great enemy of the Cheyenne. And he had counted coup.

"Sir?" a trooper asked, carbine ready.

"No," said Henry Morbitzer. "The first man who fires, I'll personally take the lash to him. Can't you see? It's over." He holstered his Colt revolver. "Over."

The Cheyenne waited where they had watched. Panther Burn felt the horse shudder beneath him. But he did not dismount. Not now, not yet. He saw Michael move toward him, but Panther Burn shook his head no, and his son stopped, face contorted with grief as he retreated back to Kate. A wind sprang up as if announcing the arrival of the one Panther Burn waited for. He saw Rebecca riding toward him through the last of the mist as the wind carried off the diaphanous strands of gold. The troopers parted, allowing Rebecca Blue Thrush to pass among them unmolested. Panther Burn kept his eyes on his wife, his back to the settlement as if scorning the future he had refused to be a part of. The earth was red beneath him. His life was seeping from the dozen wounds, his arm hung limp, his shattered legs somehow managed to grip his horse's flanks. He held himself upright, refusing to succumb. Yet. Rebecca reined her horse alongside his. Her eyes were dry, only her heart wept at the sight of him. She leaned down and took the reins from his loosened grip. The leather traces were slick crimson. Rebecca glanced at her son and smiled reassuringly, then she led her mortally wounded husband off to the forest, toward the hills and beyond to the mountains where the wind never ceases.

No one moved to stop them.

Epilogue

First silence. Then departure. Then children to race through sunlight, returning to their play. The dust from their exertions soon masked the bloody ground and their laughter lasted longer than the reverberations of gunshots or thunder in the hills. Children are the balm of history; in the young, the world heals itself and begins anew. Michael watched them from where he sat in the shade on the porch of the clinic. He felt . . . nothing. Only numbness. Kate emerged from inside, shaded her eyes, and looked toward the hills for Rebecca.

"She'll be back. After she has buried him in a place only she will know of," said Michael. He reached out and took Kate's hand in his. He looked out at the settlement and the houses scattered over Lame Deer Valley. "One day there will be a Cheyenne town on Cheyenne land and there will be no more ration Fridays."

"He died for them," Kate said, looking at the children. One of the boys pretended to be a fierce war chief, others were chasing him. The boy war chief kept falling down but he refused to be killed. Each time he fell, the boy rose again. "And we will live for them," said Michael.

"Don't ever let me go," Kate gently replied. Michael smiled. He had no intention of ever doing that. The children playing nearby noticed them, and recognizing Michael, ran over to him and crowded onto the steps leading up to the porch. Jonah Yellow Leg, Susan, and Sara Pretty on Top, and half a dozen other children crowded around the couple. Jonah was the spokesman, though several of the boys were older than he.

"Tell us about him, will you, Michael?"

"Your papa," Sara explained.

"Tell us about Panther Burn," another boy said. Michael remembered he was the one who had refused to die.

Like a legend.

Michael glanced around at Kate, who smiled, squeezed his hand, then stepped toward the door. "I think I can find a jar of peppermints," she said, and darted inside. Michael hesitated, lifted his gaze to the hills, to the trail his mother and father had taken and down which only Rebecca would return. *Yes, let it begin here.*

"My father, Panther Burn," Michael began. He sat on the top step and the children drew close on every side. "Let me tell you the story of Panther Burn." Michael stared into each intent, innocent face.

"It began with a hawk. . . ."

Author's Note

I cannot get the Northern Cheyenne out of my system. My wife Patricia and I arrived at the St. Labre Indian Mission in the summer of 1973. We came to teach and wound up being taught. Echoes of my time among the Morning Star people continue to haunt my work. I make no claim to be an authority on the Northern Cheyenne. And I beg pardon for any inaccuracies found in this novel. Although this is a work of fiction, two of the main incidents in these pages actually occurred; I have, however, altered the location as well as the names of the participants to suit my story.

On November 29, 1864, a force of seven hundred Colorado Volunteers led by Colonel John Chivington attacked a village of Southern Cheyenne encamped along Sand Creek. These Cheyenne not only had lived in peace with the white settlers, but their chief, Black Kettle, had even seen to it that an American flag flew over the village. The attack came at morning. It was sudden and brutal. By the time the militia had finished, one hundred thirty-seven Cheyenne were dead. Only twenty-eight were men; the rest were Cheyenne women and children whose bodies were mutilated beyond recognition, although portions of Indian anatomy wound up as tobacco pouches and hat bands for sale in Denver. The survivors of the bloodbath, those Southern Cheyenne who managed to gain the safety of the surrounding forest, headed North and joined with the Northern Cheyenne in Montana Territory. The Sand Creek massacre is one of the darkest entries in the annals of the history of the West. It resulted in the full-scale uprising of the Cheyenne nation and hostilities lasting almost twenty-five years.

Panther Burn and Zachariah Scalpcane are based on actual Cheyenne braves. In the fall of 1890, two men, Head Chief and John Young Mule, ran afoul of the law. By this time the Cheyenne were concentrated on their reservation in south-central Montana. The local military authority threatened to cut off rations to the tribe unless the braves surrendered. Head Chief sent word he would meet the U.S. Army in battle in the valley of Lame Deer, near Lame Deer, Montana, a reservation town. Head Chief and John Young Mule were determined to die as befitting the warriors of old. Head Chief claimed that, if the U.S. cavalry arranged itself in ranks across the valley, he would ride through their midst. On Friday, September 13, 1890, the last of the Cheyenne warriors rode down from the hills to wage war. John Young Mule had his horse shot out from under him. He continued to charge on foot until he fell, riddled with bullets. Head Chief, though dying, fulfilled his promise and rode through the soldiers before tumbling from horseback. Head Chief and John Young Mule were buried on a place called Squaw Hill. Both battle and burial site were about twenty miles from where Patricia and I lived and worked. I have walked the hilltop where the bones of Head Chief and John Young Mule bleach in the sun. There this book was born, there I heard God speak in the distant thunder, there I learned in my own poor way how sacred is the wind.

ABOUT THE AUTHOR

KERRY NEWCOMB's first book under his own name was the best-selling *Morning Star*. Writing with longtime collaborator Frank Schaefer, Kerry's novels have appeared under the names Shana Carrol *(Live for Love, Paxton Pride, Raven, Yellow Rose)* and Christina Savage *(Hearts of Fire, Love's Wildest Fires, Dawn Wind, Tempest)*. Kerry Newcomb and Frank Schaefer are also the authors of *Pandora Man* and *Ghosts of Elkhorn*. Kerry lives in Fort Worth, Texas, and is currently at work on a new historical novel.

Winner of
The National Book Critics
Circle Award
For Fiction

Love Medicine
by Louise Erdrich

"This greatly gifted first novelist seems to have come by her enormous folk wisdom instinctively, like Huckleberry Finn. She depicts the hardness of these lives with originality, authority, tenderness, and a pitiless and wild wit—in all, a terrific debut."

—Philip Roth

"The beauty of LOVE MEDICINE saves us from being completely devastated by its power."

—Toni Morrison

Award-winning storyteller and Native American, Louise Erdrich writes about survival, tenacity, and the supreme power of the heart. LOVE MEDICINE is the story of the intertwined fates of the Kashpaws and the Lamartines on and around a North Dakota reservation from 1934 to 1984. Erdrich weaves a tale of the endless snag of the flesh, the bind of blood and the love that is proved only by betrayal. Rarely has a writer created a world that matters so much to the reader who meets it for the first time.

Meet the world of
Love Medicine by Louise Erdrich
In Bantam Trade Paperback!
Available December, 1985.